At His
REVENGE

Sarah
MORGAN

Trish
MOREY

Janette
KENNY

MILLS &
BOON

Published in Great Britain 2015
by Mills & Boon, an imprint of Harlequin (UK) Limited,
Eton House, 18-24 Paradise Road, Richmond, Surrey, TW9 1SR

AT HIS REVENGE © 2015 Harlequin Books S.A.

Sold to the Enemy © 2013 Sarah Morgan
Bartering Her Innocence © 2013 Trish Morey
Innocent of His Claim © 2012 Janette Kenny

ISBN: 978-0-263-91773-4

25-0116

Harlequin (UK) Limited's policy is to use papers that are natural, renewable and recyclable products and made from wood grown in sustainable forests. The logging and manufacturing processes conform to the legal environmental regulations of the country of origin.

Printed and bound in Spain
by CPI, Barcelona

SOLD TO THE ENEMY

SARAH MORGAN

CHAPTER ONE

'NO ONE will lend you money, Selene. They are all too afraid of your father.'

'Not all.' Selene sat down on the bed and stroked her mother's hair—hair tended regularly by hairdressers in order to keep up the appearance of a perfect life. 'Stop worrying. I'm going to get you away from here.'

Her mother lay still. She said 'from here' but they both knew that what she really meant was 'from him'.

'I should be the one saying that to you. I should have left years ago. When I first met your father he was so charming. Every woman in the room wanted him and he only had eyes for me. Have you any idea how that feels?'

Selene opened her mouth to say *How could I, when I've been trapped on this island for most of my life?* but realised that would only hurt her mother more. 'I can imagine it must have been very exciting. He was rich and powerful.' She wouldn't make that mistake. She would never let love blind her to the true nature of the man underneath.

'It's stupid to talk of leaving when we both know he'll never let us go. As far as the world is concerned we're the perfect family. He isn't going to let anything ruin that image.' Her mother rolled away, turning her face to the wall.

Selene felt a rush of frustration. It was like watching

someone adrift on a raft, making no effort to save themselves. 'We're not going to ask him. It's our decision. *Ours*. Maybe it's time we told the world this "family" is a lie.'

Her mother's lack of response didn't surprise her. Her father had dictated to them and controlled them for so long she'd forgotten she even had a choice.

Despite the oppressive summer heat and the fact that their fortress home had no air-conditioning, a chill spread across her skin and ran deep into her bones.

How many years did it take, she wondered, before you no longer believed your life was worth fighting for? How many years before hope turned to helplessness, before anger became acceptance and spirit was beaten to a stupor? How many years until she, too, chose to lie on her side facing the wall rather than stand up and face the day?

Beyond the closed shutters that blotted out the only window in the tiny bedroom the sun beamed its approval from a perfect blue sky onto the sparkling Mediterranean, its brightness a cruel contrast to the darkness inside the room.

To many, the Greek Islands were paradise. Perhaps some of them were. Selene didn't know. She only knew this one, and Antaxos was no paradise. Cut off from its neighbours by a stretch of dangerous sea, rocks that threatened ships like the jaws of a monster and by the fearsome reputation of the man who owned it, this island was closer to hell than heaven.

Selene tucked the covers around her mother's thin shoulders. 'Leave everything to me.'

That statement injected her mother with an energy that nothing else could. 'Don't make him angry.'

She'd heard those words more often than she could count.

She'd spent her life tiptoeing around 'angry'.

'You don't have to live like this, watching everything

you say and everything you do because of him.' Looking at her mother, Selene felt sad. Once, she'd been a beauty and it had been that blonde, Nordic beauty that had attracted the attention of the rich playboy Stavros Antaxos. Her mother had been dazzled by wealth and power and she'd melted under his charm like candle wax under a hot flame, never seeing the person beneath the smooth sophistication.

One bad choice, Selene thought. Her mother had made one bad choice and then spent years living with it, her heart and spirit crushed by a life spent with a ruthless man.

'Let's not talk about him. I had an e-mail this week from Hot Spa in Athens.' She'd been nursing the news for days, not daring to share it before now. 'Remember I told you about them? It's a really upmarket chain. And they have spa hotels on Crete, Corfu and Santorini. I sent them samples of my candles and my soap and they *love* them. They used them in their treatment rooms and three of their top clients insisted on taking them home and paid a fortune for the privilege. Now they want to talk to me and put in a large order. It's the break I've been hoping for.' She was buzzing inside and longing to share the excitement so it came as a blow when her mother's only response was to shake her head.

'He'll never let you do it.'

'I don't need his permission to live my life the way I want to live it.'

'And how are you going to live it? You need money to set up your business and he won't give you money that enables us to leave him.'

'I know. Which is why I don't intend to ask him. I have another plan.' She'd learned not to speak without first checking to see who might be listening and instinctively she turned her head to see that the door was closed, even though this was her mother's bedroom and she'd secured the door herself. Even though *he* wasn't even on the island. 'I'm leaving tonight and I'm telling you this because I won't be able to contact you for a few days and I don't want you to worry about me. As far as everyone is concerned I am at the convent for my usual week of retreat and meditation.'

'How can you leave? Even if you could slip past his security and make it off the island you will be recognised. Someone will call him and he will be furious. You know how obsessed he is about maintaining the image of the perfect family.'

'One of the advantages of being the shy, reclusive daughter of a man feared by everyone is that no one is expecting to see me. But just to cover all eventualities I have a disguise.' And she didn't intend to share the details with anyone. Not even her mother, who was now looking at her with panic in her eyes.

'And if you do manage to make it as far as the mainland, what then? Have you thought that far?'

'Yes, I've thought that far.' And further, much further, to a future that was nothing like the past. 'You don't need to know any of this. All you need to do is trust me and wait for me to return and fetch you. I'd take you now only two of us travelling together are more likely to attract attention. You have to stay here and keep up the perfect family pretence for just a little longer. Once I have the money and somewhere to stay I'm coming back for you.'

Her mother gripped her arm tightly. 'If by any chance you manage to do this, you should not come back. It's too late for me.'

'It drives me mad when you say things like that.' Selene hugged her mother. 'I will come back. And then we're leaving together and he can find someone else to control.'

'I wish I had money to give you.'

So did she. If her mother had maintained her independence then perhaps they wouldn't be in this mess now, but her father's first and cleverest move following his marriage had been to ensure his wife had no income of her own, thus making her dependent on him in every way. Her mother had confessed that at first she'd found it romantic to have a man who wanted to care for her. It had been later, much later, that she'd realised that he hadn't wanted to care for her. He'd wanted to control her. And so her mother's independence had slowly leeched away, stolen not by a swift kill but by a slow, cruel erosion of her confidence.

'I have enough to get me to Athens. Then I'm going to get a loan to start my business.' It was the only option open to her and she knew other people did it all the time. They borrowed money and they paid it back and she would pay it back, too. All of it.

'He has contacts at all the banks. None of them will loan you money, Selene.'

'I know. Which is why I'm not going to a bank.'

Her mother shook her head. 'Name one person who would be prepared to do business with you. Show me a man with the guts to stand up to your father and I'll show you a man who doesn't exist.'

'He exists.' Her heart pumped hard against her chest and she forced herself to breathe slowly. 'There is one man who isn't afraid of anyone or anything. A strong man.'

'Who?'

Selene kept her voice casual. 'I'm going to see Stefanos Ziakas.'

The name alone drained the colour from her mother's face. 'Ziakas is another version of your father. He's a ruthless, self-seeking playboy with no conscience and not one shred of gentleness in him. Don't be fooled by that handsome face and that charismatic smile. He's deadly.'

'No, he isn't. I met him once, years ago, on the yacht on one of the occasions we were forced to play "happy families" in public. He was kind to me.' Selene was annoyed to feel herself blushing.

'If he was kind, it was because he knew it would annoy your father. They hate each other.'

'He didn't know who I was when we started talking.'

'You were the only seventeen-year-old there. It was obvious who you were.' Her mother sounded weary. 'Ask yourself why a sophisticated man like him would spend his time talking to you when he came with the actress Anouk Blaire.'

'He told me she was boring. He said she only cared about how she looked and who wrote about her and that being with him enhanced her career. He said I was much more interesting. We talked all night.' About everything. She'd told him things she'd never told anyone before. Not about her family, of course—she was too well trained to let that particular truth slip—but she'd talked about her dreams and her hopes for the future and been grateful when he hadn't laughed. He'd listened with those sexy eyes fixed on her and when she'd asked him if he thought she might be able to run a business one day he'd spoken words she'd never forgotten.

You can do anything if you want it enough.

Well, she wanted it.

Her mother sighed. 'The schoolgirl and the billionaire. And because of this one conversation you think he'll help you?'

Come back in five years, Selene Antaxos, then maybe we'll talk.

She'd wanted to do a whole lot more than talk and she suspected he'd known that, just as she suspected he'd guessed the truth about the fabricated life she led. She'd felt more of a connection with him than she had with any other human being. For the first time in her life someone had listened to her and his words had stayed with her, day and night. When life had grown hard it had been a comfort to remember that she had someone to go to if things were desperate.

And things *were* desperate.

'He'll help me.'

'That man is more likely to hurt you than help you. You have no experience of men like him. I would not put you with a man like Ziakas. I would find you someone kind and gentle who deserves you.'

'I don't want him to be kind or gentle. I need him to be ruthless or this isn't going to work. If he doesn't have the guts to stand up to my father then there is no hope for my plan. I want to run my own business and Ziakas knows more about how to do that than anyone. He did it all himself. He lost his parents when he was young. No one helped him. No one gave him a helping hand. And look at him now. He was a billionaire by the time he was thirty and he did that by himself.'

She found his story inspirational. If he could do it, why couldn't she?

Her mother struggled upright, finding energy from anxiety. 'Do you honestly think you'll just be able to walk up to a man like Stefan Ziakas and ask him for money? He is protected from the outside world by layers of security, just like your father. Getting an appointment with someone like him would be almost impossible, especially at short notice. Even if you could somehow find a way to leave the island undetected while your father is away, Ziakas won't see you.'

'He'll see me. And I have found a way to leave the island.' Determined not to reveal too much, and even more determined not to let her mother batter her confidence, Selene stood up. 'I will be back tomorrow, which gives us plenty of time to get far away before my father returns from—from his trip.' 'Trip' was the word they both used to describe her father's frequent absences from the island. It disgusted Selene that he didn't even bother to keep his infidelities a secret. Disgusted her more that her mother accepted them as part of the marriage deal.

She couldn't allow herself to think about what she'd do if her mother refused to leave, as she'd refused so many times before. All she knew was that she didn't want to spend anther day on Antaxos. She'd lived here all her life, trapped within its rocky shores, thirsty for a life other than the one she'd been given. She didn't want to spend another day in this 'family' pretending that everything was perfect.

The events of the last week had shown her that she had to do it sooner rather than later.

Bending down, she kissed her mother on the cheek. 'Dream about what you're going to do on the first day of your new life. You're going to laugh without worrying that the sound is going to draw his attention. You're going to paint again and people will buy those paintings, just as they used to.'

'I haven't painted for years. I don't feel the urge any more.'

'That's because he didn't like you doing anything that took you away from him.' The anger was like an energy source, giving her a determination that felt close to power. 'You're going to get your life back.'

'And if your father returns from Crete early and finds you gone? Have you thought of that?'

It was like stepping off a cliff or missing a step on the

stairs. Her heart bumped uncomfortably and she wanted to clutch something for support. 'He won't return early. Why would he?'

Bored out of his mind, Stefan lounged with his feet on his desk.

Far beneath the glass cocoon that housed his corporate headquarters, Athens was slowly waking up. Athens, a city in trouble, licking its wounds as the world watched in wary fascination. People encouraged him to move his base to a different city. New York. London. Anywhere other than the troubled Greek capital.

Stefan ignored them.

He had no intention of abandoning the place that had allowed him to become who he was. He knew what it was like to have everything and then lose it. He knew how it felt to go from prosperity to poverty. He understood fear and uncertainty. And he knew all about the effort required to drag yourself back from the edge. It made winning all the more satisfying and he'd won in a big way. He had money and power.

People would have been surprised to learn the money didn't interest him. But power? Power was different. He'd learned at an early age that power was everything. Power opened doors that were closed. Power turned no to yes and stop to go. He'd learned that power was an aphrodisiac and, when it needed to be, it was a weapon.

It was a weapon he wasn't afraid to use.

His phone rang for the tenth time in as many minutes but he chose to ignore it.

A tap on the door disturbed his thoughts. Maria, his PA, stood in the doorway.

Irritated by the interruption, Stefan lifted an eyebrow in question and she pursed her lips.

'Don't give me that look. I know you don't want to be disturbed, but you're not answering your personal line.' When he still didn't answer, she sighed. 'Sonya's PA has been ringing and when you didn't answer Sonya herself called. She isn't in a good mood.'

'She is phoning to give me an update on her moods? I have marginally more interest in the weather forecast.'

'She wanted me to give you a message. She said to tell you she's not playing hostess at your party tonight until you make a decision about your relationship. Her exact words were...' Maria cleared her throat. '"Tell him it's either on or off."'

'It's off. I already told her that in words that even she should have been able to understand.' Exasperated, Stefan picked up his phone and deleted all his messages without listening to them. Even without looking he could feel Maria's censorship and he smiled. 'You've worked for me for twelve years. Why the long face?'

'Doesn't the end of a relationship *ever* bother you?'

'Never.'

'That says something about you, Stefan.'

'Yes. It says I'm good at handling break-ups. Go, me.'

'It says you don't care about the women you date!'

'I care as much as they do.'

With a despairing shake of her head, Maria cleared two empty coffee cups from his desk. 'You have your pick of women and you can't find *one* you want to settle down with? You are a success in every aspect of your life except one. Your personal life is a disaster.'

'I happen to consider my personal life an unqualified success.'

'You must want more than this from a relationship.'

'I want hot, frequent, uncomplicated sex.' He smiled

at her disapproving expression. 'I pick women who want the same thing.'

'Love would be the making of you.'

Love?

Stefan felt something slam shut inside him. He swung his legs off his desk. 'Did your job description change when I wasn't looking? Has there been some EU employment law that requires you to take charge of my private life?'

'Fine. I can take the hint. It's none of my business. I don't know why I even bother.' The cups rattled in her hand as she stalked through the door but she was back moments later. 'There's someone here to see you. Perhaps she'll be able to persuade you to get in touch with your human side.'

'She? I thought my first appointment wasn't until ten o'clock?'

'This person doesn't have an appointment, but I didn't feel comfortable turning her away.'

'Why not? I employ you to be the dragon at my door.'

'I can be dragon-like when I have to be but not when the person wanting to see you is a nun.'

'A *nun*? You have to be kidding me.'

'She says she has something urgent to discuss with you.'

Stefan gave a sardonic smile. 'If she's here to save my soul, tell her she's too late.'

'I will not. To be honest I have no idea what to say to her.'

'Any combination of words would have sufficed, providing "no" and "get out" were included.'

Maria squared her shoulders. 'I can't turn a nun away. I don't want that on my conscience.'

Stefan, who hadn't made the acquaintance of his conscience for several decades, was exasperated. 'I never saw

you as gullible. Has it occurred to you she's probably a
stripper?'

'I know a genuine nun's habit when I see one. And your
cynicism does you no credit.'

'On the contrary, my cynicism has protected me nicely
for years and will continue to do so—which is just as well
given that you're turning into a soft touch.'

'I'm sorry, but there's no way I can tell a nun you won't
see her. And she has a really sweet smile.' Maria's face
softened momentarily and then she glared at him. 'If you
want it done, you'll have to do it yourself.'

'Fine. Send her in. And then take a trip to the nearest
fancy dress store and see for yourself how easy it is to hire
a nun's costume.'

Clearly relieved to have offloaded that responsibility,
Maria retreated, and Stefan felt a rush of irritation at the
thought of an interruption that would bring him no benefit.

His irritation intensified at the sight of a nun in a black
habit standing in the doorway to his office. Under the
robes he could see that she was slightly built but she kept
her head bowed, allowing him a single glimpse of a pale
face under flowing black and white.

Unmoved by her pious attitude, Stefan leaned back in
his chair and scrutinised his unwanted visitor. 'If you're
expecting me to confess my sins then I should probably
tell you that my next appointment is in an hour and that
is nowhere near long enough for me to tell you all the bad
things I've done in my life. On the other hand if you're
about to beg for cash then you should know that all my
charitable donations are handled through my lawyers, via
a separate part of my company. I just make the money. I
leave other people to spend it.'

The tone he used would have had most people back-

ing towards the door but she simply closed it so that they
were alone.

'There is no need to close the door,' he said coldly, 'because you're going to be going back through it in approxi-
mately five seconds. I have no idea what you're expecting
to gain by...' The words died in his throat as the nun removed her hood and hair the colour of a pale moonbeam
tumbled in shiny waves over her black habit.

'I'm not a nun, Mr Ziakas.' Her voice was soft, breathy
and perfect for the bedroom, a thought that clashed uncomfortably with the vision of her in a nun's outfit.

'Of course you're not,' Stefan drawled, his eyes fixed
on her glorious hair, 'but you managed to convince my
hardened PA so I suppose you should get points for that.'
Suddenly he was annoyed with Maria for allowing herself to be so easily manipulated. 'I'm used to women using
all sorts of devices in order to meet me, but I've never yet
had one stoop so low as to impersonate a nun. It smacks
of desperate behaviour.'

'I'm not impersonating anyone. But it was essential that
I keep a low profile.'

'I hate to break this to you, but in the business district
of Athens a nun's habit is *not* considered camouflage. You
stand out like a penguin in the Sahara. If you want to blend,
next time dress in a suit.'

'I couldn't risk being recognised.' Her eyes flickered
to the huge glass windows of his office and after a moment she sidled across and peered down at the city while
he watched in mounting exasperation.

Who would recognise her? Who was she? Someone's
wife?

There *was* something vaguely familiar about her face.
His mind coming up blank, he tried to imagine her without
her clothes to see if he could place her, but mentally strip-

ping a nun proved a stretch even for him. 'I don't sleep with married women so that can't be the reason for the elaborate subterfuge. Do we know each other? If so, you're going to have to remind me.' He raised an eyebrow as a prompt. 'Where? When? I admit to being hopeless with names.'

She dragged her gaze from the view, those green eyes direct. 'When and where what?'

Stefan, who hated mysteries and considered tact a quality devoid of reward, was blunt. 'Where and when did we have sex? I'm sure it was amazing but you're going to have to remind me of the details.'

She made a sound in her throat. 'I haven't had sex with you!'

'Are you sure?'

Green eyes stared back at him. 'If rumour is correct, Mr Ziakas, sex with you is a memorable experience. Is it something I'm likely to have forgotten?'

More intrigued than he would have been willing to admit, Stefan sat back in his chair. 'You clearly know a great deal more about me than I do about you. Which brings me to the obvious question—what are you doing here?'

'You told me to come and see you in five years. Five years is up. It was up last week, actually. You were kind to me. The only person who was.'

There was a wistful note in her voice that sparked all the alarm bells in his head. Trained to detect vulnerability from a hundred paces so that he could give it a wide berth, Stefan cooled his voice.

'Then this is clearly a case of mistaken identity because I'm never kind to women. I work really hard *not* to be or they start to expect it and the next thing you know they're dropping hints about rings, wedding planners and a house in the country. *Not* my style.'

She smiled at that. 'You were definitely kind to me. Without you I think I would have thrown myself overboard at that party. You talked to me for the whole night. You gave me hope.'

Stefan, all too aware that he was widely regarded as the executioner of women's hopes, raised his eyebrows. He stared at that glorious hair and filed through his memory bank. 'Definitely a case of mistaken identity. If I'd met you, we definitely wouldn't have wasted a night talking. I would have taken you to bed.'

'You told me to come back in five years.'

That news caught his attention and Stefan narrowed his eyes. 'I'm impressed by my own restraint.'

'My father would have killed you.'

My father would have killed you.

Stefan stared at her, his eyes sweeping her face for clues, and suddenly he stilled. Those beautiful washed-green eyes were a rare colour he'd only seen once before, hidden behind a pair of unflattering glasses. 'Selene? Selene Antaxos.'

'You *do* recognise me.'

'Barely. *Theé mou*—' His eyes swept her frame. 'You've—grown.' He remembered her as a gangly blonde who still had to grow into her lean body. An awkward teenager completely dominated by her overprotective father. A pampered princess never allowed out of her heavily guarded palace.

Stay away from my daughter, Ziakas.

It was the unspoken threat that had made him determined to talk to her.

Just thinking of the name Antaxos was enough to ruin his day and now here was the daughter, standing in his office.

Dark emotion rippled through him, unwelcome and un-wanted.

He reminded himself that the daughter wasn't respon-sible for the sins of the father.

'Why are you dressed as a nun?'

'I had to sneak past my father's security.'

'I can't imagine that was easy. Of course if your father didn't make so many enemies he wouldn't need an entire army to protect him.' Blocking the feelings that rose in-side him, he stood up and strolled round his desk. 'What are you doing here?'

The one thing he did remember from that night was feeling sorry for her and the reason he remembered it was because he so rarely felt sorry for anyone. He believed that people made their own choices in life, but he'd taken one look at her in all her leggy, uncomfortable misery and de-cided that being the daughter of Stavros Antaxos must be the shortest straw anyone could ever draw.

'I'll get to that in a minute.' She bent down and caught hold of the hem of her habit. 'Do you mind if I take this off? It's really hot.'

'Where did you get it? The local dressing-up shop?'

'I was educated by the nuns on Poulos, the island next to ours, and they've always been very supportive. They lent it to me but there's no point in keeping it on now I'm safe with you.'

Knowing that most women considered him anything but 'safe', Stefan watched in stunned disbelief as she wriggled and struggled until finally she freed herself and emerged with her hair in tangled disarray. Underneath she was wearing a white silk shirt teamed with a smart black pen-cil skirt that hugged legs designed to turn a man's mind to pulp.

'I almost boiled to death on the ferry. You have no idea. That's why I couldn't wear the jacket.'

'Jacket?'

'The jacket from my suit. It's designed to be worn in an air-conditioned office, not a floating tin can which is how the ferry feels.'

Stefan wrenched his gaze from those bare legs, feeling as if he'd been hit round the head with a brick. Staring into those green eyes, he looked for some sign of the awkward teenage girl he'd met years before. 'You look different.'

'I should hope so. I hope I look like a businesswoman because that's what I am.' She slid her arms into a jacket that matched the skirt, scooped up her hair and pinned it with brisk efficiency. 'When you met me five years ago I had spots and braces. I was hideous.'

She wasn't hideous now. 'Does your father know you're here?'

'What do you think?'

The corner of her mouth dimpled into a naughty smile and Stefan stared at that smile, hypnotised by her lips, trying to clear his mind of wicked thoughts.

'I think your father must be having a few sleepless nights.' The wicked thoughts still very much in play, he tried desperately to see her as she'd been that night on the boat. Young and vulnerable. 'I should offer you a drink. Would you like a—' he groped for something suitable '—a glass of milk or something?'

She pushed some loose strands of her hair away from her face in a gesture that somehow managed to be both self-conscious and seductive. 'I'm not six. Do you often offer your visitors milk?'

'No, but I don't usually entertain minors in my office.'

'I'm not a minor. I'm all grown up.'

'Yes. I can see that.' Stefan loosened his collar and discovered it was already undone. He wondered if the air-conditioning in his office was failing. 'So—why don't you tell me why you're here?'

If she wanted him to ruin her father, they might yet find themselves with a common goal.

'I'm here about business, of course. I have a business proposition.'

Huge eyes were fixed hopefully on his face and Stefan felt an instant pull of lust. The explosion of attraction was instant, unmistakable—and entirely inappropriate given the circumstances.

Apart from the obvious physical changes she still looked as innocent as she had that night on the boat. It would be asking for trouble. Even he wasn't going to stoop that low.

'I'm not known for doing favours for people.'

'I know. And I'm not expecting a favour. I know a lot about you. I know you date different women all the time because you don't want a relationship. I know that in business they call you all sorts of things, including ruthless and uncaring.'

'Those are generally good traits to have in business.'

'And you never deny any of those awful things they write about you. You're happy to be portrayed as the big bad wolf.'

'And yet still you're here.'

'I'm not afraid of you. You sat with me for seven hours and talked to me when no one else could be bothered.' Folding the nun's habit carefully, she leaned forward to stuff it into her bag, oblivious to the fact that the movement gave him a perfect view of the curve of her breasts above a hint of lacy bra.

Stefan made a valiant attempt to avert his eyes and failed. 'You were sweet.'

He emphasised the word for his own benefit. If there

was one thing designed to kill his libido it was 'sweet', so why the hell was he painfully aroused? And why was she looking at him with big trusting eyes when what he should have been seeing was an appropriate degree of caution?

Come into my house, Little Red Riding Hood, and close the door behind you.

Caution nowhere in sight, she gave him a warm smile. 'It's a bit embarrassing to remember it, to be honest. I was so upset I would have done anything just to make my father mad, but you refused to take advantage of me even though you hate him. You didn't laugh at me when I told you I wanted to set up my own business and you didn't laugh when I flirted with you. You told me to come and find you in five years, which I thought was very tactful.'

She spoke quickly, almost breathless as she got the words out, and Stefan stared at her for a long moment, all his instincts telling him that something wasn't quite right.

Was he seeing desperation or enthusiasm?

Stefan bought himself some time. 'Are you sure you wouldn't like something cold to drink?'

'I'd *love* some champagne.'

'It's ten in the morning.'

'I know. It's just that I've never tasted it and I thought this would be the perfect opportunity. According to the internet you live a champagne lifestyle.' There was a wistful note in her tone that didn't make sense. He'd assumed the Antaxos family bathed in champagne. They were certainly rich enough.

'Believe it or not I try and restrict my champagne consumption until the end of my working day.' Clenching his jaw, Stefan hit a button on his phone. 'Maria? Bring us a jug of water, or lemonade, or—' he racked his brains for a suitable soft drink '—or something soft and refreshing.

With ice,' he added as an afterthought. 'Lots of ice. And some pastries.'

'That's thoughtful of you. I'm starving.'

Stefan leaned against his desk, maintaining a safe distance. 'So—you say you have a business proposition. Tell me about it and I'll tell you if I can help.' Those words felt alien on his tongue. When did he ever help anyone but himself? He'd learned at an early age to take care of himself and he'd been doing it ever since.

'I want to set up my own business just like you did. That night on the yacht, you inspired me. You talked about how you'd done it all yourself and about how great it felt to be independent and not rely on anyone. I want that.' She dug her hand into her bag again and pulled out a file. 'This is my business plan. I've worked hard on it. I think you'll be impressed.'

Stefan, who was rarely impressed by other people's business plans, gingerly took the pink file from her outstretched hand. 'Is there an electronic version?'

'I didn't want to save it on the computer in case my father found it. It's the figures that count, not the presentation.'

So her father knew nothing about it. Perhaps that explained the hint of nerves he detected beneath all that bounce and optimism.

No doubt this was her summer project, designed to fill the long boring hours that came with being an overprotected heiress, and he was the lucky recipient of her endeavours.

Shaking off the feeling that something wasn't quite right about the whole situation, Stefan flipped open the file and scanned the first page. It was surprisingly professional. 'Candles? That's your business idea?'

'Not just candles. Scented candles.' Her voice vibrated

with enthusiasm. 'I went to school in a convent. I started making candles in craft lessons and I experimented with different scents. I have three different ones.'

Candles, Stefan thought. The most boring, pointless product on planet earth.

How the hell was he going to let her down gently? He had no experience of letting people down gently. He just dropped them from a great height and stepped over their broken remains.

Clearing his throat, he cultivated what he hoped was an interested expression. 'Why don't you tell me a bit more about what makes them special? Top line? I don't need detail.' Please, God, no detail. As far as he was concerned talking about candles would be one step down from talking about the weather.

'I've called one Relax, one Energise and one—' her cheeks turned a deeper shade of pink '—Seduction.'

Something in the way she hesitated over the word made him glance up from the file. She was trembling with anticipation, and all it took was one glance to know that his first assumption had been correct.

She was a bored heiress, playing at business.

And now she'd prompted him he could clearly remember the night they'd met.

She'd been a teenager—miserable, confused and self-conscious. An ugly duckling dumped in the middle of a flock of elite swans with a doting father who barely took his eyes off her. None of the other men had dared talk to her, none of the women had wanted to, so she'd stood alone, her awkwardness almost painful to witness.

But she was no longer that teenager. She was all woman, and she knew it.

Stavros Antaxos must be having *lots* of sleepless nights.

And now she was looking at him with those big eyes filled with unwavering trust.

Stefan knew she couldn't have found a man less worthy of that trust.

He wondered just how much she knew about his relationship with her father.

The atmosphere in the room shifted.

When he was sure he had his reactions under control, he closed the file slowly and looked at her. 'So your candles are called, Relax, Energise and Seduction?'

'That's right.'

'And just how much,' he asked slowly, 'do you know about seduction?'

CHAPTER TWO

GREAT. Of all the questions to ask, he had to ask that one.

Not market share or growth forecasts—seduction.

Selene maintained the smile she'd been practising—her business smile—while her brain raced around in crazy circles getting nowhere.

What did she know about seduction? Nothing. Nor was it a skill she was ever likely to need unless her life changed radically. What she did know was that without his help she'd never get her mother away from the island. It was up to her to prove she had a viable business. 'What do I know about seduction? Not a lot. But you know what they say— you don't have to travel the world to teach geography.'

She didn't add that she had her imagination and that was already working overtime.

She'd often wondered if her teenage brain had exaggerated his appeal or whether her own misery that night, together with his kindness, had somehow mingled together to create a god from a man. But he was as gorgeous as she remembered—power, strength and raw virility merged together in a muscle-packed masculine frame that made her feel dizzy with thoughts she couldn't seem to control.

Physically he was imposing, but it wasn't his impressive height or the width of those shoulders that shook her. It was something less easily defined. A hint of danger—

the sense that underneath that beautifully cut suit and the external trappings of success lurked a man who wielded more power than even her father.

Flustered, Selene tried to remember the way he'd been on that night five years earlier, but it was almost impossible to equate that kind stranger with this cool, sophisticated businessman standing in front of her.

And the fact that he was flicking through her amateurish document so quickly left her squirming with embarrassment. He barely took any time as he glanced at each page, nothing in his face giving a hint as to his thoughts. Clearly he thought it was rubbish.

Her mother was right. He was never going to help her.

He was right at the top of his game, a busy man with huge demands on his time. According to her research, thousands of people approached his company every year for business advice and he helped less than a handful of people.

While she waited for him to comment she sipped the lemonade but after a couple of minutes of squirming in her seat restraint left her. 'So tell me honestly—' *Is it a crappy idea?* God, no, she couldn't say that. 'Er—do you see this as an investment opportunity?' She felt like such a fraud. A total impostor, just waiting for him to laugh her out of his office. It must have been obvious to him that she'd never had a business meeting with anyone except her own reflection.

He closed the file, then turned to put it on his desk. His tailored shirt pulled across his wide shoulders, emphasising hard muscle, and her heart started to thud.

She dreamed about him all the time. Had thought about him almost every hour since that night.

'Selene?'

His voice was gentle and she looked at him, startled and embarrassed to have let her concentration lapse.

'Yes. I'm listening.'

The look in his eyes told her he was skilled at reading minds and hers was probably the easiest he'd ever read.

Suddenly her mouth felt as if she hadn't touched liquid for a week.

If he guessed how she felt about him she'd die on the spot.

Her trawl of the internet had revealed a lot about his relationship with women and every scandalous story had made her heart beat just a little bit faster because they spoke of a life so far removed from hers that it was like listening to a fairy story. Glittering parties. Opening nights. Opera. Ballet. Film premieres. The list was endless, as were the names of the beautiful women he'd paraded on his arm at one time or another, and it was all she could think about now as she stared at him, waiting for his answer.

'These candles—do you have a sample?'

'Yes.' She fumbled in her bag, trying to ignore the nerves fluttering low in her belly. It was as if just being in the same room as him had somehow triggered all the alarms in her body. The attraction was so shockingly powerful it knocked her off-balance. She definitely needed to get out more. This was what happened when a father locked a daughter away. She'd turned into a raging nymphomaniac. Stefan Ziakas was going to be lucky to escape with his clothes still on.

Disconcerted, she glanced at him but that turned out to be a bigger mistake. Thick, inky lashes highlighted eyes of molten gold and his mouth was a slim, sensual line in a face sculpted by the devil to tempt women to the dark side.

Selene was unsettled by just how desperately she wanted to be taken to the dark side.

'I know this business idea has potential.' She was brisk and businesslike and hoped he wouldn't guess that she'd practised this a hundred times in the mirror. 'I have some packaging samples, but they might need to be adapted. We live in a fast-paced, stressful world. Scented candles are an affordable luxury and I'm not the only one who thinks so. The market is currently growing at forty percent.'

His mouth was such a perfect shape, she thought. She'd noticed the same thing that night on the boat as she'd stared and stared at him, willing him to kiss her. There had been a few breathless moments when she'd thought he might do just that but he hadn't, so clearly it had just been wishful thinking on her part.

Leaning forward, he extracted the candle from her grip and turned it in his fingers. 'You're expecting me to believe that this is the next big thing?'

'Why not? Don't you like candles?'

A smile played around that sexy mouth. 'You want an honest answer?'

She remembered that this was a business meeting. That she was a businesswoman. 'Yes,' she said firmly. 'Yes, I do.'

'I'm a man. The only reason a man is ever going to like candles is if there is a power cut and the generator fails, or if he finds himself dining with a woman who is ugly.'

And she was willing to bet he never found himself in that position. 'But candles are about so much more than romantic lighting in a restaurant.' She tried not to think about him dining with a beautiful woman. 'The one I've named Seduction is scented with lotus blossom and it creates the perfect atmosphere for—for—'

'For?'

His eyes gleamed and she had a strong suspicion he

was laughing at her. 'Seduction,' she said lamely, suddenly wishing she'd called it something else.

'And you know that because...?'

His voice was disturbingly soft and the laughter had gone from his eyes. Now his gaze was intense—*serious*—and Selene felt as if she'd been seared by the flame of a blowtorch.

'Because people have told me that's the case.'

'But you've never tried it yourself.' It was a statement, not a question, and she felt her face burn along with her body.

She wished he'd stuck to a conversation about market share and forecasts. 'I've tried Relax and Energise.'

'So no market research on Seduction?'

'Yes, just not—personal research.'

There was a long, pulsing silence and then he put the candle down and leaned his hips on the desk, the movement of his trousers revealing expensive polished shoes. 'Let me tell you something about seduction, Selene.' His voice was more seductive than a thousand scented candles. 'To you it's just a word, but it's so much more than that. Seduction is about tempting, enticing and persuading until you've driven someone mad with need. Yes, scent is important, but not the artificial scent of a candle—it's the individual scent of the person you're with, and it's not just scent but scent combined with touch and sound.'

Selene couldn't breathe. 'Sound?'

'When I'm with a woman I want to hear the sounds she makes. I want to hear her pleasure as well as feel it under my lips and fingers. And then there's taste...' His voice was softer now, those dangerous eyes velvety dark as he held her gaze, 'I want to taste every part of her and encourage her to taste every part of me.'

'Y-you do?'

'Scent, touch, hearing, sound, taste—seduction uses all the senses, not just one. It's about taking over someone's mind and body until they're no longer capable of rational thought—until they want just one thing and one thing only—until they're reduced to an elemental state where nothing matters but the moment.'

Selene felt dizzy. 'I think I might need to rename my candle.'

'I'm sure there are men out there who would be only too happy to use a scented candle as a prop. I'm just not one of them.'

He wouldn't need any external props to seduce a woman. Those hands would be sure and skilled. And as for his mouth—

Realising her own hands were shaking, she tucked them firmly into her lap. 'Just because you're not my target audience, it doesn't mean I don't have a viable product.' Proud of that response, she carried on. 'Will you teach me what I need to know?' As his brows rose she continued, flustered. 'I mean about marketing. Running a business.'

'I have a question.'

'Yes, of course you do. Ask me anything.' He was so cool and sophisticated and she was no more interesting than her seventeen-year-old self. 'You want to know more about the product? It's a really good-quality candle. It's made of beeswax and it's smokeless and virtually drip-free.'

'I can hardly contain my excitement.' But he was smiling as he picked up the candle again and she had a feeling his mind was still on seduction rather than the product in his hand. 'That wasn't my question.'

'Oh. I expect you want to ask me about my revenue projections. I've had an order for five thousand from Hot Spa. They're the most exclusive chain of spa hotels in

Greece. But of course you know that…' Her voice tailed off. 'You own them.'

Stefan handed the candle back to her. 'That wasn't my question, either.'

She gulped. Licked her lips. 'Sorry—I'm talking too much. I do that when I'm—' *desperate* '—excited.'

'My first question,' he said slowly, 'is why someone like you would even want to set up a business. Are you bored?'

Bored? She bit back a bubble of hysterical laughter. 'No.'

'You're an heiress. You don't need to run a business.'

He had no idea. 'I want to prove myself.'

He stared at her for a long moment. 'Which brings me to my second question—why come to me? If you're serious about this then your father could put up the investment.'

Selene made sure her smile didn't slip. 'I don't want my father's name on it. This is my project. I want to own it. I don't want anyone doing me favours.' It was a lie, of course. She needed all the favours she could grab. 'I can't approach the banks because they won't help me without asking my father's permission. I tried to think of someone who isn't under his thumb and I came up with you. You told me to look you up in five years—'

The silence stretched between them.

Looking at his hard, handsome face she felt the confidence drain out of her. In an appalling flash of clarity she realised she'd made a monumental mistake. Losing her nerve, horribly embarrassed, she rose to her feet. 'Thank you for listening.'

He stirred, uncrossed those long, lean legs and stood up, dominating the room. 'You came to me for a business loan. Don't you want to hear my answer?'

'I—I thought you might need time to think about it.'

'I've had all the time I need.'

So the answer was no. Her shoulders sagged. Misery seeped into her veins.

'Right. Well—'

'My answer is yes.'

Because it wasn't what she was expecting to hear, it took a moment for his words to sink in.

'Seriously? You're not just saying that because I've made it hard for you to say no?'

'No is my favourite word. I don't find it hard to say.'

But he wasn't saying it to her. 'I just thought you might be agreeing to help me because you don't want me to feel bad.'

A strange expression crossed his face. 'That isn't the reason.'

His eyes were on her mouth and she saw something in his face that made her heart pound just a little harder in her chest.

I lie awake at night thinking about you.

He was silent for a long moment and then strolled to the window and stared across the city. 'It is going to drive your father crazy. Does that bother you?'

Yes, it bothered her. Her safety and the safety of her mother rested on a knife-edge, which was why she had to get away.

She had a sudden urge to tell him the truth, but years of keeping her secret and loyalty to her mother prevented her from doing it. And she knew enough about Stefan Ziakas to know that he wasn't going to be interested in the details of her personal life. He avoided all that, didn't he? He would never let anything personal interfere with business. 'He has to understand that this is my life and I want to make my own mistakes. I want to be independent.'

'So this is delayed teenage rebellion?'

Let him think that if he wanted to. 'I know you're not

afraid of going up against him. I read that article recently—the headline was "Clash of the Titans". And the mere mention of your name is enough to put my father in a bad mood for days.' She stared at his broad shoulders, wondering if the sudden tension she saw there was a product of her imagination.

'And has he ever told you why?'

'Of course not. My father would never discuss business with a woman. He won't be pleased with me but he'll have to get used to the idea.' The ache in her arm reminded her just how displeased he was likely to be. 'I hadn't thought about the implications for you. If it bothers you that he'll be angry...'

'That's not a problem for me.' There was the briefest pause and then he turned back to his desk in a smooth, confident movement and pressed a button on the phone. Without any further discussion or questions he instructed someone in his legal department to start making all the necessary arrangements to loan her whatever money she needed.

Having braced herself for rejection, or at least a load of awkward questions, Selene stared at him, unable to believe what she was hearing.

He was going to lend her the money. Just like that.

It couldn't be this easy, could it? Nothing in life was this easy.

The knot of tension that had been lodged in her stomach for as long as she could remember started to ease. Anxiety was replaced by a rush of euphoria that made her feel like dancing round the room.

Apparently unaware of the impact of his decision, Stefan ended the phone call, supremely relaxed. 'It's done. My only stipulation is that you work with one of my business development managers who will give you access to all the in-house resources of the Ziakas Corporation. That way you won't be ripped off by suppliers or customers, and basically you can draw on whatever funds you need.'

He was watching her from under those thick, dark lashes and her stomach flipped.

He was *gorgeous.*

People had him *so* wrong. It wasn't right that everyone should talk about him in hushed voices as some sort of cold, conscienceless machine when he was obviously capable of all the normal human emotions. Maybe he was hard and ruthless in some aspects of his life, but to her he'd been nothing but kind.

'I—' She was dizzy with euphoria, hardly able to get her head around what had just happened. She was going to be able to start her own business, rent a small apartment and help her mother leave her father. She wanted to fling her arms round him and then remembered that this was a business meeting and she was pretty sure people didn't do things like that in business meetings. 'That's an excellent outcome. Thank you. You won't be sorry.' She should shake his hand. Yes, that was what she should do. Shake his hand to seal the deal.

Standing up, she walked towards him and held out her hand.

His hand closed over hers, warm and strong, and suddenly what had begun as a simple handshake became something else entirely. He smelt good. She had no idea whether it was shampoo or something different but it made her want to bury her face in his neck and inhale deeply. All she had to do was lean forward and she'd be kissing him. Horrified by how tempted she was, she looked down at her hand instead and saw the expensive watch on his wrist and his lean, bronzed fingers linked intimately with hers.

Her stomach clenched.

Power and masculinity throbbed from him and suddenly all she could think about was sex—which was crazy because she knew nothing about sex.

But he did.

'So now that's out of the way,' he drawled softly, 'the question is how far are you willing to take this quest for independence?'

Busy imagining those strong, confident hands on her body, she felt her heart thud. 'Why are you asking?'

'Because I'm hosting a party tonight and I find myself minus a date. How do you feel about celebrating your new-found independence in style?'

Her eyes lifted to his and she saw amusement there. Amusement and something a little bit dangerous.

The excitement came in a whoosh that drove the air from her lungs.

Her head spun. The hungry look in his eyes was interfering with the normally smooth rhythm of her breathing. 'You're inviting me to a party?' She never went to parties unless her father decided it was time to play Happy Families in public. They were the most painful moments of her life. And the loneliest, all of them fake.

She'd never been to a party for the sheer fun of it. Never been to a party where she was allowed to be herself.

She wondered why he was asking her.

'If I say no does that mean—?'

'You have my agreement on the loan. Your answer has no effect on our deal.'

In that case she should walk away. There would be time to party once she was safely away from the island. Selene licked her lips. 'What sort of party is it?'

'A strictly grown-up event. No jelly or ice cream in sight.'

A party. *With him.*

'You're asking me to come as your date?'

'That's right.'

The excitement was sharper than when he'd agreed to lend her the money. A date. A party. With this man. She'd never done anything like that in her life.

She should say no. Now that he'd agreed to help her she should get back to Antaxos, persuade her mother to leave and be long gone before her father returned. She couldn't possibly say yes even though she wanted to more than she'd ever wanted anything in her life.

On the other hand, why not?

For the first time in her life she was free to make her own decision about something. For once her father wasn't dictating her actions, no one was watching her and her mother was safe. She had no one to think about but herself. If she wanted to go to a party, she could. And wasn't that the point of all this? To be able to live her life the way she wanted to live it?

Feeling liberated, she opened her mouth. 'I don't have anything to wear.'

'That's easily solved.'

'I have this fantasy about wearing a wicked red dress and drinking champagne from a tall, slim glass with a handsome man in a dinner jacket. Would we drink champagne?'

His mouth curved into a smile so sexy it should have been illegal. 'All night.'

'And would we—?'

The devil danced in his eyes and his mouth moved fractionally closer to hers. 'If you're asking what I think you're asking then the answer is yes, we definitely would.'

CHAPTER THREE

'How did he arrange for these dresses to be delivered so fast? And how did he guess my size? On second thoughts, don't answer that.' Confronted with a rail of the most beautiful dresses she'd ever seen, Selene felt as if she'd stepped onto a Hollywood movie set. Part of her felt anxious about her decision to stay, but another part felt wildly excited. She listened to the excited part and ignored the anxiety. That, she reasoned, came from too many years of not being allowed to make her own decisions. It was natural that it felt strange.

Maria pulled an elegant clutch bag from tissue paper. 'When Stefan picks up the phone, people respond at supersonic speed. The benefits of being a man of power.'

'Except that you were the one who did the phoning.'

'True.' Maria smiled. 'Power by proxy. Why don't you start by choosing a dress?'

'Is Stefan joining us?'

'He sends his apologies. He has one more important meeting he has to take before you leave.'

'I don't mind. I'd be too self-conscious to strip in front of him anyway and it's more fun with a woman. It was thoughtful of him to arrange for you to help me.' She saw Maria's expression change. 'You don't think he's thoughtful?'

The other woman removed a beautiful pair of shoes from a bag. 'That's certainly an adjective I've not heard applied to him before.'

'He's running a business. Of course he has to be tough. But on the two occasions I've met him he's been kind to me.'

Maria put the shoes down in front of her. 'You have no idea how pleased I am to hear that. Why don't you pick a dress and try it on? Because once he's finished his meeting he won't want to hang around. Is there anything in particular that grabs your attention?'

'The red one.' There was no other choice for her and the colour matched her mood. *Bold.* 'I've never worn anything like that in my life.' She reached for a shimmering sheath of scarlet with jewels on the strapless bodice. 'This is *gorgeous*. Will it be over the top?'

'No. It's a very glamorous party. That dress is very sophisticated.' Maria stared at it for a long moment. 'Are you sure you don't want to pick a different one? Maybe the blue?'

'You don't think Stefan will like the red one?'

'I think he might like it a little too much.'

'How can he possibly like it too much?'

'Selene…' The other woman hesitated. 'Are you sure you want to go to this party?'

'*Want* to go? I'm *desperate* to go. You have no idea how boring my life has been up to now. I'm going to dress up, drink champagne and have the most amazing night with Stefan.'

'Just as long as you know that's all it will be.' Maria cleared her throat gently. 'Stefan is the stuff of female dreams, but he quickly turns into a nightmare for most women. He isn't the happy-ever-after type—you do know that, don't you? Because you seem like a really nice girl and I'd hate to see you hurt.'

Selene paused with her hand on the dress.

She knew all about hurt and this wasn't it. 'I won't be hurt. I'm excited. It will be fun to just enjoy myself for one night.' Fun to be able to make a decision to go to a party. Fun to decide what to wear. For once, her life felt almost normal.

'You don't usually enjoy yourself?'

'I have an overprotective father.' Realising that she'd said more than she intended to, Selene draped the dress over her arm. 'Is there somewhere I can try it on?'

'You'll need underwear.' Maria handed her several boxes. 'Go and change and if you need help, call me.'

An hour later Selene was the proud owner of the most beautiful dress she'd ever seen, along with a small emergency wardrobe suitable for an overnight stay at a luxury villa on a Greek island. Ahead of her lay the most exciting night of her life, and if lurking underneath her happiness was a fear that her father might return early she dismissed it.

That wasn't going to happen.

She'd have plenty of time to get home, persuade her mother to leave and be long gone before he returned.

'You can't do this. You can't take that girl to the party. It's immoral.'

Stefan glanced up from the papers he was signing to find Maria standing in front of his desk like a general facing down an enemy army.

'Now, *that's* the look you're supposed to give unwanted visitors.' He flung down his pen. 'Do I need to remind you that *you* were the one who showed her into the lion's den?'

'I'm serious, Stefan. Take someone else. Someone more your type.'

'Just this morning you were lecturing me on picking the wrong type. Make up your mind.'

'I wasn't telling you to prey on innocent girls.'

'She's an adult. She knows what she's doing.' He picked up his pen and flicked through the papers on his desk.

'She's an idealist. She thinks you're thoughtful and kind.'

'I know.' Smiling, Stefan signed the back page. 'For once, I'm the good guy. An unfamiliar role, I admit, but I'm surprised by how much I'm enjoying the novelty.'

'You're treating her like a shiny new toy that you can play with.' Maria's mouth set in a firm line. 'Send her home to her father.'

Stefan was careful not to let the sudden flare of emotion show on his face. Slowly, he put his pen down. 'Do you know who her father is?'

'No. Although she mentioned something about him being overprotective.'

'Is that a useful synonym for "tyrant", I wonder? Her father, Maria, is Stavros Antaxos.' He watched as Maria's face lost some of its colour. 'Yes. Exactly.' He heard his voice harden and it irritated him that just saying the name was enough to do that to him. He'd had over two decades to learn how to control his response.

'How on earth can a man like that produce someone as charming as Selene?'

He'd been asking himself the same question.

'I assume she takes after her mother.'

Maria looked troubled. 'But why would someone as wealthy as her, from such a close family, come to you?'

He'd been asking himself the same question. Repeatedly. 'I'm a hero, didn't you know? I'm the first man women think of when they're in trouble.'

'You're the man who causes the trouble.'

'Ouch, that's harsh.' Stefan leaned back and stretched out his legs. 'Here I am, sword at the ready, eager to chop the head off a dragon to save the maiden, and all you can do is knock my confidence.'

She didn't smile. 'Is that really what's going on here? Because it occurred to me that maybe you're using the maiden to taunt the dragon.'

Stefan's smile didn't slip. 'When we were dishing out roles in this company I picked cynic, not you.'

'We're all cynical here. It's contagious. Does she know how much her father hates you? Does she know the story?'

No one knew the story. Not even Maria, whom he allowed more liberties than most. Oh, she *thought* she knew—thought it was all about business rivalry and two alpha males acting out their deeply competitive natures. She had no idea how far back it went, or how deep the scars. And why would she? They weren't visible. He didn't allow them to be visible.

'It's because of my relationship with her father that she chose me.'

Maria's mouth flattened with disapproval.

'Are you sure this isn't a case of out of the frying pan and into the fire?'

'You're suggesting I'm worse than Antaxos? That is hardly a complimentary view of one's boss.'

'We're not talking about work right now. My admiration for your intellect and business skills is boundless but when it comes to women you're bad news. What are your plans for her, Stefan?'

'When it comes to women I never make plans. You should know that by now. "Plan" implies a future and we both know I don't think like that. I've agreed to help her with her business—which, by the way, looks remarkably interesting on paper, particularly when you consider the product. And I'm taking her to a party. I intend to provide more fun than she's had in the rest of her life. She can make her own decisions about how she spends her time. She's twenty-two and on a quest for independence.' Stefan battled a disturbingly vivid image of her breasts revealed through a cloud of lace. 'All grown up.'

'She's very inexperienced.'

'Yes. I'm finding that unusually appealing.'

'And does that appeal have anything to do with the fact you are the *last* man her father would want her to be with? Thinking of her with you will drive him demented.'

Stefan smiled. 'I consider that an added bonus.'

'I'm worried about her, Stefan.'

'She came to me. She asked for my help. I'm giving it.' It was obvious that there was something going on beneath the surface and it intrigued him. She was playing a game, but he wasn't sure which game. 'I don't recall you ever being this protective of the women I date before.'

'That's because you normally date women who don't need protecting from anything.'

'So maybe it's time for a change.' Cutting off the conversation, he rose to his feet. 'How long until she's ready? No doubt she's still pulling clothes on and off, trying to decide what to wear.'

'She decided what to wear in less than five seconds and it took her barely more than that to try it on.'

Used to women who could waste the best part of a day selecting one outfit, he was impressed. 'I like her more and more.'

'She has a very high opinion of you.'

'I know.' He walked past her to the door and Maria made a frustrated sound.

'Where is your conscience?'

Stefan picked up his jacket. 'I don't have a conscience.'

When he'd mentioned his villa she'd imagined somewhere small. She hadn't for one moment expected this spacious, airy mansion with high ceilings and acres of glass. Here, in this testament to innovative architecture, there were no dark corners or contagious gloom, just dazzling light exploding across marble floors and picking out the warm Mediterranean colours that turned the deceptively simple interior into a luxurious sanctuary.

Outside, a vine-shaded terrace led to gardens that created a blur of extravagant colour as they tumbled down a gentle slope that led to a crescent beach. And even there the idyll didn't end. Unlike Antaxos, there were no killer rocks or dark, fathomless depths that threatened to swallow a person and leave no trace. Just sand of the softest, creamiest yellow and tiny silver fish dancing in the clear shallow water. The whole scene was so tempting that she, who avoided water, just wanted to rip off her shoes and plunge into the safe, cool shallows.

'So this is why people see the Greek Islands as a tourist destination.' She spoke without thinking and her unguarded comment earned her a questioning look.

'Was the reason for that choice in doubt?'

Staring out of huge windows across the garden to the turquoise sea, she felt something stir inside her. It was like living a life in black and white and suddenly seeing it in colour. 'Antaxos isn't anything like this. No soft sand, just nasty rocks—' She just stopped herself mentioning the rumour that a woman who'd been madly in love with her father had once fallen from those rocks and drowned.

'My father's house—our house—is built of stone with small windows.' She managed to say it without shuddering. 'The design supposedly keeps the heat out.' And it kept everything and everyone else out, too. The bleak, dark atmosphere inside the place had somehow permeated the stone so that even the building felt unfriendly. 'It's stuffy in the summer and dark and cheerless in the winter. I like the light here. You have a very happy home.'

'Happy?' He glanced up at the villa, a faint frown between his eyes. 'You think a building has moods?'

'Definitely. Don't you?'

'I think a building is a building.'

'Oh, no, that isn't true. A building can make a person feel different. Here, the sunshine makes you want to smile. And all this *space*—it feels like being free.' She spread her arms. 'I've always wanted to be a bird so I can fly.' *Fly away from the island that had held her trapped for so long.*

But she'd finally escaped. She'd done it.

This was the start of her new life.

Excited, she did a twirl. Stefan shot out a hand and steadied her before she lost her balance. 'Probably best if you don't fly here. I've seen pictures of your home on Antaxos. You live in a building the size of a castle.'

Selene was conscious of the strength of his fingers on her arm. 'It isn't anything like this. My father doesn't like spending money on material things.'

'Is there anything that your father *does* like?'

Hurting people.

She stood, searching for an appropriate response to his question, her heart a ball of pain in her chest. 'Winning,' she said finally. 'He likes winning.'

'Yes.' His hand dropped abruptly from her arm. 'Yes, he does.'

And he'd know, of course, because he was her father's

biggest business rival. She sensed the anger in him and she also sensed something more. Something dark lurked behind those sexy eyes. 'You really hate my father, don't you?'

'It's true to say he's not my favourite person in the world.' The deceptively light banter and that attractive slanting smile didn't fool her.

This man was every bit as tough as her father.

She felt a twinge of unease, but already he was strolling ahead of her. She tried to ignore the little voice in her head telling her this might not have been such a good idea after all.

It was her first party. Her first 'date' with a man. It was natural to be a little apprehensive.

She followed him through a beautiful living space with white walls and uninterrupted views of the sea into the most beautiful bedroom she'd ever seen.

Forgetting her unease, Selene stared around her in delight. 'It's gorgeous. There's a pool outside the doors and you can see the sea from the bed. It's stunning. Is this my room?'

He turned to her with a slow, deliberate smile. 'It's *my* room,' he said, his tone soft and intimate as he lifted his hand and gently pushed a strand of hair out of her eyes, 'but you're sharing it, *koukla mou.*'

She didn't know whether it was the endearment that made her heart bump harder, the seductive brush of his fingers against her cheek or the anticipation of what was to come. 'The bed looks comfortable.'

'It is. Unfortunately proving that will have to wait until later.'

'I didn't mean that.'

'I know. I'm finding your tendency to speak before you think surprisingly endearing.'

The crazy thing was she wasn't normally like that. At home she had to guard every word. She wondered why she'd suddenly lost that built-in inhibition and decided it was just because her father wasn't present. It was liberating not to have to watch what she said. 'I'm going to zip my mouth.'

That dark gaze dropped to her mouth. 'Don't. I like it.'

Heart thudding, she looked at his lips. Noticed that they were firm and slightly curved.

'No,' he said gently.

Her eyes lifted to his. 'No?'

'No, I'm not going to kiss you. At least, not yet. Tempted though I am to snatch a few moments, there are some things that shouldn't be rushed and your first time is one of them.'

The fact that he knew it was her first time should have embarrassed her but it didn't, and she didn't waste time denying something that would be obvious to a man like him.

There was an almost electric connection between them that she felt right through her body. Warmth spread through her pelvis and she felt shaky with need. She wanted him to kiss her so badly she couldn't imagine how she was going to last a whole evening without just grabbing him. 'Maybe I don't mind being rushed.'

Frowning slightly, he brushed this thumb over her lower lip, the movement slow and lingering. 'You need to be more cautious around men.'

And normally she *was* cautious, of course, not least because all the men she knew worked for her father in some capacity. But Stefan was different. He wasn't afraid of her father. And he'd got her through that horrible night when she was a teenager. 'I don't feel a need to be cautious around you. Does that sound crazy?'

'Yes.'

'I trust you.'

'Don't.'

'Why not? You're not being paid by my father.'

Silence stretched between them.

His eyes glittering, he lowered his head a fraction until his forehead was against hers and their mouths were a breath apart. The brush of his fingers against her cheek was gentle and seductive at the same time. 'You've come here with me but I want you to know it's not too late for you to change your mind.'

'I'm not going to change my mind.'

His gaze darkened. 'Maybe I should just cancel the party and we can have our own party here, just the two of us.'

Awareness twisted in her stomach. The tension was stifling. She felt as if she were standing on the edge of a deep, dark pool about to jump, with no idea whether she'd be able to save herself from drowning. 'If we have our own party here, I couldn't wear my new dress.'

'You could wear it for me.' His mouth slanted into that sexy smile. 'And I could remove it.'

Her hand was resting on his arm and she could feel the hardness of his biceps under her fingers. 'Isn't that rather a waste of an expensive dress?'

'The dress is just packaging. It's the product underneath that interests me.' His fingers stroked her neck gently and then his phone rang. He stepped back with a regretful smile. 'Probably a good thing. I need enough time to do justice to the moment. Our guests will be arriving in a few hours and in true Cinderella style *you* need to get ready.'

A few *hours*? 'How long do you think it will take me?'

'In my experience most women take a lifetime to get ready. In the hope of speeding up that process, I've arranged for you to have some help. Not only am I a knight in shining armour, I'm also a fairy godmother. In fact the extent of my benevolence is starting to astonish me.' His phone continued to ring and he dragged it out of his pocket. 'Excuse me. I need to take this.'

As the door closed behind him Selene stood still. Her cheek tingled from the touch of his fingers and the only thing in her head was the memory of hard, male muscle under her fingers.

With a shiver, she wrapped her arms around herself and turned to look at the bed. It was enormous, draped in white linen and facing the sea. Indulgent, luxurious and like nothing she'd ever seen before. Experimenting, she slid off her shoes and jumped into the middle of it, moaning with delight as she felt the soft mound of pillows give beneath her. It was like being hugged by a cloud.

She rolled onto her back and stared up at the ceiling, smiling.

She felt free.

Right this moment no one knew where she was. No one was watching her. No one was reporting her every move to her father. No one had told her where she had to be. She was here because *she* had decided she wanted to be here.

Going to Stefan for help had been her first good decision and agreeing to come to the party had been her second.

Feeling light-headed, she sprang off the bed and explored the rest of the bedroom suite.

There was a ridiculously luxurious bathroom with a wall of glass that made it possible to lie in the bath and look at the sea.

Determined to indulge herself, Selene unpacked her own candles and soap. Then she ran herself a deep bath and lay in it, enjoying the scent of the candle.

She wasn't so naïve she didn't know what was going to

happen and she wanted it to happen. She'd dreamed about Stefan for years. Had had years to think about it. *Imagine it.* It was perfect that he should be the first.

Soon, she thought. *Soon she'd know everything there was to know about seduction.*

She washed her hair and was wrapped in a soft towel, wondering why getting ready was supposed to take hours, when there was a tap on the door and two young women entered, clutching several cases.

'Selene? I'm Dana. I'm a genius with hair.' Dana pushed the door shut with the toe of her shoe. 'This is Helena—she's the make-up fairy.'

'I don't own make-up.' It was embarrassing to admit it but her father had never allowed make-up or anything that he described as 'vanity'. He'd only paid for her to have a brace because the dentist had told him it would cost him more in the long run if she didn't have one.

Dana flipped open her case. 'No problem. We have everything you'll need.'

'Do you think you can do something about my freckles and my non-existent eyelashes?'

'You're kidding, right?' Helena peered at her. 'Your eyelashes are incredible. Thick and long. What's wrong with them?'

Selene had assumed it was obvious. 'Don't you think I look a bit freakish? They're so fair they barely show up.'

'Freakish? No, I don't think you look freakish. As for being fair—that's why mascara was invented, sweetie.' With a dazzling smile, she flipped open another case to reveal an array of different make-up. 'I have everything we'll need right here.'

'Hair first.' Dana pulled a chair into the middle of the room. 'Sit. And don't look in the mirror or you'll ruin the "wow" moment and that's our favourite part. Just trust me.'

'Will I recognise myself?'

'You'll be the best version of you.'

Selene, intrigued by what the best version of herself was going to look like, sat still as the girl trimmed her hair, trying not to flinch as blonde curls floated onto her lap. 'You're cutting it short?'

'All I'm doing is taking off the ends to improve the condition and cutting in a few layers to soften it. Stefan threatened never to use me again if I ruin your beautiful hair, although if you want my personal opinion—' Dana squinted at her '—I think it would suit you short.'

He liked her hair. The thought went round and round in her head.

He liked her hair.

It was her first compliment—not actually spoken, of course, but a compliment none the less—and with it came the discovery that the feeling of flying was something that could happen inside you. Her spirits lifted and a smile touched her lips, and as well as the smile and the happiness there was something else. A lump in her throat that caught her by surprise.

'It's in great condition.' Dana's fingers moved through her hair as she snipped and combed.

He liked her hair.

The girl worked speedily and skilfully, dodging Helena, who was doing Selene's nails.

Once Selene's hair was dry Dana swept it up, twisted and pinned until finally she was satisfied. 'You're ready for make-up.'

'Can your magic make-up box get rid of my freckles?'

'Why would you want to? They're charming. Part of you. We want to keep you looking like you. That's one thing he insisted on. This is just primer I'm using, by the way.' Helena smoothed her fingers over Selene's face. 'You have beautiful skin.' The girl opened a series of pots, potions, colours, concealers, the sight of which made Selene's head spin. 'What cleanser do you use?'

'Soap I make myself.' Selene delved into her bag and pulled out a bar. 'Try it. I make candles, too, but Stefan isn't convinced there's a market for those.'

'He's a man. What does he know?'

Selene smiled and her heart pounded because finally, finally, she believed this might actually happen. Her new life was almost visible, shining like a star in the distance.

The girl sniffed the soap. Her brows rose. 'Smells good. And your skin is wonderful so that's a good advert.' She dropped it into her bag. 'I'll try it, thanks.' She turned back to Selene. 'I'm not going to use too much make-up on you because you have a wonderfully fresh look and I don't want to spoil that.'

It took ages, and Selene was just starting to fidget and wonder how much longer it was going to take when Helena stepped back.

'God, I'm good at my job. You look spectacular. Don't look in the mirror yet. Get dressed first so that you can see the full effect all at once.' She grinned. 'I almost feel sorry for Stefan.'

CHAPTER FOUR

STEFAN moved slowly among his guests, stirring up expectation.

'So who is she, Stefan?' A Hollywood actress who had been flirting with him for months didn't hide her annoyance at his hints that he'd brought a special guest. 'Not Sonya, I assume?'

'Not Sonya.'

'Why so mysterious? And why is she still in the bedroom and not out here, or is that a question one shouldn't ask?'

'Worn out from too much sex,' someone murmured. Stefan simply smiled and accepted a glass of champagne from one of his hovering staff.

'She leads a very quiet, very private life and this is all very new to her.' He'd discovered early in life that it was best to sail as close to the truth as possible and he stuck to that now as he carefully conjured suspense and interest among his guests.

Carys Bergen, a model who had been flirting with him for several months, strolled up to him. 'You're a wicked man. Who is this reclusive woman that you're about to produce like a rabbit from a magician's hat?'

He left his guests simmering in an atmosphere of expectation and strolled through the villa to the master bedroom suite, scooping another glass of champagne on the way.

At first he thought she wasn't in the room and he gave an impatient frown and glanced around him. 'Selene?'

'I'm here.'

He turned his head.

There was no sign of the awkward schoolgirl. The person standing in front of him in a sheath of shimmering scarlet was all woman.

'That dress was designed for the express purpose of tempting some poor defenceless man to rip it off.' His eyes weren't on the dress, but on the delicious curve of her narrow waist and the swell of her breasts above the tight jewelled bodice.

She smiled, clearly delighted by the effect she was having on him. '"Defenceless" is not a word anyone would use to describe you. And I know you spend your life escorting women who wear stunning dresses so what makes this one special?'

'The person wearing it.'

'Oh, *smooth*, Mr Ziakas.'

Unused to women whose response to compliments was laughter, Stefan handed her a glass. 'Champagne in a tall, slim glass, a red dress and a guy in a dinner jacket. This could be the first time in my life I've made a woman's dreams come true.'

'Mmm, thank you.' She took a mouthful of champagne, her eyes closing as if she wanted to savour the moment. 'It tastes like celebration.' Immediately she took another sip, and then another larger gulp.

Stefan raised his brows. 'If you want to remember the evening, drink slowly.'

'It tastes delicious. I love the feel of the bubbles on my tongue. And one of the best things about my new independence is being able to decide what I drink and what I don't drink.'

'That's fine. But, delighted though I am that you're clearly capable of enjoying the sensual potential of champagne, I'd rather my date wasn't unconscious. From now on take tiny sips and count to a hundred in between.' He held out his arm and she immediately put her empty glass down, took his arm and smiled up at him.

'Thank you.'

That wide, genuine smile knocked him off-balance. He was used to coy, flirtatious and manipulative. 'Friendly' was new to him and he had no idea how to respond.

She appeared to have no sense of caution. No layers of protection between her and the world. How the hell was she going to manage when she was no longer protected by her father's security machine?

'What are you thanking me for?'

'For agreeing to help me, for inviting me to this party and for arranging all these wonderful clothes. It's the perfect way to start my new life. You're my hero.' She stood back slightly, her eyes on his shoulders. 'You look smoking hot in a dinner jacket, by the way. Very macho. I bet all the dragons in Greece are trembling in their caves, or wherever it is dragons live when they're not munching on innocent maidens.'

'Heroes don't exist in real life and you've definitely drunk that too fast.' Stefan made a mental note to brief the staff to make her next drink non-alcoholic, otherwise she'd be lying face-down in a coma before the party had even begun.

'You're too modest.' Her eyes drifted from his shoulders to his mouth. 'People are so wrong about you.'

'You are *far* too trusting. What if they're right?'

Apparently undaunted by that suggestion, she closed

her other hand round his lapel and pulled him towards her. 'Do you know what I think? I think you've created this bad-boy image to keep people—women especially—at a distance. I think you're afraid of intimacy.'

Stefan felt darkness press in on him.

She'd found the one tiny chink in his armour and thrust her sword into it.

How? How had she done that? Was it a lucky guess?

It had to be a lucky guess. She didn't know anything about his past. No one did.

'I'm not afraid of intimacy and later I'm going to prove that to you, so don't drink any more or you'll fall asleep before we reach the interesting part of the evening.' Ignoring her puzzled expression, he guided her towards the door.

'I've upset you. Did I say something wrong?'

'What makes you think you've upset me?'

'Because your voice changed.'

Stefan, who prided himself on being inscrutable, started to sweat. Did she pick up on *everything*? 'You haven't upset me but I have guests, and I've already kept them waiting long enough. Are you ready?'

'Yes. Although I'm bracing myself to be hated.'

'Why would you be hated?'

'Because I'm with the hottest guy on the planet. All the women are going to hate me, but don't worry about it. When you're Stavros Antaxos's daughter you get used to not having friends.'

Her tone was light but he instantly thought of the night on the boat, when she'd found a hidden corner to sit, away from all the other guests. She'd worn her loneliness with a brave smile but she'd been almost pathetically grateful when he'd sat down and talked to her.

'Friendship is idealised and overrated. If someone wants

to be friends with you, it's usually because they want something.'

'I don't believe that.'

'You mean you don't want to believe it. You are hopelessly idealistic.' He held the door open for her and the brightness of her expression dimmed slightly.

'So you're saying that true friendship is impossible?'

'I'm saying that the temptation of money is too strong for most people. It changes things.' The scar inside him ached, reminding him of the truth of that. 'Just something to bear in mind for the future if you don't want to be hurt.'

'Is that what you do? Do you live your life protecting yourself from being hurt?'

Stefan, who was used to keeping his conversations satisfyingly superficial, wondered why every exchange with her dived far beneath the surface. 'I live my life the way I want to live it. Right now I'd like to attend my own party. Shall we go?'

Everyone was staring, some discreetly over the top of their champagne glasses and some more openly. But all the glances revealed the same emotion.

Shock.

Feeling like a caged bird suddenly released to freedom, Selene took another glass of champagne just because she could.

Stefan frowned. 'Are you sure you should drink that?'

'Do you know one of the best things about tonight? The fact that all of it is my decision. I decided to come to the party, I decided what dress I'd wear and now I'm deciding to drink champagne.'

'Just as long as you realise you're also choosing to have a crushing headache in the morning.'

'It will be worth it.' She drank half the glass and smiled

up at him. 'Champagne makes everything feel more exciting, doesn't it?'

'The second glass does that. After the third I doubt you'll remember enough about what happened to be excited. I advise you to switch to orange juice.'

'If it's going to give me a headache then I'll find that out for myself.'

'I'll remind you of that when you're moaning in the bathroom.'

She laughed up at him, forgetting the people around them. 'How many glasses of champagne do you have to drink before you'll kiss me in public?'

His eyes gleamed. 'I don't need to be intoxicated for that, *koukla mou.*'

'In that case—' her voice husky, Selene closed her fingers around the lapel of his jacket and closed her eyes '—kiss me.' *Just in case it never happened again. Just in case tonight was the only chance she was going to get to kiss a man like him.*

Anticipation washed over her skin and she waited to feel the brush of his mouth over hers, barely aware of the hum of conversation or the music around her as her imagination took over her mind. But he didn't kiss her. It was a moment of elongated suspense designed to torture her, and just when she'd started to think she was going to remember this moment as the most humiliating of her life she felt the tips of his fingers slide over her jaw.

She opened her eyes and met his, her heart pounding a crazy rhythm.

There was a brief silence and then he slid his hand behind her head and drew her face to his. 'What is it about you? I should walk away, but I can't.'

Desire was an ache low in her belly. 'I'm hanging onto your jacket. That could be the reason.'

He didn't smile. He didn't say a word.

For a breathless moment Selene saw something flicker in those dark eyes and then he lowered his head slowly, his eyes locked on hers. Until that moment she'd never known that a look could have a physical effect, but she felt that look all the way through her body in a rush of heat that spread right through her.

The anticipation was so acute it was almost painful—and he knew it because that sensual mouth curved slightly as he prolonged expectation.

And then the warmth of his breath brushed against her lips and she felt his free hand slide down her back and settle low on her waist as he drew her into contact with him.

She felt hardness and heat and suddenly doing this didn't feel like light-hearted fun any more. In his eyes she saw no trace of humour. Just raw, untamed male sexuality. She realised in a flash that he was controlling every second of this encounter. The pace. The intensity. Even her response. He was in charge of all of it.

And suddenly she knew that exploring her own sexuality with this man was like deciding to buy a pet and choosing a tiger. He was everything that wasn't tame or safe. Everything dangerous. Everything she'd dreamed of during those long nights when she'd imagined her life looking different.

Her mind in fast rewind, she tried to pull away. But his hand was hard and warm on her back and he held her exactly as she'd dreamed of being held.

'Close your eyes, champagne girl.' His soft command slid into her bones and she felt as if she'd just jumped off a high diving board with no opportunity to change her mind before she hit deep water.

And then his mouth touched hers and she forgot all of it as she melted under the skill of his kiss. He kissed her with erotic expertise, teasing her lips with his tongue, driving her wild with each movement of his mouth until her head was spinning and her thoughts were an incoherent blur.

It was, without doubt, the most perfect, exciting moment of her life and she wrapped her arms around his neck, her body quivering as she felt the evidence of his arousal pressing against her.

The fact that he wanted her was as intoxicating as the feelings he whipped up inside her with nothing but the skill of his mouth.

'Maybe you should get a room. I know the man who owns this villa. I could put in a good word for you if you like?'

A light female voice cut through her dreams and Selene would have jumped away from him had it not been for the fact that Stefan kept her locked firmly against him.

'Your timing is less than perfect, Carys.'

'I thought it was absolutely perfect.'

Bitterly disappointed by the interruption, Selene stole a glance at the other woman, wondering who she was.

The woman was stunning, her smile cool as she extended a hand to Selene. 'I'm Carys. And you're Selene.'

It gave her a jolt that someone recognised her. Stupidly, she hadn't even thought of that. 'You know me?'

'Of course. It's just unusual not to see you with your parents. You're such a close-knit family.'

Selene kept her smile in place. This was the part she was used to playing and she played it well. 'It's nice to meet you.'

'Mmm. And you.' Carys raised her glass to her lips, admiration in her eyes as she looked at Stefan. 'I have to hand it to you, occasionally you display a Machiavellian genius beyond anything I've ever encountered. Game, set and match, Stefan.'

Selene, who assumed that this coded exchange related to their relationship, stayed silent as Carys scooped two glasses of champagne from a passing waitress and handed one to her.

'Let's drink to your existence.'

She saw Stefan frown slightly and remembered what he'd said about not drinking any more champagne, but she couldn't bring herself to ask for orange juice in front of this sophisticated woman so she tapped her glass against hers and drank.

The alcohol fizzed into her veins and boosted her confidence. She wanted to dance but no one else seemed to be and when she asked why, Carys looked amused.

'Dancing makes one—hot.'

'Does that matter?' She started to sway on the spot and the other woman smiled.

'That's for you to decide, but if you can tempt Stefan onto the dance floor then you'll have succeeded where others have failed.'

Realising that she desperately wanted to succeed where others had failed, Selene watched as she walked away. 'She hates me. Not because of my father, but because of you. She's crazy about you.'

He gave her a sharp look. 'Not so innocent, are you?'

'I'm good at reading people.' She'd had to be. She'd learned to recognise everything that wasn't said, every emotion hidden beneath the surface, so that she could anticipate and deflect. It was how she lived her life and it was going to take more than one evening of freedom to undo that.

Thoughtful, she finished her champagne. He removed the empty glass from her hand and replaced it with orange juice.

'Here's a hint—alcohol makes you feel good for five

minutes, then you crash and you'll be crying on my shoulder.'

'I only cry when I'm happy. Although you should know I'm very happy tonight so you probably ought to stock up on tissues.' Laughing at the look on his face, she tugged her hand from his and spun onto the dance floor. Emerging from a pirouette, she smacked into Stefan who closed his hands around her arms to steady her.

'No more champagne.'

'Killjoy.'

'I'm preserving my sanity and your brain cells.'

'I just want to start living my life.' The thumping rhythm of the music made it impossible not to dance.

Stefan clamped his arm around her to restrict her movements. 'But you don't have to live it all in one night.'

The music slowed and he drew her against him. She sighed and slid her arms around his neck. 'You know when you have a dream and the reality turns out even better?'

He covered her lips with his fingers. 'I don't know what is coming out of your mouth next, but I suggest this would be a good moment to clamp it shut.'

'It's no wonder all the women chase after you because you are *seriously* hot.'

He shook his head in disbelief. 'Whatever happened to the shy, withdrawn nun who walked into my office?'

'I think this might be the real me, and the real me has never been let out before.'

Amusement mingled with exasperation. 'Should I be afraid?'

'You're not afraid of anything. That's why I came to you. I know it's not politically correct to admit it but I think I might be very turned on by strong men.' Dizzy from the atmosphere and the champagne circulating in her system, Selene leaned her forehead against his chest. 'And it doesn't hurt that you smell amazing.'

'Selene—'

'And you kiss like a god. You must have had hours of practice to be able to kiss like that. It's brilliant to have ticked the first thing on my wish list.'

'You have a wish list?'

'I have a list of ten things I want to experience the moment I leave the island and start my new life. Being kissed is one of them and I have to say you aced that one. I'm so glad it was you and not some slobbery amateur. Another is waking up next to a really hot guy.' She sneaked a look at him and he shook his head in disbelief.

'So this is what happens when an overprotected daughter suddenly cuts loose. Until a few hours ago you were a shy girl who had never been near a city. What else is on this list of yours?'

Selene discovered that her head was too fuzzy to remember in detail. 'Being able to make my own decisions about everything. Sex is on my list, too, obviously. Wild, abandoned sex.'

'With anyone in particular?' His mocking tone made her smile.

'Yes, you. I always wanted the first time to be you.' She saw no reason not to be honest. 'I hope I'm not giving you performance anxiety? No pressure or anything.'

His eyes glittered down into hers but he was no longer smiling. Somewhere during the course of their conversation the atmosphere had shifted subtly. 'I think the champagne is talking.'

'No, I'm pretty sure it was me, although the champagne might have prompted it. It's good at removing inhibitions.'

'I'd noticed.' With a driven sigh, he drew her off the dance floor and down a narrow path that led to the beach.

'Where are we going? You're walking too fast.'

'I'm removing you from public before you tip over the edge and do something you're going to regret.' He cursed under his breath as she stumbled and fell against him. '*Cristos*, I should have taken that third glass of champagne out of your hand.' His voice harsh, he swept her into his arms as if she weighed nothing and continued down the steps. 'Here's another tip. Next time stop drinking while you can still walk in a straight line.'

'There might not be a next time. That's why I'm making the most of this time. You have to live for the moment and I'm living for the moment. At least, I'm *trying* to live for the moment but it's hard to do that unless the other person is doing it too.'

'*Theé mou—*' Jaw tense, he lowered her to her feet and Selene collapsed onto the sand in a dizzy heap.

Shaking her head to try and dispel the swimmy feeling, she pulled her shoes off her feet. 'The world is spinning. Next time I won't drink quite as much quite as fast. And if you even mouth the words "I told you so" I will punch you.'

He swore softly under his breath. 'Do you even realise what could happen to you in this state? You virtually offered yourself to me.'

'I did offer myself to you, but obviously that was too forward of me because now you're frowning. Is it because you don't think a woman has as much right to enjoy sex as a man?'

He sucked air through his teeth. 'I don't think that.'

'Then why are you looking so disapproving? I was relying on you being as bad as everyone says you are.' She flopped back onto the soft sand and he gave a growl low in his throat.

'One of my few life rules is never to have sex with a drunk woman. You should be grateful for that. Stand up!

I can't have a conversation with you when you're lying at my feet like a starfish.'

'Why do men always compare me to animals? First my father says I'm a giraffe and now you say I'm a starfish. The day a man tells me I'm a whale, I'm killing myself.'

With an exasperated sigh he bent and lifted her and she tumbled against him, her body pressed hard against his. There was a tense, throbbing silence broken only by the soft sound of the sea on the sand and his harsh breathing in her ear.

'This,' he breathed, 'is *not* turning out the way I planned it.'

'Tell me about it. I thought amazing things would happen to a girl wearing a dress like this but all I got was lots of anticipation, an incredible kiss and a lecture.'

His grip on her tightened. 'You should be grateful I'm showing restraint.'

'Well, I'm not. I hate the fact you're so controlled. I'd do anything for you to just lose it for a moment and follow your deepest male instincts.'

He muttered something under his breath and then cupped her face in his hands and slanted his mouth over hers. Excitement flashed through her, slid through her limbs and deep into her bones until she felt the strength leaving her. As his tongue traced the seam of her lips and dipped inside Selene felt her tummy tighten and the world spin. His mouth moved slowly, expertly, over hers and she lost track of time and place, *of herself.*

Just when she'd decided that all her dreams about kissing were still intact, he released her.

The sense of loss was searing.

She stared up at him in the semi-darkness, acutely aware of the contrast between them. He was all raw power and masculinity. Despite her height, in her bare feet she barely reached his shoulder.

Without thinking she stretched out her hand and touched his face and instantly heard his sharp intake of breath.

'I'm taking you back to the room.'

'Yes. Take me back to your room so that we can try out your big, beautiful bed. Strip me naked and do unspeakable things to me,' she murmured, running her fingers over his biceps. 'You're very strong.'

'Strong enough to stop you doing something you'll regret tomorrow.'

'You see? You pretend to be bad, but then you're good. I hate to say I told you so, but I was right all along. Secretly you're a nice person, although right now...' Selene suppressed a yawn. 'Right now, I wish you weren't.'

'Stop talking, Selene. Whenever a thought comes into your head, just trap it there. Don't let it out.'

'That's what I've been doing all my life. If my brain is a computer then my hard drive is definitely full.' She gave a gasp as he scooped her off her feet and strode across the sand.

Mouth tight with disapproval, he carried her up a flight of illuminated steps to a private part of the villa. Brightly coloured bougainvillaea tumbled over whitewashed walls and he strode past the small pool she'd noticed earlier outside the doors of the master suite.

'This place is so romantic. Just in case you don't have the energy to make it to the beach, you can leap in here on the way.' Selene gazed at the smooth, floodlit surface of the water, thinking it was the most tranquil place she'd ever seen. Lush exotic plants clustered around the edge of a beautiful pool and the tantalising sound of water came from two elaborate water features. 'How long have you owned this place?'

'A long time.' His voice was terse. 'Can you walk or do you want me to carry you?'

'I definitely want you to carry me. I really like it.' Selene tightened her arms around his neck. 'I want you to carry me straight to bed, and teach me everything I don't know about seduction. We can call it market research.'

'The state you're in, you won't remember any of it in the morning.'

'If it makes you feel better, I'll make notes. I promise to concentrate and learn quickly. You won't have to tell me anything twice.'

'The first thing you should learn is that you should never, ever drink again. The next time you are given a choice of drink or no drink, choose no drink.' Casting her a look of undiluted exasperation, Stefan deposited her in the centre of the huge bed and turned to the woman who had just entered the room. He spoke in rapid Greek as Selene flopped onto her side.

'You're always giving out orders. Does anyone ever say no to you?'

'They work for me. They're paid to say yes. I ordered you a pot of coffee.'

'I can't drink coffee this late. It will keep me awake. Do you give orders in the bedroom?' She sat up and rested her chin on her knees as she watched him. 'Remove your clothes—lie like this—' Her voice was sultry and she saw that his powerful body was simmering with barely suppressed tension.

'*Stop* talking,' Stefan advised in a thickened tone.

Selene watched him hungrily, admiring the sleek, powerful lines of his body. 'Can I ask you something?'

'No.'

'Have you ever been in love?'

'*Stop* talking, Selene. Snap that pretty mouth of yours

shut and keep it shut.' He wrenched off his jacket and slung it on the nearest chair.

'I'll take that as a no.' Her head spinning, Selene flopped back against the soft pile of pillows that adorned the bed. 'I want to be in love. I really, really want to be in love. As long as he loves me back. I would never, ever be with someone who doesn't care for me. That's one of my rules.'

'Does this conversation have a point?'

'I'm just telling you more about me.'

'I don't need to know more about you. I already know all I need to know.'

'So you're a man who doesn't believe in love? I bet as far as you're concerned it's a myth right up there with the Minotaur and the legend of Atlantis.'

'You should definitely stop talking.' Stefan removed his bow tie with an impatient flick of his long fingers. 'Go into the bathroom and turn the shower to cold. It might help you. It would definitely help me.'

She rolled onto her stomach and leaned her chin in her palm. 'Do you know what this room needs? Scented candles. Studies have shown that nine out of ten men are more likely to get laid if there is a scented candle in the room.'

His mouth tightened. 'You know nothing about getting laid.'

'I'm doing my best but you're not being very accommodating.' Trying to distract herself from the spinning, Selene beckoned to him. 'Kiss me. And this time don't stop.'

He stilled, his eyes a dark, dangerous black. 'You are playing with fire.'

'I'd so much rather be playing with you...' Registering the exasperation on his face, she giggled. 'For a sophisticated man of the world with a shocking reputation, you're very restrained.'

'A drunk woman telling me she wants love tends to

do that to me.' Unbelievably tense, Stefan dropped his tie onto a vacant chair and undid the top button of his shirt, his eyes never leaving her face.

'I am definitely not drunk and I absolutely don't want love from you. I just want sex,' Selene said firmly. 'Really steamy sex. There's nothing to be afraid of. I won't hurt you. And you can walk away afterwards and neither of us will mention it again. It will be our little secret.'

The atmosphere shifted in an instant. For a moment she thought he was going to walk out of the room but instead he stared at her for a long time, as if he were making a decision about something.

Just when she'd given up on him taking it any further, he walked towards her with a purposeful stride.

As he approached her tummy tumbled and she felt a wild flicker of delicious, terrifying anticipation.

Her eyes collided with his and she struggled to sit up. 'Say something—'

'You've said more than enough already. It's time to stop talking.' His tone raw, he undid the buttons on his shirt with sure, strong fingers and her mouth dried.

Her stunned gaze rested on his wide shoulders and slid slowly down to his flat abdomen.

'I—I—'

'You issued an invitation, Selene. I'm here to take it up.'

As her eyes fixed on his he shrugged the shirt off his shoulders revealing a bare, bronzed torso that would have been the pride of any gladiator.

'That's what you want, isn't it?'

Still looking at her, he reached for the button at the top of his trousers…

CHAPTER FIVE

STEFAN lay with his hands hooked behind his head, watching as dawn sent beams of light across the bedroom. He could see a tiny bird dipping itself in the pool, playing innocently, blissfully unaware of the possibility of danger.

It reminded him of Selene.

Next to him, she stirred. With a moan, she flung her arm over her eyes. 'Turn the light off. Ugh—how can you be so thoughtless? It's giving me a headache.'

He turned his head to look at her, remembering how frank and open she'd been. He was starting to understand why her father was so overprotective. She was a sitting duck for any unscrupulous individual that happened to come along.

And now she was lying in his bed.

His bed. In his house, where no woman had stayed the night before. The house he'd built from nothing after Stavros Antaxos had ripped everything from his family.

Now he lay in silk sheets, but he never forgot how it had felt to lie on the cold, hard ground with the smell of rotting food in his nostrils. He never forgot the pain of seeing someone he loved laughing with someone he hated.

Stefan reached out and pushed her tangled blonde hair away from her face, remembering how open she'd been with him. It was the champagne, of course. 'It's called the sun. It's morning and your headache has nothing to do with the light.'

She peeled her eyelids open gingerly. For a moment she stared at him, as if trying to work something out. Those eyes slid from his bare shoulders to his abdomen and lower to—

'You're naked?' She shot up in bed and then groaned and immediately flopped back down again. 'Oh, my God, that hurts.'

There was something hopelessly endearing about her lack of sophistication. 'Yes, I'm naked. And so are you. That generally happens when two people spend the night together.' He waited for his words to sink in. Watched as her eyes widened and a faint colour touched her pale cheeks.

There would be regret, he knew. She would shoot out of his bed, accuse him of taking advantage of her and that would be the end of that. Except he would have taught her a lesson life hadn't yet taught her. To be cautious of people.

Next time she'd be more careful.

Next time she wouldn't drink so much with a man she didn't know—especially a man with his reputation.

Next time she'd know better than to trust someone like him.

'You undressed me and I don't even remember it.' Her voice was muffled by the pillow. 'I bet that was fun for you. I don't feel too good. Could I have a drink, please?'

'More champagne? That was your favourite drink last night.'

The sound from her throat was a whimper. 'No, *not* champagne. I'm never drinking again. It hurts so much. Why didn't anyone tell me it hurts afterwards? Water. Is there any water? A glass from the pool will do. I don't care. Anything as long as it isn't champagne.'

Stefan reached out a hand for the phone and spoke to someone in the kitchen, all the time aware of Selene burrowed into the pillow next to him like a very vulnerable, very sleepy kitten. She was adorable.

He frowned slightly, realising it wasn't an adjective he'd had cause to use before.

The sheet had slipped. He stared at the smooth skin of her shoulder, knowing that no other man had enjoyed the view he was enjoying now. Unable to help himself, he reached out and ran his hand down the length of her arm, feeling her tremble. But still she stayed in his bed. Even though the alcohol had to have worked its way out of her system, she wasn't showing any more caution than she had the night before.

Tenser than he could ever remember being, Stefan sprang from the bed and grabbed boxer shorts and jeans. 'My advice would be to go and take a long, cold shower.'

'That sounds like a truly horrible idea.' Selene winced as he pulled up his zip. 'Could you try and be a bit quieter? The noise is killing my head.'

And still she lay there. In his bed. In his home. Trusting him.

His fury with her father growing with every passing minute, Stefan dragged open the door of his bedroom suite, removed the tray from his staff with a nod of thanks and kicked the door shut.

Unaccustomed to playing the role of nurse, he poured iced water into a glass and handed it to her.

Run, part of him screamed. *Get out of here while you can.*

Still half under the covers, Selene eyed it doubtfully. 'I'm not sure if I'm thirsty after all. My stomach isn't happy.'

'You're dehydrated. You need fluid. And then you need food.'

'How can you mention food at a time like this?'

After a moment's hesitation, he sat down on the bed next to her and scooped her up, keeping his arm around her bare shoulders. Trying to ignore the softness of her flesh beneath his fingers, he lifted the glass to her lips. 'Drink. You'll feel better.' At least one of them would. He should never have brought her back here. It had been an appalling error of judgement on his part.

'I feel hideous. And I hate you for being so full of energy first thing in the morning.' Instead of taking the glass from him, she curled her fingers over his and took a few sips. 'Thank you. You're so kind.'

Kind.

The word jarred against his thoughts.

He felt a rush of exasperation. Somehow he had to kill this impression she had of him as some sort of god. 'You're naked in my bed and you remember nothing of last night.'

'I know. I'm *furious*.'

Stefan relaxed slightly. This was better. 'Good. You *should* be furious with me for taking advantage of you.'

'Oh, I'm not furious with *you*. I'm furious with myself. You kept telling me not to drink. I drank. My fault. How could I be furious with you? You've been amazing.'

'I was the one who stripped you naked.'

'It would have been horribly uncomfortable sleeping in that dress, so I'm grateful to you.'

He'd spent his life shattering women's illusions without trying and now, when he wanted to, he didn't seem able to manage it. Stefan shifted tack. 'It was a *very* exciting night. I am now familiar with every delicious inch of your body, and you,' he murmured, 'are familiar with every inch of mine.'

Still with her hands locked around his, Selene took a tiny sip of water. 'Really?'

'Really. You were so responsive. Unbelievably bold for someone with so little experience. When you suggested I tie you up, I admit I was surprised. I didn't think someone as innocent as you would be prepared to give a man that much power.' He'd expected shock. He hadn't expected a smile.

'I trust you. Whatever you want to do will always be fine with me.' Her simple declaration raised his tension levels several notches. Heat exploded through his body.

'*Theé mou*, I thought you were so trusting because you were drunk, but apparently not. What does it take to get you to show caution?'

'I can be cautious when I have to be. I just don't feel the need when I'm with you.'

'You should be angry.'

'I am angry. Angry with myself for ruining a really special night. You warned me to stop drinking and I didn't listen. You could have left me in a heap on the beach for anyone to take advantage of.'

Stefan couldn't believe what he was hearing. '*I* took advantage of you.'

'No, you didn't. And I'm the one who should be apologising to you for flirting and then collapsing unconscious. Hardly responsible behaviour. You were thoughtful and protective and you lay in bed all night wide awake, frustrated and determined not to touch me because that would have gone against your moral code.'

Why was it that her response was never what he expected? 'Selene, I don't have a moral code.'

'If that's true then why didn't we have sex?'

'What makes you so sure that we didn't?'

'I may be inexperienced but I'm not stupid. I'd know

if I'd had sex. And you wouldn't have done that. Not like that. Not with me. You protected me.'

Her voice husky, she turned her head to look at him and that look contained everything he'd avoided all his life. Depth. He'd always run from it because it led to something he absolutely didn't want. Not ever. He'd seen what that did. Seen lives ripped apart because of it.

'Stop turning me into a hero.'

'You could have taken advantage of me, but you didn't. You could have left me on the beach, but you didn't. You put me safely to bed where no harm could come to me.'

'*My* bed.'

'Where you didn't touch me.'

The rawness of the attraction was shocking. It pulled at the edges of his control, dragging him downwards. He no longer knew who he was protecting—himself or her.

'I was doing you a favour.'

'But you never do people favours, so that makes me feel even more special.' There was a brief pause and then she gave him a soft look that almost finished him. 'You're right. I should take that shower. It will wake me up and make me feel more human.' Her fingers uncurled from his and she slid from the bed, stood for a moment as if she were getting her balance and then walked towards the bathroom.

Naked.

Deciding that selflessness was definitely an overrated quality, Stefan was torn between a desire to flatten her back to the bed or throw a sheet over her. 'You should cover up.'

'What would be the point of that? You were the one who undressed me. You've already seen everything there is to see.'

* * *

She stood under the shower, feeling the cool water wash over her.

The drink and the tablets had cleared her head and reduced the pain to a dull ache. What couldn't be so easily erased was the knowledge she'd messed up what should have been the best night of her life so far. She almost wished he'd lived up to his reputation because then she wouldn't have been standing here bathed in regret.

Switching off the shower, she groped for the towel she'd put out for herself and instead encountered hard male muscle.

Swiping water from her eyes, she opened them. What she saw made her breath catch.

There was nothing tame there. Nothing gentle. Just raw male sexuality.

And he was naked, too.

'Maybe you should have locked the door, Selene.'

His silky voice made her stomach flip. 'Maybe I didn't see the need.'

'No?' He slid his hand behind her neck, his eyes locked on hers as he drew her head towards him. 'You need to develop a keener sense of self-preservation.'

'I can protect myself when I have to.' And she'd had to on so many occasions she didn't want to think about it. That had been her old life, and this was her new one. And because she didn't intend to screw her new life up a second time, she placed her hands on his chest.

His skin was warm. His muscles hard and smooth. The difference between her body and his fascinated her, and she explored him with her fingers and then pressed her mouth to his chest and heard his sharply indrawn breath.

'Are you afraid?' His voice was rough and she lifted her head.

'Excited, maybe a little nervous, but never afraid. Not of you.'

'And if I say that you should be?'

'I wouldn't listen. I make up my own mind. I trust myself.'

He smoothed her wet hair away from her face. 'Your hair is spectacular. You remind me of a mermaid.'

'You've met a lot of mermaids?'

'You're the first.' He lowered his head slowly, his mouth hovering just above hers. 'And I'll be *your* first so if you don't want this you'd better speak now.'

Her heart was pounding. 'I've never been more sure of anything in my life.'

'I do not come with a happy ending attached.' He spoke the words against her mouth, his fingers locked in her hair. 'There's a strong chance I'll make you cry.'

'I only cry when I'm happy. Don't worry, you're off the hook. I take full responsibility. This is my decision.' She felt the warmth of his hand at the base of her bare back as he drew her against him. Felt the hardness of his body against hers and closed her eyes, because she'd imagined it for so long in so many different ways but even her dreams had never felt as perfect as this.

'I might hurt you.'

'You could never hurt me.'

The hand on her back was now resting on the curve of her hip. 'I'm terrible at relationships.'

'I know. I don't want a relationship.' But she wanted *him* and the fact that he was still protecting her made her want him even more. 'I have a whole new exciting life ahead of me and nothing is going to get in the way.'

'You're crazy to do this—you know that, don't you? You should be slapping my face.'

'Stefan, *please*.' She gripped his biceps. 'I want this.

I want *you.* I always have.' He'd been her dream for so long, her lifeline, the one thing that had kept her going when she'd lain awake at night thinking how much she hated her life.

Something in her voice must have convinced him because he scooped her off her feet and carried her back to the bedroom.

The early morning sun beamed approval as he lowered her onto the bed.

Selene didn't care that it was daylight. Daylight meant that she could see him. All of him. Trembling with anticipation, she slid her arms around his neck, drawing him down to her. His hand locked in her hair.

'We're taking this slowly.'

'I don't want slowly.'

'I'll tie you up if I have to.'

'Then tie me up. Do it.'

His eyes darkened. 'You shouldn't say things like that.'

'Only to you.'

'You're far, far too trusting.' Something flickered in his eyes, the suggestion of a frown mingling with the blaze of raw desire.

If he changed his mind she'd die.

'Stefan—' Her hands slid down his body and she heard the sharp intake of his breath as she closed her hand around that part of him that was new to her. She felt silk over steel, experimented with the lightest of touches and heard him groan deep in his throat. The sudden switch of power was as intoxicating as the feel of him. The heady, extravagant excitement triggered by the fact that this man, this gorgeous indecently sexy man, wanted her as much as she wanted him was enough to wipe everything from her head except the moment.

Later she'd think of the future but not now, because right now her dream was finally reality.

'You have to slow down,' Stefan said in a thickened tone, closing his hand over hers to stop her. 'You've never done this before.'

'But I'm learning fast.'

'*Too* fast—' He rolled her under him and brought his mouth down on hers. She felt the erotic slide of his tongue and there was a whoosh of heat through her body that settled itself in her pelvis. The feeling was so maddeningly good that she shifted her hips against him.

He cursed softly and flattened her to the bed. 'You're beautiful.'

Without giving her a chance to answer, he continued his intimate exploration of her body, the wickedly sensual stroke of his tongue driving her wild. Pleasure arced through her as he toyed lazily with the tip of each breast and she wriggled and arched, trying to ease the growing ache low in her pelvis.

No one had told her she was beautiful before but he did so now, again and again, in English, in Greek, and with his lips and hands until she was a writhing mass of sensation.

She hadn't known it was possible to feel this good about herself.

'Stop moving,' Stefan groaned. 'You have no idea how hard you're making this for me.'

It was hard for him? For her it was torture, and when she felt him shift his weight and slide his hand over her quivering abdomen she thought she was going to explode.

'Please, now,' she begged.

He gave a ragged laugh and trailed his mouth lower. 'No way. I'm just getting started, *koukla mou*.'

'But I *really* want you to—'

'I know you do,' he growled, sheer overload of desire

lending an edge to his voice, 'but I want it to be good for you. Trust me.'

She wanted to tell him that it couldn't possibly be anything but good, but the smooth slide of his hand to the top of her thighs robbed her of the power of speech. His clever fingers lingered for a moment, tormenting her and magnifying the ache until she was no longer aware of anything except her own physical need. He touched her *there* and she sobbed with pleasure because he knew everything she didn't and wasn't afraid to show her.

She rocked her pelvis against him and instantly he moved his hand.

'Not yet. Stop moving.'

'I can't.'

'You will. Just lie there. Just—don't move.' He locked his hand round her wrists and lifted her arms above her head. 'Hold on and don't let go until I give you permission.'

Her hands touched the cool metal of the pretty iron bedframe and she curved her fingers around it, holding on as he'd ordered, out of her mind with sheer overload of sensation. She wanted it all. The scent of his skin. The feel of his hands, his mouth, his body— 'Please, Stefan—'

'I don't want to hurt you. I *won't* hurt you.'

'Please—'

'*Don't* speak.' His voice thickened with raw need, Stefan parted her thighs.

She was surprised she didn't feel embarrassed because it was full daylight, but she knew nothing she ever did with him would embarrass her—not even *this*.

This was his mouth on her, his tongue on her and in her, and she heard someone sobbing and realised that the sound was coming from her throat. He spread her wide, opening her to his gaze and his mouth, and his only concession to her innocence was his patience. With each skilled slide and lick of his clever tongue the warmth grew to heat, and it spread and consumed her until holding onto the bed felt like holding on for her life, because it was the only thing anchoring her. He demanded everything and she gave him what he demanded because she was no longer in control. He was.

It was almost a relief to feel the first fluttering of her body but he immediately stilled.

'No. Not yet.' His voice was rough. 'Relax. Do you hear me? Relax.'

She was almost crazy with the need and she tried to move her hips against his hand, but he withdrew his fingers from her gently.

'Not yet. I want to be inside you when you come. I want to feel it. Be part of it.'

Her eyes had closed but now they flickered open and she was treated to a close-up private view of sheer masculine power. Dressed, he was gorgeous, but undressed he was spectacular. Bronzed skin sheathed smooth curves of hard muscle and the dark hair that hazed the centre of his chest trailed down over his flat stomach and disappeared out of view. But she'd already seen and she knew, and she wanted to know more.

'Then do it,' she begged hoarsely. 'Do it now. Please. You're driving me crazy.'

'So impatient.' A sexy smile hovering on his mouth, Stefan shifted over her and curved her leg behind his back. 'I'm going to torture you with pleasure,' he murmured against her mouth, 'until you're mindless and begging—'

'I'm begging now.' Her gaze collided with his and every bone in her body melted under the fire in his eyes. 'It's you. You make me—crazy.'

His thick dark lashes lowered fractionally and he lowered his mouth to hers again, his kiss teasing and seduc-

SARAH MORGAN 85

tive. 'This is just the beginning.' The subtle stroke of his
tongue and his skilled exploration of her mouth left her
shaking and Selene kissed him back, her uninhibited response drawing a similar degree of reaction from him.

She was dimly aware that Stefan had pulled back
slightly—that he was reaching for something from the
table by the bed.

A moment later he slid one hand into her hair. Dazed
and desperate, Selene's eyes collided with the fierce passion in his.

'If I hurt you, tell me,' Stefan said thickly, his other hand
sliding under her writhing hips as he lifted her against him.

She could feel the male power of him but she was so
wet, so ready, and she knew he'd done that for her, done
everything he could to make her first time good.

His body felt hard, male and thoroughly unfamiliar. She
closed her eyes and held her breath, just waiting, *waiting*,
conscious of his leashed power and superior strength and
wondering how this could possibly work out well despite
his skill.

Braced for discomfort, she was surprised by his gentleness and care.

She'd expected him to thrust, but he entered her slowly,
carefully, and she held her breath, the feeling of warmth
and fullness taking her by surprise. She felt him pause
and then his mouth brushed hers as he kissed her gently.

'Relax and open your eyes. I want you looking at me.
If I'm hurting you, I want to know.'

She opened them.

Her heart slamming against her chest, Selene stared
up at him, her gaze trapped by his. It was clear how much
each slow, purposeful stroke was costing him and Selene
slid her hands over his shoulders, feeling tension under
hard, sleek muscle.

And then he did thrust, as if he could no longer help himself. He thrust deep and she held her breath because it felt like too much.

Buried deep inside her, Stefan sensed the change in her and paused, his breathing uneven and his eyes darkened to a dangerous shade of black. 'You feel incredible,' he said thickly. 'Tell me you're OK—say *something.*'

But she couldn't speak. Couldn't find any words to express what she was feeling. All she could do was move and when she did that the breath hissed through his teeth.

'I'll take that as an indication that I'm not hurting you.' He groaned, dropping his mouth to hers. His kiss was raw, passionate and hotly sexual, the skilled slide of his tongue winding the excitement tighter and tighter until Selene was aware of nothing except the building tension in her body.

Each controlled thrust of his body was designed to draw the maximum response from hers until the ache inside her grew agonising, her need for him a ravenous hunger that swept away sanity. Heat engulfed her as he drove her towards the peak with a smooth, expert rhythm and then her body tightened and she was launched into an entirely different world, a world that consisted of nothing but her and this man—just the two of them, blended in every way that mattered. Overwhelmed by sheer physical excitement, she was trapped in a vicious cycle of pleasure that sent spasm after spasm of pulsing ecstasy through her thoroughly over-sensitised body and drove him to the same point.

It was the most perfect moment of her life.

And when she finally emerged from that suspended state of erotic intensity, Stefan kissed her gently and rolled onto his side, taking her with him, stroking her hair away from her face with a hand that wasn't quite steady.

'That,' he said hoarsely, 'was incredible.'

Dazed, Selene kept her face against his shoulder, but he gave a low laugh and forced her to look at him.

'You're *not* hiding from me.' He stroked her flushed cheek with gentle fingers, his gaze searching. 'Are you OK?'

Lifting her head, Selene tumbled into that dark gaze. 'I feel amazing,' she mumbled. 'It's better than champagne.'

Humour in his eyes, he drew her head to his and kissed her. '*Much* better than champagne...'

Still dazed by her own shocking reaction to him, Selene closed her eyes.

She'd been worried her dream wouldn't live up to expectation, but it had.

He made her feel utterly desirable, irresistible and beautiful, and she'd never felt like that in her life before—had never imagined it was possible to feel like this. 'Thank you,' she murmured, wrapping her arms around his neck. 'Thank you for making it special.'

He muttered something inaudible in Greek and lowered his forehead to hers. 'I am now officially addicted to your body.'

Selene smiled up at him, feeling like a cross between a goddess and a seductress. 'I think I'm possibly addicted to yours, too.'

'Good. In that case I'm going to break one of my unbreakable rules and keep you here for another night.'

That statement was a reality check. A dark cloud passing in front of the sun. A reminder that this part of her life hadn't officially started yet. *Soon.* 'I can't do that. I have to go home.' Disappointment thudded through her and he lifted his head and frowned.

'Why?'

'I have to get back to Antaxos.'

'I thought you wanted to assert your independence?'

'I do. And to do that I have to go back to Antaxos.' She told herself that was her decision. She was going back for her mother, not her father. And nothing, not even the thought of going home, was going to spoil this moment. Her active mind quickly spun a scenario where she was living here with Stefan, spending her days with her body tangled with his.

She stared up at him, wondering if he was imagining the same thing, but his handsome face was inscrutable.

'Returning home isn't asserting your independence. It's regressing.'

'It's just a temporary thing.' She'd kept her plan secret, protected it as carefully as a mother would her child, desperate for it to grow, but all her defences were ripped away after the intimacies they'd shared. 'I have to get back to the island before my father returns and discovers I've gone. If he knows I came to you it will be difficult for me.'

'Returns?' There was a sudden tension in his shoulders. 'You mean he isn't there?'

'No. Once a year he spends a week on Crete. That's how I was able to get away.'

She wondered why they were spoiling the moment by talking about her father.

She wondered why he was suddenly so still. Why his expression was guarded.

'So you were hoping to return and leave again without him knowing?'

'Of course. Why do you think I came to you? Why do you think I dressed as a nun? He never would have let me leave had he been on the island. I've planned this for so long—you have no idea.'

'Why go back at all? Stay here with me.'

The invitation was so tempting. 'I can't do that. There are things I need from the island—' Years of playing a part stopped her revealing that final secret part of herself. It was how they lived. Pretending that this was normal. Keeping up the show for the outside world. 'Important things. But I don't plan to stay for any time at all. I have to be away again before he returns.'

'Because you're afraid he won't want you to leave? Stand up to him.' His tone cooler, Stefan eased himself away from her and sat up. 'Show him you're a grown-up and he might treat you that way.'

Missing the intimacy, Selene sat up, too. 'You don't know my father.'

'I know that being independent means taking responsibility for your actions and owning them. There is no reason to hide this from him. Tell him you're with me. Show him you're not afraid.'

She *was* afraid. She'd be a fool not to be and she wasn't a fool.

Selene thought about what happened when someone stood up to her father and she thought of her mother, alone and vulnerable on Antaxos.

'I can't do that. Not yet.' The magic had gone so she slid from the bed.

She felt different.

She felt beautiful.

She was aware of herself in a way that felt new. And she was aware of *him*. Of the way he watched her as she picked a dress from the clothes he'd bought her. Of the way he looked, his eyes hooded and his jaw shadowed by blue-black stubble.

'Come back to bed. I'll fly you back to Antaxos later if that's what you want. We'll pick up whatever it is you need and then you can come back to Athens with me. I'll help you with your business.'

'I have to do this by myself.'

She walked into the bathroom and turned on the shower, letting the jets of water slide over her body. Closing her eyes, she reached for the soap but he was there before her.

'This soap smells like you.'

She smiled and pushed her soaking-wet hair away from her face as he slid his hands down her body. 'It's my soap. It comes in the same three scents as the candles.'

'At least you know a bit more about seduction now.'

As he kissed her neck she closed her eyes, but this time the anxiety twisting inside her prevented her from relaxing.

Reluctantly, she pulled away from him and grabbed a towel.

'I have to go.'

It felt urgent now, to get this done so that she could start her new life. Excitement bubbled under the feeling of apprehension. She walked back into the bedroom and picked up the pretty linen dress she'd chosen from the clothes he'd provided. Her hesitation was driven by years of living with her father. He wasn't here, and yet she could hear his voice telling her to change into something more suitable. Telling her that the dress was too short, too eye-catching, too—everything.

Then she remembered her father wasn't going to see her wearing it.

From now on the only time she heard his voice would be in her head.

There would be no row because this was the last time she was going home and her father wouldn't be there.

Stefan strolled back into the bedroom, a towel knotted around his lean hips.

Determined not to be distracted, Selene let her own towel drop to the floor and reached for the dress.

Behind her she heard the sharp intake of his breath. Assuming his response was because she was naked, she lifted her head and smiled at him. He was looking at her body.

'*Theé mou*, did I do that? I hurt you?' He was across the room in three strides, his hands gentle on her arms as he turned her and took a closer look at her back and then her arms. 'You have bruises. Finger-marks.'

Selene twisted away from him and pulled the dress over her head quickly. 'It's fine. It's nothing.' It wasn't nothing, of course, but it wasn't anything she wanted him to know about. It was her past and she wanted it to stay in her past.

His face was suddenly pale. 'I thought I'd been gentle.'

'You were gentle. You were brilliant. Honestly, Stefan, it's nothing—' She stumbled over the words, feeling guilty that she had to let him think that but unable to give him an alternative explanation. 'And now I really need to go.'

'You should have told me I was hurting you. I would have stopped.'

'You didn't hurt me.' No way could she tell him, or anyone, the truth—and she didn't need to because she was fixing it. 'I just bruise easily, OK? It's nothing to do with you.' Not looking at him, she scooped her damp hair into a ponytail.

Now that the moment had come, she just wanted it over with. She wanted to get it done. 'I'll take the ferry to Poulos and the nuns will take me back by boat.'

'I'll take you back to Antaxos.'

'No! Someone might see you and call my father. I can't risk him knowing I've left the island. I need a head start on him.'

'Selene—' His tone raw, Stefan dragged his hand through his hair and shot her a look she couldn't interpret. 'He probably already knows.'

In the process of sliding her feet into her shoes, she assumed she'd misheard him. 'How can he possibly know?

He's with one of his women. He won't be home for another six days.'

'He knows because he will have seen the photographs.'

'Photographs?' Selene stared at him, her brain infuriatingly slow as she tried to make sense of what he was saying. 'What photographs?'

'The photographs of us together. You and me.'

'Someone took photographs?' Selene felt physically nauseated. The bag slipped from her hand. 'How could they? This is your home. There were no journalists. Please tell me you're joking.'

'I'm not joking.'

'No—' She felt the colour drain from her face, felt her fingers grow cold and her body sway. She saw the sudden narrowing of his eyes as he saw the change in her.

'I don't see why it would bother you. Nothing else has bothered you. Drinking too much champagne, waking up in my bed, having sex—'

'That's different. My father doesn't know about any of that.' Or at least she hadn't thought he did.

'So this new life of yours only works if your father doesn't know about it? The first step to independence is standing up for yourself. Just tell your father what you told me. That you want to start living your life. You're not asking him for money. You're just telling him how it is.' There was a tightness around his mouth and a coldness in his eyes. 'What can he do?'

Selene knew exactly what he could do. And she knew he wouldn't hesitate to do it.

'How do you even know there are photographs?' *Please let him be wrong.* 'Show them to me.'

Unsmiling, Stefan reached for his phone and accessed the internet. A few taps of his fingers later he was showing her photographs that snapped the leash on her panic.

'Oh, no...' Her voice was a whisper. 'It's you and I. Kissing. And it's a close-up. He's going to go wild. Who took that photo? *Who?*'

'Carys, I suppose.' The question didn't appear to interest him much. 'She writes a gossip column for a glossy magazine and for other places if the story is juicy enough.'

Selene processed that information. 'But if you know she writes a gossip column then you must have known there was a risk she'd take a photograph—that she'd tell the world about me. You must have known—you...' Her voice tailed off as her brain finally caught up. 'Wait a minute. She said something about you being a Machiavellian genius and I had no idea what she meant, but you *did* know. You did it on purpose. You invited me to the party with the express purpose of upsetting my father.'

'I invited you to the party because I needed a date and there you were, all vulnerable and sexy mixed in together—it seemed like the perfect solution.'

'And because you knew it would really upset my father?'

His eyes were cool. 'Yes, I knew it would upset your father. But presumably so did you. If he'd approved of what you were doing you wouldn't have had to come to me in the first place.'

'But I didn't want him to find out yet. It was so important that he didn't find out—why do you think I came to you in disguise?' Realising how naïve she'd been to trust him, Selene took a step backwards, stumbling over his shoes discarded on the floor. 'You warned me—everyone warned me about you—even Maria—and I didn't listen.' Because she hadn't wanted to. Because she'd spun a fantasy in her head and she'd lived with that fantasy for five years and she wasn't going to let anyone destroy it because it had been her lifeline. Her hope. Her dream. 'I thought you were being kind and thoughtful but all the time you were just making sure I came with you so that you could score a point against a business rival.'

His expression was blank. 'This is not about business. I separate the two.'

But she didn't believe him. No longer believed in anyone but herself. 'What sort of a man are you?'

'A man who isn't afraid to confront your father—which is why you came to me in the first place. I am *exactly* the person you knew I was when you walked into my office on that first day.' He snapped the words. 'It isn't my fault if you turned me into some sort of god in your head.'

'Well, don't worry. I don't think that any more.' She choked on the words. 'I can't believe you've done this. This is worse than anything.' Because now she was alone. She was on her own. There was no one out there who would help her. No one who cared. Certainly not this man.

'I've done you a favour. Your father will realise you're serious about wanting your independence. And before you get all sanctimonious can I remind you again that you came to me?' he said flatly. 'I didn't kidnap you, force you into a dress and thrust a glass of champagne in your hand. You were the one who begged me for money and you were pretty much willing to do anything to get it, I might add. If you cast your mind back to your drunken episode my behaviour was impeccable. You did everything you could to seduce me and I said no.'

Humiliation piled onto anger and misery. 'You're just a saint.'

'I never claimed to be a saint. You were the one who came to me in a nun's outfit with ridiculous expectations.'

She stared at him, mute, seeing the uncomfortable truth in everything he was saying. It had been her decision to come. Her decision to drink champagne. Her decision to kiss him and go to bed with him.

She'd wanted so badly to be able to make her own decisions and all she'd done was make bad ones. Lonely and desperate, she'd built him up in her mind as some sort of perfect being and the truth was a horrible blow.

He'd used her to score points against her father and she was the one who would pay the price. *And her mother.*

Thinking of it made her limbs shake. 'You're right, of course. From now on I'll be making more careful decisions. And the first will be to stay away from men like you. That's what you wanted, wasn't it? You wanted me to be more cynical. Well, now I am. I'm officially cynical.'

His features taut, he stepped towards her. 'Selene—'

'Don't touch me. You only invited me to the party because you knew it would upset him.'

'That isn't true. I invited you to the party because you're sexy as hell and your innocence was—refreshing.'

'Well, I'm not innocent any more.'

'You are overreacting. This will be to your advantage. Once he realises you're serious about being independent and making your business a success he'll let you go.' Those wide shoulders lifted in a dismissive shrug. 'I've done you a favour. There's no point in rebelling if no one knows you're rebelling.'

'I've told you this isn't about rebellion. It was never about rebellion.' Selene could hardly breathe as her mind ran swiftly through the possible consequences.

'If you allow your father to bully you, he will always bully you.'

'You have no idea. No idea what you've done. No idea of the consequences that this will have.' Galvanised into action, she stumbled around the room, gathering her things and stuffing them frantically into her bag. 'I have to leave, right now. Is there a ferry from here?' How long did she have? *How long?* She was panicking too much to make the calculation and truthfully it was impossible to know because she didn't know what time her father would have seen the photographs.

He swore under his breath. 'You need to calm down—'

'When would these photos have come out? What time?' Someone, somewhere would have seen them. She was sure of that. Her father was so paranoid and self-absorbed that he had whole teams of people scouring the media for mentions of himself. The moment the images had appeared on the internet someone would have seen them and would have told him. She had no doubt that he already knew everything. Nothing escaped him—especially something as catastrophic as this.

'I don't understand why you're so concerned. I've already told you I'm giving you the money. You'll be able to have the lifestyle you want. Buy what you like without your father's approval.'

All the money in the world would be useless if she couldn't get her mother away from the island. *'What time?'*

Stefan flicked his gaze back to the screen of his phone. 'This one was posted around midnight.'

'Midnight?' Hours ago. And she'd been lying in his bed, basking in the ability to make her own choices, unaware that she'd made nothing but bad ones. Fear gripped her like a nasty virus. She felt dizzy with it. Sick. 'If my father saw these at midnight then that means—' He might already be on his way back to the island and her mother was alone and unprotected. 'I have to leave now.'

Stefan swore under his breath and reached out his hand but she flinched away from him, flattening herself against the wall.

'Get away from me. Don't pretend you care about me,'

she mumbled. 'I know you don't. I don't *ever* want you to touch me again.'

'Fine. I won't touch you.' He spoke through clenched teeth. 'But at least stand still and look at me. The way to handle this is not to sprint home like a good, obedient girl.'

'You have no idea. You have no idea what you've done.'

'At worst I've annoyed your father and reinforced the message that you want to be independent.'

'You might have taken that opportunity away from me—' Her throat was thick with tears. If her father returned home before her, her mother would be too afraid to leave. She'd lose her nerve as she'd lost it so many times before. 'I want to leave. Now.'

'Fine, if that's what you want. Run home. That's clearly where you belong. You're a child, not a woman.' Stefan's face was a frozen mask as he strode across the room and opened a safe concealed in the wall. 'I promised you money. I always keep my promises.'

'Because you're such a good guy?'

'No.' His mouth twisted. 'Not because of that. Call my office any time you need business help.' He dropped the money into her bag and strode towards the door. 'I'll arrange for your transport home.'

CHAPTER SIX

'STEFAN, are you even listening to me?'

Stefan turned his gaze from the window of his Athens office to his lawyer, Kostas. 'Pardon?'

'Have you heard a word I've been saying? I've been telling you that Baxter has agreed to all our terms. We've been working on this deal for over a year. We should celebrate.'

Stefan didn't feel like celebrating. He listened to his friend offer profuse congratulations, his mind preoccupied with Selene.

What the hell had possessed him to sleep with someone as inexperienced as her?

Her overreaction to the news of the photographs had made him realise how young she was. She'd said she wanted independence, but then freaked out at the thought of her father finding out.

Clearly surprised by the lack of response, Kostas paused. 'Don't you want to hear the details?'

'No. I pay you an exorbitant amount to handle details for me.'

Was it the sex that had made her panic? Remembering the bruises made him shift in his seat but nothing relieved the guilt. He'd never bruised a woman before. A love-bite maybe, but not bruises like those. They were finger-marks, caused by someone grabbing her too roughly, and the worst thing was he had no recollection of doing it.

Kostas closed the file. 'Do you want to meet him in person?'

'Meet who in person?'

Stefan went through their encounter in minute detail, trying to identify when exactly he'd hurt her. He'd been gentle with her. Careful. At no point had he been rough and yet somehow he'd caused those sick-looking yellow bruises.

Yellow bruises. He frowned. 'How old is a bruise when it turns yellow?'

His lawyer stared at him. 'What?'

'Bruises,' Stefan snapped. 'Is a fresh bruise ever yellow?'

'I'm no doctor, but doesn't it take about a week for a bruise to turn yellow? Longer than a week?'

Theé mou.' How could he have been so dense?

Driven by a sense of urgency that was new to him, Stefan pulled out his phone and called his pilot—only to be told that he'd already delivered Selene safely to Poulos, the closest island to Antaxos. From there she'd planned to catch a boat home.

Home, where presumably her father would now be waiting.

Stefan was in no doubt as to who was responsible for those bruises.

That was why she wanted to escape from the island. Not just because she wanted her independence, but because she was afraid for her life. Afraid of her father.

The memories came from nowhere, thudding into his gut like a vicious blow.

Why doesn't she come home, Papa?

Because she can't. He won't let her. He doesn't like to lose.

The emotion inside him was primal and dangerous.

How could he have been so blind? He was probably one of the few people who knew just what Stavros Antaxos was capable of and yet he'd let his own emotions about the past blind him to the truth of the present.

'He's not going to let her go. He's never going to let her go.' He growled the words and his lawyer looked at him, startled.

'Who—?'

'I'm going to get her out of there.' Driven by emotions he hadn't allowed himself to feel for over two decades, Stefan was on his feet and at the door before his lawyer had even finished his question. 'I'm going to Antaxos.'

'There is no safe landing spot on the island of Antaxos. It's renowned for its inhospitable coastline.'

'I'll fly to the yacht and take the speedboat.' He delivered instructions to his pilot while Kostas caught up with him, following him as he took the stairs up to the helipad.

'What's going on? Is this to do with Selene Antaxos?' When Stefan looked at him, he shrugged. 'The pictures are all over the internet. Why all the questions about bruises?'

His lawyer tone was several shades cooler than usual and Stefan shot him a look. 'I don't pretend to be perfect, but I don't hurt women.' Except that he had. Not with his hands, but with his actions. And by his actions he'd made it possible for someone else to hurt her physically. A cold feeling spread down his spine.

You have no idea what you've done.

Her final words still rang in his brain and alongside was a picture of Selene stuffing her new possessions randomly into her battered bag. He'd caught a glimpse of the nun's habit and samples of her soap and candles. But it wasn't the contents of her bag that stuck in his mind as much as the look on her face.

She was a woman who wore her emotions openly and over the past two days he'd witnessed her entire repertoire. He'd seen hope, mischief, flirtation, shyness, wonder, excitement and laughter. This morning he'd seen something new. Something he hadn't understood until now.

He'd seen terror.

Suddenly his collar felt too tight and he called Takis, his head of security, and instructed him to meet him at the helicopter pad.

Kostas caught his arm. 'I have no idea what you're planning, but I advise caution where Stavros Antaxos is concerned.'

Stefan shrugged him off. 'Your advice is duly noted and ignored.'

'You have brought shame upon me and upon yourself and you did it with a man I hate more than any other.'

Selene stood stubbornly to the spot, clutching her bag like a life raft as her father vented his fury. She knew better than to answer back. Better than to try and reason because his anger was never driven by reason. And she was angry with herself, too. Angry for deviating from her original plan. If she hadn't flown to the villa with Stefan she wouldn't be in this position now.

'Why him?' Her father's eyes blazed with every emotion but love. 'Why?'

'Because he's a businessman.' Because he'd talked to her when no one else had. Because he'd paid her attention and flattered her and her stupid brain had built him up into a hero so when he'd invited her to the party it had seemed all her dreams had come true. Instead of questioning what

a man like him would see in a girl like her, she'd been
blinded by his stunning looks and masculine charisma.

She'd lived in the moment without thinking about tomorrow and now tomorrow had come.

'A businessman? And what is your "business"?' The
derision hurt more than any blow.

'I have an idea. A good idea.'

'Then why didn't you come to me?'

'Because—' *Because you'd kill it, the way you kill everything that threatens to break up our 'family'.* 'Because
I want to do this by myself.'

And she almost had.

It made her sick to think how close she'd come to a
new life.

All of this could have been avoided had she simply
shaken hands at the point where Stefan had agreed to give
her a business loan, but she'd mixed business with pleasure and even she knew you weren't supposed to do that.

'He used you. You know that, don't you? He used you
to get to me and you have no one to blame but yourself. I
hope you feel cheap.'

Selene closed her eyes, remembering the way she had
felt. Not cheap. Special. Beautiful. But it hadn't been real.
He'd done it so that he could get juicy fodder for the photographers. All those things he'd said. All those things he'd
done. It hadn't been about her—it had been about scoring
points against her father. He'd sacrificed her on the altar
of personal ambition. 'I made a mistake.'

'We'll say he forced you. Physically he's much bigger
than you, and you're so obviously innocent no one will
have any trouble believing it.'

'No!' Horrified, her eyes flew open. 'That isn't what
happened.'

'It doesn't matter what happened. What matters is what

people *think* happened. I don't want our family image tarnished with this. I have my reputation to protect.'

Image. It was all about image, not reality. 'He has his reputation, too. And he'll deny it because it isn't true.' Just thinking of that story in the papers made her feel faint because simmering beneath the layers of pain that he'd deceived her was guilt that she'd let him think he was responsible for the bruises.

Her father's expression was cold and calculating. 'Who cares what's true? Mud sticks. By the time he's proved it wasn't the case no one will remember your part in it, just his. People will always wonder. You'll be the innocent girl he used.'

'No.' Selene lifted her chin. 'I won't do that to him. I won't lie.'

There was a deadly silence. 'Are you saying no to me?'

Her stomach cramped. 'I can't do that to him.'

She had money in her bag. If she could just calm the situation there might still be a way to get away. She'd persuade her mother to leave. They could slip away at night. She'd—

He stopped in front of her, too close, his hands clenched into fists that he was getting ready to use. 'So if you liked being with him so much, why bother coming back?'

She knew better than to mention her mother. 'I left because I wanted to have some fun. Freedom. Rebellion.' She made free use of Stefan's misconception. 'I've been trapped here so long with no life and I wanted to get away. But I don't actually want to leave my home. Or my family.' She almost choked on the word because she knew that no family should be like hers. A family was supposed to be a unit knitted together by blood and love. All they had was blood, and too much of that had been shed.

'So you admit you behaved badly?' He flexed his fingers. 'You admit you need discipline?'

The thought of the money in the bag gave her renewed strength. 'I'm sorry my actions upset you.'

'What's in that bag?'

Her knees turned to water. 'Clothes.'

He grabbed it. Wrenched it from her fingers so hard that he tore the skin.

Selene put her hand to her mouth and tasted blood. Inside that bag were her hopes for the future and she held her breath as he wrenched open the zip and dragged out the contents without care or respect, forcing her to watch as every one of her dreams was slaughtered in front of her.

First to fall was the red dress. That beautiful red dress she'd stuffed into her bag in a gesture of defiance against Stefan. She wished she'd left it. If ever she'd needed proof that hope was ephemeral she had it now as her father took that dress and wrenched it from neck to hem. She couldn't even pretend that he didn't know what it meant to her because he watched her face the whole time, and with every rip as she flinched a little more his mouth grew more grim. When the dress was nothing more than torn strips at her feet he kicked the pile of belongings and found her candles.

Selene didn't realise she'd made a sound but she must have done because he glanced towards her swiftly, eyes narrowed, assessing the significance of what was in his hand.

'This is it? This is your business idea? Did he laugh at you?'

'No.' Her lips felt numb. 'He thought it was a good idea.'

'Because he thought he could make a fool of me, not because your business venture has any merit. Is that it? Candles? I'm almost embarrassed a daughter of mine couldn't have been more creative.'

He picked up the apparently empty bag and her heart stopped because she knew it wasn't an empty bag and that if he looked there...if he found...

'That's it,' she muttered. 'There's nothing else there.' And of course by saying that she pronounced herself guilty.

He stared at her for a long moment and then took another look at the bag. With those fat, muscular hands that had turned her mother from vivacious to victim he patted it down and unzipped pockets. And she wished she'd worked harder to hide what was hidden there. Because he found it, of course, under the false bottom she'd created—the thick wedge of money tied with a thong because she hadn't been able to think how else to keep so much cash together.

Her father untied the sexy thong and dropped it to the floor with revulsion. 'You wore that and he paid you in cash?'

'No. I mean...' She floundered. 'The cash was just an advance to—to—'

'To pay for sex.' He put the bag down slowly, his eyes glassy with rage. 'You disgust me.'

'I'll leave. I'll leave and you'll never have to see me again.'

'Leave?' His smile was ugly. 'Oh, no. You don't get to leave. You're part of this family, Selene, and that isn't going to change. This is where you belong and you're lucky I'm prepared to have you back under my roof when you've been with *him*.'

'I don't—'

The blow was unexpected. Because she wasn't prepared, the force of it banged her head against the wall and pain exploded through her skull.

Selene crumpled to the floor, tasting blood. She was so shocked she couldn't move and she fought waves of sickness as his words pelted her like stones.

'Your mother must have known about this.'

Your wife, Selene thought dizzily. *She's your wife.* 'She didn't know. I didn't tell her.' Touching her mouth with the tips of her fingers, she realised she'd bitten her lip. She tried to stumble back to her feet but her legs wouldn't hold her and she stayed on all fours like an animal, wishing she'd made different decisions, trying not to feel because feeling was agony.

'When I've finished with you I'll talk to her and she will tell me the truth.'

The implied threat brought her up onto her knees. 'You stay away from her! You touch her again and I'll—' she swayed '—I'll call the police.'

He laughed. 'We both remember what happened the last time you did that.'

Numb, Selene stared at the floor, knowing it was hopeless.

They hadn't believed her. Or if they'd believed her they'd refused to act. Her father was charming, powerful and able to buy his way out of trouble. At first her sense of justice had been shaken. She'd realised that she had no one until one night, lying in the darkness, she'd realised that she didn't need anyone. Maybe no one else could solve this for her, but she could solve it for herself. Which made it doubly frustrating that she'd blown her chance.

He prowled around her and she knew from the look in his eyes that the moment he'd finished with her he would start on her mother.

Something sharp pressed into her hand and she looked down and saw that she'd fallen onto one of the jagged remnants of all that was left of a glass candle-holder.

She closed her hand over it, careful to avoid cutting herself on the sharp edge. And this time when her father came in swinging she closed her eyes and plunged the glass into his wrist. He gave a howl of pain and staggered backwards. It wasn't enough to stop him but it was enough to slow him down and Selene didn't waste a moment of her advantage. She forced herself to her feet and stumbled from the room, slamming the door behind her as she ran from the villa. He would chase her, of course, and that was what she wanted. Because if he chased her then he wouldn't be going for her mother.

She just had to hope that his temper burned itself out before he killed them both.

Stefan manoeuvred the sleek speedboat as close to the rocks as he dared. He'd picked the north side of the island, judging the currents to be less savage. His yacht was moored further out to sea where the waters were deeper and he'd launched the tender and indulged himself in a few minutes of speed and spray as he'd skimmed the surface of the sparkling ocean towards the towering cliffs of Antaxos. But that spurt of adrenaline had been brief. Negotiating the rocky approach to the island had taken all his skill and concentration.

He let the engine idle as he assessed the distance between boat and rock, judging the rise and fall of the sea. Between both lay fathoms of swirling water, ready to swallow up victims, but Stefan had no intention of being anyone's victim. Judging it perfectly he sprang, lithe as a panther, landing safely and gesturing for his team to take the boat back out.

Takis followed him. His movements were clumsier and Stefan shot out a hand to steady him as he veered dangerously close to the water.

'Didn't sign up for this. You could have picked a nice girl from the centre of Athens, boss,' Takis muttered, his face scarlet as he found his balance. 'But, no, you had to go for the pampered princess guarded by the dragon. Working for you is never boring.'

Pampered princess.

Stefan felt a stab of guilt. Hadn't he made the same mistake?

Like everyone he'd been fooled by the image the tycoon had spun for the world. The adored wife. The much loved, overprotected daughter. The happy family.

He suspected the truth was much bleaker. Almost as bleak as this island.

Antaxos.

He stared at the narrow path that led up the cliffs to the grey, fortress-like building at the top.

As a child, he'd spent hours thinking about this place. Powerless, he'd conjured up images of the almost mythical island and imagined himself storming its rocky shores. Something had burned inside him and it burned still, confusing the past with the present.

He wasn't powerless now. He'd made sure of it. From the day his father had brought him the sickening news, through choking tears he'd promised himself—*promised her*—that one day he was going to be a man of power. His quest for that had become the driving force in his life, and when he'd lost his father, too, his drive had simply increased.

A sound made him look up.

Four men dressed in black approached down the path. Bulky men, built like gorillas, whose sole purpose in life was to stop people getting close to their reclusive billionaire boss. If the rocks hadn't killed you, these men probably would.

'This is a private island. You are not allowed to land here.'

Stefan stood his ground, legs spread, using that power

he'd sweated blood to gain. 'You might want to rethink the warmth of your welcome.'

They drew closer. 'There is nothing here for tourists. You need to leave right now.'

'I'm not a tourist and I'll leave when I'm ready.' Timing it perfectly, Stefan removed his sunglasses and the man stepped back. Recognition was followed by alarm.

'Mr Ziakas!' Thrown, the gorilla exchanged a dubious glance with his two colleagues. 'Mr Antaxos doesn't receive visitors here.' But the tone had changed. There was caution now. Respect for the reputation of the man facing them. Respect and just a touch of fear because there were so many rumours about the past life of Stefanos Ziakas. 'You should leave.'

'I'll leave when I have the girl. Where is she?'

They exchanged nervous glances. 'You can't—'

Judging that they were too scared of their boss to be of use to him, Stefan strode past them towards the ugly stone building perched on the hill. His insides churned.

Images blurred in his head and he paused, reminding himself that this was about Selene and no one else.

There was a commotion behind him but he didn't turn his head, knowing that Takis could handle all four of them with his eyes closed. Providing he didn't slip on the rocks and fall in the water.

A faint smile on his mouth, Stefan swiftly climbed the steep path. He was just calculating the most likely place for an overprotective father to lock away his daughter when Selene came flying down a set of steps that led to the path. There was blood on her face, on her hands and streaked through that beautiful pale hair. She was running so fast she almost crashed into him and he closed his hands round her arms to catch her, using all his strength to stop her propelling both of them off the cliff and onto the rocks below.

Her eyes were dazed, almost blank, and he could see now that the blood came from a cut on her head.

Swearing under his breath, Stefan turned his head and ordered Takis to bring the first-aid kit from the speedboat. Then he turned back to her, touching that blonde hair with gentle fingers as he assessed the damage.

Her eyes finally focused on him. 'What are you doing here?'

If he'd been expecting a warm welcome he was disappointed because she twisted in his grip, but he was so afraid she was going to go over the edge of the cliff he kept hold of her.

'Keep still. You'll fall.'

'I know this path. I've lived here all my life.'

And he couldn't bear to think of what that life had been like. 'Did he do this?' The anger roared like a beast but he kept his emotions hidden, not trusting his ability to contain what was inside him.

'You shouldn't be here. I don't want you here. This is *all* your fault.'

'*What* is all my fault?' Stefan tried to ignore the scent of her hair and the feel of her body against his. The hot sun beat down on them but everything else was dark. The rocks, the buildings, *the mood...*

'He saw the photographs. That's what you wanted, isn't it? He was waiting here when I arrived, so if you've come here to do more damage you're wasting your time because there is nothing more you can do than hasn't already been done.'

He didn't correct her assumption that he was somehow behind the photographs. Time enough for that later. His priority was to get her away from here.

Ignoring her attempts to free herself, he examined her

head. A blue bruise darkened the skin around her eye. Looking at it made him feel sick. 'He did that?'

'I fell. I was clumsy.'

She mumbled the words and Stefan bit back his instinctive response to that lie.

'We're leaving, Selene. I'm taking you away from here.'

There was a brief silence and then she started to laugh. 'I came to you for help and doing that made things a thousand times worse. I thought you were a hero—' Her voice broke on the word. 'And just when I find out how far from a hero you really are you turn up here to make things worse. I won't be part of your stupid business rivalry.'

She was so innocent, he thought. Like a child, with a talk of heroes.

She'd stood in front of him in her business suit, spouting numbers and pretending to know what she was talking about, and he hadn't looked deeper. He'd ignored all the instincts that had told him something wasn't quite right. Because he preferred all his interactions to be superficial, he hadn't probed. Like everyone, he hadn't questioned the happy-family image. Even he, who should have known better, had believed it.

'I never claimed to be a hero but I'm going to get you away from here. I promise you that.'

'Forget it, Stefan. If there's one thing I've learned over the past few days it's that the only person I can rely on is myself.'

Before Stefan could respond someone came striding out of the villa and down the path towards them. He recognised the bulky figure of her father.

Stavros Antaxos. Rich, reclusive and rotten. His features were set in a scowl that made closer to bulldog than man and his body groaned from an excess of good food and a shortage of physical exertion.

Stefan topped him by a foot but the other man didn't appear to notice him. His attention was fixed on his daughter.

'You're hurt, Selene—you shouldn't have run. You know how clumsy you are.' His concerned tone caught Stefan off-balance and he realised in those few seconds why no one had questioned the happy-family image so carefully created by this man. He was a master.

His expression was warm and caring as he stepped closer and it was only because Stefan was still holding her that Stefan felt her flinch.

Acting instinctively, he stepped in front of her, shielding her with the muscular power of his body while inside him the anger snapped at its leash. *'Kalimera.'* His voice was silky-smooth and deadly and the older man stopped and looked at him, apparently seeing him for the first time.

His expression altered. Something flickered in those eyes. Something deeply unpleasant. *'Ziakas!'* The other man's face grew ugly. 'You dare show up on my island after what you've done? You made a whore of my daughter. And you did it publicly to humiliate me. You took her innocence.'

Emotion almost blinding him, Stefan was about to answer that accusation with a few of his own when Selene pushed in front of him.

'He didn't take my innocence. *You* did that a long time ago when you became everything no father should ever be.'

Shock crossed her father's face. 'If I've been strict it's because I was trying to protect you from unscrupulous men who would use you to get to me.' His eyes bored into Stefan but Selene shook her head.

'No. You wanted to control me, not protect me. I know what you are, even if no one else will believe it. I won't do it any more. I won't pretend to be this perfect family. It's over.'

Stavros's expression changed slightly. 'You're very emotional, and I'm not surprised. You must be feeling very hurt. Used.'

Stefan saw the confusion on Selene's face and presumably so did her father because he carried on. 'I don't know what this man said to you, but I'm sure it has confused you. He used you to get at me so don't make the mistake of thinking that he cares for you.'

'I know that.' Selene lifted her chin. 'And I used him to get away from you, so that probably makes us equally manipulative. It was my choice to have sex with him.'

Her father moved quickly for a man carrying such excess bulk but Stefan was faster, blocking the blow and delivering two of his own, one low and one straight to the jaw that gave a satisfying crack and sent the other man sprawling on the path.

The Antaxos security team moved forward but Stefan turned his head and sent them a single fulminating glance because now he had evidence of why she'd been so desperate to leave home.

'You really want to defend a man who hits women? Is that in your job description?' When they hesitated, he transferred his gaze to the man now crumpled at his feet.

The man who was responsible for so much pain.

His knuckles throbbed. 'Get up.' Stefan barely recognised his own voice. It was thickened with anger and rage and suddenly he knew he wasn't safe around this man. 'This is what you do to women, isn't it? You live in this place so they can't escape and then you treat them like this. And they don't all get away, do they?'

'Stefan—'

Selene's voice penetrated that mist of fury but he ignored her, all his attention focused on her father.

'I'm taking her away from you. You've lost her. And

I'll be contacting lawyers and the police. The real police, by the way—not the ones you've bribed.'

He watched with a complete lack of sympathy as the tycoon dragged his overweight frame upright, staggering slightly as he stood. Without the support of his security team he appeared to shrink in size.

Stefan turned briefly to Selene. 'Go. Get in my boat. Takis will help you.'

He knew that, wounded and publicly humiliated, Stavros Antaxos was perhaps even more dangerous now than he'd been a few moments ago but to Stefan's surprise instead of denouncing his intention to take his daughter the man appeared to crumple, the fight draining from him.

'If she wants to go she can go, of course. I just want the best for her like any father would. But if she goes then she must live with the consequences.'

Stefan frowned. 'The only consequences will be positive ones. Get in my boat, Selene.'

But she didn't move. Her eyes were fixed on her father. 'I can't.'

He glanced at her impatiently, thinking that he must have misheard. 'What?'

'If I leave, he'll hurt her. That's what he means by living with the consequences. He'll hurt her and it will be my fault.'

'Who?'

'My mother. He'll hurt my mother.' It was a desperate whisper. 'It's what he always does when I don't do what he wants.'

'Your *mother*?'

And then it fell into place, all of it, and he wondered why on earth it had taken him so long to work it out. *This* was why she'd wanted the cash. To get her mother away from the island. And she'd wanted to do it while her fa-

ther was away in Crete. This was the plan. No rebellion.
No business plan. Just an escape plan.

An escape plan he'd wrecked.

She had no other source of income. No place to go. All
her resources cut off by this brutal tyrant.

Exasperation that she hadn't told him the truth mixed in
with another, unfamiliar emotion. *Guilt?* 'Where is your
mother now?'

'In her room.'

With a simple movement of his head Stefan indicated
that his head of security should deal with it. Reluctantly,
he let go of Selene. 'Do you feel well enough to show Takis
the way? If so, go and bring her here.'

Face pale, she glanced at her father and then back at
him. It was obvious she didn't know whom to trust and
the uncertainty in her face almost killed him.

'Just fetch her.' Unnerved by the blood still oozing from
her head, Stefan took a dressing pad from one of the security team and quickly bound her head. 'Stay close to Takis
and if you feel dizzy, tell him. I'd go with you but I have
some business to finish here.'

Switching from intimidating hulk to pussycat, Takis
smiled at Selene and took her hand. 'Which way?'

When they were a safe distance away and out of earshot,
Stefan turned his attention back to her father. Turned to
have a conversation that was long overdue. Finally he had
the power he'd wished he'd had as a child and he used it
now, feeling a rush of grim satisfaction as Antaxos's security team melted into the background, not wanting to get
between the two men. 'You and I have things to discuss.'

CHAPTER SEVEN

NUMB with shock, Selene sat in the stateroom of Stefan's luxury yacht, watching over her mother.

She knew she had to move but she ached from head to foot after her fall onto the hard floor. Every time she tried to boost her spirits panic descended, squashing her flat. She had nothing. No money, no home, no job, no means to support herself. And the craziest thing of all was that none of that depressed her as much as the knowledge that Stefan had set her up. That nothing about that night had been real.

It was humiliating to admit that she'd been so naïve it hadn't even occurred to her to be suspicious when he'd invited her to attend the party. She'd seen him as heroic instead of as he really was—a ruthless businessman who would stop at nothing to get what he wanted.

He was no better than her father.

She was going to have to try and find someone else to give her a business loan but she already knew her father would block every avenue.

In the midst of her lowest moment ever, the door to the stateroom opened.

Stefan stood there, casually dressed in dark jeans and a shirt that did little to disguise the muscular frame that even her father had found intimidating.

Ignoring the tug of lust deep in her belly, Selene started to boil inside. Misery turned to anger.

How *dared* he stand there, so cool, controlled and *sleek*, when her life was falling apart because of him? Yes, some of it was her fault, but if she'd known what he was going to do she would never have made that decision.

Anger simmering, she stalked through the door and closed it behind her, anxious not to wake her mother and determined to maintain her dignity no matter what.

Determined not to be trapped in a room with him, she chose the steps that led to the luxurious deck, relieved to find that Antaxos was no longer even on the horizon. It was gone and she hoped she'd never see it again.

Stefan strode after her. 'You and I have things to discuss.' He spoke through his teeth, as if he were hanging onto control by a thread. 'But first I want to know why you refused to see the doctor.'

'I don't need a doctor.' She was so shaken by what he'd done she could hardly bring herself to speak to him. 'But you should definitely see one because there has to be something *seriously* wrong with you to even contemplate doing what you did to me.'

The flare of shock in those fierce dark eyes revealed that her response wasn't the one he'd been expecting. 'I rescued you.'

'You rescued me from a situation of *your* making. That doesn't score you any points.' Her voice rose. 'Before St George killed the dragon did he first poke it in the eye with a burning stick and drive it mad so that he'd look good when he killed it? I don't think so.'

Stefan eyed her with the same astonishment he would have shown had the dragon in question just landed on his polished deck. '*You* are angry with *me*?'

'Furious. Livid.'

'Then that makes two of us.' He snapped out the words. 'But before we have this conversation I want the doctor to check you over. You had a nasty blow to the head. Do you have a headache? Blurred vision?'

'I'm seeing you perfectly clearly, Stefanos, and believe me you are *not* looking good.'

His jaw clenched. 'I would appreciate a professional opinion on your health.'

'You need a professional to tell you I'm steaming mad? You can't see that for yourself? If that's the case then you're even more insensitive than I thought.'

His only response to that was a slight tightening of his firm, sensual mouth. 'You received a significant blow to your head. I want him to check that you're all right.'

'Why? Because you care so deeply about my welfare? Or maybe because your master plan isn't finished yet? What am I supposed to do next? Dance naked on national TV?' It gave her some satisfaction to see the streaks of colour tracing the lines of his cheekbones. 'You used me. The whole thing was a set-up—the champagne, the dress, the… the sex.' Why on earth had she mentioned the sex? It was the last thing she wanted to think about. She wouldn't *let* herself think about it. She didn't dare. 'It was all planned so that someone could take the most incriminating photos possible.'

'That is *not* true.'

'That's why you rescued me, isn't it? To score another blow against my father.'

He threw her a simmering glance of raw emotion. 'Stop looking for conspiracy theories. None of this would have happened if you'd told someone your father was abusive.'

'I tried. No one would believe me. We are a happy family, remember? My father is a pillar of society. A philanthropist. He is ruthless, but part of his appeal has always been that he is a family man. People believe that.' She saw from the expression on his face that he'd believed it, too. 'Do you know that he even supports a charity for abused women?' The irony of it almost made her choke. 'I called the police once.'

'And?'

'He told them I was going through a difficult teenage phase. They believed him. Or maybe they didn't—' she shrugged '—maybe they were just afraid of what would happen if they arrested him. Either way, it just made it worse for me and for my mother.'

He turned away and closed his hands over the rail of the yacht. His knuckles were white.

'You let me think I caused those bruises.' The rawness of his tone caught her off-balance. 'You let me think I'd hurt you.'

A sharp stab of guilt punctured her anger. Thrown by the sudden shift in the conversation, she stared at his rigid shoulders and suddenly she was right back in his bed, naked and vulnerable. 'I—I didn't know what to say—'

'The truth would have been good. I blamed myself for being rough with you but I couldn't work out how or when. I went over and over it in my mind.'

'I didn't think it would bother you that much.'

'Why? You think all men like to bruise their women?' He turned, his voice a dangerous growl. 'Is that what you think?'

She shook her head. 'No. I just—I wasn't thinking about you. I was thinking about my mother. If I'd told you the truth you either wouldn't have believed me or you would have tried to stop me.'

'Or perhaps I would have helped you. If you'd mentioned just once when you were presenting your business plan that this was all about escaping from your father we wouldn't be here now. If you'd told me the truth instead of letting me think I'd hurt you—'

'You did hurt me.' Selene felt her insides wobble and reminded herself that everything that had happened between them had been fake. 'I thought you were such a hero. You talked to me that night on the boat. You were kind to me when no one else was. When things were terrible at home, I lay there and dreamed about you. I planned how it was going to be when I finally met you again. How I was going to look. What I was going to say. And every time I imagined it you were the hero.'

His breathing was shallow. 'Selene—'

'And when I finally planned our escape you were part of it. I'd worked through every scenario, making sure that even if it didn't work it wouldn't make things worse. I had a market for my candles, a way of earning money. I was prepared for everything. Everything except a man who lied to me. A man who used me as a pawn in his stupid business rivalry.' Dizziness washed over her like a giant wave and she swayed slightly, resisting her body's attempts to persuade her to lie down.

Dark brows brought together in a frown of concern, Stefan reached for her.

She stepped away from him. 'Do not touch me,' she said thickly. 'Do not touch me ever again, do you hear? You might not have bruised me physically but you hurt me more than my father ever did.' Because she'd cared. Oh, God, she'd really cared. But there was no way she was admitting that now. He'd already had too much of her.

Eyes wary, he watched her. 'You're bleeding.'

'Good. I hope it stains your deck.'

'*Theé mou*, you are the most stubborn woman I have ever met. Will you at least let me change the dressing on your head before we continue this conversation?'

'No. And this conversation is over.' She fixed her gaze somewhere past his broad shoulders so that she wasn't distracted by those killer good looks which could lull a woman into thinking he was a good person. 'All I want from you is to stop at the nearest port. Then you can get back to trampling the innocent as you build your empire. You and my father are each as bad as the other.'

'I'm not dropping you anywhere. Your father is being arrested as we speak. He'll be charged but we can't be sure he won't be released. As you rightly say, he has powerful friends. You're staying with me and that's non-negotiable. Now, sit down before you fall down.'

Yesterday she would have taken his words to mean he wanted her with him but she knew better now.

'If you're planning on keeping me for leverage against my father I can assure you he won't care what you do.'

'That is *not* what I was thinking.'

'Of course it wasn't. You'd never use a person like that, would you, Stefan?'

'Selene—'

'Just so that we're clear about who we're dealing with, he isn't going to care if you throw my dead body over the side of your boat even if you've packaged me in red sequins and a bow.' She was horrified to discover a lump in her throat. 'My father doesn't love me and never has.'

What was it about her that was so unlovable?

Knowing that this wasn't the time to dwell on that, she blinked and cleared her vision. But it was too late because he'd seen and instead of backing away, which was what she would have preferred, he moved closer.

His hands were gentle on her face, tilting it as he urged her to look at him. 'If that is the truth then you are better off building your life without him. I will help you do that.' The softness in his voice almost finished her.

'No, thanks. I've already experienced your idea of "help". From now on I help myself. I don't want anything to do with either of you.'

'You're not thinking the situation through. You have nowhere to go.'

The fact that it was true did nothing to improve her mood. Panic squeezed her insides. 'I wouldn't stay on this boat with you if it were the only piece of dry land in the Mediterranean. I'd rather be eaten by sharks.'

'That's extremely unlikely in these waters.'

'Are you mocking me?'

Her voice rose and he went unnaturally still.

'No. I'm merely trying to stop you making a rash, emotional decision that will harm no one but yourself.'

'So now you're saying I'm rash and over-emotional?'

'*Cristos*, stop twisting everything I say! If you had told me the truth I would have ensured your safety. And that is enough of the past. You need to think about the future. I'm willing to offer you and your mother a home—on a temporary basis, of course,' he added swiftly, 'until you can find somewhere suitable.'

Selene heard that hastily added qualifier and burst out laughing. 'I'm almost tempted to say yes. It would serve you right to find yourself living with a woman *and* her mother. That would really cramp your style. Relax, Stefan. I can't think of anything worse than living under the same roof as you.'

His jaw was clenched. 'It's probably wise to stop talking while you're this upset because you're going to say things you don't mean.'

'I mean every word.'

'I'm trying to help you.'

'You're the one who taught me to be cautious.' Her gaze lifted to his shoulders, travelled over the bronzed skin at the base of his throat and finally met those dark eyes that could seduce a woman with a single glance. 'I don't want your help. I never want to see you again.'

Below deck in the owner's suite, Stefan poured himself a large drink, but when he lifted it to his mouth his hand was shaking so badly the liquid sloshed over the side.

Cursing softly, he put the glass down and closed his eyes, but that didn't help because his mind was tortured by images. Images of her stepping back onto the island not knowing whether her father was waiting. Images of his anger spilling over. Images of that beautiful hair streaked with blood.

Gripping the glass, he drank, feeling the fire burn his stomach.

While he'd been on the island he hadn't dared let himself feel, but he was feeling now and the emotion hit him so hard he couldn't breathe. He'd never let it out before and because he'd never let it out he had no idea how to haul it back inside again.

Business rivalry. She thought this was about *business*?

He had no idea how much time had passed but eventually he heard a voice behind him.

'Boss?'

It was Takis.

Not willing to reveal even a sliver of weakness, Stefan kept his back to him. 'Problems?'

There was a brief pause. 'Possibly. The girl and her mother have gone.'

'Gone?' He was surprised how normal he sounded. Surprised by the strength of his voice given the turmoil inside him. 'Gone where?'

'Left the boat, boss.'

'How can they have left the boat? Did they swim?'

'Er—the boat docked twenty minutes ago, boss.'

Docked?

Stefan turned his head, saw the port, and realised with a stab of shock just how long he'd been down here. While he'd been trying to get himself under control they'd arrived in Athens.

'How can they have gone?'

'No one was looking, boss.'

Stefan rolled his shoulders to ease the tension. 'You are telling me that two women, at least one of whom was in a weakened state, managed to leave my boat unobserved by any of my so-called security team within two minutes of arriving at Athens?'

'It would seem so. I take all the blame.' Takis sounded sheepish. 'Fire me. Truth is, I wasn't expecting them to leave. Selene is a very determined young woman. I underestimated her.'

'You're not the only one guilty of that.' Stefan stared blindly out of the window, knowing that the blame was his.

Instead of listening, instead of proving he was someone she could trust, he'd been angry—and she had no way of knowing that the root of that anger had nothing to do with her.

No wonder she'd walked.

She'd had enough of male anger to last her a lifetime.

Takis cleared his throat. 'I'm worried he might go after her, so I've already got a team on it and I've briefed a few people. Called in a few favours. We'll find her.'

Stefan knew that the Ziakas name had influence. He had links with everyone from the government to the Athens police. But he also knew better than to underestimate his enemy, and in this case his enemy was formidable and motivated.

Stavros Antaxos wanted his wife and daughter back

and he had a web of contacts every bit as impressive as Stefan's.

Takis was watching him. 'Have you any idea where she might go? Any clues?'

Where could she go? How did she plan to support herself?

She'd left the island with nothing. Not even the battered old bag holding her candles and soap and the money he'd given her.

Tension rushed into his shoulders. She had no one to defend her. No way of earning money.

He imagined some unscrupulous man handing her a drink. Imagined him being on the receiving end of that sweet smile and quirky sense of humour. Imagined her naked with another man—

Sweat broke out on the back of his neck and he uttered just two words.

'Find her.'

CHAPTER EIGHT

THREE weeks later Selene was balancing plates in a small *taverna* tucked away in the labyrinth of backstreets near the famous Acropolis when she heard a commotion behind her.

'Hey, Lena, take a look at *him*,' breathed Mariana, the waitress who had persuaded the owner to give Selene a job when she'd appeared out of nowhere only hours after she'd slipped away from the luxurious confines of Stefan's yacht. 'That man is smoking hot. He should come fitted with air-conditioning.'

Terrified of losing concentration and dropping the plates, Selene focused on her task until the meals were safely delivered to the table. 'Two *moussaka*, one *sofrito* and one *kleftiko*.' She was so nervous of doing something wrong and losing her job she didn't even look to see who was attracting everyone's attention and anyway, she'd had enough of 'smoking hot' men. 'Can I fetch you anything else?'

'Just that indecently sexy Greek man who has just taken the table behind you, honey,' the woman murmured, her eyes fixed in the same direction as Mariana's. 'Do they all look like that around here? If so, I'm moving here. No question.'

'That would be great for the economy.' Selene added

fresh cutlery to the table and removed empty glasses. On her first day she'd dropped a tray. It had only happened once. She'd learned to balance, concentrate and not overload. 'How are you enjoying your holiday? Did you make it to Delphi yesterday?' This was the part of the job she loved most of all—talking and getting to know people, especially when they returned to the *taverna* again and again. She'd used her mother's maiden name and no one knew who she was. The anonymity was blissful, but nowhere near as blissful as being able to live her life the way she wanted to live it. 'I'm going there on my next day off.'

'We followed your advice and went early in the morning. It was perfect. It's always good to have local knowledge.'

Knowing that her 'local knowledge' had been rapidly acquired over a three-week period, Selene smiled. 'I'm glad you had a good time.'

'We did. And talking of good times—' the woman peeped over the top of her sunglasses '—that guy makes me want to forget I'm married. If he's looking for company, send him my way.'

A nasty suspicion pricking the back of her neck, Selene turned and glanced towards the man who was attracting so much attention.

Stefan lounged at a table in the far corner of the *taverna*. Even without the expensive suit there was an unmistakable air of wealth and power about him, and yet she knew women stared not because of the promise of riches but because his raw masculine appeal promised sex as they'd never had it before. He attracted women like iron filings to a magnet with no apparent effort on his behalf. Perhaps that was why, she thought numbly. Perhaps it was his supreme indifference that provided part of his appeal. Every woman wanted to be the one to catch the attention of a man whose attention wasn't easily caught. There wasn't a woman alive, even those happily married, who could look at this man and not wonder what a night with him would be like.

And *she* knew.

His gaze locked on hers and she knew her changed appearance hadn't fooled him for a moment. In that single look she was hit with the full force of his masculinity. Her body burned under his steady appraisal but even though she wanted to she couldn't look away.

Something passed between them. Something raw and primal that made it impossible to think of anything but those intense, unforgettable hours she'd spent in his bed.

Desperately, she tried to remind herself that none of it had been real. At least, not for him.

'*Kalimera.*'

He spoke softly and Selene almost stumbled, tightening her grip on the tray to stop it from crashing to the ground.

It wasn't fair that she should feel like this.

By rights she should be able to look at him and want to slap his face. Instead all she wanted to do was grab the front of his exquisitely tailored shirt with both hands and rip it open, exposing the man underneath. On the surface he seemed so urbane and sophisticated—*civilised*—and yet beneath the trappings of success was a man who had fought his way to the top with his bare hands. He had no scruples about doing what needed to be done to get what he wanted. Of course he didn't. He ran his business according to his own agenda with no thought for anyone else. He'd used her to score points against her father. Knowing that, she wanted to look away, but those dark, dangerous eyes wouldn't release her from that invisible bond that held her trapped.

Her brain appeared to have shut down and she was

breathing so fast she started to feel light-headed. 'What are you doing here?'

'Pausing for a drink in a local *taverna* after a long, stressful day at work.' He stretched out his legs, as relaxed as she was tense, those dark eyes watchful.

'Why pick this one?'

'You already know the answer to that.'

Why would he have tracked her down? Why go to that trouble?

She could feel everyone watching them, straining to hear the conversation. Saw her boss watching her with a frown and remembered just how precious this job was. 'What can I get you?'

'Just coffee.' Somehow he managed to make that instruction sound intimate. 'I like your hair. The cut shows off your face.'

The compliment threw her and she lifted her hand to her newly cropped hair.

She'd cut it herself, with blunt scissors and nothing but a chipped mirror in which to view the results. With a few hacks of those scissors she'd become Lena. And when she'd finished hacking she'd scooped up the mounds of soft golden hair and added them to the rubbish where no one would find it. It was the first thing she'd done in her new life. The second was to get a job, and she knew she'd been lucky to get this one when so many were struggling.

'What do you want, Stefan?'

'You didn't have to cut it. You don't have to hide.'

Panic gripped her and she glanced over her shoulder to check no one was listening. 'I'm not hiding. I'm working in a restaurant in full daylight. And I'd like to take your order.'

'You're trying not to draw attention to yourself. You've cut your hair. You're nervous. I can protect you.'

There was a strange fluttering low in her belly. 'Too late. I don't believe in heroes any more.'

'How about man's ability to make a mistake. Do you believe in that?'

She didn't dare listen. He was smooth, persuasive and a master negotiator. She knew he would probably be capable of convincing her of anything.

'I'll fetch your coffee.'

'What time do you finish?'

'It doesn't matter. I don't want you to come here again. You *mustn't* come here again. You're too—conspicuous.' Her heart thudded hard against her ribs. The thought that her father might find her made her feel sick. She'd contemplated hiding away but that would have made it impossible for her to work, and if she couldn't earn money she couldn't be independent. And that wasn't all, of course. She refused to live her life in hiding.

He read her mind and his gaze darkened. 'I won't let him hurt you.'

'You were the reason he hurt me last time. If you come here, you'll attract attention. I don't want you here again.'

He reached out, those long, strong fingers trapping hers. 'I repeat—he won't hurt you.'

'And how do you plan to stop him? I'd rather rely on myself, thank you.'

'The police questioned him and then released him. You haven't been out of our sight for the past three weeks.'

The shock was physical. She snatched her hand away from his. '*Our* sight?'

'I had to ensure your safety. As you pointed out when we last met, my actions put you in danger. The least I could do was fix that. He won't touch you again.'

'You've had me followed?'

'For your safety.'

The thought made her grow cold. He'd had her followed and she hadn't noticed. She'd been alert, on the look-out, but she hadn't noticed. How could that have happened?

She looked around but no one stood out. There were tourists. A group of Americans. An English couple. A bunch of local men. Two giggling teenage girls. 'How? Who has been watching me?'

'You wouldn't have seen them so stop beating yourself up for being unobservant.'

'I've been looking.'

'Takis only employs the best in his team. If you'd spotted them they would have been out of a job.'

Takis. Selene remembered how kind he'd been to her mother that day. How kind he'd been to her. 'He's…' She sighed. 'I liked him.'

'I only employ the best, too. As I said—you don't need to be afraid.'

'I'm not afraid. And I don't appreciate you interfering.'

'You accused me of putting you in danger. You have to allow me to put that right.' His tone was conversational. Casual. No one watching them would have guessed they were talking about anything more significant than the menu.

'If you don't want to put me in danger the best thing you can do is stay away.'

'We'll talk about it over dinner, Selene.'

'No way.'

'Last time we spent an evening together we had fun.' He hesitated. 'I want to see you again.'

The air left her lungs in a rush and she was so shocked she simply stared at him. Terrified that someone might have overheard, she didn't dare look at anyone. 'The last time we spent an evening together you ruined my life. And my name is Lena. I'll fetch your coffee.' She backed away from him, knocking into the table behind her.

The last time we spent an evening together we had fun.

Those words sent images rushing back into her head. Images she'd been trying to delete for the past three weeks.

She walked briskly back inside the *taverna*, shaking so badly she was convinced everyone would notice.

Fortunately they all seemed too overawed by the identity of their illustrious visitor to pay any attention to her pale face.

'Everything OK?' Mariana walked up to her, her cheeks pink from the heat. 'It's a hot one today, that's for sure.'

A rowdy group of young men took a table near to them and Selene took a step towards them, but Mariana stepped in front of her in a smooth move.

'I'll take them. They look as though they've had a bit too much to drink already. Just my type.'

Selene frowned. 'I can handle it.'

'You serve Ziakas. He's more important. Plenty of people round here wish he'd give up running his company and run Greece. He'd soon sort out our problems. You only have to look at him to know there is nothing that man doesn't do well.'

Selene stared at her for a moment, wondering how she could have been so obtuse. 'You work for him. *You're* the one who has been watching me.'

Mariana hesitated and then shrugged. 'One of them. I don't see why it has to be a secret. If a man was going to all this trouble for me, I'd want to know. I mean, the guy has done everything except call in air support. He obviously adores you.'

'I thought we were friends?'

'We are friends. Just because I'm an expert in hand-to-hand combat doesn't mean I can't have female friendships.'

Selene's head was reeling. 'So you're—?'

'Ex-military. But fortunately I also make a mean cappuccino. It's a useful skill.'

Mouth tight, Selene picked up the coffee order from the counter and thrust the cup to Mariana. 'In that case you can serve him. He's your boss.'

'A few layers above me. Technically I work for Takis. I don't understand why you're upset.' Mariana's expression was curious. 'The guy has virtually enlisted the Marines to keep you safe. And he is so tough. If a guy like him were that keen on me I wouldn't be complaining. Unfortunately I only attract losers and once they discover I can break their arm with one twist they run away terrified. No idea why.'

'He's not keen.'

'Right. So he's going to all this trouble just for his entertainment? I don't think so.' Marianna added a spoon to the saucer. 'Why not just go out with him a few times? Have some fun with his bank account?'

'The problem with rich guys,' Selene said tightly, 'is that they think all that money gives them the right to trample all over you.'

Mariana's gaze slid to Stefan. 'He can trample on me any time he likes. Sadly he hasn't looked once in my direction and that's because he can't stop looking at you. Are you seriously not going to do anything about that?'

'No, I'm not. Tell me one other thing—did he arrange for me to have this job?'

Mariana pulled a face. 'I—'

'Great. So I didn't even get this on my own merits.' Furious, confused, she walked over to the group of men. 'What can I get you?'

They were rowdy but good-natured, and this was their third trip to the *taverna* in the same week so she recognised them immediately.

'Hey, Lena—' one of them winked at her '—what are the specials tonight?'

She told them, handing out menus and taking their drinks order, shifting slightly to one side when the man's hand covered her bottom.

'I recommend the lamb.'

'We're going clubbing later. Will you come?'

'I'll be too tired after working here all day, but thanks for the invitation.' She was used to deflecting invitations and she kept it light and friendly, kept the smile on her face, all the while aware of Stefan seated two tables away, listening to every word.

She felt him watching her. Felt those sinfully sexy eyes following her every move as she moved between tables serving tourists and locals.

He sat still as Mariana delivered his coffee, and continued to watch Selene until her nerves were shredded and she hardly dared hold a plate in case it slipped from her sweaty fingers.

The fact that they'd been watching her without her knowledge freaked her out.

Who else was watching her?

Suddenly she made a decision.

Walking through to the bar area, which couldn't be seen from the restaurant, she smiled sickly at the owner and told him she was feeling unwell. The job wasn't real anyway. He'd only given her the job because the Ziakas machine had swung into action.

She went to the bathroom, pushed open the window, climbed through it and dropped onto the street outside.

Brushing off the dust, she derived some small satisfaction from the knowledge that she wasn't making it easy for him. No doubt he'd track her down again in no time if he wanted to, but that didn't mean she had to hand herself over.

Heart pounding, she sprinted along the maze of streets that led back to the tiny room she was renting, all the time expecting to hear the heavy tread of masculine footsteps behind her.

She was just congratulating herself on successfully slipping away when a male hand curved over her shoulder.

Terrified that it might be her father or one of his men, Selene turned round swinging but it was Stefan who caught her arm.

'It's all right. It's just me.' His voice was roughened with concern. 'But it might not have been. Why are you doing this to yourself? Why are you making it hard for us to protect you?'

'I've been followed and watched over for the whole of my life. I am trying to escape from that.'

'I offered you my help but instead you choose to spend your day working in a *taverna* being propositioned by sleazy men in Hawaiian shorts.'

'And what are you, Stefan? A sleazy man in an expensive suit? At least they're honest about what they want.' Still shaken by the panic that had gripped her when he'd touched her shoulder, she pressed herself against the wall. 'I really have no idea why you're even here. I've served my purpose and we both know you're not interested in anything or anyone unless it serves a purpose.'

'Since when did you become so cynical?'

'Since I accepted that you're a cold, emotionless megalomaniac with no redeeming qualities. Now, if you'll excuse me, I'll—'

'No.'

He planted his arms either side of her, caging her, and she gasped, shoving him hard.

'Don't *ever* trap me like that.'

'Then don't run.' But he lowered one of his arms. It made virtually no difference because he was standing so close to her there was no way she could move. 'I did *not* invite you to that party because of your father. I invited you because you were sweet and sexy and because I wanted to spend time with you.'

'I don't want to talk about this. It's too late, Stefan.'

'Journalists take photographs of me all the time. It's part of my life. So much a part of it I didn't think of it. Had you explained to me the importance of your father not knowing, it might have occurred to me.'

'I arrived in your office in disguise. Didn't that give you a clue?'

'You told me he disapproved of what you were doing and I had no reason not to question that. You were dressed in a nun's outfit—' his eyes gleamed with self-mockery, '—I assumed that what came out of your mouth was the truth.'

'But you knew I wanted to keep my visit to you a secret.'

'I didn't even think about it. There is a world of difference between a disapproving father and an abusive father. I thought you wanted to make your mark on the world. I didn't know he was leaving marks on you.' There was a brief pause. His mouth tightened. 'You should have shared that with me.'

'Apart from that one abortive attempt to tell the authorities, I've never shared it with anyone.'

'But you shared something else with me you've never shared with anyone.' His fingers brushed her cheek, surprisingly gentle. 'You could have trusted me, Selene.'

She felt her body respond instantly and knew that the biggest danger to herself came from him.

'So you're saying what happened is my fault?'

'No, it was mine.' His hand dropped. 'And I apologise because the possibility of photographs should have occurred to me and it didn't. But the reason it didn't was because I've lived with it for so long I don't notice it any more.' His leg brushed against hers. Her mind blurred.

Melting inside, Selene pressed herself hard against the wall in an attempt not to touch him. 'It really doesn't matter. I've moved on.'

'But you've moved on without me,' he said softly, 'and that isn't what I want. Your mother seems well.'

'She's very well. She's been staying in the same artists' community she lived in when she first arrived in Athens as a teenager. She's painting again and her confidence is returning. It's wonderful to see that after—' She broke off, eyes wide. 'Wait a minute, how do you know she's well? You've followed her, too?'

'Naturally we are concerned. Unlike you, she welcomes the protection. It has allowed her to relax and enjoy her new life and her old friends.'

Selene thought about how frightened her mother had been. 'All right—' her voice sounded stiff '—maybe I'm grateful to you for helping my mother, but don't think it's going to change the way I feel about you.'

'You're very cynical all of a sudden, *koukla mou*. It doesn't suit you. It isn't who you are.'

'It is now. And it was being with you that made me this way.'

'So you've changed personality in a matter of weeks? I don't believe that. You are the most open, trusting person I've met.'

'You mean I'm stupid.'

A frown touched his brows. 'No. I do not mean that.' He took a deep breath. 'I realise we have some obstacles to overcome, but it would be much easier to overcome them if I wasn't worrying about your safety all the time. I want you to come and stay at my villa, at least for a while.'

The temptation was so great it horrified her. 'No, thanks.'

'I don't want you living on your own.'

'Well, I want it. I've lived under my father's rules for so long I want the freedom to come and go as I please. I can wear what I like. See whoever I like. Be who I want to be.'

'And who do you want to be?'

She'd thought about nothing else.

'Myself,' she said simply. 'I want to be myself. Not someone else's version of who they think I should be.'

'So if I ask you—the real you—out to dinner, will you say yes?'

Selene swallowed, unsettled by how much being this close to him affected her. What scared her most in all this was how badly she lost her judgement around him. She didn't want to be the sort of woman who lost her mind around a man. 'Why are you bothering? Why are you so persistent?'

'When there is something I want, I go for it. That's who I am.'

'And you're pretending that's me? Come on, Stefan, we had one night. A whole night. I'm already the longest relationship you ever had.'

'And I'm the only relationship *you've* ever had.' His eyes were dark and not once did they shift from hers. 'Are you telling me you don't want to explore that? Are you telling me you don't think about it?'

The heat went right through her body. 'I try not to because when I remember I also remember how you used me to score points with my father.'

A muscle flickered in his jaw. 'You don't believe that it was not intentional?'

'No, I don't.' She didn't dare. She was *not* going to be gullible. 'I think you're trying to talk your way out of trouble.'

He stared down at her for a long moment. 'Even if you don't want to eat with me you're working yourself to the bone trying to afford to live. Let me help you.'

'I don't need or want your help. I'm doing fine by myself.'

'Working in a *taverna*?' He lifted his hand and touched her cropped hair. 'What about your scented candles? What happened to the dream?'

'The dream is still there. I'm working to get the money I need to set up in business.'

'You're determined to do things the hard way?'

'I'm determined to do things myself.'

'I said I'd give you a business loan. That offer still stands.'

'I no longer want anything from you.'

His gaze was suddenly thoughtful. 'You're worried you can't control your feelings around me?'

'You're right about that. There's a possibility I could punch you. I can't be sure it won't happen.'

For some reason that made him smile. He stepped back and glanced up at the run-down building. 'This is where you're living?'

'Where I'm living is none of your business. Neither is where I'm working or who I'm seeing. This is my life now and I'm not sharing the details with anyone.'

His mouth tightened as he took in the paint blistering on the woodwork. 'I want to help you and that help is not linked to what happens between us.'

'Nothing is going to happen between us. Next time I get involved with someone it will be with a man who has

strong family values and who doesn't treat commitment
as a contagious disease to be avoided at all costs.'

'Family. You still believe in family after what he did
to you?' Lifting his hand, he traced her lower lip with
his thumb, a brooding look in his eyes. 'Love just makes
you vulnerable, *koukla mou*. You are hurting because you
loved.'

'I'm not hurting.'

'I saw your face that day on the island. I saw the way
you looked at him.'

'He's my father. You can't just undo that.' How did they
come to be talking about this? It was something she'd
never talked about, not even to her mother. It felt wrong
to want love from someone for whom you had no respect.
'But it's—complicated.'

'Emotions are always complicated. Why do you think
I avoid them?'

Despite herself, she found herself wondering about him.
She saw the shadow flicker across those moody eyes and
the sudden tension in his shoulders as he let his hand drop.

'My advice? Forget your father. He isn't worth a single
tear from you. And as for family—' he eased away from
her '—travel through life alone and no one can hurt you.'

His words shocked her. 'Thanks to my father I've been
alone for the best part of twenty-two years and that sucks,
too. He alienated everyone. My life was a lie. For the first
time ever I'm making friends and I'm loving it. No one
knows that my surname is Antaxos. No one cares. I'm
Lena.'

A noisy group of tourists surged down the narrow street
and she flinched.

He noticed her reaction instantly. 'And you're looking
over your shoulder all the time. Come with me and you
won't have to look over your shoulder.' He stepped closer

to her, protecting her from the sudden crush of people. His thighs brushed against hers and her stomach clenched. 'I can protect you from your father.'

But who would protect her from Stefan?

Suffocated by the feelings inside her, Selene lifted her head and their eyes met.

The noise of the crowd faded into the background and all she could think was that he was the most insanely good-looking man she'd ever seen. And then he was kissing her, his mouth possessive, skilled, explicit as he coaxed her lips apart in echoes of what they'd shared that night at his villa.

When he finally lifted his head she had to put her hand on his chest to steady herself.

'I want to start again,' he said roughly, cupping her face in his hands and lowering his forehead to hers. 'I've never felt this way about a woman before. Everything that happened between us was real. All of it. And deep down you know it. Give me a chance to prove it to you.'

His body was pressed up against hers, and it was an incredible body. Hard muscle, height, width—he was exquisitely proportioned. Even though the night was oppressively warm, she shivered.

He lifted a hand to her short hair, toying with the ends. 'I'm attending a charity ball tomorrow on Corfu. It's going to be glamorous. Men in dinner jackets, champagne in tall, slim glasses. Your kind of evening.'

Once again temptation pulled at her but this time she pulled back. 'No, thank you.'

His eyes gleamed with exasperation. 'What happened to the sweet, trusting girl who drank too much champagne and tried to seduce me? She would never have said no to a good night out.'

'She grew up the night you used her to score points over a business rival.' Terrified by her own feelings, she pushed past him but he caught her arm, his fingers holding her still.

'What if my feelings for your father have nothing to do with our conflicting business interests?' He spoke in a tone she'd never heard him use before and it made her pause.

'Of course they do. You're just two alpha males who have to win, and because two people can't both win it's never going to end.'

'Your father ruined my father.' His voice was hoarse and not entirely steady. 'He took everything from him, starting with my mother.'

When Selene simply stared at him, he carried on. 'I was eight years old when Stavros Antaxos landed in his flashy yacht and tempted her away with the promise of a lifestyle beyond her imagination. And just in case she ever changed her mind and considered returning to her husband and son he made sure there was nothing to return to. He destroyed my father's fledgling business, his self-respect and his dignity, and the irony was he didn't need to. The day my mother walked out my father lost everything that mattered to him. He loved her so much that his life had no meaning once she'd gone. So before you judge me remember I have more reason than most for knowing just how low your father will stoop.'

Selene was welded to the spot—and not just by the shock of that unexpected revelation and by the pain she saw in his face. It was the first time she'd seen him display any real human emotion. 'I—I didn't know.'

'Well, now you do.' His tone was flat. His expression blank.

'There have always been women, of course. Before his marriage and afterwards.' She said the words to herself as much as him. 'It was one of the things I hated most— that my mother just accepted it as part of her marriage. I wanted her to have more self-respect, but she was dazzled by him to begin with and then ground down by him. He sucked the personality from her.'

'Yes. That's how he operates.'

'It's driven by insecurity.' She saw it clearly now and wondered why she hadn't before. 'He doesn't believe someone will stay with him if they can leave, so he stops them leaving. He makes them feel weak. As if they can't survive without him.' And suddenly she knew and the realisation made her feel sick. 'There was a woman—a woman who was in love with him years before my mother ever came on the scene—and she drowned on the rocks off Antaxos.'

He released her suddenly. 'We never knew if it was an accident or if she jumped.'

Without waiting for her to respond he strode away from her, leaving Selene staring after him in appalled silence.

Your father ruined my father.

The woman who had drowned was his mother.

'Stefan, wait—*Stefan*.' But her voice was lost in the crowd and he was already out of sight, his long, powerful stride eating up the ground as he walked out of her life, leaving her with nothing but the knowledge she'd been terribly, horribly wrong about him.

CHAPTER NINE

STEFAN sat sprawled in his chair at the head of the table, his features stony as he listened to his executives discussing a business issue that should have interested him but didn't. His mind was preoccupied with memories he himself had unlocked. It was like ripping open an old wound, tearing through healing tissue and exposing raw flesh. It wasn't just pain, it was screaming agony. But worse than that was the thought of Selene struggling on her own, looking over her shoulder all the time, never able to relax and just enjoy her new life.

Despite the efficient air-conditioning, sweat beaded on his brow.

As well as watching Selene they'd been watching Antaxos but her father hadn't shown his face since their encounter on that day.

What the hell had possessed him to get involved with Stavros Antaxos's daughter? It was a decision that had 'trouble' written all over it.

'Stefan—?'

Hearing his name, he glanced up and saw Maria in the doorway.

It was unheard of for her to interrupt him in a meeting and Stefan rose to his feet in a cold panic. He told himself that Takis would not have let anything happen to Selene, but still his limbs shook as he walked to the door.

'What's wrong? Have you heard from her?' His voice trailed off as he saw Selene standing in his office, the sun sending silver lights shimmering through her newly shorn hair. She wore a simple cotton strap top and a pair of shorts that revealed endless length of tanned leg.

Tears streaked her pretty face.

His world tilted. '*Theé mou*, what has happened?' He was across the room in two strides, his hands on her arms. 'Has he found you? If he's threatened you in some way then I'll—'

'He hasn't threatened me. I haven't seen him.' She choked out the words. Sniffed. 'Nothing like that.'

'Then what the hell is wrong? Tell me.'

The quiet click of the door told him that Maria had left the room, which meant that he was alone with someone who repeatedly made him feel as if he were poised on the top of a slippery slope about to plunge to his doom.

'I was so wrong about you and I'm sorry.' Her eyes lifted to his. 'I— This is *all* my fault. After I met you that night and you were so nice to me I built you up in my head as some sort of hero. I thought about you all the time, I dreamed about you, and then I met you and you were this amazing guy—' Her voice cracked. 'And we had that night, and it was fun, and you were so incredibly sexy, and being in your bed was—well, I just—I never thought anything could feel like that—'

'You need to breathe, *koukla mou*.'

'No, I need to tell you this because I feel *horrible* and I'm not going to stop feeling horrible until I've said what I have to say and you have to listen.'

'I'm listening,' Stefan assured her, 'but I need you

to calm down. I thought you only cried when you were happy?'

'Turns out that's another thing I was wrong about. But mostly I was wrong about you. I was so panicked when I saw those photos, and you were so unconcerned about it I assumed you were responsible. I didn't even think about it from your point of view. Of course you didn't know about my father. Why would you? And I was so used to playing my part in this so-called happy family that I didn't even know how to tell someone that it was all fake.'

'None of this matters now. It's fine.'

'No, it isn't fine. Because you came to that island to rescue me and all I did was yell at you, and then I found out you'd got me the job and had people watching me so that I was safe, but did I thank you?' Her voice rose. 'No! I yelled at you again.'

'You wanted to be independent. I understand that.'

'I was embarrassingly unrealistic. I have no experience, no credentials, nothing that would make an employer take me on, and yet I thought I'd be able to just walk into a job and when I did I didn't even question it. If it hadn't been for you I probably would have been sleeping rough—'

'I've done that and I didn't want it for you.' He wiped that image from his mind.

'You've been so kind to me,' she mumbled, 'and I didn't deserve it. I was mean and I'm not a mean person. But I can see it all more clearly now.'

'You have been through more than anyone should have to. Why would you trust me? I was your father's enemy— that's why you came to me in the first place.'

'But I never saw you as that. I knew you weren't. I knew you were good. You *are* good.' She was standing so close to him he could smell the scent of her hair and see the flecks of black in her green eyes.

'*Don't* start that again.'

'I'm not. I know you're not a hero, but you are good. I also understand now that your mother walking off like that when you were so young must have put you off relationships for life.'

'I have had plenty of relationships.'

'I mean real ones, not just sex. You don't let anyone close because of it and that breaks my heart, because you deserve to have a lovely family.'

Stefan felt a flash of panic. 'Believe me that is *not* what I want. You are far more sensitive about this than I am. It was a long time ago and my mother was just another of your father's many conquests. It happened long, long before he met and married your mother.'

'But you're still hurting. Of course you're hurting. You brush it away like dust on your sleeve but we both know you haven't left it behind. You're carrying it with you into everything you do—your business and your relationships. It's the reason you work so hard and it's the reason you don't get involved with women. It's the reason you don't have a family. You're afraid of losing what you love.'

Her insight shocked him. 'I really don't—'

'I was the one who opened the wound. I pushed you and pushed you and suggested it was just because you were fighting over business—as if you could be that superficial.'

Stefan, who had spent his life being exactly that superficial was floored. 'Selene—'

'I'm sorry.' She flung her arms round him and hugged him tightly.

He stood immobile, the feel of her softness against him driving the breath from his body. And there was that smell again. The smell of her soap that always drove him wild. He closed his eyes and clenched his teeth to try and hold back the rush of feeling.

He couldn't remember being hugged by a woman except as part of foreplay. He stood rigid, unsure what to do next. 'I should probably get back to my meeting.'

'Couldn't they have the meeting without you? We could go somewhere private.' Her voice was muffled in his chest. 'We could have fun and do a few more things on my list.' She was still hugging him, her body warm against his, her arms wrapped around him.

'If we're doing things on your list why do we need to be private?'

'Because most of them involved getting naked with you.'

Stefan gave an incredulous laugh. 'You are the most confusing woman I've ever met.'

'I'm the least confusing woman you've ever met. I'm honest about what I want.'

'And what *do* you want?' He forced himself to ask the question even though he wasn't sure he wanted to hear the answer.

'I want quite a lot. First I'd like you to help me with my business.'

'I thought you didn't want my help?'

'It was incredibly stupid and childish of me to say that. Of course I want your help. I'd be mad to turn it down, wouldn't I? You know more about business than anyone and although candles make you wince I know I have a viable business. But I have no idea how to make it reality. If you're still prepared to help me, I'd be grateful.'

Stefan relaxed slightly. Business was the easy part. 'I'll help you.'

'I'm prepared to work as hard as I have to. I'm excited about it.' Her eyes sparkled. 'I've given up the job in the *taverna*—they only took me on because of you so I felt bad taking a job from someone else. I want to concentrate on my business and if you could loan me enough to live on while I get everything off the ground I'd consider myself fortunate. But I will pay you back. It's a loan, not a gift. No more money tied in a thong.'

Stefan lifted his brows. 'That is a creative way of keeping money in one place.'

'With hindsight it wasn't such a clever idea. My father found it.'

The thought horrified him. 'It's a good job you ran from him when you did.'

'It's a good job you turned up when you did. Thank you for that, too. And I was very impressed that you managed to land a boat on that side of the island without sinking it. That will go down in Antaxos legend, I can tell you.'

'I don't understand how you could have lived with that man all your life and escaped unscathed.'

'I'm not unscathed. I dreamed of heroes. It made me unrealistic. I created a mythical person who could defeat my father and leave him grovelling with apology—' She frowned. 'Come to think of it, you did leave him groveling.'

'But there was no apology.'

'That would have been asking for a miracle.' Her hand was resting on his chest. 'Aren't you going to ask me what else I want apart from help with my business?'

'Go on.'

'I want to be with you. I want to go on dates like normal people. I want to have lots of sex.'

Stefan breathed deeply. 'You shouldn't say things like that—'

'I'm just saying it to you. I know I'm asking a lot because you don't normally date women. This is the part where you tell me you'll break my heart, you don't want happy-ever-after and that the longest relationship you've ever had lasted three courses over dinner.' Her arms slid round his neck. 'And this is the part where I tell you I just want to have fun with someone I trust. I want to explore the chemistry with someone I feel safe with. I want to make love with you the way we did that night at the villa and this time I don't want to have to rush off in the morning.'

Heat spread through his body. 'Selene—'

'But if you'd rather go back to your meeting...' Her finger trailed down his neck. 'Or if being hugged is making you uncomfortable and you'd rather go back to living your life in an isolated bubble, that's fine with me. Actually it's not fine with me, and if that's what you decide you'll probably find I'm just as persistent as you are when I want something.'

He caught her hand in his. 'You're driving me crazy.'

'Good. Because I haven't slept since that night at your villa. I've turned into a sex maniac. If you could do something about that, I'd appreciate it.' Her fingers tangled with his. 'Look at it this way—if it doesn't work out you can just dump me and move on. Isn't that what you always do? It's never caused you a problem before. What's different this time?'

His collar was constricting his throat and he extracted himself from her arms, yanked at his tie and flipped open the top button of his shirt. 'Your first instinct was probably the right one. You should stay away from me. I'm not good for you.'

'Maybe you are. And maybe I'm good for you. But if we don't do this we'll never find out.'

'I know that this product is special. It's a luxury. A treat. Something to make a woman feel pampered. If we sell it in supermarkets as an everyday item, it loses its appeal. It's a high-end product. I thought maybe if we made it exclusive to your spa hotels to begin with it might add to the feel that this is a superior product.'

Selene stopped talking, aware of the twelve people in the room all watching her. It should have felt daunting, but only one person interested her and that was the man who lounged at the head of the table. Stefan hadn't spoken a word since the meeting began and yet it was obvious from the body language of everyone in the room that his opinion was the one that mattered.

He'd removed his jacket. On the surface he was no different from anyone else, and yet he throbbed with authority and power. Even without speaking he commanded the room and Selene felt something stir inside her.

He was shockingly handsome, those dark lashes framing eyes that looked at her with raw sexual promise.

Imagining that mouth on hers, she lost the thread of her speech.

He smiled, and the fact that he so clearly knew what she was thinking infuriated her and at the same time made her insides turn to jelly.

She didn't want to be that predictable, but she loved the fact he could read her. She didn't want him to be so sure of her, but she wanted him to know her. She wanted that intimacy.

'Exclusive,' she said firmly. 'That's the approach I think we should take. By making it hard to get, people might want it more.'

His eyes held hers. Amusement danced there, along with something infinitely darker and more dangerous.

There was an expectant silence. Heads turned to Stefan and finally he stirred.

'It's a high-risk strategy but I like it. Put it into five of our hotels to test it and if it's successful we'll roll it out across the whole group.'

Selene felt the tension ooze out of her. She'd presented her ideas to a commercial task force put together by Stefan and they'd discussed everything from packaging options and advertising to demographics and market forces until her brain was a blur.

'Start exclusive.' Adam, head of Ziakas Business Development, picked up one of the candles and nodded. 'I can work with that. Jenny?'

Jenny was head of public relations for the Ziakas Corporation. 'Yes, our campaign should focus on the luxury element. We'll invite a few journalists for pamper days—they can share their experiences. Spread the word. Create demand. I'll have some companies pitch ideas.'

By the time the meeting eventually finished Selene had been on her feet for almost four hours, but she'd learned so much and her head was buzzing.

'We're done here.' Stefan rose to his feet, dismissing everyone, but as Selene closed her laptop—her brand-new laptop—he stopped her. 'Not you.'

Finally the room cleared and it was just the two of them left alone.

'So…' Stefan strolled round the table, his attention focused on her. 'By making it hard to get, people might want more? I can confirm that's the case. Do you have any idea how much control I had to exercise today?'

Shaken by the look in his eyes, she swallowed. 'Did you?'

'Yes. Normally I like to pace during a meeting. Sitting still drives me mad.'

'So why did you?'

'Because you look disturbingly hot in your suit and I've been aroused for the entire meeting. *Not* comfortable.' He slid his hand behind her neck and drew her face to him. 'Are you wearing stockings under that skirt?'

'Maybe. Possibly.' Her heart was pounding. 'So you would have said yes to anything? Does that mean you thought my ideas were rubbish?'

'No. It means I thought your ideas were excellent but you talk too much.' His eyes were on her mouth. 'You had me sold in the first ten minutes. You could have stopped then and I could have taken you to bed and avoided this prolonged torture.'

'I needed to convince the rest of your team.'

'You only needed to convince me. I'm the one who counts. And now I've had enough of talking about candles.' His eyes gleamed. 'I'm all burnt out.'

'Very funny. Are you laughing at me?'

'I never laugh at business. You have a good product. A product you believe in. You should be proud, *koukla mou*.'

'You shouldn't call me that when we're working. I don't want people to think this is favouritism.'

'I don't care what people think, but just for the record I can tell you that everyone who works for me knows I'm incapable of favouritism.' He slid his fingers into her cropped hair. 'I like it like this.'

'So do I. It was a bit of an impulse but now I've got used to it I think it suits the new me.' She was so aware of him, her body stirring at the memories of how it felt to be with him, and her heart went crazy as he curved his hand around her face and kissed her gently.

'Pack up your things. We're leaving on a market research trip.'

'What sort of market research?'

'You want to sell your product in my exclusive hotels. You've never even stayed in one. So we're going to take your Seduction candle to a hotel and see how it performs in a field test.'

She gave a gurgle of laughter. 'Where?'

'Santorini. You once told me you didn't know Greek Islands could be beautiful. I'm going to broaden your education. It's time you experienced sex against a backdrop of dramatic views and spectacular sunsets.'

'What? Right now?'

'Yes, now. We're going to spend time alone together. Just me, you—' he kissed the top of her nose '—and your candle.'

'And my soap. Don't forget the soap. It's a useful addition to the range.'

'How can I forget the soap?' His hands slid into her hair and his mouth hovered close to hers. 'I smell it on you and it drives me crazy because it makes me think of you naked in my shower.'

'You have a focused mind, Mr Ziakas.'

'I do indeed. And right now it's focused on you.'

They flew to Santorini in his private jet and Selene was dazzled by her first views of the stunning volcanic island with its pretty whitewashed houses and blue-domed churches overlooking the sparkling Aegean Sea.

'It's stunning. I didn't even know places like this existed.'

'Did you never travel anywhere with your father?'

'No. He liked to give the impression of being loving and protective, keeping us out of the media glare, but in reality he just didn't want us to cramp his style. I think he probably stayed in places like this all his life, but without us.'

'This' was the Ziakas Hot Spa, an exclusive hotel consisting of individual private suites nestling into the hillside overlooking the Caldera.

'I never imagined anywhere as romantic as this existed,' Selene murmured as she walked onto their private terrace and stared across the sea.

'You surprise me. Your brain appears to have infinite capacity for dreaming.'

'I know. It's what kept me sane. But this...' She sighed happily and picked up a card from the table placed in a strategic position overlooking the sea. 'This place even has...' She read the card and looked at him in astonishment. 'A pillow menu?'

'Duck as the starter, goose as the main, hypo-allergenic for dessert.' Smiling, he stripped off and dived into their private pool, soaking Selene in the process.

She stood there, gasping, showered in droplets. 'Thank you. Now I'm wet.'

'Good. Join me.'

'We're in public.'

'We are not in public. This is their best suite and it isn't overlooked. And I am the boss.' He gave her a slow, wicked smile. 'No one will dare disturb us, and if they do you have a choice of over seven different pillow types with which to assault them. Are you going to join me voluntarily or do I have to fetch you?'

She put down the pillow menu. 'This is my work suit. It's wet.'

'I'll buy you another. You have to the count of three to get naked. One—'

'But—'

'Two—'

Selene toed off her shoes and wriggled out of her skirt and jacket.

Stefan groaned as he saw her stockings. 'You're killing me.'

'Good.' She slid the stockings down her legs slowly, enjoying his reaction. 'By the way, I'm keeping my underwear on.' As she held her breath and jumped in she thought she heard him mutter 'Not for long…' but the cool water closed over her head and felt blissful on her heated skin.

She surfaced to find him right next to her.

His hand was on her hip and then her waist, and a fierce stab of excitement shot through her body and pooled in her pelvis.

I love you.

The words flew into her brain but for once she managed to stop her thoughts popping out through her mouth because she knew this one would send him running.

Instead she stayed still and savoured the contrast between the cool of the water and the heat of his mouth.

She was here. She had now.

That was enough.

Behind them, the setting sun was dipping down to the sea, but neither of them noticed the spectacle that drew tourists from all over the world. Their focus was on each other.

Her mouth was as urgent as his, her hands as desperate to touch and explore, and this time it was all the more exciting because she used the knowledge he'd given her. When she ran her tongue along the seam of his sensual mouth he groaned and tried to take possession, but she held back just a little bit, enjoying the feeling of power that came from knowing she was driving him crazy. But holding back only worked as long as he allowed it, and when he clamped his hand on the back of her head and held her for his kiss it was her turn to moan. His kiss was deliberate and unashamedly erotic, each skilled slide of his tongue a tantalising promise of things to come.

When he closed his hands over her bottom and lifted her she instinctively wrapped her legs around him. Her sensitive skin brushed against his solid, muscular thighs and she realised she was naked—that somehow in the heat of that kiss he'd removed the last of her clothing and she hadn't even noticed. But she noticed now, felt the heat of him brush against her, and the contrast drove her crazy. She dug her fingers into his shoulders, felt resistance and hard muscle beneath sleek bronzed skin.

'I want you.' His eyes were so dark they were almost black, his voice a low growl. 'Here. Now.'

Maybe had she been more coherent she would have worried about the danger of being spotted, but she was beyond caring and simply moved her hips against him in a desperate attempt to relieve the ache between her thighs.

When his hand slid between her legs she gasped against his mouth. The gasp turned to a moan as his fingers explored her with all the intimate knowledge that had driven her wild the first time. His breathing was harsh and shallow, tension etched in his features as he turned her mindless.

And then he shifted her slightly and surged into her. He was hot, so hot in contrast to the cool water, and it felt so impossibly good that she sucked in air and stopped breathing.

'*Cristos*—' His voice was hoarse, his mouth warm on her neck as he struggled to breathe, too. 'You feel—'

'Don't stop. Please, Stefan—' The need in her was so primal she could do nothing but move her hips.

With a soft curse his fingers tightened on her, his grip almost painful. 'Just—wait—'

'Can't—' Eyes closed, she arched into him, took him deeper if that were possible, and he groaned and gave in to it.

He felt smooth, hard, powerful, and the excitement spread through her until there wasn't a single part of her body that couldn't feel him. She tried to rock her hips but his hands were clamped on her, holding her, limiting her movements, so that he was the one who controlled the rhythm. He was merciless with each stroke until the orgasm ripped through her and she sucked in gasping breaths, only dimly aware that he was gripped in his own fierce climax. And then his mouth was on hers and he kissed her through the whole wild experience, swallowing her cries, her gasps, words she wanted to speak but couldn't until the whole thing was nothing but a blur of sexual pleasure.

And when it was over, when her body finally stopped shuddering, he cupped her face in his hands, staring down at her with a stunned look in his eyes.

'That was—'

'Incredible,' she muttered and he lowered his head and kissed her. But it was a gentle, lingering kiss designed to soothe not seduce.

'I don't know what you do to me—'

'You were the one doing it to me—you wouldn't let me move.'

'I didn't dare.' He caught her lower lip gently between his teeth, his eyes fixed on hers. 'You are the sexiest woman I've ever met.'

'You better not have lied about the fact we're not overlooked or I just might turn into the most self-conscious woman you've ever met.'

He closed his hands around her waist and lifted her easily onto the side of the pool. 'Let's take a shower. I think it's time to put in an order from the pillow menu.' He vaulted out of the pool after her, water streaming from his bronzed, powerful shoulders.

It was impossible not to stare and of course he caught her staring. *'Don't* do that.' Snatching a towel from the nearest sun lounger, he pulled her to her feet and wrapped it around her. 'I have to— I can't think when you're naked—'

She was about to ask why he wanted or needed to think but his hand was in his hair and he was clearly striving for some semblance of control.

'You're incredible.' She could say that, surely, without freaking him out? It wasn't what was in her heart but it was all she dared say at this stage. Apparently it was the right thing because he scooped her off her feet and carried her through to the bedroom.

'I'll demonstrate just how incredible—'

She giggled and tightened her grip on him. 'You're going to do your back in.'

'It's not my back I'm worried about. It's other parts of me.'

'Really? Because I might be able to help you with that.' She slid her arms round his neck and pressed her lips to the damp skin of his throat. Then she lifted her head and looked around the bedroom, with its glorious views over the sea. 'I love it here. I could stay forever.'

She felt the change in him. Felt it ripple through him as he lowered her to the ground.

'Why don't you take the first shower? While you're doing that I'll check my e-mails.'

His tone was a shade cooler. Another person probably wouldn't have noticed but she was so tuned in to every subtle shift in her father's moods that she sensed the change instantly.

Confused, she stood for a moment clutching the towel, watching as he strolled to the bed and pulled his phone out of his abandoned trousers.

A moment ago he'd been focused on her and now his focus was on his phone. His business. His world. He'd shut her out as clearly as if he'd closed a door between them.

And she didn't understand it.

Selene cast her mind back to try and work out what

she'd said. 'I love you' had stayed firmly in her head, so it definitely hadn't been that.

All she'd said was that she loved it here so much she could stay forever. And that couldn't possibly—

Forever.

Her head snapped up and she stared at the ceiling, wondering how she could have been so stupid. She'd used the word 'forever' and it had to be his least favourite word in the English language.

The fact that it had been a throwaway comment didn't make a difference. It had triggered alarm bells and he'd backed off—withdrawn as quickly as if she'd booked the church. And now his attention was focused on his e-mails as if their steamy, erotic encounter in the pool had never happened.

Selene took a step towards him, then changed her mind and instead walked quietly into the shower and closed the door.

If she brought it up, tried to talk about it, she would just make it worse.

She understood that he was running from attachment. She understood that he kept his relationships short and superficial. She knew all that so it wasn't fair of her to feel this sick disappointment, was it? She knew *him*.

Reminding herself of that, she hit the buttons on the shower. There was an assortment of expensive, exclusive bath products but she ignored them and reached for a bar of her own soap from the bag she'd packed. *Relax*, she thought numbly, letting the scent of it flow over her and into her. It was what she needed.

And tomorrow she'd give him some space.

Show him she wasn't going to crowd him.

CHAPTER TEN

STEFAN lay in the dark, wide awake as she slept. She'd fallen asleep snuggled next to him and now one slender arm was wrapped around his waist and her head was buried in his shoulder as she breathed softly.

The scent of her soap—*that smell that he associated only with her*—slid into his brain and blurred his thinking.

He wanted to extract himself from her grip but he didn't want to risk waking her.

The night was warm but he was cold with panic.

He shouldn't have brought her here. He'd sent out all the wrong messages and then compounded it by not even waiting for her to undress before having sex with her in the pool.

The intensity of it made him uncomfortable. He was used to being in control, not losing control. He was used to walking away. Used to keeping himself separate. And yet here he was, his limbs tangled with hers, anything but separate.

Tomorrow, he promised himself as he stared into the darkness, when she woke he'd make some excuse. Take her back to Athens and explain he couldn't mix business with pleasure.

Having decided on that approach, he fell asleep—and

woke hours later to find the sun blazing into the room and the bed empty.

'Selene?' Assuming she was in the bathroom, he called her name, but there was no response. He sprang from the bed, prowled out to the terrace area and found no sign of her.

Alarm flashed through him and he reached for his phone and called hotel security, who told him that Selene had been in the hotel spa since it had opened.

Slightly unsettled by just how relieved he felt hearing that, Stefan relaxed and decided to take the opportunity to work. No doubt she was enjoying a massage or something similar and would be back shortly. Then they'd have the conversation he'd been planning. He'd emphasise that this was just fun, not anything serious, and they'd go from there.

Hours later he started to worry that she still hadn't returned.

He was about to call the spa when the door opened and Selene walked back into the suite, wearing a pristine white uniform presumably supplied by the staff of the spa.

His eyes slid to her wonderful curves. 'Where have you been? You've been gone all day.'

'I've been working. Wasn't that why we came here? Market research?' She put her bag down on the sun lounger and slid off her shoes—white pumps that had obviously been provided along with the uniform. 'I've spent the day in the spa, talking to the staff and the customers. It's been so useful. They loved the candles, by the way, and the whole approach of exclusive seems to work for them.' She ran her hands through her hair. 'It's so hot. I'm going to change out of my uniform and then take a dip in the pool.'

'Selene—'

'And I wanted to talk to you.' Her hands were on the buttons of her dress and he felt heat whoosh through him.

This was it.

This was the moment when she talked about the future. Where she tried to turn today into tomorrow and the day after.

'Selene—'

'I felt really strange talking to them about business when they know I'm sharing your suite. It doesn't feel professional. So I propose we end the personal side of our relationship right now. It's been fun, but we don't want to ruin everything.' She poured herself a glass of iced water from the jug on the table. 'Do you want water? I'll pour you some. It's important to drink in this heat and, knowing you, you've been working so hard you've forgotten to drink.'

'End our relationship?' Having planned to suggest exactly the same thing, Stefan was thrown by how badly he didn't want to do that. 'Why would you want to end our relationship?'

'Because I want to be taken seriously in business and that isn't going to happen if I'm having sex with the boss.'

'I don't like hearing you describe it in those terms.'

'Why not? I'm just describing exactly the way it is.'

She drained her glass and he found himself staring at her throat. And lower.

'It isn't awkward and I'm not your boss. You don't work for me. I'm simply investing in your business. It's different.' He wondered why he wasn't just jumping through the escape hatch she'd opened and perhaps she did, too, because she looked surprised.

'It's not that different. I just don't want things to be awkward.'

'I don't have that word in my vocabulary. I do what

suits me and if people don't like it that's their choice.' He
watched as she lowered the glass.

'I wasn't talking about things being awkward with other
people. I was talking about being awkward between us.'
She put the empty glass down on the table. 'It was fun,
but I think we should call it a day. Move on.'

'Well, I don't.' Furious, almost depositing his laptop on
the terrace, Stefan rose to his feet, dragged her into his
arms and kissed her. Her mouth was soft and sweet and
the more he tasted, the more he wanted. Desire clawed at
him, brutal and intense, driving out every thought he'd
had about cutting the threads of this relationship. Usually
he was wary of anything that threatened his sense of purpose, but in this case she'd *become* his purpose. He lifted
his head. 'You're not moving on. *We're* not moving on.'

She looked dazed. Dizzy. 'I—I assumed that was what
you wanted.'

So had he. 'Well, it isn't.'

He wondered if 'moving on' meant seeing other men.
The thought had him scooping her up and taking her back
to bed.

He was a mass of contradictions, she thought days later
as she sat across from him in the pretty restaurant that
overlooked the bay and the sunset. She'd been so sure that
he'd been freaked out when she'd said the word 'forever'
and she'd intentionally stayed out of his way, giving him
space, only to return and have him behave as possessively
as if their relationship were serious.

She wondered if she'd overreacted. If she'd imagined it.

Candles flickered in the faint breeze and sounds of
Greek music played in the background.

It felt so far from her old life. 'Has anyone heard anything of my father?'

Stefan frowned. 'You don't need to be worried about your father.'

'I just wondered. I know you're in constant touch with Takis.'

'Of course. He's my head of security.'

'And you briefed him to tell you where my father is at all times.'

'He told you that?'

'He didn't want me to keep looking over my shoulder and worrying.'

Stefan hesitated and then reached for his wine. 'Your father hasn't left Antaxos since that night, although he did have a visit from the police.'

'He will have seen more photographs of us together.'

'But he hasn't acted. He knows he can't touch you. I won't let him touch you.'

The savage edge to his tone shocked her. 'You're so angry with him. Is it because of your mother?'

'No. My mother was an adult. She made a choice and left of her own free will.' He frowned into his glass. 'It took me years to see that.'

'That must have been painful.'

'Because I had to come to terms with the fact she chose him over my father and me? Yes, it was painful. I'd spent years planning how I could become more powerful so that I could storm the island and free her. It took me too long to realise she wouldn't have wanted to be freed.'

That was what had driven him, she realised. He'd wanted power. He'd wanted to be able to wield whatever power he needed.

'But you're still angry—'

'I'm angry because of the way he treated you.' Slowly, he put the glass down on the table. 'My mother had a choice. You didn't. You were trapped there.'

His words warmed her and confused her.

They suggested he cared and yet she knew he avoided that degree of emotional attachment to anyone. She wondered if he was driven by guilt. If he was still blaming himself for exposing her to danger.

She didn't dare hope it was anything else and she certainly didn't dare ask him.

She was just enjoying the moment, and if a part of her wanted it to be more than a moment—well, she ignored it.

She had now. She had him.

'But you rescued me.' Ignoring the envious glances of the other women in the restaurant, Selene lifted her glass. 'I can't believe you're giving me champagne after last time. You swore you'd never do it again.'

'You can drink it as long as you're with me.' His fingertips slowly caressed her wrist and she felt his touch right through her body.

It terrified her that she felt like this. It made her vulnerable, she realised. For her, this had moved beyond fun. It was the most intense experience of her life and the thought of losing it was terrifying.

'It seems ages ago,' she murmured, 'that night at your villa.'

'A lot has happened since then.' His eyes were on hers and then on her mouth and she knew he wanted exactly what she wanted.

'Stefan—'

'Let's go.' Without releasing her hand, he flung money down on the table and propelled her out of the restaurant, either oblivious or indifferent to the interested looks of the other diners.

He released her hand just long enough to ease his car out of its parking space and then slid his fingers into hers again and pressed her hand to his knee, driving one handed through the narrow streets. She probably should have been worried, but the only thing she could focus on was the hardness of his thigh under her hand and the firm grip of his fingers as they held hers.

Her breathing grew shallow. She tried not to look at him but lost the battle and turned her head briefly at the exact time he turned to look at her. Their eyes clashed. Their gazes burned and he cursed softly and brought the car to a ragged halt outside the hotel.

Throwing the keys to the parking attendant, Stefan strode directly to their suite.

They were barely through the door before his hand came behind her neck and he was kissing her.

Mouths fused, they stumbled back and the door slammed shut.

He braced one hand against the door, his other hand holding her face for his kiss, and she wanted it so badly, was so desperate for his touch, his kiss, his body, that her fingers fumbled on the buttons of his shirt. She tore it, sent buttons flying, slid her hands down hard, male muscle and then dragged her mouth from his and kissed her way down his bronzed chest.

She heard the breath hiss through his teeth as she moved lower. Heard him swear softly as she flipped open the button of his trousers, slid the zip and freed him.

She ran her hands over him, loving his body, savouring each moment as she took him in her mouth, first the tip and then as much of him as she could. He gave a harsh groan, both hands braced against the doorframe, as she explored him with the same intimacy with which he'd explored her.

'Selene—' His voice was ragged, his hands unsteady as he lifted her, kissed her hard and backed her towards the bed.

They fell, rolled, and rolled again until she was straddling him. He slid her skirt up her thighs, his hands urgent, his eyes dark with raw need as he wrenched her panties aside. She lowered herself fractionally, held his gaze as she paused and then took him in, took him deep, felt her body accommodate the silken power of him and saw the effort it took him not to thrust, to stay in control.

His eyes closed. His jaw tensed. His throat was damp with sweat, his struggle visible in every gorgeous angle of his sexy face, but she didn't want him to struggle against it. She wanted him to let go of that control and she wanted to be the one who made him do it.

'Stefan...' She murmured his name, leaned forward and licked at his mouth, her body hot and tight around his until he moaned and caught her hips in his hands, trying to slow her down.

She grabbed his hands and pushed them upwards, locking them above his head. He could have stopped her, of course. He was infinitely stronger. But either he was past defending himself or he realised how badly she wanted to take charge because he didn't fight her, just let her hold him there as she slid deeper onto his hard shaft.

'Wait—you have to—'

'Can't wait—' She was past waiting, or slowing down, or stopping or anything else, and so was he. When he thrust hard and deep she felt the power of it right through her body, felt the first fluttering of her own release and then his.

They exploded together, the ripple of her orgasm stroking the length of his hard shaft and taking him with her, on and on, until she collapsed on top of him, spent and stunned.

Weak and disorientated, she tried to roll away from him but he curled his arms around her and pulled the covers over them both.

'Where do you think you're going?'

It was the first time he'd held her like this.

The first time their intimacy had continued after sex.

Drugged with happiness, Selene smiled but didn't say anything. She wondered if he even realised what he'd just done. If not, then she didn't want to risk spoiling it by pointing it out.

He cared for her. She was sure of it.

It was true he hadn't actually said that in as many words, but he'd shown it in a million ways. He'd come after her and rescued her from the island. Then, when she'd escaped from him, he'd made sure she was all right. He'd got her a job and had people watching her so that her father couldn't get to her. And when she'd suggested they end their personal relationship and just focus on the business side of things he'd dismissed the idea instantly.

'I think you might just have killed me,' he murmured, turning his head to look at her.

His eyes were a dark, velvety black and she stared at him and felt something shift inside her.

'I love you.' She said it softly, without thinking, and immediately wanted to snatch the words back because he tensed for a second and then lifted his hand and stroked her hair gently.

'Don't say that.'

'Even if I mean it?'

'You don't mean it. You just feel that way because I'm your first lover. And because you had five years to build me up as a hero in your head.'

'That isn't—' She was going to say that wasn't why she loved him, but she didn't want to risk ruining the moment, so she simply smiled and closed her eyes, keeping her thoughts to herself. 'Let's go to sleep.'

But she was awake long after he was, staring into the

darkness, telling herself that if she kept saying it maybe a time would come when he wanted to hear it. When he might even say it back.

After a blissful week at the spa on Santorini they flew back to Athens and Stefan was sucked back into work, spending long hours in the office and travelling while Selene focused all her attention on the launch of her business.

She missed the intimacy of their suite on Santorini, missed the time when they'd been able to focus only on each other. She wondered if he'd suggest going again, but he was buried under work and the next time she flew to one of his hotels she did it alone.

Of course 'alone' never really was alone, because if he couldn't be with her himself then Stefan made sure Takis was with her. Her protection was something he wouldn't delegate to anyone else and she was touched by the evidence of how much he cared for her. It was there in everything. From the way he held her, confided small details of his life growing up, and from the way he made love to her.

But he never said he loved her and had made it clear he didn't want her to say it either.

Two weeks after they'd arrived back from Santorini they were both due to attend a charity ball and she dressed carefully, excited at the prospect of spending a whole evening with him even if it was in the company of other people.

'I've missed you,' she said cheerfully, taking his arm as they walked to the car.

'I've been hideously busy.'

'I know. I've been worried about you.' She saw him frown briefly as he slid into the car after her.

'Why would you be worried?'

'Because you work too hard,' she said softly. 'Because I care about you.'

'You don't have to worry about me.'

'Why not? Presumably you worry about me or you wouldn't arrange for someone to be with me all the time— and not just someone: Takis. It's all part of caring.'

His eyes were fixed straight ahead, his profile rigid and inflexible. 'I put you in danger. It's up to me to make sure you don't suffer for that.'

'That's all it is? Guilt?' Suddenly it upset her that he couldn't at least admit to caring just a little bit. 'You care about me, Stefan, I know you do.'

'We've arrived.' His tone cool, he unsnapped his seat belt and opened the door even though the car had barely come to a halt.

Exasperated, Selene started to speak, but he was already out of the car and standing on the red carpet waiting for her while the paparazzi crowded together to take photographs.

More photographs, she thought dully. More photographs of another fake life. Another evening where she had to pretend that what was on the surface reflected reality. Another evening of lies and never saying what she really felt. Fortunately this was her particular area of expertise, so she smiled dutifully, held his hand, posed for photographers, ate a reasonable quantity of her meal, listened attentively to speeches and did everything she was expected to do— just as she had for her father.

And all the time she felt numb inside.

'Do you want to dance?' Stefan rose to his feet and frowned when she didn't respond. 'Selene?'

She rose automatically. 'Yes, of course.'

His eyes narrowed on her face but she ignored him and walked onto the dance floor, then stopped dead. 'Actually, no.'

'No?' He drew her into his arms but she stayed rigid.

'I can't do this.'

'I thought you'd enjoy it, but if you don't want to dance you just have to say so.'

'Not the dancing. All of it.' She lifted her eyes to his. 'I can't be fake any more. I won't live a false life. I've done it for as long as I can remember and it stops now. This is who I am. This is what I feel. I'm not going to hide any more.'

His expression was guarded. 'Hide what?'

'The way I feel about you.' The look in his eyes should have silenced her instantly but she was beyond being silenced. 'I tiptoed round a man for twenty-two years of my life, Stefan, watching every word I said, trying not to upset him. I won't live like that again. I want to be able to express how I feel without worrying that I'm upsetting the person I'm with.'

His eyes darkened. 'Are you suggesting I'd hurt you?'

His interpretation shocked her. 'No, of course not. But the fact that you don't want me to tell you how I feel is making me miserable.'

'You're miserable?'

'Yes,' she whispered. 'Yes, I am. Because I love you and you don't want to hear it. I have to bite my tongue and squash everything I'm feeling down inside and I hate that.'

He didn't answer her. Just stared at her in silence while the couples around them moved slowly on the dance floor.

And suddenly she realised she'd done it again. She'd created something in her head out of nothing. When was she going to realise that just because she wanted something to happen it didn't mean she could think it into happening?

She could want him to open up, but that didn't mean he ever would.

And she could live with that or she could make a different choice.

A choice that didn't need her to compromise everything that mattered to her.

Music flowed around her but all she was aware of was him and the huge pain pressing down on her chest. 'I can't do this...' Her words were barely audible but clearly he heard her because his face seemed set in stone. 'I can't be with a man who is afraid to feel. And I can't be with a man who doesn't want to hear how I feel. I thought I could, but I can't. I'm sorry.' Mumbling the words, she pulled away from him. 'I hope you find someone. I really do. I want that for you.'

Heart breaking, knowing she had to get away before she made a terrible fool of herself, she forged her way through the crowded dance floor, slipped through a side door into a carpeted corridor and walked slap into her father.

'Hello, Selene.'

Her legs turned to water. Seeing him here was the last thing she'd expected. Since she'd been with Stefan she'd stopped looking over her shoulder. Behind her she could hear music from the dance floor, but this part of the corridor was empty and he was between her and the only exit. 'I didn't know you were here.'

'So you're still trying to make a fool of me?'

'I'm not trying to make a fool of you. I'm just living my life.'

'You came here in public with that man. He is setting you up in business. How do you think that looks to people? My biggest competitor sponsoring my daughter in her pathetic business venture.'

It was always about him, she thought dully. Always about his public image. Never about anyone else.

'It has nothing to do with you and the only reason I had to ask him is because you wouldn't help me. This is my business and it isn't pathetic. It's real. That's why he's helping me. He's sees the potential.'

'Potential?'

His laughter made Selene flinch.

This was what had drained her mother's confidence. The consistent drip of derision that eroded like acid.

For the past month she'd lived in a protected bubble. She'd forgotten what it felt like to be put down all the time. She'd forgotten how it felt to watch every word she spoke and feel her way through every conversation. 'He's helping me because I have a really good business idea that is going to make him money.'

'You're still as naïve as ever. His only interest in you is as a weapon to strike me.'

'Why do you always think everything is about you?' The words flew from her mouth and she immediately clamped it shut, cursing herself for not thinking before she spoke. Once it had been second nature to do that but with Stefan she spoke freely about everything. Well, everything except one thing. The most important thing. And she couldn't think about that now.

As always her father pounced on weakness. 'Has he ever said he loves you?'

As always he picked the words designed to do maximum damage. To inflict maximum pain.

His timing was so perfect this time she even wondered if he'd somehow overheard their exchange on the dance floor. No. He couldn't have done. If he'd been anywhere near the dance floor she would have seen him.

Or would she?

She'd been so wrapped up in her own misery she hadn't been paying attention to anyone around her.

'What Stefan says or doesn't say to me is none of your business.'

'In other words he *hasn't* told you he loves you. And now you're fooling yourself that he will say it given time.'

'I won't talk about this with you.'

'He's using you. And when he's got what he wants he'll dump you just as he's dumped every woman before you. Women are a short-term distraction, nothing more.'

She had no intention of telling him she'd just ended it.

'Don't you even care?' Horrified, she heard her voice crack. 'You're supposed to be my father. You're supposed to love me and want me to be happy. Instead you only ever smile when my life is falling apart. It pleases you that I'm unhappy.'

'If you're unhappy then it's your own fault.' There was no sympathy in his face. 'If you'd stayed at home with your family instead of destroying it, your life wouldn't be falling apart.'

'I did *not* destroy our family! You did that.'

'You are a hopeless dreamer. You always have been. You're a sitting duck for the first guy who comes along and shows you some attention.'

'That is enough.' A cold, hard voice came from behind her and Selene turned to see Stefan standing there in all his powerful fury, that angry gaze fixed on her father. 'You don't speak to her again—ever.'

'And why would you care, Ziakas? You used her.'

'No. It was you who used her. You used her to project the image of a happy family but you've never been a father to her. And I care because I love her and I won't let you upset someone I love.'

Selene couldn't breathe.

She'd wanted so badly to hear him say those words. Even though she knew he'd only said it to protect her from her father, she felt something twist inside her.

There was a long silence and then her father laughed. 'You don't believe in love any more than I do.'

'Don't bracket us together.' Stefan's voice was pure ice. 'I am nothing like you.' He took her hand, his touch firm and protective as he drew her against him. 'Let's go. There's nothing for you here.'

Stefan steered her through the crowd and down into the gardens. She was pale and unresponsive, walking where he led her but not paying any attention. Only when he was sure they were in private did he stop walking and that was when he saw the tears.

Her face was streaked with them, her eyes filled with a misery so huge that it hurt him to look at it.

'He's not worth it.' He cupped her face in his hands, desperate to wipe away those tears while everything inside him twisted and ached just to see her so unhappy. 'He isn't worth a single tear. Tell me you know that. *Theé mou*, I wish I'd punched him again just for having the nerve to approach you.'

'He waited until I was alone.'

'Like the coward he is.' Seriously concerned, he gathered her close, hugged her tightly. 'I had no idea he was even here or there is no way I would have let you walk away from me. Takis is here, but because you were with me—'

'I can protect myself. I've done it my whole life.'

'And the thought of you alone with him, growing up with him, horrifies me. I can't bear to think of it.'

'You grew up alone. That's worse.'

'No. It was easier. All I had to do was move forward. You had to escape before you could do that. Every time I think about how I messed that up I go cold.'

'It was my fault for not telling you. Don't let's go over that again.' She eased out of his grasp and brushed the heel of her hand over her cheeks. 'Sorry for the crying. I know you hate it.'

'Yes, I hate it—I hate seeing you unhappy. I never want

to see you unhappy.' He realised that he'd do anything, *anything*, to take those tears away.

'Thank you for what you said in there. For standing up for me when he said all those awful things about you just being with me to get back at him.'

When he thought of the contempt in her father's eyes he felt savage. Shocked by the extreme assault of emotion, he pushed aside his own feelings and concentrated on hers. 'What he said wasn't true. You do know that, don't you? Tell me you're not, even for a moment, thinking to yourself that he might have been right.'

'I'm not thinking that. I know what we had was real.'

The fact that she put it in the past tense sent a flash of panic burning through him. 'It *is* real.'

But she wasn't listening. 'He called my business pathetic.'

'He will eat those words when he sees the success of your business, *koukla mou*. And he *will* see it.'

'Thank you for believing in me. You're the first person to ever do that. Even my mother didn't think I could do it.'

'But you believed in yourself. You came to me with your candles and your soap and the beautiful packaging you'd made yourself. You are *so* talented. Your business idea is clever and you work harder than anyone on my team. If you weren't already making a success of being an entrepreneur, I'd employ you straight away.'

Her hand rested on his chest, as if she couldn't quite bear to let him go. 'But you probably wouldn't have offered to help me if I hadn't been who I was.'

'I probably would.' He gave a half-smile. 'I'm a sucker for a woman dressed in a nun's costume.'

There was no answering smile and he was shaken by how badly he missed that ready smile. He'd taken it for granted. She was always so bouncy and optimistic and yet now she just stood there, shivering like a wounded animal.

'Selene—'

'I should go. Someone might see me and take a photograph.' Finally she smiled, but it was strained. 'See? I'm learning. I don't want my father knowing he made me cry. That's one act I'm prepared to keep up until the day I die.' She rubbed her hand over her face again. 'It was kind of you to come to my defence. Kind of you to tell him our relationship meant something.'

'It wasn't kindness.' He'd realised it the moment she'd walked away from him. 'I do love you.'

'Yes, I know.' There was no pleasure in that statement. Her face didn't light up. She just looked incredibly sad. 'I know you do, Stefan. But you don't want to. It scares you.'

'Yes, it does.' He didn't deny it because he knew only honesty would save him now. 'I didn't want it to happen. I've done my best not to let it happen by picking women I couldn't possibly fall in love with. I controlled that.'

'I know that, too. I know *you*.' She eased out of his arms. 'I really do have to go. I don't want anyone taking a photograph of me like this.'

'I'll take you home. Then we'll fly to my villa.' He saw her hesitate and then shake her head.

'No, not this time. I'll see you in the office on Monday. We have the ad agency pitch.'

'I'm not talking about business. I'm talking about us.' It was a word he'd never used before. 'I've just told you that I love you.'

'But you don't want to. You don't want to feel that way and I can't be with a man who always holds part of himself back. Even though I understand all your reasons and I'm sympathetic, I want more. I know love makes a person vulnerable but I want a man who is prepared to risk everything because the love is more important than protecting himself. And I want him to value my love and allow me to express it.'

'Selene—'

'Please don't follow me. Not this time. I'll see you in the office on Monday.' Mumbling the words, she hurried away from him, walking so fast she almost stumbled.

She applied layers of make-up, added blusher, but still she looked pale when she walked into the Ziakas building.

The glamorous receptionist smiled at her. '*Kalimera*. They're all waiting for you in the conference room.'

But when she walked in the room was empty apart from Stefan, who was pacing from one end of the room to the other.

When he saw her, his face paled. 'I was afraid you wouldn't turn up.'

'Why? Today is important.' Horrified by how hard it was to see him, she glanced around the room. 'Where is everyone?'

'I sent them to get breakfast. They're coming back in an hour. I need to talk to you. I need you to hear what I have to say.'

Her heart clenched at the thought of going over it again. 'There really isn't—'

'You were right—I do love you.' Tension was stamped in every line of his handsome face. 'I think I've loved you from the day you walked into my office dressed as a nun, determined to find a way through my security cordon. Or maybe it was before that—maybe a part of me fell in love with the seventeen-year-old you—I don't know.'

She'd never seen him look like this. Never seen him so unsure of himself. 'Stefan—'

'You were so open about your feelings. I'd never met

anyone like you. It frightened me and it fascinated me
at the same time. I liked the fact that you spoke openly
without guarding every word. It made me realise the other
people in my life were—' he frowned as he searched for
the word '—fake.'

'So was I.'

'No. I saw *you* that night. The real you. And when you
walked into my office that day and pulled out your candles and asked for a loan I was so cynical, so sure I knew
everything there was to know about women and had it all
under control. I didn't look deeper. I judged you based on
everything that had gone before. But the truth was I knew
nothing about you. You shook every preconceived idea
I had about women. That night when you had too much
champagne—'

'You were so kind to me.'

'You have no idea how much self-control it took to
keep my hands off you.' He groaned, dragging his fingers through his hair. 'You were sweet and sexy rolled
into one and so unbelievably curious—'

'Why was it unbelievable? You're the most gorgeous
man I'm ever going to meet. I wanted to make the most
of it.'

'When I worked out your reasons for wanting to leave
the island I couldn't believe I'd been so blind. I couldn't
believe I hadn't worked it out.'

'Why would you? My father can be very persuasive.'

'And I have more reason to know that than most.'

'None of this matters now.'

'No, it doesn't, because you're mine now and I'm never
letting you go.' His voice hoarse, he crossed the room
in three strides and took her face in his hands. 'Until I
met you all I knew about love was how much damage it
could do. I didn't want that. I spent my life avoiding that.

I couldn't understand why anyone would take that risk and I certainly didn't want to, so I kept my relationships short and superficial—and then I met you and suddenly I didn't want to do either of those things. For the first time ever I cared whether I saw a woman again. I wanted to see you again.'

'And you were scared.'

'Yes, and you knew that. You knew I was scared. You knew I loved you.'

'I thought you did. I hoped you did. But I never thought you'd admit it. Or want it.'

'I do want it. I want you.'

He kissed her gently, his mouth lingering on hers, and her head reeled and her thoughts tumbled as she tried to unravel the one situation she hadn't prepared for.

'I— It's too complicated. You hate my father.'

'It's not complicated. I'm not marrying your father and I'm hoping you won't want to invite him to our wedding.'

Her heart thudded and skipped. 'Is that a proposal?'

'No. I haven't reached that part yet but I'm getting there. I have something for you.'

He reached for a box on the table and her brows rose because she recognised the packaging.

'That's one of my candles.'

'Close. It's one I had developed just for you. You already have Relax, Energise and Seduction. This one is called Love.'

Love?

He wanted to marry her?

Hands shaking, Selene opened the box and saw a diamond ring nestling in a glass candle-holder. 'I don't know what I'm more shocked about—the fact that you're asking me to marry you or the fact that you've actually given me a candle. Does this mean I'm actually allowed to light it in the bedroom?'

'You can do anything you want with me in the bedroom,' he said huskily, sliding the ring onto her finger and then kissing her again. 'Just don't tell me it's too late. Don't tell me you've given up on me for taking so long to discover what you knew all along.'

'I'm not telling you that. It's not too late. It's never too late.' She stared down at the ring on her finger, hypnotised not just by the diamond but by what it symbolised.

'How did you end up such an optimist with a father like yours?'

'I refused to believe that all men were like my father. I knew they couldn't be—especially after I met you. I believed in something better and I wanted that. Why would someone want to repeat the past when the future can be so much better?'

His lips were on hers. 'You are an inspiration, *koukla mou.*'

'Not really.' She melted under his touch. 'I'm just trying to have the life I want. Which probably makes me horribly selfish.'

'Then we're a perfect match, because you know I don't think of anyone but myself.'

But he was smiling as he said the words and so was she, because the happiness was too big to keep inside.

'You kept shutting me out.'

'You were so affectionate. So open. I kept shutting you out and when you said those words I panicked.'

'I know.'

'I'm not panicking now.' He trailed his fingers down her cheek. 'So any time you want to say them again, that would be good.'

She smiled again. 'What words?'

'Now you're torturing me, but I suppose I deserve it.'

'I'm not torturing you—' she wrapped her arms round his neck '—I just don't know which words you mean.'

'You're a wicked tease.' His mouth was hot on hers and she gasped as he lifted her onto the table.

'Any moment now thirty people are going to walk into this room.'

'Then you'd better say those words fast—unless you want to say them in front of an audience.'

'Which words?'

He cupped her face. 'The ones where you tell me how you feel about me.'

'Oh, *those* words.' She loved teasing him. 'I've forgotten how to say them because you didn't want to hear them. They've vanished from my brain.'

'Selene—'

'I love you.' For the first time she said it freely, and she smiled as she did so because it felt so good to be truly honest about her feelings. No more hiding. No more pretending. 'I really love you and I'll always love you.'

They kissed, lost in each other, until they heard applause and both turned to see a crowd in the doorway led by Maria, who was smiling. Behind her stood Takis, Kostas and all the other members of Stefan's senior team.

Blushing, Selene slid off the table and Stefan muttered under his breath.

'What does a guy have to do to ensure privacy round here?'

'We came to congratulate you.' Maria produced two bottles of champagne which she put on the table and then turned to hug Selene. 'I'm so delighted. I know it's a little early in the day, but we thought it was appropriate to celebrate the occasion with champagne.'

Stefan eyed the bottles with incredulity. 'You shouldn't

even have been aware of the occasion. Were you listening at the door?'

'Yes.' Maria was unapologetic.

Takis eyed his boss cautiously and then slid into the room, put a tray of glasses on the table and hugged Selene, too.

Choked, Selene hugged them both back. 'Thank you for watching over me and being so kind.'

'If everyone could stop hugging my future wife,' Stefan drawled, 'I'd quite like to hug her myself. But it appears I no longer have any influence in my own office.'

'This is a special occasion, boss,' Takis muttered, releasing Selene. 'Some of us had given up on ever seeing this day.'

Unbelievably touched, Selene slid her hand into Stefan's as his executive team piled into the room. 'This is so great! Can we open the champagne? I always wanted to live a champagne lifestyle—although preferably without the headache.'

Takis reached for the nearest bottle. 'Champagne in a breakfast meeting. A typical working day in the Ziakas Corporation.'

Stefan rolled his eyes. 'Clearly you've never seen what happens to Selene when she drinks champagne.'

'I'm lovely when I drink champagne—and anyway I have Takis to extract me from danger.'

'That's *my* job now. I'm signing on full-time.' Stefan pulled her back into his arms and kissed her, ignoring their audience. 'Which is just as well if you intend to go through life with a glass of champagne in your hand.'

She smiled up at him. 'Good things happen when I drink champagne. You know that.'

'Yes.' His eyes glittered into hers. 'I do.'

There was a thud as the champagne cork hit the ceiling,

and Selene beamed as Takis handed her a glass of champagne. 'We have four advertising agencies sitting in the lobby, waiting to pitch to us. They're going to think we're very unprofessional.'

'They can think what they like.' Stefan tapped his glass against hers and bent his head to gently kiss her mouth. 'Just this once I'm mixing business with pleasure.'

* * * * *

BARTERING HER INNOCENCE

TRISH MOREY

Trish Morey is an Australian who's also spent time living and working in New Zealand and England. Now she's settled with her husband and four young daughters in a special part of South Australia, surrounded by orchards and bushland, and visited by the occasional koala and kangaroo. With a lifelong love of reading, she penned her first book at the age of eleven, after which life, career, and a growing family kept her busy until once again she could indulge her desire to create characters and stories – this time in romance. Having her work published is a dream come true. Visit Trish at her website, www.trishmorey.com

To Jacqui, Steph, Ellen and Claire,
Four gorgeous girls who have grown up amidst
the mess and chaos and deadline-mania of a
writer's life, and who somehow still managed to
turn out all right.

I am so proud of the beautiful, talented, warm
and wonderful young women you have become.

I am so looking forward to seeing all
that you can be.

luv nun

xxx

CHAPTER ONE

THE last time Tina Henderson saw Luca Barbarigo, he was naked. Gloriously, unashamedly, heart-stoppingly naked. A specimen of virile masculine perfection—if you discounted the violent slash of red across his rigid jaw.

As for what had come afterwards...

Oh God. It was bad enough to remember the last time she'd seen him. She didn't want to remember *anything* that came after that. She must have misheard. Her mother could not mean *that man.* Life could not be that cruel. She clenched a slippery hand harder around the receiver, trying to get a better grip on what her mother was asking.

'Who...who did you say again?'

'Are you listening to me, Valentina? I need you to talk to Luca Barbarigo. I need you to make him see reason.'

Impossible. She'd told herself she'd never see him again. More than that. She'd *promised* herself.

'Valentina! You have to come. I need you here. Now!'

Tina pinched the bridge of her nose between her fingers trying to block the conflicting memories—the images that were seared on her brain from the most amazing night of her life, the sight of him naked as he'd risen from the bed, all long powerful legs, a back that could have been sculpted in marble, right down to the twin dimples at the base of his spine—and then the mix master of emotions,

the anger and turmoil—the anguish and despair—for what
had come afterwards.

She pinched harder, seeking to blot out the dull ache
in her womb, trying to direct her shocked emotions into
anger. And she was angry, and not just about what had
happened in the past. Because how typical was it that the
first time her mother actually called her in more than a
year, it wasn't to wish her a belated happy birthday, as she'd
foolishly imagined, but because Lily needed something.

When did Lily not need something, whether it was attention, or money or adulation from a long and seemingly
endless line of husbands and lovers?

And now she foolishly imagined Tina would drop everything and take off for Venice to reason with the likes
of Luca Barbarigo?

Not a chance.

Besides, it was impossible. Venice was half a world
away from the family farm in Australia where she was also
needed right now. No, whatever disagreement her mother
had with Luca Barbarigo, she was just going to have to
sort it out for herself.

'I'm sorry,' she began, casting a reassuring glance towards her father across the room to signal everything was
under control. A call from Lily put everyone on edge. 'But
there's no way I can—'

'But you have to do something!' her mother shrieked
down the telephone line, so loud that she had to hold the
receiver away from her ear. 'He's threatening to throw
me out of my home! Don't you understand?' she insisted.
'You have to come!' before following it with a torrent of
French, despite the fact that Lily D'Areincourt Beauchamp
was English born and bred. The language switch came as
no surprise—her mother often employed that tactic when
she wanted to sound more impassioned. Neither was the

melodrama. As long as she had known Lily, there was always melodrama.

Tina rolled her eyes as the tirade continued, not bothering to keep up and tired of whatever game her mother was playing, suddenly bone weary. A long day helping her father bring in the sheep in preparation for shearing wasn't about to end any time soon. There was still a stack of washing up waiting for her in the kitchen sink and that was before she could make a start on the piles of accounts that had to be settled before her trip to town tomorrow to see the bank manager. She rubbed her brow where the start of a headache niggled. She always hated meetings with their bank manager. She hated the power imbalance, the feeling that she was at a disadvantage from the get go.

Though right now the bank manager was the least of her problems...

Across the room Tina's father put down his stock journal on the arm of his chair where he'd been pretending to read and threw her a sympathetic smile before disappearing into the large country kitchen, no real help at all. But then, he'd broken ties with Lily almost twenty-five years ago now. It might not have been a long marriage but, knowing her mother, he'd more than served his time.

She was aware of the banging of the old water pipes as her father turned on the tap, followed by the thump of the kettle on the gas cooker and still her mother wasn't through with pleading her case. 'Okay, Lily,' she managed while her mother drew breath. 'So what makes you think Luca Barbarigo is trying to throw you out of the palazzo? He's Eduardo's nephew after all. Why would he threaten such a thing? And in English, please, if you don't mind. You know my French is rusty.'

'I *told* you that you need to spend more time on the Continent,' her mother berated, switching grievances as seamlessly as she switched languages, 'instead of burying yourself out there in the Australian outback.'

'Junee is hardly outback,' she argued of the mid-sized New South Wales town that was less than two hours from the semi-bright lights of Canberra. Besides, she hadn't exactly *buried* herself out here, more like she'd made a tactical withdrawal from a world she wanted no further part in. And then, because she was still feeling winded by her mother's demands, she added, 'It's quite civilised actually. There's even talk of a new bowling alley.'

Silence greeted that announcement and Tina imagined her mother's pursed lips and pinched expression at her daughter's inability to comprehend that in order to be considered civilised, a city needed at least half a dozen opera theatres, preferably centuries old, at a bare minimum.

'Anyway, you still haven't explained what's going on. Why is Luca Barbarigo threatening to throw you out? What kind of hold could he possibly have over you? Eduardo left you the palazzo, didn't he?'

Her mother fell unusually quiet. Tina heard the clock on the mantel ticking; heard the back door creak open and bang shut as her father went outside, probably so he didn't have to hear whatever mess Lily was involved in now. 'Well,' she said finally, her tone more subdued, 'I may have borrowed some money from him.'

'You what?' Tina squeezed her eyes shut. Luca Barbarigo had a reputation as a financier of last resort. By all accounts he'd built a fortune on it, rebuilding the coffers of his family's past fortune. She swallowed. Of all the people her mother could borrow from, of all the contacts she must have, and she had to choose *him*! 'But why?'

'I had no choice!' her mother asserted. 'I had to get the money from somewhere and I assumed that being family he'd take care of me. He promised he'd take care of me.'

He'd taken care of her all right. And taken advantage into the deal. 'You had to get money for what?'

'To live, of course. You know Eduardo left me with a fraction of the fortune he made out that he had.'

And you've never forgiven him for it. 'So you borrowed money from Luca Barbarigo and now he wants it back.'

'He said if I couldn't pay him, he'd take the palazzo.'

'How much money are we talking about?' Tina asked, pressure building in her temples. The centuries-old palazzo might be just off the Grand Canal, but it would still be worth millions. What kind of hold did he have over her? 'How much do you owe him?'

'Good God, what do you take me for? Why do you even have to ask?'

Tina rubbed her forehead. 'Okay. Then how can he possibly throw you out?'

'That's why I need you here! You can make him understand how unreasonable he is being.'

'You don't need me to do that. I'm sure you know plenty of people right there who can help.'

'But he's *your* friend!'

Ice snaked down Tina's spine. *Hardly friends.* In the kitchen the kettle started to whistle, a thin and shrill note and perfectly in tune with her fractured nerves and painful memories. She'd met Luca just three times in her life. The first in Venice at her mother's wedding, where she'd heard his charming words and felt the attraction as he'd taken her hand and she'd decided in an instant that he was exactly the kind of charming, good-looking rich man that her mother would bend over backwards to snare and that she wanted no part of. And when he'd asked her to spend the night with him, she'd told him she wasn't interested. After all, Lily might be her mother, but no way was Tina her mother's daughter.

The second time had been at Eduardo's seventieth birthday, a lavish affair where they'd barely done more than
exchange pleasantries. Sure, she'd felt his eyes burn into
her flesh and set her skin to tingling as they'd followed
her progress around the room, but he'd kept his distance
and she'd celebrated that fact, even if he hadn't given her
the satisfaction of turning him down again. But clearly her
message had struck home.

The third had been at a party in Klosters where she'd
been celebrating a friend's birthday. She'd had one too
many glasses of champagne and her guard was down
and Luca had appeared out of the crowd and suddenly
his charm was infectious and he was warm and amusing
and he'd taken her aside and kissed her and every shred
of self-preservation she'd had had melted away in that one
molten kiss.

One night they'd spent together—one night that had
ended in disaster and anguish and that could never be blotted from her mind—one night that she'd never shared with
her mother. 'Who said we were friends?'

'He did, of course. He asked after you.'

Bastard! As if he cared. He had never cared. 'He lied,'
she said, the screaming kettle as her choir. 'We were never
friends.'

Never were.

Never could be.

'Well,' her mother said, 'maybe that's preferable under
the circumstances. Then you'll have nothing to risk by intervening on my behalf.'

She put a hand to her forehead, certain the screaming
must be coming from somewhere inside her skull. 'Look,
Lily, I don't know what good I can do. There is no way my
being there will help your cause. Besides, I can't get away.

We're about to start shearing and Dad really needs me here right now. Maybe you'd be better off engaging a lawyer.'

'And just how do you think I'll be able to afford to pay for a lawyer?'

She heard the back screen door slam and her father's muttered curse before the screaming abruptly tapered off. She shook her head. 'I really don't know.' And right now she didn't care. Except to ensure she didn't have to go. 'Maybe…maybe you could sell one or two of those chandeliers you have.' God knew, from the last time she'd visited, it seemed her mother had enough of them to fill a dozen palazzos. Surely if she owed a bit of money she could afford to dispense with one or two?

'Sell my Murano glass? You must be mad! It's irreplaceable! Every piece is individual.'

'Fine, Lily,' she said, 'it was just a suggestion. But under the circumstances I really don't know what else I can suggest. I'm sorry you're having money troubles, but I'm sure I'd be no help at all. And I really am needed here. The shearers arrive tomorrow, it's going to be full-on.'

'But you have to come, Valentina! You must!'

Tina put the phone down and leaned on the receiver a while, the stabbing pain behind her eyes developing into a dull persistent throb. Why now? Why him? It was likely her mother was exaggerating the seriousness of her money problems—she usually managed to blow any problem right out of proportion—but what if this time she wasn't? What if she was in serious financial trouble? And what could she do about it? It wasn't likely that Luca Barbarigo was going to listen to her.

Old friends? What was he playing at? Ships that crashed in the night would be closer to the mark.

'I take it your mother wasn't calling to wish you a happy

birthday, love?' Her father was standing in the kitchen doorframe, a mug of coffee wrapped in each of his big paw-like hands.

She smiled, in spite of the heaviness of her heart and the sick feeling in her gut. 'You got that impression, huh?'

He held up one of the mugs in answer. 'Fancy a coffee? Or maybe you'd like something stronger?'

'Thanks, Dad,' she said, accepting a mug. 'Right now I'd kill for a coffee.'

He took a sip. Followed it with a deep breath. 'So what's the latest in Circus Lily then? The sky is falling? Canals all run dry?'

She screwed up her face. 'Something like that. Apparently someone's trying to throw her out of the palazzo. It seems she borrowed money from Eduardo's nephew and, strangely enough, he wants it back. Lily seems to think I can reason with him—maybe work out some more favourable terms.'

'And you don't?'

She shrugged her shoulders, wishing she could just as easily shrug off memories of a man who looked better naked than any man had a right to, especially when he was a man as cold and heartless as he'd turned out to be. Wishing she could forget the aftermath… 'Let's just say I've met the man.' *And please don't ask me how or when.* 'I told her she'd be better off engaging a lawyer.'

Her dad nodded then and contemplated his coffee and Tina figured she'd put a full stop on the conversation and remembered the dishes still soaking and the accounts still to be paid. She was halfway to the sink when her father said behind her, 'So when do you leave?'

'I'm not going,' she said, her feet coming to a halt. I don't want to go. *I can't go.* Even though she'd told her mother she'd think about it, and that she'd call her back, when she'd never had any intention of going. She'd promised herself she'd never have to see him again and that was a promise she couldn't afford to break. Just thinking about what he'd cost her last time... 'I can't go and leave you, Dad, not now, not with the shearing about to start.'

'I'll manage, if you have to go.'

'How? The shearers start arriving tomorrow. Who's going to cook for a dozen men? You can't.'

He shrugged as the corners of his mouth turned up. 'So I'll go to town and find someone who can cook. You never know, I hear Deidre Turner makes a mean roast. And she might jump at the chance to show off her pumpkin scones to an appreciative audience.' His smile slipped away, his piercing amber eyes turning serious. 'I'm a big boy, Tina, I'll manage.'

Normally Tina would have jumped at her father's mention of another woman, whatever the reason—she'd been telling him for years he should remarry—but right now she had more important things on her mind—like listing all the reasons she couldn't go.

'You shouldn't have to manage by yourself! Why waste the money on flights—and on paying someone to cook—when we're already begging favours from the bank manager as it is? And you know what Lily's like—look at how she made such a drama about turning fifty! Anyone would have thought her life was coming to an end and I bet this is exactly the same. I bet it's all some massively overblown drama, as per usual.'

Her father nodded as if he understood, and she felt a surge of encouragement. Because of course her father would understand. Hadn't he been married to the woman? He, more than anyone, knew the drama queen stunts she was capable of pulling to get her way.

Encouragement had almost turned to relief, and she

was more than certain he would agree. Until he opened his mouth.

'Tina,' he said, rubbing the stubble of his shadowed jawline, 'how long is it since you've seen your mum? Two years? Or is it three? And now she needs you, for whatever reason. Maybe you should go.'

'Dad, I just explained—'

'No, you just made an excuse.'

She stiffened her shoulders, raising her chin. Maybe it was an excuse, and if her father knew the truth, surely he would understand, surely he would be sympathetic and not insist she go. But how could she tell him when she had kept it secret for so long? Her shameful secret. How could she admit to being as foolish and irresponsible as the woman she'd always told herself she was nothing like? It would kill him. It would kill her to tell him.

And when defence wasn't an option, there was always attack...

'So why are you so keen to ship me off to the other side of the world to help Lily? It's not like she ever did you any favours.'

He wrapped an arm around her shoulders and hauled her close, holding her just long enough for her to breathe in his familiar earthy farm scent. 'Who says I'm keen? But she's still your mum, love, and whatever happened between the two of us, you can't walk away from that. Now,' he said, putting his mug down to pick up a tea towel, 'what's this about a new bowling alley in town? I hadn't heard that.'

She screwed up her nose and snatched the tea towel out of his hands, not because she couldn't do with the help or his company, but because she knew he had his own endless list of chores to finish before he could collapse into bed, and partly too because she feared that if he lingered, if he asked her more about her mother's predicament and how she knew the man Lily owed money to, she wouldn't know how to answer him honestly. 'How about that?' she said much too brightly as she pushed him towards the door. 'Neither had I.'

He laughed in that deep rumbling way he had and that told her he knew exactly what she'd been doing. 'Your mum's not going to know what hit her.'

'I'm not going, Dad.'

'Yes, you are. We can check about flights when we go into town tomorrow.' And he came back and hugged her, planting a kiss on her strawberry-blonde hair the same way he'd done ever since she was old enough to remember and probably long before. 'Goodnight, love.'

She thought about her father's words after he'd gone, as she chased cutlery around the sudsy sink. Thought with a pang of guilt about how long it had been since she'd seen her mother. Thought about how maybe her father might be right.

Because even though they'd never seen eye to eye, even though they never seemed to be on the same wavelength, maybe she couldn't walk away from her mother.

And neither did she have to run from Luca Barbarigo.

She had been running. She'd run halfway around the world to forget the biggest mistake of her life. She'd run halfway around the world to escape.

But some mistakes you couldn't escape.

Some mistakes followed you and caught up with you when you least expected it.

And some mistakes came with a sting in the tail that made you feel guilty for wishing things had been different. They were the worst mistakes of all, the ones that kept on hurting you long, long after the event.

She pulled the plug and stood there, watching the suds gurgle down the sink, suds the very colour of the delicate iron lace-work that framed a tiny grave in a cemetery in far distant Sydney.

Tears splashed in the sink, mixing with the suds, turning lacy bubbles pearlescent as they spun under the thin kitchen light. She brushed the moisture from her cheeks, refusing to feel sorry for herself, feeling a steely resolve infuse her spine.

Why should she be so afraid of meeting Luca again? He was nothing to her really, nothing more than a one-night stand that had ended in the very worst kind of way. And if Luca Barbarigo was threatening her mother, maybe Lily was right; maybe she was the best person to stand up to him. It wasn't as if there was a friendship in the balance. And it certainly wasn't as if she was going to be charmed by him.

Not a second time.

She wasn't that stupid!

CHAPTER TWO

SHE WAS COMING.

Just as her mother had said she would.

Luca stood at the darkened balcony overlooking the Grand Canal, his senses buzzing with the knowledge, while even the gentle slap of waters against the pilings seemed to hum with anticipation.

Valentina was coming to save her mother. Expecting to rescue her from the clutches of the evil banker.

Just as he'd intended.

A smile tugged at his lips.

How fortuitous that her mother was a spendthrift with a desperate need for cash. So desperate that she was not bothered to read the terms of any loan agreement too closely. How naive of her to assume that marrying his uncle somehow made her eligible for special treatment.

Special treatment indeed.

And now the noose he'd tied was so tight around the neck of the former beauty that she was about to lose her precious palazzo from beneath her once well-heeled feet.

A water taxi prowled by, all sleek lines and polished timbers, the white shirt of the driver standing out in the dark night, before both taxi and driver disappeared down one of the side canals. He watched the wake fan out across the dark canal and felt the rhythm of water resonate in the

beat of his blood; heard it tell him that the daughter was
drawing ever closer.

He searched the night sky, counting down the hours,
imagining her in the air, imagining her not sleeping because she knew he would be here in Venice, waiting for
her to arrive.

Waiting.

He smiled, relishing a sense of anticipation that was
almost delicious.

It was delicious.

He was no gambler. Luck was for suckers. Instead he
thrived on certainty and detail and left nothing to chance.
His version of luck happened when excellent preparation
met with sublime opportunity.

The seeds for both had been sown, and now it was time
to reap the harvest.

The palazzo had been his uncle's once, before that
woman had stuck her steely claws into him and hung
on tight, and now it was as good as back in the family
fold again. But the satisfaction of returning the palazzo
to the family fold was not what drove him now. Because
Lily Beauchamp had something far more valuable that
he wanted.

Her precious daughter.

She'd walked out on him once. Left the mark of her
hand bright on his jaw and walked away, as if she'd been
the one on high moral ground. At the time he'd let her
go. Waved good riddance. The sex had been good but no
woman was worth the angst of chasing her, no matter how
good she was in bed.

He'd put her from his mind.

But then her mother had called him, asking for help
with the mire of her finances, and he'd remembered the
daughter and a night of sex with her that had ended way

too prematurely. He'd been only too happy to help then. It was the least he could do for his uncle's widow, he'd told her, realising there might be a way to redress the balance.

So now fate was offering him the chance to right two wrongs. To get even.

Not just with the spendthrift mother.

But with the woman who thought she was different. Who thought herself somehow better.

He'd show her she was not so different to her mother after all. He'd show her he was nobody to walk away from.

And then he'd publicly and unceremoniously dump her.

CHAPTER THREE

ARRIVING in Venice, Tina thought, was like leaving real life and entering a fairy tale. The bustling Piazzale Roma where she waited for her bag to be unloaded from the airport bus was the full stop on the real world she was about to leave behind, a world where buildings were built on solid ground and transport moved on wheels; while the bridges that spanned out from the Piazzale crossing the waterways were the 'once upon a time' leading to a fairy tale world that hovered unnaturally over the inky waters of the lagoon and where boats were king.

Beautiful, it was true, but as she glanced at the rows of windows looking out over the canals, right now it almost felt brooding too, and full of mystery and secrets and dark intent...

She shivered, already nervous, feeling suddenly vulnerable. Why had she thought that?

Because he was out there, she reasoned, her eyes scanning the buildings that lined the winding canal. Luca was out there behind a window somewhere in this ancient city. *Waiting for her.*

Damn. She was so tired that she was imagining things.

Except she'd felt it on the plane too, waking from a restless sleep filled with images of him. Woken up feeling almost as if he'd been watching her.

Just thinking about it made her skin crawl all over again.

She pushed her fringe back from her eyes and sucked in air too rich with the scent of diesel fumes to clear her head. God, she was tired! She grunted a weary protest as she hauled her backpack over her shoulder.

Forget about bad dreams, she told herself. Forget about fairy tales that started with once upon a time. Just think about getting on that return plane as soon as possible. That would be happy ending enough for her.

She lined up at the vaporetto station to buy a ticket for the water buses that throbbed their way along the busy canals. A three-day pass should be more than adequate to sort out whatever it was her mother couldn't handle on her own. She'd made a deal with her father that she'd only come to Venice on the basis she'd be back at the farm as soon as the crisis was over. She wasn't planning on staying any longer. It wasn't as if this was a holiday after all.

And with any luck, she'd sort out her mother's money worries and be back on a plane to Australia before Luca Barbarigo even knew she was here.

She gave a snort, the sound lost in the crush of tourists laden with cameras and luggage piling onto the rocking water bus. Yeah, well, maybe that was wishful thinking, but the less she had to do with him, the better. And no matter what her frazzled nerves conjured up in her dreams to frighten her, Luca Barbarigo probably felt the same way. She recalled the vivid slash of her palm across his jaw. They hadn't exactly parted on friendly terms after all.

Tourists jockeyed and squirmed to get on the outer edge of the vessel, cameras and videos at the ready to record this trip along the most famous of Venice's great waterways, and she let herself be jostled out of the way, unmoved by the passing vista except to be reminded she was on Luca Barbarigo's patch; happy to hide in the centre of the boat under cover where she couldn't be observed. Crazy, she knew, to feel this way, but she'd found there were times that logic didn't rule her emotions.

Like the time she'd spent the night with Luca Barbarigo.

Clearly logic had played no part in that decision.

And now once again logic seemed to have abandoned her. She'd felt so strong back home at the kitchen sink, deciding she could face Luca again. She'd felt so sure in her determination to stand up to him.

But here, in Venice, where every second man, it seemed, had dark hair or dark eyes and reminded her of him, all she wanted to do was hide.

She shivered and zipped her jacket, the combined heat from a press of bodies in the warm September air nowhere near enough to prevent the sudden chill descending her spine.

Oh God, she needed to sleep. That was all. Stopovers in Kuala Lumpur and then Amsterdam had turned a twenty-two hour journey into more like thirty-six. She would feel so much better after a shower and a decent meal. And in a few short hours she could give in to the urge to sleep and hopefully by morning she'd feel halfway to normal again.

The vaporetto pulled into a station, rocking sideways on its own wash before thumping against the floating platform and setting passengers lurching on their straps. Then the vessel was secured and the gate slid open and one mass of people departed as another lot rushed in, and air laced with the sour smell of sweat and diesel and churned canal water filled her lungs.

Three days, she told herself, as the vessel throbbed into life and set course for the centre of the canal again, missing an oncoming barge seemingly with inches to spare. She could handle seeing Luca again because soon she would be going home.

Three short days.

She could hardly wait.

The water bus heaved a left at the Canale di Cannaregio and she hoisted her pack from the pile of luggage in the corner where he'd stashed it out of the way. And this time she did crane her neck around and there it was just coming into view—her mother's home—nestled between two well-maintained buildings the colour of clotted cream.

She frowned as the vaporetto drew closer to the centuries-old palazzo. Once grand, her mother's house looked worse than she remembered, the once soft terracotta colour faded and worn, and with plaster peeling from the walls nearly up to the first floor, exposing ancient brickwork now stained yellow with grime at the water level. Pilings out the front of a water door that looked as if it had rusted shut stood at an angle and swayed as the water bus passed, and Tina winced for the once grand entrance, now looking so sad and neglected, even the flower boxes that had once looked so bright and beautiful hanging empty and forlorn from the windows.

Tourists turned their cameras away, searching for and finding more spectacular targets, an old clock tower or a passing gondola with a singing gondolier, and she almost felt ashamed that this was her mother's house, such an unworthy building for a major thoroughfare in such a beautiful city.

And she wondered what her mother could have done with the money she had borrowed. She'd said she'd needed the money to live. Clearly she hadn't spent much of it on returning the building to its former glory. She disembarked at the next stop, heading down one of the narrow *calles* leading away from the canal. The palazzo might boast its own water door but, like so many buildings fronting the canals, pedestrian access was via a rear courtyard, through an ornate iron gate in yet another steeply walled lane, squeezing past clumps of strolling tourists wearing their cruise ship T-shirts and wielding cameras and maps, or being overtaken by fast moving locals who knew exactly where they wanted to go and how to get there in the shortest possible time.

For a moment she thought she'd found the right gate, but ivy rioted over the wall, unkempt and unrestrained, the ends tangling in her hair, and she thought she must have made a mistake. Until she peered closer through the grille and realised why it looked so wrong.

She remembered the courtyard garden being so beautifully maintained, the lawns mowed, the topiary trees trimmed to perfection, but the garden looked neglected and overgrown, the plants spilling from the fifteenth century well at its centre crisp and brown, the neat hedge along the pathway straggly and looking as if it hadn't been clipped for months. Only two bright pots spilling flowers atop the lions guarding the doorway looked as if anyone had made an effort.

Oh, Lily, she thought, looking around and mourning for what a sanctuary this garden had once been. What had happened to let it go like this?

There was no lock on the gate, she realised, the gate jammed closed with rust, and she wondered about her mother living alone, or nearly alone in such a big house. But the gate scraped metal against metal and creaked loudly as she swung it open, a sound that would no doubt frighten off any would-be thief.

It wasn't enough to bring her mother running, of course—Lily was too much a lady to run—but Carmela, the housekeeper, heard. She bustled out of the house rubbing her hands on her apron. Carmela, who she'd met a mere handful of times, but greeted her now with a smile

so wide she could have been her own daughter returning home.

'Valentina, *bella*! You have come.' She took her face
between her hands and reached up to kiss each cheek in
turn before patting her on the back. 'Now, please...' she
said, wresting her backpack from her. 'I will take this. It
is so good you have come.' A frown suddenly came from
nowhere, turning her face serious. 'Your mother, she needs
you. Come, I take you.'

And then she smiled again and led the way into the
house, talking nonstop all the time, a mixture of English
and Italian but the meaning perfectly clear. And Tina, who
had been on edge the entire flight, could finally find it
in herself to smile. Her mother would no doubt treat her
daughter's attendance upon her as her God-given right;
Luca Barbarigo would probably see it as a necessary evil,
but at least someone seemed genuinely pleased to see her.

She followed Carmela across the threshold and, after
the bright autumn sunshine, the inside of the house was
dark and cool, her mother still nowhere to be seen. But,
as her eyes adjusted, what little light there was seemed to
bounce and reflect off a thousand surfaces.

Glass, she realised, remembering her mother's passion
for the local speciality. Only there seemed to be a lot more
of it than she remembered from her last visit.

Three massive chandeliers hung suspended from the
ceiling of the passageway that ran the length of the building, the mosaic glass-framed mirrors along the walls making it look as if there was at least a dozen times that. Lily
blinked, trying to stick to the centre of the walkway where
there was no risk of upsetting one of the hall tables, also
heavily laden with objets d'art, trying to remember what
this hallway had looked like last time she was here. Certainly less cluttered, she was sure.

Carmela led her through a side door into her kitchen that smelt like heaven, a blissful combination of coffee and freshly baked bread and something savoury coming from the stove, and where she was relieved to see the only reflections came from the gleaming surfaces, as if the kitchen was Carmela's domain and nothing but the utilitarian and functional was welcome.

The older woman put down Tina's pack and wrapped her pinny around the handle of a pan on the stove. 'I thought you might be hungry, *bella*,' she said, placing a steaming pan of risotto on a trivet.

Tina's stomach growled in appreciation even before the housekeeper sliced two fat pieces of freshly baked bread and retrieved a salad from the refrigerator. After airline food it looked like a feast.

'It looks wonderful,' she said, pulling up a chair. 'Where's Lily?'

'She had some calls to make,' she said, disapproval heavy in her voice as she ladled out a bowl of the fragrant mushroom risotto and grated on some fresh parmigiano. 'Apparently they could not wait.'

'That's okay,' Tina said, not really surprised. Of course her mother would have no compunction keeping her waiting after demanding her immediate attendance. She'd never been the kind of mother who would actually turn up at the airport to greet her plane or make any kind of fuss. 'It's lovely sitting here in the kitchen. I needed a chance to catch my breath and I am so hungry.'

That earned her a big smile from the housekeeper. 'Then eat up, and enjoy. There is plenty more.'

The risotto was pure heaven, creamy and smooth with just the right amount of bite, and Tina took her time to savour it.

'What happened to the gardens, Carmela?' she asked

when she had satisfied her appetite and sat cradling a fragrant espresso. 'It looks so sad.'

The housekeeper nodded and slipped onto one of the stools herself, her hands cupping her own tiny cup. 'The *signora* could no longer afford to pay salaries. She had to let the gardener go, and then her secretary left. I try to keep up the herb garden and some pots, but it is not easy.'

Tina could believe it. 'But she's paying you?'

'She is, when she can. She has promised she will make up any shortfall.'

'Oh, Carmela, that's so wrong. Why have you stayed? Surely you could get a job in any house in Venice?'

'And leave your mother to her own devices?' The older woman drained the last of her coffee and patted her on the hand as she rose to collect the cups and plates. She shrugged. 'My needs are not great. I have a roof over my head and enough to get by. And one day, who knows, maybe your mother's fortunes will change.'

'How? Does it look like she'll marry again?'

Carmela simply smiled, too loyal to comment. Everyone who knew Lily knew that every one of her marriages after her first had been a calculated exercise in wealth accumulation, even if her plans had come unstuck with Eduardo. 'I meant now that you are here.'

Tina was about to reply that she doubted there was anything she could do when she heard footsteps on the tiles and her mother's voice growing louder... 'Carmela, I thought I heard voices—' She appeared at the door. 'Oh, Valentina, I see you've arrived. I was just speaking to your father. I would have told him you were here if I'd known.'

Tina slipped from her stool, feeling the warmth from the kitchen leach away in the uncomfortable assessment she gauged in her mother's eyes. 'Hello, Lily,' she said, cursing herself for the way she always felt inadequate in her mother's presence. 'Did Dad call to talk to me?'

'Not really,' she said vaguely. 'We just had some… business…to discuss. Nothing to worry about,' her mother assured her, as she air-kissed her daughter's cheeks and whirled away again with barely a touch, leaving just a waft of her own secret Chanel blend that one of her husbands had commissioned for her in her wake. Lily had always loved the classics. Labels and brand names, the more exclusive the better. And as she took in her mother's superbly fitted silk dress and Louboutin heels, clearly nothing had changed. The garden might be shabby, but there was nothing shabby about her mother's appearance. She looked as glamorous as ever.

'You look tired,' Lily said frankly, her gaze not stopping at her eyes as she took in her day-old tank top and faded jeans and clearly found them wanting as she accepted a cup of tea from Carmela. 'You might want to freshen up and find something nicer to wear before we go out.'

Tina frowned. 'Go out?' What she really wanted was a shower and twelve hours sleep. But if her mother had lined up an appointment with her bank, then maybe it was worth making a head start on her problems. 'What did you have in mind?'

'I thought we could go shopping. There's some lovely new boutiques down on the Calle Larga 22 Marzo. I thought it would be fun to take my grown-up daughter out shopping.'

'Shopping?' Tina regarded her mother with disbelief. 'You really want to go shopping?'

'Is there a problem with that?'

'What are you planning on spending? Air?'

Her mother laughed. 'Oh, don't be like that, Valentina.

Can't we celebrate you being back in Venice with a new outfit or two?'

'I'm serious, Lily. You asked me to come—no, scrub that, you *demanded* I come—because you said you are about to be thrown out of this place, and the minute I get here you expect to go shopping. I don't get it.'

'Valentina—'

'No! I left Dad up to his neck in problems so I could come and sort yours out, like you asked me to.'

Lily looked to Carmela for support but the housekeeper had found a spot on her stove top that required serious cleaning. She turned back to her daughter, her voice held together with a thin steel thread.

'Well, in that case—'

'In that case, maybe we should get started.' And then, because her mother looked stunned, and because she knew she was tired and jet-lagged and less tolerant than usual of her mother's excesses, she sighed. 'Look, Lily, maybe once we get everything sorted out—maybe then there'll be time for shopping. I tell you what, why don't you get all the paperwork ready, and I'll come and have a look as soon as I've showered and changed? Maybe it's nowhere near as bad as you think.'

An hour later, Tina buried her head in her hands and wished herself back on the family farm working sixteen-hour days. Wished herself anywhere that wasn't here, facing up to the nightmare that was her mother's accounts.

For a moment she considered going through the documents again, just one more time, just to check she wasn't wrong, that she hadn't miscalculated and overestimated the extent of her mother's debt, but she'd been through everything twice already now. Been through endless bank and credit card statements. Pored over loan document after loan document, all the time struggling with a dictionary alongside to make sense of the complex legal terms written in a language not her first.

She had made no mistake.

She rubbed the bridge of her nose and sighed. From the very start, when she'd seen the mass of paperwork her mother kept hidden away in an ancient ship's chest—almost as if she'd convinced herself that out of sight really was out of mind—the signs had been ominous, but she'd kept hope alive as she'd worked to organise and sort the mess into some kind of order—hope that somewhere amidst it all would be the key to rescuing her mother from financial ruin.

She was no accountant, it was true, but doing the farm's meagre accounts had meant she'd had to learn the hard way about balancing books, and as she'd slowly pieced the puzzle together, it was clear that there was no key, just as there would be no rescue.

Her mother's outgoings were ten times what was being earned on the small estate Eduardo had left her, and Luca Barbarigo was apparently happily funding the difference.

But where was Lily spending all the money when she was no longer paying salaries? She'd sorted through and found a handful of accounts from the local grocer, another batch from a clutch of boutiques and while her mother hadn't stinted on her own wardrobe, there was nowhere near enough to put her this deep into financial trouble. *Unless...*

She looked around the room, the space so cluttered with ornaments that they seemed to suck up the very oxygen. Next to her desk a lamp burned, but not just any lamp. This was a tree, with a gnarled twisted trunk that sprouted two dozen pink flowers and topped with a dozen curved branches fringed with green leaves that ended in more pink flowers but this time boasting light globes, and the entire thing made of glass.

It was hideous.

And that was only one of several lamps, she realised, dotted around the corners of the room and perched over chairs like triffids.

Were they new?

The chandelier she remembered because it was such a fantastical confection of yellow daffodils, pink peonies and some blue flower she had never been able to put a name to, and all set amidst a flurry of cascading ivory glass stems. There was no way she could have forgotten that, and she was sure she would have remembered the lamps if they had been here the last time she had visited.

Likewise, the fish bowls dotted around the room on every available flat surface. There was even one parked on the corner of the desk where she was working. She'd actually believed it was a fish bowl at first, complete with goldfish and bubbles and coral, rocks and weed. Until she'd looked up ten minutes into her work and realised the goldfish hadn't moved. Nothing had moved, because it was solid glass.

They were all solid glass.

Oh God. She rested her head on the heel of one hand. Surely this wasn't where her mother's funds had disappeared?

'Are you tired, Valentina?' asked Lily, edging into the room, picking up one glass ornament after another in the cluttered room, polishing away some nonexistent speck of dust before moving on. 'Should I call Carmela to bring more coffee?'

Tina shook her head as she sat back in her chair. No amount of coffee was going to fix this problem. Because it

wasn't tiredness she was feeling right now. It was utter—
downright—despair.

And a horrible sinking feeling that she knew where the
money had all gone...

'What are all these amounts in the bank statements,
Lily? The ones that seem to go out every month—there
are no invoices that I can find to match them.'

Lily shrugged. 'Just household expenses. This and that.
You know how it is.'

'No. I need you to tell me how it is. What kind of household expenses?'

'Just things for the house! I'm allowed to buy things for
the house, aren't I?'

'Not if it's bankrupting you in the process! Where is the
money going, Lily? Why is there no record of it?'

'Oh—' she tried to laugh, flapping her hands around as
if Tina's questions were nothing but nuisance value '—I
don't bother with the details. Luca keeps track of all that.
His cousin owns the factory.'

'What factory? The glass factory, Lily? Is that where
all your money is going as quickly as Luca Barbarigo tops
you up? You're spending it all on glass?'

'It's not like that!'

'No?'

'No! Because he gives me a twenty per cent discount, so
I'm not paying full price for anything. I've saved a fortune.'

Tina surveyed her mother with disbelief. So very beautiful and so very stupid. 'So every time you get a loan top-
up from Luca Barbarigo, you go shopping at his cousin's
factory.'

Her mother had the sheer audacity to shrug. Tina
wanted to shake her. 'He sends a water taxi. It doesn't
cost me a thing.'

'No, Lily,' she said, pushing back her chair to stand.

There was no point in searching for an answer any longer. Not when there wasn't one. 'It's cost you everything! I just don't believe how you could be so selfish. Carmela is working down there for a pittance you sometimes neglect to pay. You can barely afford to pay her, and yet you fill up this crumbling palazzo with so much weight of useless glass, it's a wonder it hasn't collapsed into the canal under the weight of it all!'

'Carmela gets her board!'

'While you get deeper and deeper into debt! What will happen to her, do you think, when Luca Barbarigo throws you both out on the street? Who will look after her then?'

Her mother blinked, her lips tightly pursed, and for a moment Tina thought she almost looked vulnerable.

'You won't let that happen, will you?' she said meekly. 'You'll talk to him?'

'For all the good it will do, yes, I'll talk to him. But I don't see why it will make a shred of difference. He's got you so tightly stitched up financially, why should he relax the stranglehold now?'

'Because he's Eduardo's nephew.'

'So?'

'And Eduardo loved me.'

Indulged you, more like it, Tina thought, cursing the stupid pride of the man for letting his wife think his fortune was bottomless and not bothering to curb her spending while he was alive, and not caring what might happen to his estate when he was gone.

'Besides,' her mother continued, 'you'll make him see reason. He'll listen to you.'

'I doubt it.'

'But you were friends—'

'We were never friends! And if you knew the things he said about you, you would know he was never your

friend either, no matter how much money he is so happy
to lend you.'

'What did he say? Tell me!'

Tina shook her head. She'd said too much. She didn't
want to remember the ugly things he'd said before she'd
slapped his smug face. Instead she pulled her jacket from
the back of her chair. 'I'm sorry, Lily. I need to get some
fresh air.'

'Valentina!'

She fled the veritable glass museum with the sound of
her mother's voice still ringing in her ears, running down
the marble steps and out past the five-hundred-year-old
well with no idea where she was going, simply that she
had to get away.

Away from the lamps that looked like trees and the
goldfish frozen in glass and the tons of chandeliers that
threatened to sink the building under their weight.

Ran from her mother's sheer naivety and her unbelievable inability to read the terms of an agreement and then
to blithely disregard them as unimportant when she did.

Fleeing from her own fear that there was no way she
could sort out her mother's problems and be home in a
mere three days. Her mother was drowning in debt, just
as the ancient palazzo itself was threatening to collapse
into the canal and drown under the weight of tons of expensive but ultimately useless glass.

And there was not one thing she could do about it. This
trip was a complete waste of time and money. It was pointless. There was nothing she could do.

She turned left out of the gate, heading back down the
narrow *calle* towards the canal and a vaporetto that would
take her somewhere—anywhere—her mother was not.
And at the next corner she turned tight left again, too
suddenly to see anyone coming, too consumed with her

thoughts to remember she should be walking on the other side of the path. And much too suddenly to stop until his big hands were at her shoulders, braking her before she could collide headlong into his chest, punching the air from her lungs in the process. Air that had already conveyed the unmistakable news to her brain.

Luca.

CHAPTER FOUR

His eyes were shuttered behind dark glasses, and still she caught a glint of something behind the lenses as he recognised her, some flash of recognition that was mirrored in the upwards tweak of his lips, and she hated him all the more for it. Just as she hated the sizzle where his long fingers burned into her skin.

'Valentina?' he said, in a voice that must have been a gift from the gods at his birth, stroking like a pure dark velvet assault on her senses. 'Is it you?'

She tugged fruitlessly against his steel grip to be free. He was too close, so close that the air was flavoured with the very essence of him, one hundred per cent male with just a hint of Bulgari, a scent that worked to lure her closer even as she struggled to keep her distance. A scent that was like a key opening up the lid on memories she'd rather forget and sending fragments from the past hurtling through her brain, fragments that contained the memory of that scent—of taking his nipple between her teeth and breathing him in; of the rasp of his whiskered chin against her throat making her gasp; and the feel of him driving into her with the taste of his name in her mouth.

And she cursed the combination of a velvet voice and an evocative scent; cursed that she remembered in way too much detail and the fact that he still looked as good as he always had and hadn't put on twenty kilos and lost his hair since she had last seen him.

Cursed the fact that there was clearly no justice in this world.

For instead he was as beautiful as she remembered, a linen jacket over a white shirt that clung to his lean muscled chest as if it were a second skin, and camel-coloured linen trousers bound low over his hips by a wide leather belt.

He looked every bit the urbane Italian male, as polished and sleek as the streamlined water taxis that prowled the canals, the powerful aristocrats of this watery world. And she was suddenly aware of the disparity between them, with her raw-faced from her shower and dressed in faded jeans and a chain-store jade-coloured vest that was perfectly at home on the farm or even in town but here and now in his presence felt tired and cheap.

'But of course it is you. My apologies, I almost didn't recognise you with your clothes on.'

And a velvet voice turned to sandpaper, to scrape across senses already reeling from the shock of their meeting and leaving them raw and stinging.

'Luca,' she managed in an ice-laden voice designed to slice straight through his smugness, 'I'd like to say it's good to see you again, but right now I just want you to let me go.'

His smile only widened, but he did let her go then, even if his hands lingered at her shoulders just a fraction longer than necessary, the shudder as his thumbs swept an arc across her skin as they departed and left her shivery just as unwelcome. 'Where are you off to in such a hurry? I understood you had only now arrived.'

There was no point being surprised or asking how he knew. Her mother had been making calls when she'd arrived. One of them was to her father, her mother had said, but was another to Luca Barbarigo, sorting out the next instalment of her loan so she could purchase a new barge-ful of glassware? She wouldn't be surprised. For all her mother's protests about the unfair actions of the man, she needed him for her supply of funds like a drug addict needed their supply of crack cocaine. She didn't waste time being polite. 'What's it to you where I am going?'

'Only that I might have missed you. I was coming to pay my respects.'

'Why? So you could gloat to my face about my mother's pathetic money management skills? Don't bother, I've known about them for ever. It's hardly news to me. I'm sorry you've wasted your time but I'll be heading back to Australia the first flight I can get. And now, if you'll excuse me...' She made to move past him but it wasn't easy. In the busy *calle* he was too tall, too broad across the shoulders. His very presence seemed to absorb what little space there was. But as soon as this next group of tourists passed...

He shifted to the right, blocking her escape. 'You're leaving Venice so soon?'

She tried to ignore what his presence was doing to her blood pressure. Tried to pretend it was anger with her mother that was setting her skin to burn and her senses to overload. 'What would be the point of staying? I'm sure you're not as naive as my mother, Signore Barbarigo. You must know there is nothing I can do to save her from financial ruin. Not after the way you've so neatly stitched her up.'

His eyes glinted in the thin light, and Tina had no doubt the heated spark came not from what was left of the sun, but from a place deep inside.

'So combatative, Valentina? Surely we can talk like reasonable people.'

'But that would require you to be a reasonable person, Signore Barbarigo and, having met you in the past, and having examined my mother's accounts, I would hazard the opinion that you have not one reasonable bone in your body.'

He laughed out loud, a sound that reverberated between the brick walls and bounced all the way up to the fading sky, grinding on her senses. 'Perhaps you are right, Valentina. But that does not stop your mother from believing that you will rescue her from the brink of ruin.'

'Then she is more of a fool than I thought. You have no intention of letting her off the hook, do you? You won't be happy until you have thrown her out of the palazzo!'

Heads turned in their direction, ears of passing tourists pricking up at her raised voice, eager to happen upon a possible conflict to add colour and local spice to their Venetian experience.

'Please, Valentina,' he said, pushing her back towards the wall and leaning in close, as if they were having no more than a lovers' tiff. 'Do you wish to discuss your mother's financial affairs in a public street as if it is fodder for so many tourists' ears? What will they think of us Venetians? That we are not civilised enough to conduct our affairs in private?'

Once again he was too close—so close that she could feel his warm breath fanning her face—too close to be able to ignore his scent or not feel the heat emanating from his firm chest or to be able to think rationally, other than to rebut the obvious.

'I am no Venetian.'

'No. You are Australian and very forthright. I admire that in you. But now, perhaps it is time to take this conversation somewhere more private.' He indicated back in the direction she had come. 'Please. We can discuss this in your mother's house. Or, if you prefer, you can come with me to mine. I assure you, it is only a short walk.'

And meet him on his territory? No way in the world. She might have been trying to escape her mother's house, but it was still the lesser of two evils. Besides, if there were going to be some home truths flying around, maybe it was better her mother was there to hear them. 'Then the palazzo. But only because I have a few more things I want to tell you before I leave.'

'I can hardly wait,' she heard him mutter as she wheeled around and headed back in the direction she had come. So smug, she thought, wishing there was something she could do or say to wipe the expression from his face. Was he so sure of Lily's hopelessness that he had known her trip here was futile from the start? Was he laughing at her—at the pointlessness of it all?

She almost growled as she headed back down the *calle*, her senses prickling with the knowledge he was right behind her, prickling with the sensation of his eyes burning into her back. She had to fight the impulse to turn and stare him down but then he would know that she felt his heated gaze and his smugness would escalate from unbearable to insufferable, so she kept her eyes rigidly ahead and tried to pretend she didn't care.

Carmela met them at the palazzo door, smiling uncertainly as she looked from one to the other. But then Luca smiled and turned on the charm as he greeted her in their own language and even though Carmela knew that her future in this place was held by little more than a gossamer thread this man could sever at any time, Tina would swear the older woman actually blushed. She hated him all the more for it in that moment, hated him for this power to make women melt under the sheer onslaught of his smile.

'Your mother has taken to her bed,' Carmela said, apologising for her absence. 'She said she has a headache.'

Luca arched an eyebrow in Tina's direction. She ignored him as Carmela showed them upstairs to the main reception room, promising to bring coffee and refreshments. It was a massive room with high ceilings and pastel-decorated walls that should have been airy and bright but was rendered small by the countless cabinets and tables piled high with glass ornaments, figurines and crystal goblets and lamps of every shape and description, glass that now glinted ruby-red as the setting sunlight streamed in through the wide four-door windows.

It was almost pretty, she thought, a glittering world of glass and illusion, if you could forget about what it had cost.

'You've lost weight, Valentina,' came his voice behind her. 'You've been working too hard.'

And it rankled with her that all the time he'd been following her he'd been sizing her up. Comparing her to how she'd been three years ago and finding her wanting. No doubt comparing her to all his other women and finding her wanting. *Damn it, she didn't want to think about his other women! They were welcome to him.* She spun around. 'We've all changed, Luca. We're all a few years older. Hopefully a bit wiser into the deal. I know I am.'

He smiled and picked up a paperweight that glowed red from a collection from a side table, resting it in the palm of his big hand. 'Some things I see haven't changed. You are still as beautiful as ever, Valentina.' He smiled and examined the glass in his hand before replacing it with the others and moving on, finding a slow path around the cluttered room and around her, pausing to examine a tiny crystal animal here, a gilt-edged glass plate there, touching just a fingertip to it before looking up at her again. 'Perhaps, you are a little more prickly than I remember. Perhaps there is a little more spice. But then I recall you were always very...*passionate*.'

He lingered over the word as if he were donning that velvet glove to stroke her memories and warm her senses. She swallowed, fighting back the tide of the past and a surge of heat low in her belly. 'I don't want to hear it,' she said, turning on the spot as he continued to circle the room, touching a hand to the head of a glass boy holding a lantern aloft as if the golden-skinned child was real and not just another of her mother's follies. 'Instead, I want to tell you that I know what you're doing.'

He tilted his head. 'And what, exactly, am I doing?'

'I've been through Lily's accounts. You keep lending her money, advance after advance. Money that she turns straight around to purchase more of this—' she waved her hand around the room '—from your own cousin's glass factory on Murano.'

He shrugged. 'What can I say? I am a banker. Lending people money is an occupational hazard. But surely it is not my responsibility how they see fit to use those funds.'

'But you know she has no income to speak of to pay you back, and still you loan her more.'

He smiled and held up his index finger. 'Ah. But income is only one consideration a banker must take into account when evaluating a loan risk. You are forgetting that your mother has, what we call in the business, exceptional assets.'

She snorted. 'You've noticed her assets then.' The words were out before she could snatch them back, and now they hung in the space like crystal drops from a chandelier, heavy and fat and waiting to be inspected in the light.

He raised an eyebrow in question. 'I was talking about the palazzo.'

'So was I,' she said, too quickly. 'I don't know what you're thinking about.'

He laughed a little and ran the tips of his fingers across the rim of a fluted glass bowl on a mantelpiece as he passed, continuing his circuit of the room. Such long fingers, she couldn't help but notice, such a feather-light touch. A touch she remembered on her skin. A touch she had thought about so often in the dark of night when sleep had eluded her and she had felt so painfully alone.

'Your mother is a very beautiful woman, Valentina. Does it bother you that I might notice?'

She blinked, trying to get a grip back on the conversation, tilting her head higher as he came closer. 'Why should it?'

'I don't know. Unless you're worried that I have slept with Lily. That maybe I am sleeping with her?' He stopped before her and smiled. 'Does that bother you, *cara*?'

'I don't want to know! I don't care! It's no business of mine who you sleep with.'

'Of course not. And, of course, she is a very beautiful woman.'

'So you said.' The words were ground out through her teeth.

'Although nowhere—*nowhere*—near as beautiful as her daughter.'

He touched those fingers to her brow, smoothing back a wayward strand of hair. She gasped, shivering at the touch, thinking she should stop him—that she should step away—when in truth she could feel herself leaning closer.

It was Luca who stepped away, dropping his hand, and she blinked, a little stunned, feeling as if she had conceded a point to him, knowing that she had to regain the high ground.

'You told my mother we were old friends.'

He shrugged and sat down on a red velvet armchair, his long legs lazily sprawled out wide, his elbows resting on the arms. 'Aren't we?'

'We were never friends.'

'Come now, Valentina.' Something about the way he said her name seemed almost as if he were stroking her again with that velvet glove and she crossed her arms over her chest to hide an instinctive and unwanted reaction. 'Surely, given what we have shared...'

'We shared nothing! We spent one night together, one night that I have regretted ever since.' *And not only because of the things you said and the way we parted.*

'I don't remember it being quite so unpleasant.'

'Perhaps you recall another night. Another woman. I'm sure there have been so many, it must get quite confusing. But I'm not confused. You are no friend of mine. You are nothing to me. You never were, and you never will be.'

She thought he might leave then. She was hoping he might realise they had nothing more to say to each other and just go. But while he pulled his long legs in and sat up higher in the chair, he did not get up. His eyes lost all hint of laughter and took on a focus—a hard-edged gleam—that, coupled with his pose, with his legs poised like springs beneath him, felt almost predatory. If she turned and ran, she thought, even if there was a way to run in this cluttered showroom, he would be out of his chair and upon her in a heartbeat. Her own heart kicked up a notch, tripping inside her chest like a frightened gazelle.

'When your mother first came to me for a loan,' he said in a voice that dared her not to pay attention to each and every syllable, 'I was going to turn her down. I had no intention of lending her the money.'

She didn't say anything. She sensed there was no point in asking him what had changed his mind—that he intended telling her anyway—even if she didn't want to know. On some very primal level, she recognised that she did not want to know, that, whatever it was, she was not going to want to hear this.

'I should see about that coffee—' she said, making a move for the stairs.

'No,' he said, standing and barring her exit in one fluid movement, leaving her wondering how such a big man could move with such economy and grace. 'Coffee can wait until I've finished. Until you've heard this.'

She looked up at him, at the angles and planes of his face that were both so beautiful and so cruel, looked at the place where a tiny crease betrayed a rarely seen dimple in his cheek, studied the shallow cleft in his chin, and she wondered that she remembered every part of him so vividly and in such detail, that nothing of his features came as a surprise but more as a vindication of her memory.

And only then she realised he was studying her just as intently, just as studiously, and she turned her eyes away. *Because she had stared at him too long*, she told herself, *not because she was worried what he might be remembering about her.*

'I didn't have to lend that money to your mother,' he continued. 'But then I remembered one long night in a room warmed by an open fire, with sheepskin rugs on the floor and a feather quilt to warm the wide bed. And I remembered a woman with skin the colour of cream with amber eyes and golden hair and who left too angry and much too soon.'

She glared at him, clamping her fists and her thighs and

refusing to let his words bury themselves in the places they wanted to go. 'You lent my mother money to get back at me? Because I slapped you? You really are mad!'

'You're right. I can't give you all the credit. Because in lending your mother money, I saw the opportunity to take back Eduardo's home—this palazzo—before it collapsed into the canal from neglect. I owed Eduardo that, even if I wanted nothing to do with his wife. But that wasn't the only reason. I also wanted to give you a second chance.'

'To slap you again? You make it sound so tempting.' Right now her curling fist ached to lash out at something. Why not his smug face?

He laughed at that. 'Some say a banker's life must be dull: days filled with endless meetings and boring conversations about corporate finance and interest rate margins. But it doesn't have to be like that. Sometimes it can be much more rewarding.'

'By dreaming up fantasies? Look, I don't care how you while away your hours—I really don't want to know—just leave me out of them.'

'Then you are more selfish than I thought—' his voice turned serious '—your mother is in serious financial trouble. She could lose the palazzo. In fact she *will* lose the palazzo. Don't you care that your mother could be homeless?'

'That will be on your head, not on mine. I'm not the one threatening to throw her out.'

'And yet you could still save her.'

'How? I don't have access to the kind of funds my mother owes you, even if I did want to help.'

'Who said anything about wanting your money?'

There was a chilling note to his delivery, as if she should indeed know exactly what kind of currency he was considering. But no, surely he could not mean *that*?

'I have nothing that would interest any banker and convince them to forgive a debt.'

'You underestimate yourself, *cara*. You have something that might encourage this banker to forgive your mother's debt.'

She shook her head. 'I don't think so!'

'Listen to what I offer, Valentina. I am not a beast, whatever you may think. I do not want your mother to suffer the indignity of being thrown out of her home. Indeed, I have an apartment overlooking the Grand Canal ready and waiting for your mother to move into. She will own it free of any encumbrance and she will draw a monthly pension. All that stands in the way is you.' He smiled, the smile of a crocodile, the predator back in residence under his skin.

Her own skin prickled with both suspicion and fascination. He was a beautiful specimen of a man. He always had been. But she'd known the man, she'd known what he was capable of, and her self-protection senses were on high alert. 'And are you going to tell me what I have to do in order to win this happy ever after for my mother?'

'Nothing I know you will not enjoy. I simply require you to share my bed.'

She blinked, expecting to wake up at any moment. For surely she was so jet-lagged that she'd fallen asleep on her feet and was busy dreaming a fantasy. No, not a fantasy. *A nightmare.* 'As simple as that?' she echoed. 'You're saying that you will let my mother off the hook, you will gift her an apartment in which to live and pay her an allowance, and all I have to do is sleep with you?'

'I told you it was simple.'

Did he imagine she was? Did he not realise what he was asking her? To sell herself to him like some kind of whore—and all to save her mother? 'Thank you for coming, Signore Barbarigo. I'm sure you don't have to trouble Carmela to find your way out. I'm sure you can find the way.'

'Valentina, do you know what you are saying no to?'

'Some kind of paradise, apparently, the way you make it sound. Except I'm not in the market. I'm not looking for paradise. I certainly wouldn't expect to find it in your bed.'

'You might want to reconsider your options. I do not think you are giving this offer the serious consideration it deserves.'

'And I don't think you're giving me any credit for knowing when I've heard enough.'

'And your mother? You care not for what happens to her?'

'My mother is a big girl, Mr Barbarigo. She got herself into this mess, she can damned well get herself out of it.'

'And if that means she loses the palazzo and ends up homeless?'

'Then so be it. She'll just have to find somewhere else to live, like anyone else who overspends their budget.'

'I'm surprised at you. Her own daughter, and you will do nothing to help her.'

'You overplayed your hand, Luca, imagining I even cared. I will play no part in your sordid game. Throw my mother out if you must. Maybe then she might learn her lesson. But don't expect me to prostitute myself to bail her out. When I said what we had was over, I meant it.'

He nodded then, and she felt a rush of relief like she had never known before. She had just consigned her mother to her fate, it was true, but it was no worse a result than she had come here half expecting. Perhaps if her mother had been more of a mother, one who inspired loyalty and affection, she might even consider Luca's barbaric bargain. For five minutes at least. Then again, a mother like that would never put her in a position such as this. A mother like that would never have fallen victim to such an opportunistic despot.

'In that case you give me no choice. I will go. And I will call your father and let him know the bad news.'

'My father?' she asked, with an ice-cold band of fear tightening around her chest. Lily had been talking to her father on the phone when she'd arrived and she'd never got around to finding out exactly why, even though it had seemed odd. What had they cooked up between themselves? 'Why would you call him? What's Mitch got to do with this?'

'Does it matter? I thought you wanted no more part of this.'

'If it's about my father, then of course it concerns me. Why would you need to call him?'

'Because Lily spoke to him today.'

'I know that,' she snapped, impatient. 'And?'

'And he didn't want to see your trip wasted. Lily told me he would do anything for you, and apparently she was right. He offered to put up the farm as security if you could not find a way to help.'

CHAPTER FIVE

'I CAN'T believe you dragged my father into this!' Tina burst into her mother's room, livid. There was no risk of waking her, she'd just ordered Carmela to bring her brandy. 'What the hell were you thinking?'

Luca had departed, taking his smug expression with him but leaving a poisoned atmosphere in his wake and now Lily wasn't the only one with a headache. Tina's temples pounded with a message of war.

'What are you doing in here? What's all this screaming?'

Tina swiped open the curtains in the dark room, letting in what little light remained of the day. Too little light. She snapped on a switch and was rewarded by a veritable vineyard lighting up above her mother's bed head, clusters of grapes in autumn colours, russets and pinks and golds, dangling from the ceiling amid wafer-thin 'leaves' of green and pink. For a moment she was too blindsided to speak.

'What the hell is that?' she demanded when at last she'd found her tongue.

'You don't like it?' her mother said, sitting up, looking up at the lights, sounding surprised.

'It's hideous. Just like everything else in this glass mausoleum.'

'Valentina, do you have to be so rude? I'll have you know I don't buy things to please you.'

'Clearly. But right now I'm more concerned about whatever it was you got Dad to agree to. Luca said he'd put the farm on the line. For you. To bail you out. If I couldn't find a way.'

'You saw Luca?' Lily scambled from the bed, pulled on a rose-pink silk robe that wafted around her slim body as it settled. 'When? Is he still here?'

'He's gone and good riddance to him. But not before he put his seedy deal on the table. Were you in on it, mother dearest? Was it you who came up with the idea of swapping your daughter for your debt?'

Lily blinked up at her. 'He said that?' And her mother looked so stunned Tina knew there was no way she could have been in on it. 'That does explain a few things, I suppose. Well, aren't you the lucky one. And I thought he wasn't interested in sex.'

'You didn't! Oh, please God, tell me you didn't proposition him.'

She shrugged, sitting at a table, picking up a cloth in one hand, a glass dolphin in the other, absently rubbing its head. 'Turning fifty is no joy, Valentina, you mark my words. Nobody wants you. Nobody sees you. You might just as well be invisible when it comes to men.'

'There's nothing flattering about being asked to be someone's mistress, Lily!'

'But of course there is. He's a very good-looking man.' And then she stopped rubbing and stared into the middle distance as if she was building an entire story around the possibilities. 'Just think, if you play your cards right, he might even marry you…'

'I told him I wouldn't do it.'

Her mother looked at her, and Tina saw an entire fantasy crashing down in her eyes. 'Oh.'

'And that's when he told me about Dad, and agreeing to put up the farm. Is that why you were on the phone to him, Lily? Looking for a Plan B in case I couldn't save you? Begging for favours from a man you abandoned with a baby more than twenty-five years ago? A man who by rights should hate your guts.'

'He doesn't, though. I think Mitchell was the only man who ever really loved me.'

'Well, you sure made a mess of that.'

'I still don't understand what your problem is. People would kill to sleep with Luca Barbarigo.'

And the desire to shock her mother just for once, instead of being the one who was always shocked, was too great. 'That's just it. I *have* slept with him.'

'You sly girl,' she said, swapping the dolphin for another, this one with a baby swimming alongside. 'And you never let on? So why make such a big deal out of it now?'

And that simple question told her more about her mother than she ever wanted to know. 'It ended badly.'

'Because he didn't express his undying love for you? Oh God, Valentina, you're so naive sometimes.'

Her mother's words stung, deep inside where she'd promised she'd never hurt again. And maybe that was why she said it. Because she didn't want to be the only one hurting here. 'He said I was a chip off the old block. That, like you, I did my best work on my back!'

Her mother paused, forgetting momentarily about the delicate glass dolphin in her lap that she'd been lovingly dusting till then. And then she laughed, absolutely delighted. 'He said that? And you didn't take it as a compliment?' She took one look at her daughter's stricken face. 'You didn't, did you?' She shrugged and started polishing again, before she gave it a final check in the light and replaced it with another ornament. Rub rub rub. Polish polish polish. And the more she polished, the more Tina's nerves screamed.

'Would you please stop doing that?'

'Doing what?'

'Dusting those wretched ornaments of yours.'

'Valentina,' her mother said, incensed, rubbing on, 'they're Murano glass, they deserve to be shown to best advantage. Of course I have to dust them.'

'I was pregnant, you know!'

Lily looked up at her, and this time she put the ornament right back on the side table where it had come from. Finally, Tina thought. Finally she managed to look aghast. 'You were pregnant? To Luca Barbarigo?'

Tina nodded, a sudden tightness in her throat, a sudden and unbidden urge to cry stinging her eyes as she released a secret she had been holding inside for too long. Finally her mother might understand.

Finally.

Lily just sat there and shook her head. 'So why didn't you make him marry you?'

'What?'

'Don't you know how rich he is? His family were once Doges of Venice. He's Venetian nobility and you didn't marry him?'

'Lily, we had a one-night stand. One night. A baby wasn't part of the deal. Anyway, I lost the baby. And thank you so much for asking about the fate of your grandchild!'

'But if you'd married him,' her mother continued, unabashed, 'then we wouldn't be in this mess now.'

Tina's world reeled and spun. 'Didn't you hear me? I lost the baby. At twenty weeks. Do you have any idea what that's like, giving birth to a child that is destined to die?'

Lily flicked away the argument as if it were no more than a speck of dust on one of her ornaments. 'You didn't really want a child, did you? Besides, you could have been married by then. You would have been, if you'd told me at the time. I would have arranged your marriage within a week.'

'And what if I didn't want to get married?'

'That's hardly the point. You should have made him do the honourable thing.'

Tina doubted she had ever hated her mother quite so much. 'Like you made Mitch do when you got pregnant? Tell me, Lily, were you hoping for a miscarriage once you had that ring on your finger? Were you hoping to escape the birth once you had the husband, given you never really wanted a child?'

'That's not fair!'

'Isn't it? Sorry I didn't oblige. Lucky, though, in a way, given the mess you're in now.'

She turned to leave. 'Goodbye, Lily. I don't expect to see you again while I'm here.'

'Where are you going?'

And she looked back over her shoulder. 'To hell. But don't go thinking it's on your account.'

The taxi dropped him back at the water door of his own palazzo overlooking the Grand Canal. Aldo came down to meet him, swinging open the iron gate as he alighted from the vessel. 'And the company you were expecting?'

'A change of plan, Aldo. I will be dining alone tonight. I will eat in the study.'

Luca crossed the tiled floor and took the marble steps up into the house three at a time. A temporary change of plan, he had no doubt. Once Valentina slept on the choices she had, she would see she had no choice at all. She would soon come crawling, begging for him to rescue her family from the nightmare of her mother's making.

He entered the study, but eschewed the wide desk where his computer and work waited patiently and went straight to the windows instead, opening a window door leading to a balcony and gazing out over the canal at night, the vaporettos lit up with the flash of a hundred cameras, the heavy barges that performed the grunt work in place of trucks. Never did he tire of the endless tapestry of life in Venice, the slap of water against the pilings, the rich tenor strains of a gondolier as he massaged his gondola's way along the canals. But then his family had been here for centuries after all. No wonder he sometimes felt his veins ran not with blood but with water from these very canals.

It spoke to him now. Told him to be patient. That he was closer than he thought.

He saw the colour of her eyes in the golden light from a window across the canal. Amber eyes and hair shot with golden lights—she might have lost weight, she might have been travelling for more than a day and the skin under her eyes tired, but the intervening years had been good to her. She was more beautiful than he remembered.

And he hungered for her.

But she would soon come crawling.

And he would have her.

She got the address from Carmela, who hugged her tight to her chest before putting her at arm's length and kissing her solemnly on both cheeks. 'You come back if you need anything, anything at all. You come back and see Carmela. I will help you, *bella*.'

She hugged the older woman back, clutching the piece of paper with the address and the rough map Carmela had drawn for her. Luca had said it wasn't far. It didn't help that evening had closed in and that the canals were inky-black ribbons running between islands of jam-packed buildings, it didn't help that she knew she had been awake for a dozen hours too many to feel alive, but she was running on anger now, her veins infused with one hundred per cent fury, and there was no way she was staying in her mother's house a moment longer and no way she could have slept if she tried.

She made a mistake with the vaporetto, boarding the wrong one in her rush to get away and she had to get off at the next stop and backtrack to find another. She found herself lost in the dark *calles* three times, stumbling onwards as if she were blind until she found a sign on a wall with a name she recognised, telling her she was on the right track.

But all of these inconveniences just gave her the time to think. To reconsider why she was so prepared to jump into the lion's den—a place she had promised herself never to go again.

It wasn't for her mother, she knew. She'd been prepared to turn her back and walk away and leave her mother to her own devices.

It wasn't for herself. Oh God, no. She hated him after what he'd said, and what he'd done. Hated him for not caring when he could have. Hated him for the unsettling, unwanted effect he had on her, even in the midst of hating him. She wanted nothing more to do with the man.

No, this was for her father, who somehow thought that if he helped Lily in this current crisis, he was making it easier on his daughter. What had Lily told him of her plight? What dramas had she woven around the thin ribbons that still bonded them together, even after a divorce of more than twenty years?

But their property was operating on a shoestring, already mortgaged heavily to the banks. Another mortgage, another bad season would see her father's dream ruined.

She could not let him do that, for whatever misguided sense of loyalty he still had.

She could not let it happen.

She made another wrong turn and swore under her breath as she retraced her steps again. But all of the inconveniences of her journey, all these frustrations fed into her anger. So by the time she reached the sign on the locked gate that announced she was at the right number of the right street, she felt ready to tear the gate apart with her bare hands. Instead she pressed a buzzer, waited impatiently the few seconds for a response and asked to see Luca Barbarigo.

When she met with hesitation, she countered it with, 'Tell him it is Tina Henderson…*Valentina* Henderson. He will see me.'

A few moments later the gate clicked open and a stony-faced valet met her at the door, giving her a once-over that told her that in faded jeans and a cheap zip-up jacket she was seriously underdressed for a meeting with his boss. But that was okay because she had plans for her wardrobe. 'Signore Barbarigo will receive you in the study,' he said, before gesturing for her backpack. 'If you would care to leave your bag?'

'I'm good with it,' she said, her hand on the shoulder strap, 'if it's all the same to you.' Luca would be under no misapprehension why she was there if she had anything to do with it. He would know she meant business if she turned up with her pack. Besides, if she was going to be sharing the master's bedchamber, it was going to have to be carried upstairs at some stage.

The valet nodded, his disapproval clear on his set features, and led the way up the wide flight of stairs leading to the noble floor. A stunning palazzo, she registered as they climbed, with terrazzo floors and stuccoed walls and heavy beamed ceilings so high they were in no way oppressive.

Or were they?

Only one flight of steps, but suddenly she needed oxygen, as if the air was thinner the higher they climbed. But it wasn't the air, she knew. It was being here, in the lion's den, about to take on the lion at his own game.

It was anticipation, both terrifying and delicious, for what would come next.

And what could have been a spike of fear and the chance for cowardice to surface and set her fleeing down the stairs turned into a surge of strength. Did he really think she could be forced into something, to tumble meekly into his bed? Damn the man but she would not crawl to him like some simpering virgin begging for favours.

The stairs opened to a sitting room so elegant it could feature in a magazine—maybe the sofas and dark timber leant towards the masculine—but the overall effect was of light and space.

How her mother's house was meant to look, it occurred to her. Probably had looked, before Eduardo had taken her for his wife and she'd become addicted to the factory shops of Murano and let her passion for glass suck up every last euro and every available inch of space.

Through a set of timber doors, the valet led her, and yet another reception room until finally they were at another set of sculpted timber doors where he knocked and showed her in, pulling the door closed behind him as he left.

Her heart kicked up a beat when she saw him.

The lion was in.

He sprawled arrogantly in a chair behind an acre of desk across a room that went on for ever and then some. And still he owned the room. It was an extension of him, paying tribute to his inexorable power. She wrenched her eyes from his and studied the desk before him. Antique if she wasn't mistaken, but masculine and strong and with legs that were solid and built to last whatever the ages would throw at it.

It would do nicely.

'Valentina,' he said, without standing, his voice measured, his dark eyes waiting for answers. 'This is a surprise.'

'Is it?' She looked around at the door. 'Does that lock from the inside?'

He cocked his head, the shadow of a frown pulling his brows closer together. 'Why do you ask?'

She shrugged the straps of her backpack from her shoulders, hoping no hired help was about to rush in—not with what she had planned—before letting the weight drag it to the ground at her feet, making no move to stop it hitting the floor. She summoned up confidence along with a smile she didn't feel. 'It would be a shame to be interrupted.'

'Would it?' he asked, as if he didn't care one way or the other, and she almost panicked and fled while she could. It was so long since she'd last made love. Years since that last unforgettable night with Luca. Was she kidding herself that she could pull this off? She was so unpractised in the arts of the seductress, so unskilled.

And she almost did flee.

Except she noticed the way he'd already eased his body a fraction higher in his seat, his limbs a little less casually positioned.

And so she licked her lips in preparation for the show. Oh God, she was such an amateur! Such a fake! But still she touched a finger to the zip of her jacket and toyed with it a while, teasing it lower—she was way out of her depth and it had to show!—until she was certain he was watching. 'It's warm in here. Don't you think it's warm in here?'

'I can open a window,' he said guardedly, his eyes not leaving her fingers, no part of him looking like it was willing to move far enough to open a window any time soon.

'It's fine,' she said, feeling suddenly empowered, sliding the zip all the slow way down, peeling it from her shoulders lovingly, like a lover would do from behind, sighing a kiss against one bare shoulder. 'It's probably just me.'

'Why are you here?' The words were short, but his trademark velvet voice was thick and already curdling at the edges from heat.

She smiled and flicked off her sandals, cursing when one needed another kick, feeling clumsy. Inadequate for the task. But he wasn't looking at her feet and so she pressed on. 'You offered me a position,' she said, letting him wait for the rest. She tugged the hem of her singlet free from her belted jeans, waited just a moment to ensure she had his full, undivided attention, before pulling it over her head, letting her hair tumble free over her bare shoulders. She put her hands to the belt at her belly, letting her arms frame her breasts, clad in their white T-shirt bra. It was probably the plainest, dullest bra he had ever seen, but right now it was all she had and it was too late to worry about her underwear. Besides, from the glint in Luca's eyes, he probably hadn't even noticed that she was wearing one. That glint gave her the courage she needed if she was going to do this, courage to bare a body nobody had seen for three long years. A body that had been shut away from the world lest it betray her again. Was she asking too much of it now?

She held her breath as she slid the leather of her belt through the buckle and popped the button on her jeans. 'I'm accepting it.'

She slid the zip down, gave a wiggle of her hips to help push them down and hesitated, leaning forward just enough to turn cotton-clad breasts into a cleavage. He wasn't looking relaxed any more, she noticed. He was sitting up. Paying attention. 'Oh. I thought of something,' she said.

'What?' he croaked, his eyes not shifting.

'Conditions.'

Was that a groan she heard or a growl? It didn't matter. Either worked for her. 'Tell me,' he said.

'How long am I supposed to be your mistress? Only you didn't say.'

'I hadn't thought about it. However long it takes.'

'I thought a month.'

'A month?'

'A month would be more than adequate. I mean, I don't know what the going rate for mistresses is, but I'm thinking high end, late model, low mileage—well, that has to be worth more. Right?'

'If you say so.'

'Only I have work to do back home. And I'm sure you have something to be going on with. And it's not like we want this thing messing with our lives, right?'

'Right.'

Her hands lingered at her hips. She looked at him, watching her, feeling the power of his need feeding the anger that had been building ever since that phone call from Lily, the anger that had worked itself into a volcano set to erupt today, and smiled knowingly. *You utter bastard*, she thought with satisfaction. *And you thought you were going to have this all your own way.*

It was almost too good to be true. *Almost.*

'And you will never contact or threaten my father with anything financial or otherwise. Never again.'

'Never.'

It wasn't just too good to be true. It was perfect.

'You have such a lovely big desk, Luca.' She edged her jeans a fraction lower, spun around to give him a view from the back as she eased the soft denim lower, making sure her underwear went with it, and looked at him over her shoulder. 'It would be such a shame to waste all that glorious space on work, don't you think?'

'I think,' he said, standing awkwardly, kicking off his loafers while he attacked the buttons of his own shirt, shrugging it off to expose a chest made in heaven and stolen from the gods. 'I think you need help getting those jeans off.'

CHAPTER SIX

CONTROL. It was one of the things Luca prided himself on. He had patience. He had nerve. He had control of his life and his world. It was the way he liked things to be. It was the way things had to be.

But watching a flaxen haired, amber-eyed minx from Australia strip down to her underwear in his study was threatening to bring him undone.

If only she could get those damned jeans off.

She laughed when he picked her up, the sound half-hysterical, half-intoxicated, wild and free, and he was intoxicated as he spun her around and headed for the desk, sweeping it clear with one arm, sending papers and pencils and phones scattering in all directions before he planted her hard upon the desk and ripped off her jeans, tearing the bra from her breasts with a snap in the next testosterone-fuelled action.

That gave him pause. Naked on his desk, her legs parted by his, she was almost too much to take in with his eyes, too much for one hand to drink in as it swept over creamy skin from knee to thigh to belly to cup one perfect breast.

She stopped laughing then, her breath coming fast and furious, her eyes wide as he pulled his belt free, tugged his zip down and kicked off his pants, her eyes so suddenly cold as he freed his aching erection that she looked almost...*angry*.

'I hate you,' she said, confirming it, her lips tight around the words, baring her sharp white teeth, and that was fine. That was good, because for a moment she'd blindsided him with that impromptu striptease and he'd felt a glimmer of...*something*...that had hovered and curled around uncomfortably in his gut. But hatred he could work with.

Hatred would make her submission all the more satisfying.

And then he would dump her and she could hate him even more.

'Excellent,' he said, slamming open a drawer and rummaging through the contents until he found what he was looking for, shaking a packet free one-handed from the box. He tore it open with his teeth and had it on in record time, spreading her thighs wider to find her centre.

Slick and hot. Oh God.

He calmed himself long enough to stay poised at her entrance, his thumb working at that sensitive nub, watching the hatred in her amber eyes muddy with need, sensing the panting desperation of her breathing. *Oh yes, she hated him all right*.

'I'm so glad we understand each other,' he said, and he drove into her in one long exquisite thrust.

She cried out, her back arching on the desk like a bow, her hair rioting around her head, her eyes stuttering closed.

Hate was definitely underrated, he thought, as he braced her hips and drew slowly back, feeling involuntary muscles protest around him, try to keep him, seeing her eyes flicker open, confused and bereft and wanting more.

He gave her more. The second lunge took him deeper. She cried out again and this time when she bowed her back, he scooped her up from the desk so that she was sitting astride him, her breasts pressed against his chest, her legs curled around him and as he lifted her hips and let her fall, it was his turn to groan.

She needed no help to find the rhythm. She damn near set about setting it. She might have looked stunned before, but now she squirmed her bottom in his hands and braced herself on his shoulders, levering herself higher, letting herself take him in, increasing the speed, driving it, while her mouth worked at his throat, sharp teeth finding his flesh, every nip and bite timed to perfection, agony melding with ecstasy.

She was like a wildcat in his arms, untamed and unleashed, and it was all he could do to hang onto her while she used her body against him—all he could do to hang on, full stop.

Until she pumped him one too many times and any vestige of control vanished as he exploded inside her, the fireworks of her own orgasm ricocheting, magnified, through his.

Gasping and sweat-slicked, he hung on, her limbs heavy now, her head low on his chest, carrying her through an adjoining door to his suite. Awkwardly he pulled back the covers and then eased her onto the bed, where she closed her eyes and sighed into the mattress.

No tears, he thought, no recriminations? Half expecting both. That was a bonus. Though there probably wasn't a whole lot more to say after *I hate you.*

Unless it was *I still hate you.* He smiled as he headed for the bathroom, already contemplating round two. He could think of worse ways to spend the night. That first coupling had been so fast and furious, already he was contemplating the pleasures to be had in other, slower, methods. Next time he would take his time. Explore her body in more delicious detail. Next time he would be the one to set the pace.

He caught a glimpse of his neck and shoulder in the mirror, shocked at first at the marks of her teeth standing out bright and red. He smiled as he fingered them, the skin tender where she had left her brand. He remembered her biting him, but nowhere near this many times. Foremost in his mind had been the ecstasy. She was a tigress all right. Wild and untamed, and as unexpected as her surprise arrival tonight.

But then not entirely a surprise. Clearly he'd hit on the one thing that she held dear.

She'd surprised him with her vehemence. She'd been so prepared to walk away from her mother—to let her face the consequences of her overspending and be thrown out onto the streets if it came to that. He'd misjudged the relationship between mother and daughter badly. But then he'd only really had Lily's side of it to go by and in Lily's world, it was all about Lily.

But suggesting Lily ask her first husband to help, that had been a stroke of genius. Finally he'd found the one person Valentina did care about—the one she would do anything to rescue—even if it meant sacrificing herself to his bed.

Everyone had their price, it was said. He had just found Valentina's.

He padded back from the bathroom to find her curled kitten-like into a ball in the centre of his bed, her breathing even and deep and fast, fast asleep.

So much for round two.

Bemused, he climbed in alongside. She stirred and murmured something in her sleep and he wasn't planning on holding her but she curled herself against him and settled back into her dreams on a sigh.

It wasn't what he'd been expecting. He wasn't used to holding anyone when he slept. He wasn't used to anyone sleeping on him. Certainly not a woman he wasn't done with yet. He willed away an erection that was more wishful thinking than opportunity and tried to relax. She was warm and languid and, for all her muscled leanness, she was soft too, and in all the right places.

Relax? Fat chance.

But at least he could think about what might happen when she woke up.

One month she'd agreed to stay.

It had seemed more than ample when she'd suggested it. He'd only ever planned to keep her long enough that she thought she was safe, that maybe he might provide the answer to all her needs. Long enough to feel secure and so comfortable in her position as Venice's first lady that she wouldn't see it coming. Her public humiliation.

And then he remembered what had happened in his study and how she had turned the tables on him and milked him for all he was worth. And the thought of thirty nights of Valentina hating him and proving it every night in his bed—or on his desk for that matter—seemed nowhere near long enough.

She came to gently, slowly, with the strange feeling she was still moving, and for some vague period of half-sleep, she believed herself back on the plane.

Until logic interceded and she realised that last-minute bargain economy seats on passenger planes did not come complete with sublime mattresses and pillows big enough to land that plane on.

Venice.

She sat up in bed, realising she was hearing the chug of a passing vaporetto rather than the constant hum of jet engines, and she remembered the argument with her mother, and an explosive session on Luca's desk. And then—*nothing*.

She dropped her head into her hands.

What had she done?

She lifted the covers. Of course she would be naked. And of course it had been no dream. She'd performed some kind of amateur striptease in front of him. She'd offered herself as a conscientious objector instead of him taking her as an unwilling sacrifice. And she remembered a desk and the feel of him inside her.

How could she ever forget the feel of him inside her, the sense of fullness and completion and the exquisite side effects of friction?

In three years she hadn't forgotten and nothing, it seemed, had changed. Her memories were true.

But she couldn't for the life of her remember a bed. Luca's bed, she recognised, not only by his lingering scent and the presence of a jet-black hair on the pillow, but the sheer masculinity of the room, as if he'd stamped his personality on it by the sheer force of it. She'd slept in his bed and he'd slept alongside her and, surprisingly, that act seemed even more intimate than the one they'd shared on the desk.

But where was he now?

A robe lay on the coverlet. Silky and jade-coloured. She snatched it up and wrapped it around her in case he suddenly appeared. Strange, to feel shy after what she'd done last night, but she wasn't practised in negotiating a deal while taking off her clothes. She'd never expected to seal one in such a way. But last night fury had given her courage to do what she had done; rage had given her purpose. This morning she was still angry with both her mother and with Luca, but now there was wonderment too at her brazen behaviour. Not to mention a little fear, for what she might have let herself in for.

One month of sleeping with Luca Barbarigo. Thirty nights of sex with a man who knew how to blow every fuse in her body and then some. Thirty whole nights after three years of abstinence—she shivered—it was almost too much to think about. It was almost, so very almost, *delicious*.

The silken robe whispered against her breasts. Her nipples tightened into buds. She could not let him see her like this. He'd think she was primed and ready for a second course. He might even be right to think that.

But Luca didn't arrive and the only sounds she heard were the sounds of Venice coming from outside the windows. The only movement she felt seemed to come from the very foundations, the gentle sway of time and tide.

And only then did she notice the clock on a mantel-piece. *Three o'clock?*

She'd slept the entire day?

She padded from the bed and located the bathroom, and then found the study through another door with no sign of her pack and no trace of anything that had happened last night, the floor cleared of abandoned clothing, the desk restacked with pens and phones and files and so neat that she wondered for a moment if she'd dreamed it all. But no, there was no dreaming the tenderness of muscles rarely used. No dreaming the sense of utter disbelief—wonderment—at what had occurred.

For her hastily concocted plan—a plan made in fury and rage—a plan that in the cold light of day seemed impossible and unimaginable—had come off.

She'd come to Luca Barbarigo not as his victim, but as his seducer. Laying before him her own terms, not being forced blindly to accept his. And she seemed to recall it working. Or so she'd thought before sleep had claimed her. Some seductress she'd turned out to be.

She was still searching when there was a knock on the door, and Luca's manservant swept in a few seconds later, bearing a steaming tray laden with both coffee and tea, together with an assortment of rolls and pastries. If he was unfamiliar with finding women in his master's bedroom, it didn't show.

She clutched the sides of her robe more tightly around her. She needn't have bothered. His eyes avoided landing anywhere near her. She shoved aside the niggling thought that this wasn't the first time, but there was no point dwelling on it. Her deal was for one month. She didn't care who filled his bed all the other nights of the year.

'Would the *signorina* like anything else?' he asked, putting down the tray and moving towards the window. 'Signore Barbarigo said you would be hungry.'

It's so long since I've eaten, she wanted to add. 'That looks perfect,' she said, because the contents of the tray looked more than adequate, but also because clearly somewhere along the line she'd been promoted to something a little higher than something that the cat had dragged in.

'Where is the *signore*—Luca, I mean?' as the man swept rich vermillion curtain after rich vermillion curtain open, splashing light into the room with every broad sweep of his hands.

'Signore Barbarigo is of course, at his offices at the Banca d'Barbarigo.'

'Of course,' she said, but the sound came out wrong. She hadn't meant to sound disappointed. She'd meant to sound relieved. Hadn't she? It wasn't as if she expected him to hang around and wait until she woke up. After all, he'd got what he wanted, hadn't he? And he knew she wasn't going anywhere for at least a month. He knew where to find her when he wanted her.

The thought rankled, even though she'd known what she was letting herself in for.

'If there is nothing else?'

The valet was standing at the door, ready to take his leave. 'Actually there is.' She felt herself colour when she remembered where she'd left them. 'I can't seem to find my clothes.'

'The clothes you were wearing last night?'

And left scattered indecorously across the study floor? He didn't have to finish the sentence so she chose to answer it with another question. 'And my bag. I couldn't find it.'

He showed her into an adjoining dressing room and pushed against a panel in a stuccoed wall that she'd assumed was just a wall, revealing a closet secreted behind. And there, tucked away, was her pack, with yesterday's clothes folded neatly on a shelf. 'Your clothes have been laundered and pressed. Unfortunately the brassiere could not be saved.'

'Never mind,' she said too brightly, secretly mortified as she remembered the snap and tear when Luca had all but wrenched it from her, while Luca's valet seemed not to blink an eyelid at the carnage.

'The rest of your wardrobe should be here shortly.'

She frowned, searching for meaning. 'But I left nothing at my mother's.'

'The *signore* has organised a delivery for you. I am expecting it at any time.'

A delivery? To replace one plain old bra that had seen better days? He needn't have bothered, she thought, rummaging in her pack after the valet had departed. It wasn't as if she travelled without a spare.

Half an hour later she emerged from the bathroom wearing a floral miniskirt that she loved for the way it flirted around her legs and a cool knitted top and found the delivery man had been. Or men, plural, because it must have taken an entire team to cart the lot filling the dressing room wardrobe.

A veritable boutique was waiting for her, dresses of all descriptions, from day dresses to cocktail dresses to ball gowns. She flicked through the rack, many of the items still in transparent protective sleeves, along with racks of shoes—one pair for every outfit, by the look of it—and the drawers filled with lingerie of every imaginable colour.

And not a T-shirt bra in sight.

So much for imagining Luca wanted to replace her bra. He wanted to replace her entire wardrobe. She almost laughed. Almost. Because it was ridiculous.

Not to mention unnecessary.

More than that. It was downright insulting.

She pulled open the bedroom door and called for the valet. Who the hell did Luca Barbarigo think he was?

She was writing an email to her father on her clunky old laptop, pounding at the space bar that only worked when it wanted to, when the double doors to the living room opened. She didn't have to turn her head to know it was Luca. The way her heart jumped and her skin prickled was enough to tell her that. And the way heated memories of last night and a certain desk jumped to centre stage in her mind, she was grateful to have something to focus on so she didn't have to look at him until she'd wiped all trace of those pictures from her eyes. She banged her thumb once again on the space bar, trying to appear unmoved, while feeling the weight of his gaze on her back.

'What are you wearing?'

'I'm trying to get this space bar to work. It sticks all the time.' She pounded on the key again, hoping it covered the thump of her heart and this time it worked and she managed to rattle off another few words before she noticed her fingers were on the wrong keys and she'd written nonsense.

'No. Not, what are you doing. What are you *wearing*?'

The correction took her by surprise. She forgot the email and looked down at her simple outfit and then around at him. She almost wished she hadn't. The dark business suit and snowy white shirt made him look powerful. The five o'clock shadow darkening his olive skin turned that power into danger. Or was that just the way his eyes narrowed as they assessed her? She might just as well be a butterfly pinned in a display cabinet, being examined for the colour of its wings. Being found wanting.

'Just a skirt and top.' And she half wondered whether he was still seeing her in those jeans, as she edged them down over her hips. Had he been expecting to find her wearing them again? Had he been hoping for a repeat performance? She shivered in anticipation—suddenly half hoping... 'Why do you ask?'

'What happened to the clothes I ordered? Did they not arrive?'

Oh. She'd forgotten the clothes. She swivelled out of her chair and stood, keeping hold of the desk behind her, solid and strong. Sitting down he loomed too tall and imposing, but standing up wasn't as easy as it looked. Not when it looked as if the Furies were about to descend upon her. 'They came.'

'Then why aren't you wearing something from that collection?'

She hitched up her chin. 'How do you know I'm not?'

He snorted. 'Believe me, Valentina, it shows.'

'So what's wrong with what I'm wearing, anyway?'

'Nothing, if you want to look like a backpacker. Go and get changed.'

'Excuse me? Since when did you tell me what to wear?'

'Ever since you agreed to this deal.'

'I never—'

'You made your conditions known last night, if I recall rightly. I remember nothing about choosing what you wear being one of them. In which case…'

'You can't make me—'

'Can't I? I have a dinner reservation in one hour. At one of the most exclusive restaurants in Venice. Do you expect to accompany me wearing those rags?'

'How dare you?' They weren't rags to her. Maybe nothing in her wardrobe cost more than fifty dollars, maybe they weren't weighed down in designer labels, but they were hardly rags. She bundled up her outrage and fired it straight back. 'Anyway, those clothes you had delivered…'

'What about them?'

She allowed herself a smile. 'I sent them back.'

'You *what*?'

'You heard me. I sent them back. I didn't ask for them, I didn't want them, so I told Aldo to send them back.'

Luca stormed to the door. 'Aldo!' he yelled, his booming voice echoing around the palazzo, before turning around and striding across the room, eating up the length of it in long powerful strides, wheeling around when he reached the end. 'I can't believe you would do such a stupid thing.'

'And I can't believe you would order clothes for me like I was some kind of doll you want to dress up and play with!'

He stopped right in front of her. 'You will be seen on my arm. You will look the part.'

'As your strumpet, you mean. As your whore!'

'I didn't see you complaining last night when you

agreed to this deal. You seemed quite willing to spread your legs for me then.'

The crack of her palm against his cheek filled the room, the resultant sting on her hand a mere shadow of what he must be feeling.

He rubbed his face, his cheek blooming dark beneath his hand. 'You seem to have an unfortunate habit of slapping me, Valentina.'

'What a coincidence. You seem to have an unfortunate habit of provoking me.'

'By calling a spade a spade? Or by buying you clothes and insisting you wear them? Most women would not object. Most women would be delighted.'

'I'm not most women and I am not your whore. And I agreed to share your bed, yes. But that doesn't mean I'm happy to be paraded on your arm like some kind of possession.'

'Did you expect to stay one month chained to my bed? While I must admit the idea appeals on some primitive level, given I have your agreement to this arrangement, it seems such drastic measures will not be necessary.'

'What a shame,' she snapped. 'I imagine someone like you would get a real kick out of that.'

'I don't know,' he countered. 'Why would I restrict you to my bed when you have already shown such willingness for spontaneity?'

Aldo coughed at the door, signalling his presence, and two heads swivelled simultaneously. Tina wanted to curl up and die while Luca might just as well have been talking about the weather for all the embarrassment he showed. *'Prego,'* said Luca. 'I'm looking for the clothes that were sent, Aldo. The ones Valentina says she had sent back.'

'They are downstairs in the studio. I thought, under the circumstances, it might be wise to wait.'

Tina forgot her embarrassment. 'What? I told you to send them back. You told me you'd take care of it.'

He bowed his head. '*Scusi*. If that is all?'

'No,' Tina said, 'that's not all—'

'What Aldo is saying—' Luca interrupted '—is that I am master of this house. You are a guest and an honoured one, but you would do well to understand that I make the decisions here. Not you.'

He turned to his valet. '*Grazie*, Aldo. Perhaps you might be so good as to select a few outfits for our guest to choose from. It seems designer fashion is not one of her strong points. She may need your assistance.'

'I don't want to go out.'

'Find her something sexy, Aldo,' he said, as if she hadn't spoken. 'Cocktail length would be perfect. High heels. Choose something that shows off her figure. I want every man in that restaurant to be salivating for her and every woman to be hating them for it.'

Aldo bowed and turned, a man on a mission, clearly unsurprised by his master's bizarre request and equally clearly expecting her to follow meekly along now that they had both been given their orders.

She stood her ground. 'And meanwhile,' she said, 'while all these people are busy either drooling or planning to murder their partners, what will you be doing?'

His smile returned, and a flare of something hot and dangerous in his dark eyes sent a bolt of heated anticipation coursing straight through her. 'I'll be imagining bringing you back here and tearing whatever it is you're wearing right off you until you are lying naked and spreadeagle on my bed.'

She shivered at his words, even as his smile widened dangerously. 'And now,' he said, his white teeth almost glinting, 'so will you.'

CHAPTER SEVEN

How was a girl supposed to think of anything after that?

Numbly Tina followed Aldo down the marble staircase, wishing she had a way to prove Luca wrong and wipe that knowing smile from his face, but there was no denying the delicious thrill of anticipation that had accompanied Luca's dark promise. And it was a promise, for it could hardly be called a threat. Not when her blood fizzed at the knowledge that in a few short hours he wanted her back in his bed.

Was it wrong to look forward to sex with a man that you hated, who held you hostage to a debt you hadn't yourself incurred? But maybe that was the wrong question to ask, for that question led to more questions, and all kinds of answers she didn't want to think too much about.

Maybe it was simply better to ask if it was wrong to look forward to an act that you knew would blow your mind and your world apart—an act that your body hungered for on a scale you had never known—an act you had already agreed to undertake for one entire month and so what was the point of asking anyway?

Surely that was the better question.

It felt better, from where she was standing.

'This one,' said Aldo, intruding into her thoughts as he handed her a dress, feverishly intent on his task and already searching for the right accessories as she took the hanger. He soon found what he was looking for and before she knew it she was back in her dressing room and wearing a dress that fitted as if it had been made for her.

And in spite of her protests that she didn't want any of Luca's clothes and her order to send everything back, she adored the dress the moment she slipped it over her head. It felt delicious and sinful and decadent all in one go.

Cocktail length, the cobalt satin dress skimmed her shape without a ridge or seam in evidence beneath— perhaps because she was wearing gossamer-thin silk underwear instead of her usual plain, cotton bras—or perhaps because it was so superbly right for her, the dress nipping in at the waist to make the most of her curves, hugging her shape like a caress.

Aldo had somehow even managed to conjure up earrings to match, sapphires set with diamonds that sparkled when they caught the light, the blue stones echoing the rich colour of her dress. A touch of make-up and a simple uptwist of her hair were all she needed to do herself, and even she was astounded by the results. The rich colour of the dress did something to her eyes, turning amber into gold, although maybe it was the thoughts of what would happen later that seemed to turn them molten.

'You look amazing,' Luca said when she emerged, his rich deep voice working its way down to her bones, and he made her believe it. When she looked into his dark eyes, she felt his desire. When he took her hand to step down into the water taxi, she felt the spark of his need ignite her own.

Mad, she thought, as he finally let her hand go so she could precede him into the interior; she must be mad to feel this schoolgirl breathlessness, this overwhelming sense of anticipation. It was not as if she was going on a date with a man she wanted to be with. It was not as if they hadn't already made love. In fact he was really nothing to her but an obligation—thirty days and nights to spend in his bed—a deal made with the devil.

But knowing that was somehow still not enough to stop the racing of her pulse as he ducked his head and curled his long body onto the leather divan alongside her. Knowing that was no protection against the lure of his signature scent or the sheer magnetism of his body heat. In fact, logic seemed pathetically irrelevant when the devil looked like Luca Barbarigo.

The water taxi cruised slowly down the Grand Canal, past yet more examples of Venice's architectural treasures, and out past the crowded St Mark's Square with its magnificent Doge's Palace and towering Campanile. Across the basin, the church of San Giorgio Maggiore and its belltower stood majestically on their own island.

She'd come here not as a tourist. She'd come to Venice with no thought of sightseeing, but it was impossible not to drink in the sights and be awed by the spectacle.

How could anyone remain unmoved, when the shifting view revealed such a feast for the eyes with every turn? And then Luca turned his head and she caught his profile and the feasting continued.

Such sculpted perfection, she thought, such classical chiselled features. He belonged here in Venice, amongst the beautiful and the magnificent. He was a part of it. And as she drank his dark beauty in, she wondered…

Would their son have grown up to look like him?

Pain, sharp and swift, lanced her heart and so suddenly that she gasped with the intensity of it. A single tear squeezed from each eye and she had to cover her mouth with her hand to prevent her grief escaping via that route.

'What's wrong?' he asked, but all she could do was shake her head as she remembered.

Their tiny son.

Born too early to save. Born too late not to love. A child lost.

A child his father knew nothing about.

'It's nothing,' she lied, knowing that the only good thing she had taken from their baby's premature death was the relief that she would never have to tell him—that it didn't matter because she would never see him again.

But where was that relief now that she was here in Venice, forced to share a month with the father of that child? Where was the certainty now, that what she had decided back then was right?

She'd been a fool to ever believe it would be that easy. For the relief had turned to guilt, certainty had turned to fear, as the secret she had tried to lock away now hung over her like the sword of Damocles.

How could she begin to tell him the truth about their child now? Where would she start?

'It's the wake from the vaporetto,' he said alongside her, misinterpreting her distress. 'We're over it now.'

She nodded and smiled thinly, and wondered if she ever would be.

The water taxi berthed a few minutes later down a side canal at a plushly canopied hotel landing.

'Feeling better?' he asked, as he handed her out of the taxi.

'Yes.' And she was, if only because she was surprised by his concern. It wasn't one of the things she associated with the man. Arrogance was a given. Lust she expected. But concern hadn't figured on her list of Luca's character traits. Then again, maybe he was just worried that his playmate might be too ill to play games tonight. And that sounded so fitting that she even managed to dredge up a smile. 'Much better, thank you.'

Through an elegant arched doorway and the hotel lobby opened up like an Aladdin's Cave. Ceilings soared, magnificently decorated with gold leaf, while pink marble columns stretched high to reach them and a wide red carpeted staircase wound around the walls on its way heavenwards.

'It's stunning,' she said.

'You are.' And when she turned to look at him, he simply gestured around. 'Every head is turned your way. Hadn't you noticed?'

No. 'If they are, it's because I'm with you.'

'They're all wondering who you are, it's true,' he told her as he led her towards the magnificent staircase, 'but every woman in this hotel wishes she looked like you.'

'It's the dress,' she countered, needing to change the subject, before she started believing him. 'However did you know what size to have delivered?'

'Wouldn't you expect a man like me to know what size his lover wears?'

She shivered. His lover? That seemed too personal. Too intimate. Theirs was a business arrangement. A deal. So she schooled her features, aiming for cool and unaffected and definitely uncaring. 'Clearly you've had plenty of practice to be so good at it.'

'Clearly.' His smile widened. 'Does that bother you?'

'Why should it? I don't care who you sleep with. I don't want to know.'

'Of course,' he said. 'Although perhaps I am not so expert as you would like to believe. Aldo found your clothes. The tags were still readable apparently. But only just.'

Another reminder of her wanton behaviour. Yet another reminder of the age of her clothes. And she had no comeback either, other than to blush. So she concentrated on the stairs beneath her feet and just hoped her face didn't clash with her dress.

The restaurant ran the length of the building, half enclosed, half terrace, all understated elegance with red upholstery and cream linen tablecloths, with touches of gilt for highlights around artfully placed mirrors. Heads turned as they passed, men greeted Luca like an old friend, women preened for him and stared openly and questioningly at her. He swept through the room like a rolling wave, refusing to be distracted for longer than a second, even when it was clear that he was being welcomed to share someone's table for the evening.

Clearly Luca had other plans.

Through wide glass doors they were led onto the broad terrace, where Luca's table stood waiting for them at the far corner, boasting uninterrupted views over the San Marco Basin and the Gulf of Venice. Below them tourists paraded along the Riva degli Shiavoni enjoying the balmy September evening while water craft darted across the basin lit up like fireflies.

Luca sat back in his seat and smiled. The views from the terrace were sublime, it was true, but then his view was even better. He hadn't lied. She looked amazing tonight. There was something about the colour of her cat-like eyes. And there was something about the colour of that dress, the way the shadows danced across it in the light whenever she moved. His fingers envied those shifting shadows and itched to dance their own way across her skin. 'Are you hungry?' he asked as they were handed their menus. He was, but what he wanted to feast upon had nothing to do with his stomach.

She'd left him hungering for more last night. He'd imagined a second course before leaving for work, but she'd been so deeply asleep this morning that letting her sleep had seemed the far wiser action. He wanted her wide awake when he made love to her again. And this time he wanted her to last all night.

This night.

The thought was as delicious as anything offered on the menu, which suddenly seemed too long and filled with far too many courses. He lost interest in the choices, returned to watch her instead, enjoying the tilt of her head and the curl of slim fingers angled around her menu.

'A little,' she said, her eyes drifting upwards, widening when they caught him watching her. She swallowed and he watched the slight kick of her chin and the movement down her throat. 'Is there something special you can recommend?'

Plenty. But if she was talking food—he skipped straight to the main courses, already impatient to be home. Surprised a little by how much. 'The monkfish is excellent here, or there is always the rabbit.'

Something flared in her eyes, something challenging, as if she could read his thoughts. 'I think the beef,' she said, and he smiled.

'Excellent choice,' he said, thinking she would need it and ordered for them both.

Sparkling prosecco arrived, poured into glasses spun with gold. 'A toast,' he said, lifting his glass to her. 'To...' She arched one eyebrow, waiting. He smiled, a long, purposeful smile. '...anticipation.'

Her expression gave nothing away. Only her eyes betrayed the fact she felt it too, this thread between them, as fine as that trace of gold spun in their glasses, pulling inexorably tighter. 'To anticipation,' she echoed, a husky quality infusing her voice as she lightly touched her flute to his.

Giddy.

She hadn't even had one sip of the wine and she already felt giddy. But how could she not? The setting was sublime, the view magical and the man opposite was looking at her as if she was more tasty than anything on the menu.

And no matter what she thought of him, she could not help but like the way he looked at her and what it did to her body. She liked this delicious heat simmering under her skin and the way his eyes warmed her from the inside out. She liked the way he seemed impatient to have this meal over with when he had been the one who had insisted on coming out. There was something empowering about his need, something that meant he didn't hold all the cards.

Yes, she had agreed to his deal. She was his for the month, it was true, but did he not realise that by dressing her up and turning her into something worthy of his attention he was handing her a decent measure of his power?

All she had to do was play her part. It wasn't hard. Whatever she thought of Luca Barbarigo and his ruthless determination to get his own way, there was no hardship in anticipating the pleasures of the night to come. Just as there was no hardship in anticipating the pleasures of walking away one short month from now.

Oh yes, she'd drink to anticipation.

'So this is where we make small talk,' Luca said, breaking into her thoughts. 'Where we sit and converse like two civilised people when there is somewhere we would both rather be and something we would both much prefer to be doing.'

There was no need to ask what he would rather be doing, not when his dark eyes were thick with desire. But if he wanted small talk… 'Maybe we could talk about the weather,' she suggested. 'It's a beautiful night.'

'The weather does not interest me.'

'No? Then we could talk about the view. You could point out the places of interest. There seems to be no shortage of those.'

He shook his head. 'I could do that. But that would be dull. We would just be marking time. I would rather talk about you. How long is it since that night? Two years? More?'

That night. What an appropriate way to put it. 'Three years come January.'

'So many.' He took a sip of his wine and sat back, his dark eyes searching hers. 'Which begs the question: what have you been doing all that time?'

Well, now there was a simple question. How to find a simple answer for all she had been doing?

Nursing a bruised ego.

Discovering that she was pregnant.

Grieving the loss of that child.

Hating...

She picked up her water glass, a tumbler that bore the swirling logo of the restaurant, clearly made locally in Murano, and she wondered that, for all her vast collection, her mother had never managed to find anything near as simple or as beautiful. She studied the piece so that she didn't have to look at the man sitting opposite. She stared at it so he wouldn't know how much his questions unsettled her. 'Working on my father's property, mostly.' The mostly was important. She wasn't about to confess that for the first few months she'd been holed up in a friend's one-bedroom flat in Sydney while her life lurched from one turmoil to the next.

'What kind of property? Lily said something about wool?'

She buried the spike of resentment that rose at the mention of Lily and the farm in the same sentence. 'Yes. Sheep and some cropping. Lucerne mainly.' She looked around at their watery world, lined with buildings that went back at least five centuries. Some years the farm didn't see rain, the dams dried up and the sheep turned red with dust. The last drought had lasted so long, some local kids had grown up thinking sheep were supposed to be red. 'It's different from here,' she said, making a massive understatement, 'that's for sure.'

'So you're close to him, then. Your father.'

She shrugged. 'Of course. He was the one who brought me up after Lily walked out.' Whereas Lily, she thought, had been a some time holiday destination—her visit usually coinciding with a wedding. There'd been two more of those before her marriage to Eduardo. One to a Swiss ski school owner. Another to an Argentinian polo player. Neither of them had lasted either.

Funny, she thought, how life ran in circles sometimes.

She'd met Luca at her mother's wedding to Eduardo. By then, aged seventeen, she'd well and truly realised that her mother's life was as empty and pointless as they came. And by then she was hardly going to fall into bed with someone who happened to be Eduardo's nephew, even if he was the most perfect male specimen she had ever laid eyes upon and even if he made no bones about his attraction to her...

Luca snapped a breadstick, jolting her back to the present. 'I have trouble picturing Lily on a farm.'

'They should never have married. I'm sure she imagined she was going to end up some rich farmer's wife and play tennis and drink tea all day.'

'But it didn't turn out that way?'

She shook her head. 'She hated it, apparently—the flies, the heat—she left when I was six months old. Just packed up and left Mitch with a baby and a hole where his heart had been.'

'It seems—' he hesitated a moment, as if searching for the words '—an *unlikely* match. Someone like Lily with someone who works on the land.'

'I think their differences were what attracted them to each other. She was the original English flower, on holidays to visit an old maiden aunt. He was the rugged Australian right down to his leather workman boots and as exotic to her as she was to him. When they met at some charity event in Sydney, it was lust at first sight.' She sighed. 'In normal circumstances it would have run its course and they would have both gone back to their separate worlds but Lily ended up pregnant with me and before you know it they were married. Pointlessly as it turned out.'

'You don't approve?'

'I don't think an unplanned pregnancy is any reason for a marriage! Do you?'

Maybe she'd sounded too strident. Maybe her question had sounded too much like a demand because she needed him to agree with her. But across the table from her, Luca merely shrugged instead of agreeing. 'I am Italian. Family is important to us. Who's to say if it's the right or wrong thing to do?'

'Me,' she said, knowing that if he knew—*if he had only known*—he would think differently. 'I've lived my life knowing their marriage was futile, a disaster from start to finish. I would never do that to a child of mine. I might be Lily's daughter, but I am not Lily!'

'And yet here you are, still picking up after her.'

'I'm not doing this for Lily,' she hissed, with rods of steel underpinning her words, 'but you threatened to bring my father into this and there is no way on this earth I am going to let you suck him into Lily's nightmare. He's worked hard for every cent he has and I won't let him lose any of it on her account!'

She was breathless after her outburst. Breathless and breathing fire, but she was glad too, that he had reminded her of all the reasons she hated him, that he thought he could manufacture the result he wanted by manipulating people and using them for his own ends.

'Do you realise,' Luca asked, leaning forward and cradling his wine glass in his hands, 'how your eyes glow when you are angry? Did you know they burned like flames in a fire?'

She sucked in air, blindsided by the change in topic, but more so because she had expected anger back in return. She had been prepared for Luca to fight, expecting him to fight, if only to defend his low actions. Whereas his calm deliberations and an analysis of her eye colour had knocked the wind from her sails.

'I was angry,' she said, uncomfortable and unnerved that he could find things about her that nobody else had ever told her. Things that she herself didn't know. 'I still am.'

'It's not just when you're angry though,' he continued as their meals arrived, the waiter placing their plates with a flourish before disappearing on a bow. 'They glowed like that last night when you came. I look forward to seeing them burn that way for me again tonight.'

She wasn't sure which way was up after that. The meal passed in a blur, she ate and the beef melted in her mouth, but five minutes after her plate was whisked efficiently away, she couldn't have described how it tasted. Five minutes after he said something, she couldn't have remembered his words. Not when her whole being seemed focused not on the meal, but on the senses he stirred and by the knowledge of what would come afterwards.

Every word he spoke stroked her senses. Every heated look stoked the fire burning deep inside her belly. Every single smile had the ability to worm its way under her skin.

God, but he looked so good when he smiled. Generous lips swept open to reveal white teeth. Not perfect teeth, she noted with some satisfaction, for one eye tooth angled and hugged too close to one of his front teeth to be absolutely perfect. And yet somehow that made him more real than make believe. Somehow that only worked to make him more perfect. And still he looked so good that logic got spun on its head and she might even imagine for one infinitesimal moment that...

But no.

She brought herself up with a thump. Took a drink of *frizzante* water to cool her heated senses. There could be no imagining. Not where Luca Barbarigo was concerned.

But there could be tonight.

An entire month of tonights.

Her body hummed as dessert was short-circuited for coffee.

Anticipation built to fever pitch in her veins, as lingering to enjoy the view was short-circuited for the promise of pleasure.

The boats were still darting across the basin like fireflies; most of the tables around them were still full, when Luca had clearly had enough. 'It's time,' he said throatily, and there seemed nothing left to say when the hunger in his eyes told her all she needed to hear.

He guided her through the restaurant, the touch of his hand at her lower back no more than the graze of his fingertips, and yet every part of her body seemed focused on that spot, as if he'd tied a ribbon between them that kept her close.

And this time Luca all but ignored the greetings that were called out to him. He ignored the eye contact that would ensure recognition and guarantee acknowledgement. He stopped not once in his quest to get her out of the restaurant and down the stairs and into the waiting water taxi.

For me, she told herself. He is avoiding them for me, and that knowledge was as empowering as it was intoxicating.

All the more empowering given he had forgiven a debt—a massive debt—for the pleasure of her company.

And a question that had been niggling away at her wanted answering.

What was this all about?

Why her? Sure, her mother owed him a fortune, but surely there were plenty of women who would be prepared to grace Luca's arm and his bed for however long it took without sacrificing a cent of her mother's debt. Why did he want her? What was his game?

On the taxi he suggested they stand outside and watch the moving light show along the canal, and he took her hand and led her through to the rear deck. 'You're frowning,' he noticed, wrapping his arms around her as she held onto the rail as the taxi moved away from the dock.

She stiffened a little. 'Maybe because I don't understand you.'

She felt him shrug against her back. 'What's so hard to understand?'

'Why you want me.'

'I'm a man who likes women,' he said, peeling her away to spin her around to face him. 'And you are—' his eyes lowered, raking over her, and they might just as well have been raking hot coals over her skin '—unmistakably all woman. Why wouldn't I want you?' He leant down closer, his lips drawing closer, and fear the size of a football kicked off in her gut. She turned her head away.

'Don't do that. Don't kiss me.' People who liked each other kissed. People who were in love.

'Why not?'

Because kisses were dangerous. You could lose yourself in a kiss, and she didn't want to be lost with Luca Barbarigo.

'Because I hate you and I don't think you particularly like me that much. It just seems false.'

'And sex doesn't?'

'Not when it's just sex.'

'Just sex. Is that what you thought we were having last night—just sex?'

'What would you call it?'

'Mind-blowing. Earth-shattering. Maybe even some of the best I've ever had.'

She gasped, her eyes searching his face for laughter, finding no trace. It had been like that for her...but for him? And whether it was the sudden acceleration of the taxi as it joined the main canal, or because she didn't want to prevent it, but this time when his mouth came closer—so close that his lips brushed hers—all the air disappeared from her lungs in a rush of heat, leaving a vacuum that could be filled only by him.

He filled that vacuum with the more solid press of his lips upon hers. He filled it with the taste of him in her mouth.

Coffee and wine and heat combined in a knee-trembling cocktail that threatened to bring her undone, and only his arms around her kept her standing. And as his lips made magic against her mouth, it occurred to her that she'd been right to worry, because a girl could not only get lost, but drown in a kiss like that.

She was already drowning—in sensation. There was nothing between them but silk and cloth and the knowledge that when they came together it would be explosive.

His hands moved over her like both a caress and a demand. His kiss promised her his soul while it wrenched free her own.

She could not afford to let go of her soul.

She turned her head away and pushed against his chest, determined to show him she was unmoved while she still could, before she got lost for ever in his kiss. Before she believed its promise.

He let her go and she spun away, grabbing hold of the railing like a lifeline. 'I wish you hadn't done that,' she hissed.

'Do you?'

'Yes! Because this whole thing still makes no sense, when you could have your pick of any woman in Venice. Any woman anywhere for that matter and without having to blackmail them into the deal.'

'But I didn't want any other woman,' he said, peeling her away from the railing and back in his arms. 'I wanted you and you alone.'

'Lucky me.'

He laughed. 'And would you have come to me if I hadn't blackmailed you into my bed?'

'No,' she said breathlessly, still trying to grapple with the sense of it all. 'I wouldn't have come to you if you were the last man left on earth.'

'Then there you have it,' he said with another of those deadly smiles, his lips pressing to her forehead. 'You gave me no choice. Your not wanting it makes having you all the more satisfying.'

CHAPTER EIGHT

ANGER was good. Anger she could harness and mould and shape into something to sling right back at him. And it would not be simpering submission, but forged in hatred, and it would be slung back at him on her terms.

Anger coloured desire and turned it into a weapon. Anger shaped passion and turned it into something much more dangerous, much more lethal.

So that by the time the water taxi arrived back at the palazzo she didn't feel fearful or afraid or vulnerable.

Instead she felt stronger than she had ever done. She had survived his kiss, she had suffered his taunts, and if he thought he was going to take and take freely of her, he was very much mistaken.

Because she'd make damn sure she would take more than she would give. No, there was nothing to fear from Luca Barbarigo.

Aldo greeted them discreetly at the water door, just as discreetly evaporating as Luca ushered her upstairs, every slight caress of the hand at her back a siren's call to her senses while ratcheting up her simmering resentment; every silken whisper of his presence both a caress and a curse.

And it didn't matter any more that she didn't understand

whatever game Luca was playing. Because she knew what was expected of her as they climbed the stairs.

And what was expected of her was the easy bit.

It was just sex, after all, whatever he wanted her to believe. It wasn't as if she needed to put on a special performance. All she had to do was take off her clothes and get into bed with him. Nothing to it.

Dinner had been interminable. He'd wanted to be seen. He'd planned to give time for his dinner companion to have been photographed and image searched and found to be someone with links to him. But still it had taken too long—far too long when what he most wanted was to have her in his bed. But it had been necessary.

It shouldn't take anyone curious too long to work out.

His uncle's widowed wife's daughter.

She wouldn't be hard to trace, not with today's search technology. Soon there would be articles in newspapers and magazines. Soon the world would know she was living in his palazzo and that they were an item.

A few more outings and the papers would blow it out of all proportion and wedding bells would be predicted and gambled upon.

And she would start believing it herself.

That was when she would be the most vulnerable.

That was when she would be starting to believe the fairy tale. And she would. Even now, for all her protests of hating him, she melted in his arms like wax.

She was his.

She'd made that plain last night with her impromptu striptease, when she'd offered herself to him on his desk. She'd made that plain the way she'd stunned herself with the force of her orgasm.

Soon she would forget all about hating him and start believing in dreams.

And that was when he would unceremoniously dump her.

But that was later.

First there were more carnal pleasures to be enjoyed.

Starting now.

The bedroom lighting was low, the air body temperature, the wide bed turned down on both sides. He smiled as he closed the door to the suite behind him, watching the seductive sway of her hips as she headed across the room, liking the way the dress clung to her curves. He liked her in that dress. It would be such a shame to tear it off.

Then again...

'Where are you going?'

She stopped, looked over her shoulder at him. 'My dressing room. I'm guessing you expect me naked for tonight's performance.'

'What? No impromptu striptease tonight?' he asked, flicking open the top button of his shirt, tugging at his tie. 'No office antics?'

She blinked, golden eyes glinting and hard, watching him remove the cufflinks from his shirtsleeves. She made a move to walk away.

'Come here.'

'I don't take orders from you.'

'Come here,' he repeated, his voice velvet over steel.

'Why? So you can rip this dress off like you would... like the caveman you like to keep dressed up under those fancy Italian suits of yours? Nobody's fooled, Luca, least of all me.'

'Maybe you should come here and find out.'

Fire flared in her eyes, shooting flames straight to his groin.

'I like this dress, I don't want it ruined.'

'I like it too, as it happens. Maybe I just want the pleasure of peeling it from your body.'

'Fine,' she snapped, 'have it your way.' But there was a husky edge to her grudging agreement that signalled she wasn't as in control as she made out, even as she crossed the room and spun around in front of him, presenting her back.

Not so fast, he thought. Instead of reaching for the zip, he put his hands on her shoulders and dipped his mouth to the place where her throat met her shoulder. Her gasp was his reward, her tremor was his vindication.

'You see,' he murmured against her throat, 'even the caveman can play nice.' And she trembled again.

He ran his hands down her arms, taking his time to drink in the feel of her smooth, toned limbs, curling his fingers possessively around hers before starting the long road up. There was plenty to enjoy. There was plenty of time. Last night's lovemaking had been so rushed, he'd missed a lot.

And there was so much more to explore. His fingers found the catch of her zip and he slid it slowly down, letting just one fingertip trail a line down the skin beneath. Another involuntary gasp from his reluctant playmate and the temptation to slide his hands underneath the fabric and ease it over her shoulders and be done with it was almost too much.

Almost.

Instead he spun her around and cradled her jaw in his hands, lifting her face towards his. Her lips were parted, her breathing shallow and fast and her amber eyes swirled with confusion. There was resentment there and heated anger, but there was a flicker of vulnerability too in those amber depths, a flicker that was almost endearing.

'Where is your caveman now, Valentina?' he asked, searching her face, watching her mouth and those lips, parted and panting and just begging to be kissed. He wasn't about to disappoint them. He dipped his head and brushed her lips with his and sighed with the simple, exquisite pleasure.

Just sex, she told herself. It was just sex. His kisses meant nothing, the tenderness meant nothing.

It was just sex.

It meant nothing.

So why did it feel so very good?

His lips moved over hers like a piece of music, a symphony that built and grew and slowed to tender lows and soared to great heights and everywhere in between.

His hands traced a path down her throat. She felt the brush of silken straps over her shoulders and the slip of her dress as it fell to the floor. She felt air that cooled and caressed her naked breasts and turned her nipples even harder.

She felt his hands slide down her bare back and pull her against him.

She felt him, long and hard against her belly. Felt the aching need for him between her thighs and her hand moved of its own volition, unable to resist the temptation to curl her fingers over that rigid column.

Breath hissed through his teeth. He lifted her from the circle of her dress and into his arms, took three long strides and tossed her into the centre of the waiting bed. Chest heaving as if he'd run a marathon, he looked down at her on the bed, eyes raking down over a body clad in nothing but gossamer-thin shreds of silken underwear, a pair of killer heels and a pair of earrings, while his hands were busy pulling off his shirt, his shoes, his trousers.

She could not take her eyes from him, from the lean and

sculpted perfection of his body, from the heart-stopping size of his erection as it sprang free. Looking at him made her blood fizz and her flesh ache.

And then he kneeled alongside her on the bed and slipped off first one shoe and then the other, kissing the soles of her feet, sliding his hands up her legs to catch the scrap of silk that was her underwear, sliding it down and tossing it over his shoulder.

'Did anyone ever tell you,' he said, his voice thick with need as he gazed down upon her naked form, 'that you look amazing in sapphires?'

She was sure she would have remembered if someone had, but right now there was no space for raking up memories, no room for anything that might have happened in the past. This moment was all about what was happening now.

He lowered his head and put his mouth to her breast, drawing it in, rolling his tongue around her nipple while one hand swept down her body from neck to breast to thigh to knee, his long fingers spread wide, missing nothing, leaving no part of her untouched, leaving no part of her to his imagination. Through his scorching touch, he drank her in until she felt more liquid than solid, her senses flowing, eddying.

She shuddered under the heated assault, her senses alive, her need building like a whirlpool; spinning as he rained hot kisses down her belly; spinning as he spread her legs wide and dipped his head between her aching thighs.

The first touch of his tongue was electric, sending her arching against the mattress. She cried out, something incomprehensible—meaningless—other than as a reflection of the exquisite agony of his hot tongue circling her pulsing core, and his clever lips toying with that screamingly tight bud of nerve endings. And all the while the whirlpool built inside her, sucking her deeper, rendering her senseless, her world ever shrinking, until it consisted of nothing more than a spinning sea of sensation.

She was lost in that sea. Cast adrift. And still it wasn't enough. Still she needed more.

'Tell me that you want me,' he murmured, sensing her distress, and she felt his words on her secret flesh.

Her head thrashed on the pillow. 'I hate you.'

He caught her between his lips, suckled harder.

'Tell me that you want me.'

'I want you,' she half cried, half sobbed, the confession wrenched bodily from her as he continued to work magic with his mouth, as the circling storm inside her wound tighter and inexorably tighter like a coiled spring until she would die with it.

'I want you now!'

And his mouth was gone and she had one moment of relief, one moment of loss, before she felt him nudge at her core and drive himself home.

It was the trigger she needed, the trigger that released that achingly tight coiling spring and sent her soaring. She exploded around him as he held her and filled her and completed her.

'You should hate me more often,' he joked as she came down from the high, her body slick and hot and humming in secret places.

'I do,' she said, panting, hating him right now for his ability to do that to her, to turn her incendiary with his clever hands and clever mouth.

'Good,' he said, moving inside her, making her gasp as she realised he was still hard. 'Keep on hating me.'

She could do that. But there was no time to tell him, no time to get her breath back. He leaned back, lifted a lifeless leg and flipped her neatly onto her front before she knew what was happening, all the time still buried deep inside her.

Shock rendered her speechless, not only at his sudden manoeuvre, but at the tightening and dance of muscles she'd thought wasted, muscles that welcomed another chance to play.

Large hands anchored her hips as he drew back and she hated his leaving almost as much as she hated him. *Maybe more.*

He took his own sweet time coming back, inch by excruciating inch until she thought she would go mad with want, until he was seated deep inside her, his thighs pressed hard against hers.

She sighed with the exquisite fullness of it. Oh God, he felt so good this way, so deep.

And when he moved it was even better. He started slowly, inviting her into the rhythm of his dance, taking her with him. His hands grew hungrier, sliding down her spine, curling around a breast, slipping around a thigh to stroke her sensitive nub. He was everywhere around her. He was inside her. He possessed her.

The rhythm built, the pace increased, the slide of flesh against flesh set to the sound of the slap of skin against skin and the feverish need for air as he wound her need around him, tighter and tighter than it had been before and left her teetering on the edge of a precipice.

He paused, leaving her on the brink. She heard a sound like a whimper, needy and desperate, before she realised it had come from her own throat.

And then it was his turn to cry out—a cry of triumph borne of pain—as he thrust one last desperate time and sent her to that place where hate and want coalesced in a fireball that consumed her.

He followed her over the edge, pumping his release and catching her to ride the wave together.

I hate you, she thought, as he collapsed alongside and gathered her close.

I hate you, she thought, as a single tear rolled down her cheek. *I need to be able to hate you.*

But after what they had just shared, the sentiment rang hollow and empty.

CHAPTER NINE

Luca couldn't remember the last time he'd slept late. Not that he hadn't woken earlier. But this morning she'd stirred too and she'd been warm and malleable in his arms and it had been inevitable that they'd made love again.

But then instead of rising like he'd planned, he'd fallen back to sleep. If Aldo hadn't woken him with a subtle knock at the door, he'd still be sleeping.

'What time is it?' he asked as Aldo placed a tray of coffee and rolls on a table. Beside him Valentina stirred, still sprawled on her stomach, her hair in disarray around her head, testament to the riotous night they'd spent rediscovering each other's bodies. How many times had they made love? Was it four? Or five? He'd lost count along with his sleep.

'Ten o'clock,' the valet said in response to a question Luca had forgotten he'd asked. 'I wouldn't have disturbed you but Signore Cressini called and said he needed to talk to you.'

'Matteo called?' he asked, lashing a gown around himself while Aldo opened the curtains.

Aldo nodded. 'He said it was important.'

He left the room as Valentina lifted her head from the pillow and sniffed. 'Mmm, coffee,' she muttered before dropping her head back on the pillow and Luca smiled and reached for the pot, filling them both a cup while he wondered what Matteo wanted.

Mind you, he owed his cousin a call—he had, after all, put paid to the spending habits of his best customer. Matteo, no doubt, wanted an update.

He reached for his phone and immediately thought better of it. He was already late for the office and it wasn't as if there was anything pressing or that there weren't any number of bright young things who wouldn't be happy to cover for him for the day. Besides, right now bright autumn sunshine was flooding the room with light. Late September and the weather was still holding. Any time now the storm clouds of a European winter would come sweeping down from the north, and the heavens would turn grey and dark and open up and turn Venice from a watery wonderland into a rain-lashed water world.

Maybe he should to take a little time out while his guest was here before that happened. A run out to the island of Murano wouldn't take that long. It would make for more photo opportunities of them together for a start. And then afterwards there'd be time for a late lunch and a long afternoon siesta. He might not be Spanish, but there were plenty of reasons to like the practice. Making love in the middle of the day was one of them. Thirty nights could stretch a little that way.

But not if she was going to spend it all sleeping. He pulled off the covers and slapped her bare rump, almost tempted to linger at the sight of her creamy flesh. 'Wake up, Sleeping Beauty. I've got plans for you.'

She didn't exactly jump at his suggestion of visiting Murano and his cousin's glass factory. The glass that formed her mother's addiction was not something that held her fascination—she'd seen enough of it at Lily's palazzo to last a lifetime. And it wasn't as if she needed a reminder of how her mother had been manoeuvred into debt—yes, because she was feeding a compulsion of her own making—but also by probably two of the best in the business.

After all, who else to feed a glass-infatuated woman's habit but a financier who wanted to steal her house out from under her and his cousin, the man who owned the factory and who supplied her fix?

What worried her more, she reflected as she tied back her hair and swiped gloss over her lips, was spending time with Luca—time when they were not making love. It was one thing to share his bed and his nights—that had been the deal she'd made. She just wasn't sure she wanted to share his days. Because she needed time alone. Time to think. Time to regroup.

Time to put into perspective their love-making, to bundle it up in a box marked *meaningless* and shove it under the bed until the next night.

It was harder to do than she'd thought. Harder to separate the passionate Luca from the hated. Harder to hold herself together, even when she was coming apart.

No, she didn't need to be reminded in the daylight hours of the tender caress as he'd stroked her skin or the way he'd turned her molten with one flick of his clever tongue. She needed the lid put on that box and put on firmly and for it to be all tied up tight.

But he'd insisted. Why? To rub her nose deeper in her mother's mess by taking her to the scene of the crime? Surely he knew better now than to think that she cared enough about Lily's foolishness for that.

So he'd insisted and she'd relented. Besides, the weather was sunny, the skies clear blue, and she'd found a gorgeous floral print sundress that was just begging to be worn. Why shouldn't she see something of Venice while she was here?

And if Luca could put up with her daylight company for a few hours, she could hardly confess that she was afraid to do the same. She would just have to work harder to keep a lid on that box.

And when all was said and done, what was she afraid of, anyway? Actually liking the man? There was no chance of that, not after all the things he'd done.

Luca was in his study making calls when she emerged, so she pulled out her laptop and curled into a chair to try to finish the email to her father. He would be wondering what was happening over here and when she was planning on coming home. She was wondering how best to tell him without having him launch himself halfway around the world brandishing a shotgun to save his daughter from the clutches of the evil Luca.

She smiled at the thought as she pounded on the space bar, trying to imagine him in Venice, surrounded by water, practically living on top of the water. He'd taken her to the beach for a holiday once, when she was ten. A wide, sandy beach framed by rocky cliffs and wild waves and an endless, endless sea. He hadn't stopped staring at the sea for days, and when she asked what he was looking for, he'd just shaken his head and muttered, 'All that water.'

A bubble of sadness rose up unbidden to sully the memory and she felt a familiar pang of loss. And then the space bar stuck again and she wrote a line of jibberish and she cursed, distracted. The damn key was getting worse. No question about it.

'You look good enough to eat.'

Her mouth went dry. She swallowed, suddenly reminded of another time, another feast, the lid well and truly ripped from the box.

Was he thinking about last night too?

She took her time closing her laptop, wishing away the burning in her cheeks. She didn't dare meet his eyes. 'I didn't hear you come in.'

'I'm not surprised. Is that a computer or a brick you're banging away on?'

'It's all right,' she said, putting it down, happy to talk about anything other than the reason for her blushing. 'It does the job. Most of the time. It's just seen better days, that's all.'

He came closer, picked it up and tested its weight with one hand before discovering he needed two. 'It's seen better centuries.'

'It's fine,' she said, even though it weighed a ton and was so slow it was good for little more than the occasional email.

He grunted and put it down. 'The driver's here, if you're ready.'

Beyond the crowded canals of Venice, the driver opened up the engines. The sleek timber craft's nose leapt clear of the water, the boat skipping over the surface of the lagoon in a rush of power.

Luca asked her if she wanted to go inside, but it was exhilarating standing at the back of the vessel, the wind tugging at her hair, and she shook her head. Besides, the view outside was just too good. There was something about seeing Venice from the water, buildings standing where by rights there should be none, rising vertically from the lagoon like a mirage.

But the city was real. Just as the man standing at her side was real. Heart-stoppingly, devastatingly real, when she thought about their love-making last night; ruthlessly, unscrupulously real when she remembered why she was here, and if there was a mirage anywhere, it was this game they were playing, pretending to be lovers.

He'd told her last night he wanted her so badly that he would use her mother's debts to blackmail her into his bed. Then, with the wick of anticipation already lit and burning down towards their inevitable coupling, it had almost seemed reasonable. Today logic demanded a better explanation. Because she wasn't that special. What was really going on?

He put a lazy arm around her shoulders and she looked up at him. 'Why am I here?' she asked, her words tugged away by the wind. 'The real reason this time.'

His eyes were masked by dark glasses. 'Don't you want to see Murano?'

'No,' she said, not knowing if he had deliberately chosen to misunderstand her question, 'I don't mean that.' But, before she could clarify, he squeezed her shoulders and pointed ahead. 'Look, we're almost there.'

They slowed and landed at a small dock where a man stood waiting for them. He waved as they pulled alongside and she had no doubt who he was. Cousins could be brothers, both lean and long-limbed and good-looking enough for a dozen men. 'Matteo,' called Luca as he bounded onto the dock. The pair embraced before he turned to offer Tina his hand.

'And this,' he said as she joined him on the deck, 'is Valentina Henderson, Lily's daughter.'

Matteo smiled and greeted her like a traditional Italian, a kiss to each cheek before standing back, a wide smile on his handsome face. 'Lily's daughter, yes, I see it, but much more beautiful too. Do you share your mother's passion for our local glass, Valentina?'

'No,' she said, ignoring the compliment and hoping to knock on the head any hope he might hold that he had gained himself a new client. 'It holds no interest for me at all.'

'Valentina has—' Luca looked at her and smiled '—other passions, don't you, Valentina?'

One day she would grow out of blushing, she swore, as she tried to look anywhere but at the two men standing opposite. Maybe just not today.

'Come,' said Matteo, clearly enjoying the joke as he clapped his cousin on the shoulder, 'let's see if we can change that.'

She wasn't about to have her mind changed. Not when she was led into the large warehouse room, warm from the heat of at least four fiery kilns. Men worked there, doing whatever it was they did, but it was the chandeliers she noticed hanging from the warehouse ceiling, magnificently ornate and totally incongruous examples of the glassmakers' craft in the yawning airspace above her, that made up her mind.

So this was where her mother had found her inspiration for her disparate collection.

'If you would excuse me,' Luca said, 'I have to talk with my cousin. Would you mind waiting here for a few minutes? The glassmakers are about to put on a show. You might enjoy it.'

She raised her eyebrows. They did a show? Bring it on, she thought cynically, but still she welcomed this brief respite from Luca's presence. She welcomed the chance to breathe in air not tainted by the scent of him in space he didn't own. So she let herself be led to a small stand of tiered seating where a couple of other family groups were already seated, ready and waiting. There was space in the front row still, and she sat down and almost immediately wished she hadn't.

A toddler was sitting on the floor to her side, his mother

nursing an infant behind him, his father on the other side. The child looked up at Tina as she sat down, all huge eyed, mouth gaping, clearly wondering who she was to be invading their space.

He would be about the right age, she reasoned with a sizzle of recognition, feeling her stomach churn. *Their son would have been about the same age as this child.*

She looked away, thought about leaving, her palms suddenly damp with sweat before his big dark eyes drew her back like a magnet.

Dark eyes. Long lashes.

She had seen her baby's eyes open, and they had been dark too, like this child's. Like his father's.

The boy looked up at his mother, who was still busy tending the baby, before he looked back at her, blinking.

She smiled thinly, trying to will away the churning feeling in her gut, trying not to hurt herself more by thinking about their son growing up. But it was impossible.

She'd read the books, even before he was born. He would be two now. Full of life. Inquisitive. Driven to explore his new world. Sometimes challenging.

This child was no doubt all of those things and more. He was beautiful as he looked at her, his expression filled with question marks, and so distracted that the toy bear in his hands slipped from his grasp to the floor.

Without thinking, she reached down and scooped it up and for a moment, when he realised, he was all at war, mouth open with brimming outrage, little arms pumping fisted hands.

Until she handed back the toy and he looked almost shocked, before his face lit up with a smile as he clutched the teddy to his chest and squeezed it for all it was worth.

And that smile almost broke her heart.

Somehow she managed a tentative smile back, before

she had to wrench her eyes away from the child who reminded her of too much, from the child who was not hers.

From the ache in her womb that would never let her forget.

Tears pricked her eyes as she looked plaintively up at the high ceiling, to where the gaudily coloured chandeliers hung bold and totally shameless, mocking her, and she wished to hell she'd never come.

A collective gasp from the crowd and she turned to see one of the workmen wielding a rod tipped with molten glass dancing at its end. White-hot and fringed with red it glowed, fresh from the fire, stretching down long in its melted state before the artisan used a blunt implement and smacked it short.

The blob seemingly complied, buckling under the commands of a stronger force, melting back into itself.

From then on it was a dance of heat and fire and air, the sand turned molten glass, the rod spun and spun again over rails of steel, cooling the liquid magma until it was cool enough to be tweaked, a tweezer here and there to tug upon the glass and pull a piece outwards, a prod there to push it in, seemingly random.

She watched, but only half-heartedly, determined not to be impressed, finding a welcome distraction when she noticed the craftsman was wearing nothing on his feet. Molten glass and bare feet, she thought with horror, but happy to think of anything that would provide a distraction from the child alongside her, watching now from his father's knees in open-mouthed fascination.

She clasped her hands together tightly on her empty knees.

And then, as she watched, the bare-footed artisan's purpose became clear. A leg, she realised. Two legs, fine and slender. A roundness and then two more legs, with a twist to make a neck before the tweaking continued, the artist's movements now almost frenetic, working the glass before it cooled too much and set before he was finished.

She gasped when she realised. A prancing horse had emerged from the glass, with flowing mane and tail, and mouth open to the air, alive.

With a snap it was free, set down on a table where it stood balanced on its back legs and tail, front hooves proudly held high in the air.

She applauded louder than anyone and, when the glass had cooled, the artisan presented it to her.

'For the beautiful *signorina*,' he said with a bow, and she held the creation still warm in her hands, blinking away tears she hadn't realised she'd shed.

'It's magical,' she said, turning it in her hands, marvelling at the detail—the tiny eyes, the shaped hooves—the glass glinting in the light. 'You are a true artist.'

He bowed and moved away, back to the kiln for his next work of art.

She turned to the family alongside, who were all watching with admiration and held it out to the mother. 'You take it, please,' she said to the startled woman, pressing it into her hand. 'For your son, as a memento of this day.' *For the tiny child who could never receive her gift.*

The woman smiled and thanked her, the husband beamed and the little boy just blinked up at her with those beautiful dark eyes.

She couldn't stay. She fled. She strode away, feigning interest in a cabinet filled with numbered jars of coloured sand, with curled samples of glass hanging from a board, her back to the family, arms wound tight around her belly, trying to quell the pain. Trying not to cry.

'Did you enjoy the demonstration?' she heard Matteo ask. 'Did you like your souvenir?'

She had to take a deep breath before she could turn and face anyone, let alone them. She plastered a smile on her face that she hoped looked halfway to convincing.

'She gave it to the boy,' called the artist before she could say anything, gesturing with a grin towards the family, who were all still gathered around admiring it.

Luca laughed and slapped his cousin on the back. 'I told you she doesn't like glass.'

His cousin shrugged as a woman came running from another room, a large bunch of flowers in her arms that Matteo took from her, thanking her for remembering.

'Thank you for delivering these,' he said, handing Luca the flowers. 'Tell her I will come and see her soon.'

They left then, Matteo kissing her cheeks again as he bade them farewell, before the boat set off, the flowers lying inside on one of the long loungers.

'Who are they for?' she asked, curious, when Luca hadn't spoken for a while.

He looked straight ahead, his jaw grimly set. 'Matteo's mother. It's her birthday today but he has to take his daughter to the hospital for an appointment. He won't have time to visit her.'

'Where does she live?'

'There,' he said, pointing to a walled island she belatedly realised they were heading towards.

She shuddered. 'But surely that's…'

'Yes,' he said grimly. 'Isola di San Michele. The Isle of the Dead.'

CHAPTER TEN

THE brick walls loomed larger the closer they got, dark walls with white detail in which was set a Gothic gateway framing three iron gates.

Behind the walls the heavy green stands of cypress and pine did nothing to dispel the sense of gloom and foreboding.

She shivered.

'You must have been here before,' he said as the boat pulled alongside the landing.

She shook her head. 'No. Never.'

He frowned. 'I remember now. You didn't come to Eduardo's funeral.'

She sensed the note of accusation in his voice. 'I didn't make it in time. My flight had engine trouble and was turned back to Sydney. By the time I arrived, the funeral had already been held and Lily was barely holding herself together. There was no chance to pay my respects.'

He studied her, as if trying to assess if she was speaking the truth. Then he nodded. 'So you can pay your respects now, if you wish. Or you can stay with the boat if you prefer. Some people are not fond of cemeteries.'

'No,' she said, thinking nothing could be more forbidding than those imposing gates. Nothing could be worse than waiting to the accompaniment of the endless slap of water against the boat. 'I want to come, if you don't mind. I liked Eduardo. I'd like to pay my respects.'

Once again he paused, as if testing her words against what he knew of her. Then he gave a careless shrug. 'Your choice.'

Inside the imposing walls she was surprised to find the gloom fall away, replaced by a serenity that came with being in a well-tended garden. The sounds of motors and the chug of passing vaporettos seemed not to permeate the thick walls. Only birdsong and the crunch of gravel underfoot punctuated the silence. Here and there people tended graves, or just sat under the shade of the cypress trees in quiet reflection.

Luca led the way, past rows of neat graves adorned with marble cherubs and angels and freshly cut flowers. Everywhere she looked seemed to be bursting with the colour of fresh flowers.

He carried the bunch in his arms almost reverently. Flowers might soften a man, she thought, but not Luca. They only served to accentuate his overwhelming masculinity. Big hands, she thought, and yet so tender, the way they cradled the flowers.

Like he might cradle a child.

What would have happened had their child lived? If he had not been born too prematurely to be saved? Luca would not have welcomed the news that their one night of passion had ended with more than a face slap and that he was a father, but would he have wanted to meet his child? Would he have cradled him in those big hands as gently as he cradled those flowers and smiled down at him? Could he have loved him?

She dragged in air, shaking her head to escape the thoughts. There was no point in thinking what-ifs. Nothing to be gained but pain layered on pain.

Through different garden rooms they walked, and around them the closely packed lines of graves went on.

'It's quite beautiful,' she said softly, so as not to interrupt the pervasive sense of calm. 'So peaceful and well maintained. More like a garden than a cemetery.'

'Their families look after the graves,' he said, turning down a side path. 'They are all recently deceased. Space is limited, they can only stay here a few years before they are moved on.'

She remembered reading something of the sort. Probably around the time Eduardo had died. It seemed strange in one way, to disturb the dead and move their remains, but then again, who wouldn't want a chance to rest, at least a while, in such a beautiful setting, with the view of Venice just over the sea through the large iron gates?

'Matteo's mother died recently then?'

'Yes, two years ago, although space is not an issue for my family,' he continued, leading her towards a collection of small neoclassical buildings. 'The Barbarigo family has had a crypt here since Napoleonic times when the cemetery was created.'

Of marble the colour of pristine white sheep's wool, the crypt stood amongst others, but apart, more the size of a tiny chapel, she felt, no doubt demonstrating the power and wealth of his family through the centuries. Two praying angels, serene and unblinking, overlooked the gated entry, as if watching over those in their care, guarding who went in and who came out. Tiny pencil pines grew either side of the door, softening the look of the solid stone.

She took the flowers for him while he found the key and turned the lock. The door creaked open and cool air rushed out to meet them. He lit a candle either side of the door that flickered and spun golden light into the dark interior and took the flowers from her. And then he bowed his head for a moment before stepping inside.

She waited outside while he said some words in Italian, low and fast, she heard Matteo's name and she knew he was talking to his mother, passing on his cousin's message.

So true to his word.

So honourable.

So...*unexpected.*

She didn't want to hear any more. She breathed in deep and moved away, faintly disturbed that it should bother her.

It was peaceful and quiet in the gardens, dappled sunlight filtering through the trees, leaves whispering on the light breeze—so serene and unpopulated when compared to the crowded Centro, and she thought what an amazing place Venice was, to have so many unexpected facets, so many hidden treasures in such a tiny area.

She found another treasure amongst the trees—a gravestone she'd happened upon with a sculpture of a child climbing a stairway to heaven, fresh flowers tied onto his hand, an offering to the angel smiling down on him, waiting patiently for him at the top. She knelt down and touched the cool stone, feeling tears welling in her eyes for yet another lost child.

'Would you like to pay your respects now?'

She blinked and turned, wiping a stray tear from her cheek, avoiding the questions in his eyes. 'Of course.'

She followed him into the tiny room, the walls filled with plaques and prayers to those buried here over the years.

'So many,' she said, struck by the number of name plates. Flowers adorned a stone on one side—Matteo's mother, she reasoned.

'Eduardo is here,' he said, pointing to a stone on the other wall. 'His first wife, Agnetha, alongside.'

She moved closer in the tiny space, Luca using up so much of it, and wishing she had stopped to buy a posy of flowers to leave in the holder attached to the stone.

'I'll leave you to it,' he said, and moved to go past her. She stepped closer to the wall to let him, and it was then she noticed the names on the wall alongside. 'Your grandparents?' she asked and he stopped.

'My parents,' he said, stony-faced, pointing to a spot lower down on the wall. 'My grandparents are in the row below.'

He turned and left her standing there watching his retreating back. His parents? She looked again at the plaques, saw the dates and realised they'd died on the same day as each other nearly thirty years before.

Luca must have been no more than a few years old…

He was cold and distant when she emerged a few minutes later, his sunglasses firmly on, hiding his eyes. 'Ready to go?' he said, already shutting the door behind her, key to the lock.

'Luca,' she said, putting a hand to his arm, feeling his corded strength beneath the fine fabric of his shirt. 'I'm sorry, I had no idea that you'd lost both your parents.'

'It's not your fault,' he snapped.

'But you must have been so young. I feel your grief.'

He pulled his arm away. 'You feel my *what*? What do you know of my grief?'

The pain of loss sliced through her, sharp and deep as he walked away. 'I know loss. I know how it feels to lose someone you love.'

More than you will ever know.

'Good for you,' he said, and headed back towards the boat.

* * *

She found a box waiting for her on their return, on the table next to the bed. 'What's this?' she asked. 'I didn't order anything.'

'Open it up and find out,' he snapped, before disappearing into the bathroom, the first words he'd spoken since the cemetery. His silence hadn't bothered her during the journey home. Instead she'd welcomed it. It restored him to the role of villain. It balanced any glimpse of tenderness he might have shown—the reverent way he'd carried the flowers for his aunt—the quiet respect he'd shown when he'd entered the crypt.

It helped her forget how good he could make her feel in those moments where she could put aside thoughts that this was all a pretence, all a hoax.

And she didn't need to find things to like about him. She liked him being cold and hard and unapproachable and totally unforgivable.

It was better that way, she reasoned, as she tackled the box, looking for a way in.

Easier.

Necessary.

She found the end of one tape, ripping it from the seam of the box. Found another and swiped it off, opening a flap and then another layer of packing.

No!

Luca returned, his tie removed, his shirt half unbuttoned, exposing a glimpse of perfect chest. She tried not to look and failed miserably as he kicked off his shoes. And then she remembered the box.

'Where did this come from?'

He shrugged, and pulled his shirt off over his shoulders. 'You needed a new computer.'

'My computer is fine!'

'Your computer is a dinosaur.'

'You're a dinosaur!'

He paused, halfway to tugging off his trousers, and in spite of herself, she couldn't help but feel a primitive surge of lust sweep through her as she considered all the reasons he might be undressing, her mind lingering longingly on one particular reason... 'And there was me thinking you considered me a caveman.'

'Dinosaur. Caveman,' she said, trying not to notice the bulge in his underwear, trying to hide the faltering sound of her voice, 'It's all the same to me. All prehistoric.'

'Surely not the same,' he said with a careless shrug of his shoulders that showed off the skin over the toned muscle of his chest to perfection as he turned towards her. 'I would have thought a dinosaur would be lumbering and slow, and awkward of movement. Whereas a caveman could have more fun, don't you think, clubbing women over the head to drag them back to his cave to have his wicked way with them.'

She swallowed as he reached out a hand and stroked back the hair from her brow, winding a tendril of it around his finger. It was hard to think with a naked man standing in front of her, his proud erection almost reaching out to touch her. The caveman taunting her with his club. Making her hungry for him. 'You're right,' she said. 'You do the caveman thing particularly well.'

He smiled, and tugged on the curl of hair he had wound around his finger and drew her mouth closer to his. 'Surely not the only reason you're here, Valentina? Don't you enjoy being with me?'

'No,' she said, as he tugged on her hair and drew her still closer to his mouth. She held her breath. 'I'm counting down the days until I will be free.'

He smiled as if he didn't believe a word of it. 'In which

case,' he said, 'I'd better make the most of the days that are left.'

He pulled her face to his, his lips meshing with hers, insistent but still coaxing, inviting. And when he finally took his mouth away and she breathed in again it was to have her whole body infused with his scent and his taste.

He sighed. 'I'm sensing a problem here.'

It was impossible to make sense of his statement through the thick fog of desire clouding her brain. She licked her lips, tasting him on her tongue. 'What problem?'

He put a hand to her breast, cupped the aching weight of her through her dress. 'You're wearing far too many clothes.'

And she almost sighed with relief as she gave herself up into his kiss. Of all the problems in her life right now, an excess of clothes was one problem she could fix.

She'd imagined he wanted quick sex, fast and hot and furious. What he did was make love to her as if she were as fragile as that tiny glass horse.

His hands were slow and hot, his mouth scorchingly tender, his tongue an instrument of exquisite torture, and with all these things he spun a web of silken arousal around her, so that when she came, it wasn't wrenched from her or like being caught in the maelstrom of a storm, but almost like an admission. A confession. A giving up of herself to him.

She lay there panting, eyes open and afraid, staring at the ceiling.

Because sex was one thing. She could handle sex. Rationalise it. Treat it as a currency if she must. And she could stick it in that imaginary box under the bed in the cold light of day and shove the lid on and divorce herself from what was happening.

But giving herself up to him, losing herself in him when

she knew she was going to walk away empty-handed in a few short weeks, that scared her.

It wasn't just the sex that was making her feel this way, she knew. It was Luca himself who was changing. Showing concern when she felt shell-shocked on the boat—buying her a new computer because her old one was decrepit and inefficient. She knew he could afford it a million times over—she knew a few hundred euro would mean nothing to him—but it was the fact he'd even bothered that cut her deepest. For he didn't have to do those things. He didn't even need to find Lily an apartment when she already owed him so much.

Why did he have to appear half human when she wanted him to stay one hundred per cent monster? Why did he make it so hard to keep hating him?

She wanted to hate him.

She had to hate him.

She closed her eyes and sent up a silent entreaty to the gods. Because if she was ever to walk away from here with her head held high and her ego intact, she needed a reason to hate him.

Now, more than ever.

He should take more days off. He lay in bed listening to the rumble of his stomach—he would have to get up and have lunch soon, he supposed, before it turned on him and ate him alive—but there was something so utterly decadent about spending the middle of the day in bed. Especially when you had a good reason not to get out of it.

Like Valentina.

Idly he stroked her hair, listening to her soft breathing as she lay alongside him. He liked that she didn't feel the need to chat incessantly or ask him if it was good for him. What he liked even better was watching her eyes when she tipped over the edge. He shifted one leg, making room. God, but just thinking about it made him hard all over again.

He should do this more often.

Then again he could, at least for the next month. Or what was left of it. Plenty of time yet. Maybe even tomorrow. Thinking of which…

'I'm seeing your mother for lunch tomorrow,' he told her. 'Would you like to come with me?'

He felt her body tense. Wary. 'Why are you seeing my mother?'

'There are some papers to be signed, to finalise the transfer of the properties, the palazzo to me, the apartment to your mother.'

'And you want me there why exactly?' She sat up clutching the sheets to her chest, her golden eyes bright with argument and accusation. 'So you can gloat about how clever you are in front of us both?'

He blinked. Where had that come from? He'd thought her half asleep and she'd come out fighting.

'I thought you might like to see your mother.'

'Like hell, you did.' She clambered from the bed, dragging the bedding with her, uncaring that she was pulling the sheets from him at the same time. He grabbed hold and pulled back and the sheets snapped tight between them, caught in the crossfire, stopping her in her tracks.

She spun around, trapped in the tangle of sheets. 'You've got what you wanted. You've tricked my mother out of her house and why—' she waved her hand around the room '—when you obviously need another house like a hole in the head? You've got a playmate in your bed for a month because it's what *you* wanted and bugger what anyone else wants. What kind of sick person are you that you need to see us together like some kind of weird trophies?'

'I thought you'd like to see your mother,' he said through a jaw so stiff it could have been made with the same Istrian stone that formed the foundations of Venice itself. 'I know I'd give the world to be able to visit mine somewhere other than in a cemetery.'

She seemed to cave in before his eyes, the fight evaporating from her in a heartbeat. 'Luca,' she said softly, making a tiny move closer to the bed.

'Forget it,' he said, throwing off the sheet. 'It was a lousy idea anyway.'

He stormed off to the bathroom. *So much for enjoying a lazy day in bed.*

She didn't see Luca after that and she suspected he'd taken himself back to the office. She couldn't blame him. She'd jumped down his throat at the suggestion of visiting her mother as if it was for his spurious pleasure to have them in one room at the same time. But then, after such tender love-making, after his impromptu gift, the foundations under her seemed to be shifting and she'd needed to see him as the villain. She needed to reclaim the anger she'd felt when she'd marched into his study and practically demanded he make love to her.

Instead she almost felt sorry for the way she'd snapped at him.

She felt as if she'd let him down.

She felt as if she'd let herself down and failed some kind of test.

Crazy.

It wasn't as if she even cared what he thought of her. Her relationship with her mother was her business. He wouldn't know about the way they'd last parted, the argument that had sent her foaming mad to his door to almost dare him to take her. He wouldn't know the fractured history that lay festering like the worst of Venice's rotting piles between them.

But his gut-wrenching admission that he'd adore the opportunity to see his mother if only she were alive...

And regardless of what she thought of Luca, regardless of her justification for acting this way, it shamed her that her relationship with her own mother was so appalling.

Maybe there was just cause given the events of the last few days. But equally maybe, now that the dust had settled on the deal that had been made, perhaps while she was in Venice she should try to heal that rift, even just a little.

She heard her father's words come back to her, the rationale he'd used when she'd tried to wiggle out of coming to Venice in the first place.

'She's still your mum, love...you can't walk away from that.'

She's still your mum.

Maybe her dad was right. Maybe Luca was right. Maybe she should make an effort after all.

While she was still in Venice.

While she was lucky enough to still have a mother.

CHAPTER ELEVEN

'You're sleeping with him, then?'

Carmela had her back to Lily as she poured Tina a cup of coffee and threw her a sympathetic smile. Tina smiled back, appreciating the shared moment, regretting just a little that it had to be with the housekeeper rather than her mother, but then again, so far the visit had been surprisingly pleasant, given all the places it could have gone. They'd talked about the weather, and all about the new apartment Lily had visited just this morning. The biggest surprise had been finding the boxes and tissue paper scattered around the floor and learning that Lily was already sorting through her trinkets and thinking about which pieces to keep and which to sell through consignment with a local gallery owner. Tina's unexpected visit and coffee had come, she'd said, as a welcome respite.

So yes, it was progress of sorts, that Lily was accepting the inevitability of her move, even if there was remarkably little so far in the 'sell' box.

Of course, she was still railing on about the injustice of the whole thing and how could she possibly fit into a 'tiny' six-room apartment? But Tina was still glad she'd come, although she'd always figured she was never going to dodge the bullets for ever.

'It's true, Lily,' she admitted, wondering how many

other daughters were interrogated so openly on who they might be having sex with. But then, what was the point of avoiding the truth? It wasn't as if it was a secret. Everybody in Venice who wanted to know must know. 'I'm sleeping with Luca.'

Her mother sniffed as she sat back in her chair, and it was hard to tell whether she was pleased or disappointed. It was obvious she wasn't surprised. 'So, will it lead anywhere this time, do you think?'

That one was easier to answer. 'No.'

'You seem very sure.'

'I am sure.'

'What about Luca?'

'He's sure too. We're both sure. Can we just leave it at that?'

'Of course,' she said, putting her cup down on its saucer with barely a clink, and Tina hoped that was the full stop on that particular conversation.

But then her mother sighed. 'And yet,' she continued, 'it seems to me that for a man to come back for a second bite of the cherry, there must be something he finds... compelling about a woman. I mean, if a man comes looking for an encore, then surely he must be—'

'—looking for an easy lay. Leave it, Lily. I don't want to hear it. It's not leading anywhere. At the end of the month I walk away. Luca stays here.' She shrugged. 'End of story.'

'Well, it just seems such a waste. I don't know why you're not taking advantage of this arrangement. You could do a lot worse for a husband.'

Tina rubbed her forehead. Why did headaches so often coincide with visits to Lily? 'I'm not actually in the market for a husband.'

'But if something were to happen...'

'Like what? Like a baby, you mean? I'm hardly going

to fall pregnant. Not twice to the same man. I'm not that stupid.'

Her mother shrugged and stood, looking around the room. 'It's lovely you dropped by, but I should do some more sorting, I suppose. Luca is sending an army of men to do the chandeliers, but I don't want them touching my precious ornaments and there's such a lot to do.' She looked up at her daughter, a decided gleam in her eyes. 'I don't suppose you could help?'

Tina blinked, not really surprised that her mother would ask for help, more surprised she wanted her to help with her precious glass. 'Are you sure? I'm hardly going to be able to decide what you want to keep.'

'Oh, I'll decide what to keep,' she said, handing over a bundle of tissue. 'You can wrap.'

Tina smiled in spite of herself, liking her mother's succinct and pointed delineation of their duties.

And because it wasn't as if she didn't have time on her hands and because maybe it would offer them a chance to talk, maybe even to get to know each other a little better than they did, she agreed. 'You're on.'

Two hours later they'd barely made a dent on the collection and there was still precious little in the 'sell' box. Lily gave a sigh of contentment as if she'd just cleared an entire room when all they'd touched was a couple of side tables. 'Well, I think that's more than enough for the day.'

Tina looked around at what was left. At this rate it would take six months to clear the room, and then there was still the rest of the palazzo.

'Oh no,' her mother said, passing an ornament across. 'This one can go.'

Tina took it from her, a strange shivery sensation zipping out along her nerve endings. It was a prancing horse,

just like the one the glassmaker had made at the factory.
'Luca took me to Murano this morning,' she said, holding
the horse up to the light. 'They made one of these there
while we watched.'

'I suspect that's probably where it came from. You
might as well throw that one away. Nobody will buy it.
They're a dime a dozen.'

Tina held the fragile glass horse. Thought of the boy
with big brown eyes. Thought of another child who would
have grown up with horses on the property, who would
have ridden before he could walk, who would never get
the chance to have his own horse.

Her son should have his own horse.

He deserved it.

'Can I have it?'

'Of course you can have it. But I thought you didn't
like glass.'

'Not for me,' she said, already wrapping it carefully in
layers of tissue. 'It's for…a friend.'

Carmela appeared, brandishing a tray with drinks for
them both, and it was only then, thinking about the trip out
to Murano, that she remembered what she had meant to tell
her mother. And what she most wanted to ask. 'Oh, I meant
to say, Luca's cousin asked him to drop off some flowers
on the way home from Murano at Isola di San Michele.
I took the opportunity to pay my respects to Eduardo.'

'Oh poor Eduardo,' Lily said on a sigh, looking wist-
fully out of the window. 'I do wish he hadn't left me like
he did. None of this would be happening if he was still
around.'

'Do you miss him?'

'Of course I do.' Lily sounded almost offended. 'Besides
which, it's such a difficult business trying to find a new
husband at my age. It's not easy when you're over fifty.'

She turned to her daughter. 'And that's why you should take your chances while you have them. You're young and pretty now, but it won't last, let me tell you.'

In spite of herself, Tina smiled. 'The World According to Lily' would make a fabulous book if her mother ever thought to write it. It wouldn't be a thick book, certainly, but part fashion advice, part self-help, with a big dollop of how to marry into money, and all put together by someone who had lived by its principles and—mostly—prospered, it would be a guaranteed bestseller.

But just right now she didn't want her mother's advice. What she wanted was her knowledge to answer a question that had been burning away in the back of her mind ever since her visit to the cemetery island.

'I visited the crypt, of course. I couldn't help but notice Luca's parents were both dead. I had no idea and he didn't seem to want to talk about it. What happened to them?' she ventured cautiously. 'Do you know?'

Lily sipped her gin, looking thoughtful. 'That was way before my time. Must be twenty years ago now. Maybe more. Some kind of boating accident here on the lagoon if I remember rightly. It was the reason Luca came to live with him and Agnetha, of course.'

Tina's ears pricked up. 'He lived with Eduardo? Here?'

'He grew up with them. Of course he lived here, although he'd already moved on by the time we married. I'm sure Eduardo told me. Let me see…' She hesitated a while, blinking into the distance. 'From what I remember him saying, Matteo's family offered to take him in but because Eduardo and Agnetha had no children of their own, it was decided he should go to them.'

Tina drank in the details, holes in her knowledge filling with new information. Holes filling with even more questions.

So this had been his home then.

Where he had lived with his uncle and aunt before his aunt had died and before Lily had come along…

Was that why he seemed to resent Lily so much? Because by marrying Eduardo she had stolen his inheritance out from underneath him?

Was that the reason he was so desperate to get it back?

Where the hell was she?

Luca stood at the balcony overlooking the Grand Canal wondering where she'd disappeared to. Sure, they'd had an argument, but they had a deal. One month she'd agreed to and she'd been the one to set the term. He'd checked her wardrobe. The clothes seemed untouched, her pack still there stowed in one corner. So she hadn't just decided to take advantage of his absence and renege on their deal.

So where the hell was she?

Sightseeing?

Or just blowing off steam?

He looked out over the canal that was the lifeblood of Venice, feeling sick to his stomach and desperately scanning the faces on every passing vaporetto, searching for a glimpse of Australian sunshine in a size-eight package. She was out there somewhere. She had to be.

But where?

It wasn't an excuse for the way he'd behaved, Tina thought, as she hurried along the shadowed *calles*, even if it helped explain his actions. But it still didn't excuse them. To go the lengths he had gone to get back a house simply because in other circumstances it might one day have been his—it made no sense.

Lamps were coming on around her. She looked up at the darkening sky, thinking that she'd stayed much longer at her mother's than she'd intended to, so arriving back at Luca's palazzo much later than she'd expected, the tiny horse tucked safe and sound in a stiff shopping bag Carmela had found for her.

She buzzed the bell on the gate and it clicked open, and it wasn't Aldo who greeted her at the door, but Luca.

She swallowed. After the bitter way they'd parted earlier, she wasn't sure how happy he'd be to see her.

And after what she'd learned about him, she wasn't sure she knew what to say. He saved her from having to decide.

'Have you been shopping?' he asked, looking at the bag in her hand, and after the way they'd parted she couldn't help but notice a tense note in his voice; couldn't help but feel a tinge of resentment that there would be something wrong if she had gone shopping. 'Aldo said you've been gone for hours.'

'No.' She started working herself up into righteous indignation. 'As it happens, I've been helping Lily pack some things. I didn't realise I was expected to ask for permis—'

'You were at your mother's the whole time?'

She blinked up at him. 'Do I know another Lily in Venice?'

He regarded her through eyes half-shuttered, assessing. 'You surprise me, Valentina. You constantly surprise me. You seemed so vehemently opposed to meeting with your mother.'

'I don't know why you should be so surprised,' she said, hitching up her chin as she made a move to walk past him. 'We're practically strangers. You don't know the first thing about me.'

'Don't I?' he asked, lashing out a hand to encircle her wrist, blocking off her path with the subtle shift of his body, a body built for sex, the subtle movement enough to remind her of all the heated moves it was capable of. 'And yet I know how to make the lights in your eyes explode like fireworks. I know how to turn you molten with one flick of my tongue. I know what you like and I'm thinking that's probably slightly more than the first thing about you, wouldn't you agree, Valentina?'

He was so intense. Too intense, the way his words worked in concert with his eyes, getting under her skin and worming their way into her very bones. She could scarcely breathe in his presence, so focused was his gaze upon her, the fingers wrapped around her wrist so tightly clenched.

'You can call me Tina, you know,' she whispered, desperately needing a change of subject, her words almost crackling in the heated air of his proximity. 'You don't have to do the whole Valentina thing every time. Tina works for me just fine.'

He blinked. Slowly. Purposefully. 'Why would I call you something short and sharp, when your full name is so lush and sensual? When your full name holds as many seductive hills and valleys as your perfect body?'

She couldn't answer. There were no words to answer. Not when instead of counteracting his intensity, she had inadvertently ramped it up tenfold.

'No,' he stated, with an air of authority that both infuriated her and rocked her to the soles of her feet as he pulled her close for his kiss, 'Tina does not work for me at all.'

They dined in that night, but only after they'd made love late into the night. She couldn't tell whether it was anger or relief that tinged his love-making but, whatever it was, it gave yet another nuance to the act of sex. Worst of all, it gave her reason for not hating the fact she had to be here.

Later, when still she couldn't sleep worrying about it, she slipped from the bed to stand in the big *salone* and look out through the set of four windows overlooking the Grand Canal, watching the reflection of light onto water.

Watching the seemingly endless activity of a water-borne society while her mind wandered and wondered.

What was happening to her?

She'd spent one night with him three years ago and she hadn't seen him since. After what had happened, she hadn't wanted to see him again. But sex with Luca was like an addiction that had been suppressed, a drug refused, and one taste had sent her back to that feverish place where need was paramount and hunger would not be denied.

And maybe, if she was honest with herself, she hadn't lived those three years at all.

Maybe she'd only existed in the shadow of one perfect night, one perfect night that had all too rapidly turned toxic.

Maybe she'd only barely survived.

Despite her misgivings, they seemed to slip into a routine after that. Tina would go and help her mother sort her belongings in preparation for the upcoming move. Some days Lily would be more receptive to her help than others, but she felt that finally they were building some kind of fragile rapport as they worked room by room through the maze of glass.

She still couldn't forgive her mother entirely for landing her in Luca's bed, but neither could she honestly say she wasn't enjoying the experience—at least a little.

Well, maybe more than just a little.

There was something about being with Luca that made her feel alive and sexy, vibrant and feminine, and all at the same time. It was no hardship to be seen on his arm, to feel the envy from other women, envy she enjoyed all the more because she knew it would be short-lived. It was no hardship to feel his heated glances and know what was on his mind.

And the sex was good too.

Just sex, she'd remind herself, putting the lid back on that imaginary box and tucking it under the bed when Luca went to work in the mornings.

Just sex. And in a few short weeks she would return home and it would all be a distant memory. Why shouldn't she enjoy it while it lasted?

A week after she'd arrived in Venice, she turned up at her mother's house. She heard Lily the moment she entered the rapidly emptying palazzo. The echoing torrent of French coming from upstairs almost had her turning her back and fleeing, until she realised from the few impassioned words she could understand that it wasn't fury her mother was radiating, but delight.

'What's going on?' she asked Carmela, peering suspiciously up the stairs as she peeled off her jacket.

The housekeeper took it to slide over a hanger. 'She's talking to the gallery owner, the one who has agreed to take her glass on consignment. There must be good news.'

Lily came bounding down the stairs a minute later, her eyes bright, looking more like a schoolgirl than a fifty-something woman. But then she'd changed her hair too, Tina realised, so that now it framed her face more softly, stripping years from her face.

'What is it?' Tina asked.

'You'll never guess. Antonio has a contact in London. They're doing a display of Venetian glass and they want everything I can send. Antonio thinks it will make a fortune!'

'Antonio?'

Her mother actually looked coy, her hands tangling in front of her. 'Signore Brunelli, of course, from the gallery handling the sale.'

Tina glanced across at the housekeeper, who gave a

quick nod before bustling back in to pack up the last of the kitchen, and suddenly her mother's change of mood in the last few days made some kind of sense.

And even though that was what her mother did, finding her next partner with unerring precision, Tina couldn't help but smile at seeing her so happy. 'That's great, Lily.'

'That's not all,' her mother continued, her eyes sparkling. 'He wants me to come to London with him. He says I will be the bridge between the Venetian and the British, unifying the collection and giving it purpose. He's taking me to dinner tonight to talk about the details. He thinks we should be there for a month at least.'

She took a deep breath, looking around her as if trying to work out what she'd been up to before the call. 'Well, I guess we should get to work. It will be such a relief when it's all done.'

Relief? The one hundred and eighty degree change in her mother's mood from when she'd first arrived in Venice would be something worth celebrating if only Tina wasn't left with a bad taste in her mouth. Where was her relief? Where was her upside?

She'd been the one to make the sacrifice here—forced to spend a month with a man she hated while her mother not only got on with her life but prospered. Where was the justice?

'Don't you mind about the move any more? When I came here, you were so angry with Luca, with me, with your situation—with everything! How can you be so happy now?'

'Don't you want me to be happy?' There were shades of the Lily of old in her question, shades of indignation that once would have been the spark set to combust into something more.

'Of course I do, Lily. It's just that—' She threw her

hands out wide in frustration. 'It's just that I'm still stuck with Luca while you seem to be getting on with your life now as if this is nothing but a minor inconvenience.'

'Oh, Valentina.' Her mother nodded on a sigh. 'Please don't be angry with me. Sit down a moment.' She pulled her down alongside her on a sofa. 'I have something I should say to you—Carmela will tell me off if I don't.'

She frowned. The idea of Carmela reprimanding her mother was too delicious. 'What is it?'

Lily shook her head and took her daughter's hand. 'I know we haven't always been close, but I do know I treated you appallingly when you arrived. Even before you arrived. But I was so scared,' she implored, 'don't you see? I had nobody else to turn to and Luca was threatening to throw me out onto the streets and I believed him. I had no idea he would come up with the apartment—he never hinted. I believed he would do his worst.'

Tina nodded. 'I know.' And it was good to be reminded of how afraid they'd both been; of how Luca had ruthlessly manipulated them both to get what he wanted. It was such a short time ago and yet just lately it had been so much harder to remember. 'It's okay.'

'No,' she said. 'Don't say anything. This is hard for me and you have to listen. I'm sorry I haven't been a better mother to you. I'm sorry I got you involved in all my mess. But please don't begrudge me this slice of happiness. It's been so long since I felt this way about a man.'

'I'm happy for you, Lily, truly I am. But please be careful. You've only just met the man, surely?'

Her mother smiled and shrugged, looking into the middle distance as if she was seeing something that Tina couldn't. 'Sometimes that's all it takes. Little more than a heartbeat and you know that he's the one.'

'Is that how you felt with Dad, then? And Eduardo and Hans and Henri-Claude?'

Lily dropped her head and sighed. 'No. I'm ashamed to say it's not. I'm not proud of my track record, but this time it's the real thing, Valentina. I know it. And what I want for you is to know this same happiness. Is there no chance that you and Luca—'

Tina stood, unable to sit, needing to move. 'No. None.'

'Are you sure? Has he said nothing about staying?'

'Of course I'm sure, and no he hasn't. Because he won't. He's not a man to change his mind, Lily, and I don't want him to. In fact, I can't wait for this month to be over. I can't wait to get home and see Dad again.'

'Oh. I see. It's a shame, though. Especially after what you've been through, losing his baby and everything. Surely he realises he risks putting you through all that again.'

'He doesn't know!' she said, wishing to God she'd never told her mother about her baby. 'And he won't know. There's no point in him knowing. It's…history.'

'But surely it's his history too.'

'It's too late for that,' she said, running her hands through her hair and pulling her ponytail tight, pulling her fraying thoughts tight with it and plastering a smile on her face that touched nowhere near her heart. 'Now, where do we start today?'

'You didn't have to blackmail me to get my mother out of the palazzo, you know.'

Luca and Tina had made love long into the night and now they lay spooned together in that dreamy place between sex and sleep while their bodies hummed down from the heights of passion.

He pulled her closer and pressed his lips to her shoulder. 'What do you mean?'

'All you had to do was wave that gallery owner, Antonio Brunelli in front of her nose and she would have done anything you wanted in a heartbeat.'

He stilled alongside her. 'Lily and Antonio Brunelli? Is that so?'

'I suspect she already believes herself in love with him. So you see, you could have saved yourself all this trouble if you'd just introduced her to Antonio in the first place.'

He breathed out on a sigh, warm air fanning her skin. 'I never realised it would be that easy or maybe I would have.'

It irked her that she felt deflated. She shouldn't feel deflated. She hadn't wanted to be here after all. 'So maybe you should have.'

'Ah,' he said softly, cupping one breast so tenderly in his warm hand, 'but then I wouldn't have you.'

She squeezed her eyes shut, trying to sort out the tangle of her thoughts. He meant he wouldn't have her for sex, he meant. Nothing more.

It was ridiculous to imagine he meant any more than that when his intentions had always been so clear from the start.

All the same, she wished she hadn't pushed him. She wished she'd left him saying maybe he wouldn't have bothered. She wished she didn't secretly yearn for things to be different.

And she wished to hell she understood why she wanted them to be so.

CHAPTER TWELVE

TINA checked her watch and pulled her new computer onto her lap. As much as she'd protested when Luca had given it to her, she loved what it could do. Talking face to face with her father for one. It would be around eight p.m. at home now and Mitch would be finished work and hanging around the study waiting for her call. It was good to hear how everything was going on the farm. It grounded her, and made her realise how much a fantasy her life in Venice was.

They talked of the now completed shearing, which had gone better than anticipated and Tina was already calculating what the bales of wool would bring in when she heard it in the background—a female voice.

'Who's there with you, Dad? I didn't know you had company or I wouldn't have called.'

'Oh, it's just Deidre, love. By the way, when are you coming home?'

'Deidre? Deidre Turner, you mean? But surely the shearing's finished. Why's she still there?'

'She's…er…she's helping out with the cooking, just while you're away. Now, when are you coming home?'

'Oh Dad,' she said, distracted by thoughts of Deidre Turner and what might really be going on at home while she was away. Deidre was a widow, she knew, her childhood sweetheart husband of twenty years killed in a tractor accident a few years back. She'd never so much as looked at another man. Or so Tina had thought. But maybe she was looking now.

She smiled as she framed her next question. 'Are you sure you really want me home?' adding before he could answer, 'Don't worry, Dad. There's ages yet. I'll let you know when I've booked.'

'Tina, you've already been away three weeks. If you don't book a flight soon, you won't get one.'

Shock sizzled down her spine.

Three weeks?

That couldn't be right, could it? No. Surely it was more like two?

But when she looked at the calendar she saw he was right. Eight days she had left.

Eight nights.

And then she would be free to leave, her end of the bargain satisfied.

'Tina? You okay?'

She blinked and turned back to her father. 'Sorry, Dad,' she said, shaking her head. 'Of course you're right. I'll book. I'll let you know.'

She ended the call, stunned and bewildered. How could she have so lost track of time? When she'd first arrived in Venice she couldn't wait to get away. But now—when she could count the days and nights remaining on her fingers— now the thought of leaving ripped open a chasm in her gut and left her feeling empty and bereft.

One month she'd agreed to and now that month was nearly up and, as much as she looked forward to seeing her father again, the thought of leaving Venice…

Leaving Luca…

Oh God, no, she thought, don't go there. She'd always

been going to leave. She'd been the one to set that condition and Luca had agreed. He expected her to go. Clearly she was simply getting used to dressing up in beautiful clothes and living as if she belonged here. But she didn't belong here. She didn't belong with Luca. She would book her flight home and think about how good it would be to see her father again. She'd feel better once she'd booked.

She was sure she would.

'I booked my flight home today.'

Luca stilled at the cabinet where he was pouring them both a glass of sparkling prosecco. The pouring stopped. This wasn't how he'd planned tonight to go. The trinket in his pocket weighed heavy like the ball in his gut. 'So when do you go?'

'A week tomorrow. I was lucky enough to get a seat. Flights are pretty fully booked this time of year.'

Lucky.

The word stuck in his throat. Was she in such a goddamned hurry to leave? He'd thought she was enjoying their time together. She'd certainly given him that impression in bed.

And while he'd always planned to dump her, the thought that she might hang around a little longer would have meant putting off the inevitable just that bit longer too.

But now she'd booked, he'd have to bring his plans forward. A shame when she'd provided such a useful distraction from the working day.

He finished pouring his drink and turned around, handing her a glass. 'Very fortunate,' he said, raising his glass to her. 'In which case I propose a toast—to the time we have left. May we use it wisely.'

She blinked up at him as she sipped her wine, her amber eyes surprisingly flat, with less sparkle than the wine in her glass, and he wondered at that. Wondered if she'd been hoping he'd changed his mind and might ask her to stay.

He might have. But not now, not now she'd taken the initiative.

'And we might as well start tonight,' he said, putting down his glass to reach into his pocket. 'I have a surprise for you. Tonight I have tickets to the opera, and I want you to wear this...' From a black velvet box, he extracted the string of amber beads, a large amber pendant in the middle that glinted like gold as he laid it over her hand.

Her eyes grew wide. 'It's beautiful,' she said.

'The colour matches your eyes.' He turned her gently, securing the gems around her throat, turning her back around to see. He nodded. 'Perfect. As soon as I saw them, I knew they would be perfect for you. Here, there are earrings too.'

She cupped them in her hand. 'I'll take good care of them.'

He shrugged, reaching for his wine, wanting to fill this empty hole in his gut with...*something*. 'They are yours. Now, we need to leave in half an hour. It's time to get dressed.'

Luca's unexpected gift had thrown her off balance, the gems sitting fat and heavy upon her neck, weighing her down, anchoring her to a false reality.

Nothing in Venice was real, she decided, as she caught a final glimpse of herself in the floor to ceiling gilt-framed mirror. Nothing was as it seemed.

Least of all her.

In an emerald-coloured gown, the amber necklace warm and golden at her throat, she looked as if she could have stepped out of a fairy tale, a modern day princess about to be swept off to the ball with the charming prince.

As for Luca, just one glance at him in his dark Italian designer suit, all lean, powerful masculinity, waiting for her to take his arm, was enough to make her heart pound.

She'd be gone in a week.

Returned to the dusty sheep and their wide brown land. *Gone.*

Why did that thought set her heart to lurch and her stomach to squeeze tight when home was where her heart was? What was happening to her?

'Ready?' he said, a kernel of concern in his dark eyes, and she smiled up at him tremulously.

'I've never been to the opera before,' she offered by way of explanation. 'Never to a live performance at a real opera house.'

'You've never seen *La Traviata* then?'

She shook her head, never more conscious of their different lives and backgrounds. 'I don't know anything about it.'

'And did you never see the film, *Moulin Rouge*?'

'I saw that, yes.'

'Then you know the story. It was based on the opera.'

'Oh,' she said, remembering, 'Then it's a sad story. It seemed so unfair that Satine should find love when it was already too late, when her time was already up.'

He shrugged, as if it was of no consequence. 'Life doesn't always come with happy endings. Come,' he said, slipping her wrap around her shoulders, 'let's go.'

The entrance to the opera house at the Scuola Grande di San Giovanni Evangelista was set inside a small square, made smaller this night by the glittering array of people who stood sipping prosecco in the evening air. Heads turned as Luca arrived, heads that took her in almost as an afterthought, heads that nodded as if to say, *She's still here then*.

Tina smiled as Luca made his way through the crowd, stopping here and there for a brief word, always accompanied by a swift and certain appraisal of the woman on his arm. It didn't bother her any more. She was getting used to the constant appraisals, the flash of cameras going off around them. She was getting used to seeing the pictures of them turning up in the newspapers attending this function or that restaurant.

What they would say when she was gone didn't matter. Except there was that tiny squeeze of her stomach again at the thought of leaving.

She would miss this fantasy lifestyle, the dressing up, being wined and dined in amazing restaurants in one of the most incredible cities in the world.

But it wasn't just that.

She would miss Luca.

Strange to think that when at first she had been desperate for the month to be over, desperate to get away. But it was true.

She would miss his dark heated gaze. She would miss the warmth of his body next to hers in bed at night, the tender way he cradled her in his arms while he slept, his breathing slow and deep.

She would miss his love-making.

For there was no point pretending it was "just sex" any longer.

No point pretending it was something she could compartmentalize and lock away in a box and shove under the bed. It was too much a part of her now. It had given her too much.

'Just sex' could never feel this good.

He led her inside the building, more than five hundred

years old and showing it, the wide marble steps to the first floor concert hall worn with the feet of the centuries, gathering in this place to listen and enjoy and celebrate music and song.

And art, she realised, looking around her.

The ceiling soared, the height of another two storeys above them, held up by massive columns of marble, the panels of the walls filled with Renaissance art featuring saints and angels and all manner of heavenly scenes, framed in gold.

Here and there the floor dipped a little, rose again as they walked; here and there a corner looked not quite square, a column not quite straight.

Unconsciously she clutched Luca's arm a little tighter as he led her to her seat, fazed by the sensation of the floor shifting beneath her feet, as if the weight of the marble was pushing the building into the marshy ground beneath.

'Is something wrong?' Luca asked beside her, picking up on her unease.

'It is safe, isn't it? The building, I mean.'

He laughed then, a low rumble of pleasure that echoed into her bones. 'The opera house has been here since the thirteenth century. I'm sure it will manage to remain standing a couple more hours.' And at the same time she realised he was laughing at her, he squeezed her hand and drew her chin to his mouth for an unexpected press of his lips. 'Do not be afraid. I assure you it is safe.'

Was it?

Breathless and giddy, she let herself be led to their seats.

Was it simply the ground shifting beneath her feet, or was it something more?

Please, God, let it be nothing more.

Heels clicked on marble floors and then stilled, the hum

of conversation dimming with the lights until finally it was time.

The music started, act one of the famous opera, and in the spacious concert hall the music soared into the heavens, giving life to the angels and the cherubs in the delicate stuccoes, taking the audience on a heavenly journey.

The singers were sublime, their voices filling the air, and it was impossible not to be carried along with the tragic story of Violetta, as she discovered the heroine was called in this original version, and her lovers, warring for the affections of the dying courtesan. And yet, through it all, she had never been more aware of Luca's heated presence at her side, at the touch of his thigh against hers, to the brush of his shoulder against hers.

She wanted to drink in that touch while she still could. She wanted to imprint it on her memory so she could take it out and remember it on the long nights ahead, when she was home and Venice and Luca was a distant memory.

The story built, the young lovers united at last, only to be forced apart by family.

She seemed more acutely aware of Luca than ever. The score was in Italian and, while she caught only a snatched phrase here and there, she understood the passion, she felt the pain and the torment.

How ironic, she thought, that he had brought her here tonight, to hear the story of a fallen woman for whom love was painful and hard won and ultimately futile.

Had he brought her here as some kind of lesson?

That life, as he had told her before they had left the palazzo, did not always have a happy ending?

The third act came to an end. Despite bursts of elation, bursts of happiness, Violetta's death had always been a tragedy waiting to happen.

She felt tears squeeze from her eyes at the finale, wondering why this story affected her so deeply. It was just a story, she told herself, just fiction. It wasn't true.

And yet she felt the tragedy of Violetta's wasted love to her core.

Why?

When in a few days, little more than a week, she would be free to return home.

Free.

There was no chance she would end up like Violetta. She wouldn't let it.

And yet, increasingly, she felt herself tipping, tripping over uneven ground, trying pointlessly to keep her balance and all the while hurtling towards that very same finale.

'What did you think?' he asked her as they rose to their feet, the audience wild, celebrating a magnificent performance. 'Did you understand it?'

And she sniffed through her tears as she nodded and clapped as hard as anyone.

More than you will ever know.

That night sleep eluded her. She lay awake listening to the sound of Luca's steady breathing, the sound of the occasional water craft passing and all overlaid by the tortured ramblings of her own mind.

In the end she gave up on sleep entirely, slipped on the jade silk gown and resumed her vigil at the windows, feeling strangely forlorn and desolate as she stared out over the wide canal, drinking in a view that would all too soon be nothing more than a fond memory.

And even though she tried to tell herself it was the opera that was to blame for her mood, she knew it was more. She knew it came from deep inside herself.

She sighed as the light curtains puffed in the breeze and floated around her. The evenings were distinctly cooler now, clouds more frequent visitors to the skies blocking the moon and sun, the wind picking up and carrying with it the scent of a summer in decline. She stood there at the open windows and drank it all in, building an album in her mind of the scents and sounds and sights that she would be able to pull out and turn the pages of when she was home.

Next week.

Anguish squeezed the air from her lungs.

Suddenly it was all too soon.

She heard a movement behind her. She heard a noise like something tearing and she made to turn her head.

'Don't turn,' he instructed.

'What are you doing?'

'What I knew I had to do when I saw you standing framed in the window,' he said, and something in his voice gave her a primitive thrill, a delicious sense of anticipation that made her turn her face back towards the darkened canal. 'Keep watching the water, and the water craft.'

'As you wish,' she said, a smile curling her lips as she felt the heat at her back as he came close and joined her on the balcony, a smile that turned distinctly to thoughts of sex when she felt him hard and ready between them. She sighed at the feel of him. God, she would miss this. She put a hand to the nearest curtain, meaning to pull it closed.

'Leave it,' he said. 'Leave the curtains. I want your hands on the balcony.'

And with a rush of sizzling realisation, his meaning became crystal clear. 'But we can't…not here…not on the balcony…with the boats.'

He dropped his mouth to the curve of her neck, kissing her skin, his teeth grazing her flesh, stoking a fire that burned much, much lower. 'Yes. Here, on the balcony. With the boats.'

She gasped. 'But—'

'Keep watching,' he said when she tried to turn, to re-
monstrate, but he was right behind her and she was pinned
up against the cool marble balustrade, cool at her front,
hot where he pressed against her back, as another craft
chugged slowly by. 'They can't see us,' he said, as she felt
the slide of her gown up her calves, his fingertips tickling
the sensitive skin at the back of her knees, making her
shiver in her secret pleasure. 'Even if anyone looks, all
they will see will be shadows at a window. One shadow,
where you and I join.'

The craft disappeared, the chug of its engines replaced
by the slap of water against the foundations as air curled
around her legs and his fingers eased the silk of her gown
higher to find the cleft between her legs and slide one
long finger along that sensitive seam, teasing with just
a whisper of a touch, making her nerve endings scream
with impatience.

'You're beautiful,' he whispered against her throat, his
teeth grazing her skin, his finger delving deeper, and it
was all she could do to keep her knees locked in place and
not sag boneless to the balcony floor.

Unfair, she thought on a whimper as she felt herself
being angled over the balustrade, felt the delicious press
of his hardness at her very core, that he could do this to
her, reduce her to a mass of tangled nerve endings that
spoke the same message—need. Pure and simple, unadul-
terated need.

For she needed him inside her just as she needed the
oxygen in her lungs. Needed him inside her and all around
her just as she needed the sun and moon and sky.

He gave her what she needed, pressing into her in one
fluid stroke that filled her in all the places that ached but
one. Because there was no filling the ache in her heart.

For in a few short days she was leaving. And she couldn't bear the thought of it.

Couldn't bear the thought of leaving Luca.

God help me, she thought, as he moved inside her, taking her once again to that amazing place, a tear sliding unbidden down her cheek, but this was more than just need.

I love him.

CHAPTER THIRTEEN

HER period arrived midway through the next day and Tina couldn't suppress a bubble of disappointment. Now there was a way to celebrate their final few days together.

Not.

But there was an upside of course, she reasoned, because at least it meant that this time she wouldn't be going home with any surprises.

And why that thought didn't please her more than it did made no sense at all.

She rested her head against the bathroom mirror, feeling the familiar ache deep inside, a niggling question she'd been avoiding all the time she'd been in Venice now gnawing at her to be noticed.

Should she tell Luca about their lost baby?

It had been so easy to avoid the question at first, when she'd thought she'd never see him again. It had been easy when she'd arrived in Venice, and when mutual resentment and a deal the devil would have been proud of had been the thing that bound them together. It had been so easy to ask herself what would be the point of rehashing the past by telling him? What purpose would it serve? It wasn't as if she owed him after what he had done.

But now, after these last weeks with him, she wondered how long she could avoid telling him—that there was a headstone on a grave in Australia with his child's name on it.

How could she not tell him?

Wouldn't she want to know if their positions were reversed?

Wouldn't she have a right to know?

She peeled herself away from the bathroom mirror and drifted through the bedroom. Strange, she mused, how love could change your view on the world.

Because suddenly there were no more reasons to avoid the truth. She wanted Luca to know everything.

And even though the news would no doubt come as a shock and he would be entitled to be angry at her for not telling him earlier, she didn't want secrets between them.

Not any more.

She'd lived with this secret too long.

As for her love? Well, that would hardly be welcome news either—for had Luca once tried to talk her out of booking her flight home?

That was one secret she could keep.

Besides which, she would have more than enough trouble working out how to tell him the first.

Luca scanned the papers and swore out loud. His assistant came running. 'I thought you said you'd checked these signatures!' he yelled. 'Didn't you notice there was one missing?'

The assistant dithered and flapped and promised to fix whatever was wrong right away and Luca swept his offer aside and snatched up the papers himself. 'I'll do it!' he growled. He could do with a walk. He'd been in a hell of a mood all day and he couldn't really put his finger on why.

Yes, he could!

He didn't want her to damned well go, that was why.

She'd melted into his arms last night on the balcony as if she'd been made of honey, golden and sweet, and he'd never wanted to let her go.

But he had to. He had no choice. There was no other choice.

And in a way he was grateful for his flustered assistant for finding him something to legitimately take his anger out on, because he'd been spoiling for a fight ever since he'd left Valentina this morning.

What better reason? Because without Lily's signature in that spot on that contract, the palazzo was still legally hers, regardless of all the other papers that had been signed and countersigned. Regardless of the fact that his people had been working on the palazzo to shore it up and get it stable before the real work began. And despite the fact that she now owned the apartment lock, stock and barrel.

Maybe it was his fault for taking too much time off lately to spend with Valentina and trusting his staff to do the jobs they should, and that thought didn't make him any happier.

He needed that signature.

Carmela let him into the apartment and showed him to the *salone*, where he paced its length while he waited. He glanced at the caller ID when his cellphone rang and pressed the receive button. 'Matteo. *Sì!*'

He grunted when Matteo complimented him on the photograph of him and Valentina at the opera in the on-line papers this morning. He didn't want to be reminded of Valentina, even if his plan to have their romance followed by the papers and have them openly speculating about the possibilities of a new Barbarigo bride had worked supremely well. 'But that's not why I'm calling,' Matteo continued. 'I was wondering if you and Valentina would come to dinner on Friday evening.'

'*Sì*. I can make it, but Valentina will be gone by then.'

'Gone? Gone where?'

'Home.'

'A shame. So when is she coming back?'

'Never.'

'Why? I like her, very much. It's time you settled down,' Luca. She seems perfect for you.'

Luca laughed. 'Forget it, Matteo, I'm not looking for a wife. Least of all someone like Valentina.' He tried to remember why. Tried to dredge up all the reasons why it had once seemed so true. Tried to bundle them all up into some kind of argument that might convince his cousin. Failed, and changed tack. 'This is sport, nothing more. Rest assured, she won't be in Venice come Friday. I'm making sure of it.'

He heard a polite cough behind him and turned. 'You wanted to see me?' Lily offered, one eyebrow arched, her fingers laced elegantly together in front of her.

He cut the call and slipped his phone into his pocket and pulled out an envelope from another. 'I have some paperwork for you to sign,' he said, wondering how much she'd heard. 'It seems you missed a signature before.'

'I spoke to Valentina yesterday,' she said, ignoring him as he placed the paper down on a nearby desk and held out a pen for her. 'Her flight is on Monday. What exactly is this "sport" you are planning?'

'Who says I was talking about Valentina? Now, if you would just sign here…'

'I heard what you said. What game are you playing, Luca?'

'Just sign the form, Lily.'

'Tell me. Because if you are planning on hurting my daughter…'

'You expect me to believe you, of all people, care? You,

who shipped her out here to bail you out of the mess you'd made of your own life? You, who would sell your daughter to the devil if it profited you?'

'Guilty,' she said, 'on all charges,' surprising him with her easy admission. 'But these last few weeks I've got to know my daughter properly, and I like her. I like her a lot, so much so that I will miss her terribly when she's gone. And I know I have no right to even ask, but I so wish she did not have to go.'

The world had gone mad! Nothing was as he had thought it would be. Nothing was how it should be. Valentina was going. He should feel happy. He would be happy. Just as soon as this black cloud lifted from his shoulders.

But Lily, he'd expected to be happy too—a new house, money, a new man—the Lily he knew should not need her daughter's presence a moment longer. And yet here she was practically despairing that she was leaving.

What the hell was happening?

'Promise me you won't hurt her, Luca,' Lily inserted into the weighted silence. 'Please promise me that.'

And the frustrations of the last twenty-four hours—the news that Valentina was leaving—a night at the opera with a woman who looked like a goddess followed by a night of exquisite love-making—the missed signature—all coalesced to form one molten rage. 'I'm not promising anything!'

'But she doesn't deserve to be hurt. She's done nothing—'

'You've got no idea what she did! This is no more than she deserves!'

And her mother grew claws before his eyes. 'Oh, I'd say it's clearly much less than she deserves, after the misery you put her through.'

'What are you talking about? I gave her the best night of her life!'

'You clearly gave her one hell of a lot more than that!'

The thump in his temples thundered out a warning that pieced together in ugly sequence in his brain. 'What do you mean? What are you saying?'

She shook her head, hand over her mouth. 'I'm sorry, I shouldn't have said that. If you don't know, then maybe there's a reason for that.'

A reason for not knowing?

Not knowing *what*?

What the hell had he given her?

Why wouldn't he be told?

Unless...

And as his blood surged loud in his ears, a drum call to war, a drum call to action, the thumping beat of his heart pounded out the only possible answer and he felt sick to his very core.

'Are you saying Valentina was pregnant—pregnant with my child?'

Lily stiffened where she stood, but her eyes were wide and fearful, the fingers of one hand clutching at her throat. 'I didn't tell you that.'

He turned, already on his way out. Already with one mission in mind.

'Luca—wait! Listen to me!'

But there was no waiting. No listening. Because for three weeks he had harboured this woman in his house, treated her like a princess, made love to her like she actually meant something, and all the time she had been harbouring the ugliest of secrets.

Had she been laughing all this time? At him not knowing? At him, thinking he had the upper hand when all the while she'd already exacted her revenge in the worst possible way?

Now it was time to find out the truth.

The truth about what she had done to his child!

CHAPTER FOURTEEN

HE FOUND her curled into a window seat tapping away on the laptop, her hair hanging loose, the ends flicking free around her face, and wearing *gelato*-coloured clothes, looking like innocence personified.

Innocence?

Oh no.

He felt like growling.

Once he might have been taken in. But not now.

Because now he knew better.

She looked up as he approached and an electric smile like he hadn't seen before lit up her face for just a moment, until she blinked and the smile turned to a frown. The laptop got forgotten on a cushion beside her as she sat up. 'What's wrong, Luca? Why are you home so early?'

'All this time...' He dragged in air, needing the time and the space to get the words out in the order he wanted when so many were queued up ready and willing to be fired off. 'All this time, I never imagined you were capable of such a thing.' He shook his head from side to side as he looked at her, seeing a new Valentina where once he had seen a goddess, seeing finally the spiteful, vengeful bitch that she really was. 'When were you planning on telling me? Or was it your dirty little secret?'

The blood drained from her face, guilt leaching her

face. 'Luca?' And from where he was standing the pathetic whimper of his name on her lips sounded like a confession.

He shook his head, blood pounding in his temples, pounding out a call to war, the sound stealing the volume from his voice until his words came out rasping against the air. 'You don't even try to deny it!'

Her hand plastered over her mouth. More denial. *More proof.*

'Luca,' she implored from behind her hand as the tears started to fall. He was unmoved. Of course there would be tears. He'd expected them. Because she had been found out for what she really was.

'How long,' he demanded, 'were you going to keep it a secret?'

'Who told you?' she asked. 'Was it Lily?'

And her words damned her to a hell worse than anything he could devise. He felt sickened by her confession. Sickened that the denial he hadn't realised he'd been secretly hoping for did not materialise.

Sickened that she could have done such a thing.

'Does it matter?' He strode away, unable to look at her for a moment longer, clawing fingers through his hair until his scalp burned with the pain. And still it wasn't enough. Then he spun back. 'Why didn't you tell me?'

She looked as if she'd lost her place in the world.

She looked as if she was wondering what had gone wrong.

She looked as guilty as hell.

'I was going to!'

'Like hell!'

'I was!' And then she was up from the couch, clutching at his arm. 'Luca, you have to believe me, I was going to tell you. I know I hadn't before, but I decided this morning that you should know.'

'This morning! How convenient! What a shame some-one else got there first.' He brushed her hand away. 'I don't want anyone like you touching me. Not after what you've done.'

She blinked up at him, all big golden *fake* eyes. 'But you wouldn't have wanted to know, surely? You wouldn't have wanted to know I was pregnant, not after the way we'd parted.'

He looked down at her with all the hate in the world on his face. 'I might at least have wanted a say in how our baby met its end. Don't you think I was entitled to at least that much?'

Tina stopped and stared, sideswiped by the ugliness of his words. She'd been defending one charge—that she had never told him about their child, a charge she'd known would be difficult enough. But suddenly the argument, like the ground beneath her, had shifted again and Luca was accusing her of...what?

'What are you saying? What exactly are you accusing me of?'

'Don't pretend you don't know! Because you know what you did. You murdered my child!'

The clocks stopped, while the magnitude—the sheer injustice—of his allegation rolled over her like waves upon a beach, dumping her head first into the sand, only to come up barely alive, barely breathing.

'No,' she muttered, from that vague, shell-shocked place she was. 'No, that's not how it was.'

'You as much as admitted it!'

'No! Our baby died.'

'Because you made it happen!'

'No! I did nothing! I know I didn't tell you about our baby, but I did nothing—'

'I don't believe you, Valentina. I wish I did, but you

damned yourself when you pretended you were going to tell me today. You never made any effort to tell me. You were never going to tell me.'

'Luca, listen to me, you've got it all wrong.'

'Have I? I curse myself for taking a woman like you back into my bed, knowing now what you did that first time. Knowing what you might be capable of again.'

'I had a miscarriage! Our baby died and it was nothing to do with me. Why won't you listen to me?'

'A miscarriage? Is that what they call it where you come from?'

'Luca, don't be like this. Please don't be like this. I could never do such a thing!'

But dark eyes bore coldly down upon her, judge, jury and executioner in two deep fathomless holes. 'Then why did you?'

And she knew there was only one card left to play.

'I love you,' she said, hoping to reach some part of him, hoping to appeal to whatever scrap of his heart might hear her pleas. Might believe her.

She didn't know how he would respond. Disbelief. Horror. Indifference. She braced herself for the worst.

But the worst was nothing she could have imagined. He laughed. He threw back his head and laughed, and the sound rang out through the palazzo, filling the high-ceilinged room, reverberating off the walls. A mad sound. A sound that scared her.

'Perfect,' he said, when the fit had passed. 'That's just perfect.'

'Luca? I don't understand. Why is that so funny?'

'Because you were supposed to fall in love with me. Don't you see? That was all part of the plan.'

Ice ran down her spine, turning her rigid. 'Plan? What plan?'

'You still can't work it out? Why do you think I asked you here?'

'To pay off my mother's debt. On my back. In your bed.' The words came out all twisted and tight, but that was how she felt, like a mop squeezed and wrung out and left out to dry in a twisted, tangled mess.

'But it wasn't only her debt,' he said in a half snarl. 'It was your debt too. Because nobody walks out on me. Not the way you did. Not ever.'

'All of this because I slapped you and walked out?' She was incredulous. 'You went to all this trouble to settle the score?'

'Believe me, it was no trouble given Lily's predilection for spending.'

'So why,' she asked, her hands fisting, her throat thick, but damn him to hell and back, she refused to give in to the urge to cry, not before she knew all of the awful truth, 'why did you want me to fall in love with you? Why was that part of your so-called plan?'

'Oh,' he said, 'that's the best bit. 'Because once you fell in love with me, it would make dumping you so much more satisfying.'

'But why, when I was leaving anyway?'

'Do you think I was planning to wait until your flight to cut you loose? Not a chance. And now, after finding out the kind of person you really are, I'm glad to see the back of you.' He dragged in air. 'What a fool I was. To think I let you back into my life after what you'd done. What were you hoping this time? To do it all again? To go home with another child in your belly—another child on whom you could exact your own ugly revenge?'

She blinked against the wall of hatred directed her way, as his words flayed her like no whip ever could. They scored her and stung her and ripped at her psyche.

And there was nothing she could say or do, nothing but feel the weight of her futile love for this man sucking her down into the depths of one of Venice's canals. Knowing there would be no rescue.

'I'll go, Luca. You clearly want me gone and I don't want to stay so I'll pack up and leave now and consider myself duly dumped.'

She walked to the door, holding her head, if not her heart, high. And then she turned. 'There's one more thing I should have told you about our baby. Add it to my list of crimes if you must, I don't care. I named him Leo.'

He wandered the palazzo like a caged lion. He felt like a caged lion. He wandered through his bedroom, he wandered past the windows where they'd made love, he wandered out of his home and out through the *calles* of Venice, past the scaffolding around Eduardo's old palazzo, where the engineers and builders were already hard at work shoring up the foundations, and back again and still he couldn't get her out of his mind.

Still she was gone.

But he'd got what he wanted, hadn't he? He still wanted her gone, given what she had done.

He'd got what he had wanted all along. He'd got rid of her. He'd got even.

So why the hell wasn't he happy now she was gone?

Why was he so miserable now she was gone?

Damn the woman! He'd almost wanted her to stay. He'd almost figured she'd meant something to him before her betrayal. He'd almost factored in a measure of longevity before he'd learned the truth about what she really was. He didn't want to think about the kind of person she really was.

He got back to his study and looked at the file someone had placed on his desk while he'd been away. A file he'd asked for. A file that bore a name tag he wasn't sure he entirely recognised.

Leo Henderson Barbarigo.

Why did that name send shivers down his spine? And then he opened the file and read and realised why he'd felt so sick all this time.

Because it was true that mad in that night of love-making that he and Valentina had conceived a child.

A son.

Because it was true that the child had been lost.

Their son.

But not because Valentina had brought an end to that pregnancy, as he'd so wrongly accused her of.

Valentina had been speaking the truth.

Oh God, what had he done?

Suddenly all the injustice in the world swirled and spun like threads and blame and hope all intermingled and tangled.

And he hoped to God it was not too late to do something to make up for it.

CHAPTER FIFTEEN

LUCA had figured a chartered jet should give him a fighting chance of catching her given a commercial flight's connections along the route. A chartered jet, a fast car and a GPS set for somewhere called Junee, New South Wales—with any luck he'd be right behind her.

So when he arrived at the gate marked 'Magpie Springs' and rattled the car across the cattle grid, he thought he'd done it, that soon he would see her. That soon he would have a chance to make up for it all.

He followed the bumpy dirt track, sheep scattering in his path and increasingly wondering where the hell any house might be and if he'd taken a wrong turn, when he rounded a bend and there was the house, nestled under a stand of old shade trees.

He pulled the BMW to a stop, sending up a cloud of dust that floated on the air. He climbed from the car, never more acutely aware of the expanse of blue sky than at this far-flung end of the world, and an October that felt more like April to him, with its promise of coming heat rather than a final farewell in the sun's rays.

A screen door opened and a man emerged, letting the door slam shut behind him. Tall, rangy and sun-drenched, he stopped to assess the new arrival, his eyes missing nothing. *Her father*, he guessed, and felt himself stand taller under his scrutiny.

'*Signore*—Mr Henderson?'

'Are you that Luca fella my Tina's been talking about?'

He felt an unfamiliar stab of insecurity. *What had she told him?*

'I am he,' he said, introducing himself properly as he held out his hand.

The other man regarded it solemnly for just a moment longer than Luca would have liked, before taking it in his, a work-callused hand, the skin of his forearm darker even than Luca's, but with a distinct line where his tan ended where his shirt sleeve ended between shoulder and elbow.

'I'm here to see Valentina.'

The older man regarded him levelly, giving him the opportunity to find the resemblance, finding it in a place that made the connection unmistakable—in his amber eyes—darker than Valentina's, almost caramel, but her eyes nonetheless.

'Even if I wanted to let you see her,' he started in his lazy drawl, and Luca felt a mental, *male*!, 'she's not here. You've missed her.'

Panic squeezed Luca's lungs. He'd been so desperate to track her home to Australia, he'd never thought for a moment she'd take off for somewhere else. 'Where has she gone?'

Her father thought about that for a moment and Luca felt as if he were being slowly tortured. 'Sydney,' he finally said. 'A couple of hours ago. But she wouldn't tell me where or why. Only that it was important.'

Luca knew where and he had a pretty good idea why.

'I have to find her,' he said, already turning for the car. If she was two hours ahead he could still miss her...

'Before you go...' he heard behind him.

'Yes?'

'Tina was bloody miserable when she came home. I only let her get on that bus because she insisted.' He hesitated a moment there, letting the tension draw out. 'Just don't send her home any more miserable, all right?'

Luca nodded, understanding. There was an implicit threat in his words, a threat that told him that this time was for keeps. 'I can't guarantee anything, but I will do my best.' And then, because he owed it to the man who had been prepared to put his own property on the line to bail out a sinking Lily, even when there was no way he could, 'I love your daughter, Signore Henderson,' he said, astounding himself by the truth of it. 'I want to marry her.'

'Is that so?' her father said, scratching his whiskered chin. 'Then let's hope, if you find her, that that's what she wants too.'

The cemetery sat high on a hill leading down to a cliff top overlooking a cerulean sea that stretched from the horizon and crashed to foaming white on the cliff face below. The waves were wild today, smashing against the rocks and turning to spray that flew high on a wind that gusted and whipped at her hair and clothes.

Tina turned her face into the spray as another wave boomed onto the rocks below, and drank in the scent of air and sea and salt. She'd always loved it here, ever since her father had brought her here as a child for their seaside holiday and he'd wondered at the endless sea while they'd wandered along the cliff-top path.

They'd come across the cemetery back then, wandering its endless pathways and reading the history of the region in its gravestones. Then it had been a fascination, now it was something more than just a cemetery with a view, she thought, reminded of another time, another cemetery, that one with a stunning view of Venice through its tall iron gates.

She wandered along a pathway between old graves with stones leaning at an angle or covered in lichen towards a newer section of the cemetery, where stones were brighter, the flowers fresher.

She found it there and felt the same tug of disbelief— the same pang of pain—she felt whenever she saw it, the simple heart-shaped stone beneath which her tiny child was buried, the simple iron lace-work around the perimeter.

She knelt down to the sound of the cry of gulls and the crash of waves against the cliffs. 'Hello, Leo,' she said softly. 'It's Mummy.' Her voice cracked on the word and she had to stop and take a deep breath before she could continue. 'I've brought you a present.'

Bubble wrap gave way to tissue paper as she carefully unwrapped the tiny gift. 'It's a horse,' she said, holding the glass up to the sunlight to check it for fingerprints. 'All the way from Venice. I saw a man make one from a fistful of sand.'

She placed it softly in the lawn at the base of the simple stone. 'Oh, you should have seen it, Leo, it was magical, the way he turned the rod and shaped the glass. It was so clever, and I thought how much you would have enjoyed it. And I thought how you should have such a horse yourself.'

He watched her from a distance, wanting to call out to her with relief before she disappeared again, but he saw her kneel down and he knew why.

His son's grave.

Something yawned open inside him, a chasm so big and empty he could not contemplate how it could ever be filled.

From his vantage point, he saw her lips move, saw her work something in her hands, saw the glint of sunlight on

glass and felt the hiss of his breath through his teeth—
heard the crunch of gravel underfoot as his feet moved
forward of their own accord.

She heard it too, ignored it for a second and then glanced
his way, glanced again, her eyes widening in shock, her
face bleaching white when she realised who it was.

'Hello, Valentina,' he said, his voice thick with emotion. 'I've come to meet my son.'

She didn't reply, whether from the shock of his sudden
appearance or because there was nothing to say. He looked
down at the stone, at its simple words.

Leo Henderson Barbarigo, it read, together with a date
and, beneath it, the words: *Another angel in heaven.*

And even though he'd known, even though it had made
his job easier to find the grave, it still staggered him. 'You
gave him my name.'

'He's your son too.'

His son.

And he fell to his knees and felt the tears fall for all
that had been lost.

She let him cry. She said nothing, did nothing, but when
finally he looked up, he saw the tracks of her own tears
down her cheeks.

'Why didn't you tell me?' The words were anguished,
wrenched from a place deep inside him, but still loaded
with accusation. 'Why didn't you tell me?'

She didn't flinch from his charges. 'I was going to,'
she said, her voice tight, 'when our child was born. I was
going to let you know you were a father.' Sadly she shook
her head. 'Then there didn't seem any point.' She shrugged
helplessly and he could see her pain in the awkward movement. And in this moment, under the weight of his guilt,
he felt just as awkward.

'In Venice,' he started, 'I said some dreadful things. I accused you of dreadful deeds.'

'It was a shock. You didn't know.'

'Please, Valentina, do not feel you must make excuses for me. I didn't listen. You tried to tell me and I didn't listen. I didn't want to listen. It was unforgivable of me.' He shook his head. 'But now, knowing that he was stolen from us before his time, can you tell me the rest? Can you tell me what happened?'

She blinked and looked heavenwards, swiping at her cheek with the fingers of one hand. 'There's not a lot to tell. Everything was going to plan. Everything was as it should be. But at twenty weeks, the pains started. I thought that it must have been something I'd eaten, some kind of food poisoning, that it would go away. But it got worse and worse and then I started to bleed and I was so afraid. The doctors did everything they could, but our baby was coming and they couldn't stop it.' She squeezed her hands into balls in her lap, squeezed her eyes shut so hard he could feel her pain. 'Nothing they did could stop it.'

'Valentina...'

'And it hurt so much, so much more than it should, for the doctors and midwives there too, because everyone knew there was nothing they could do to save him. He was too early. Too tiny, even though his heart was beating and he was breathing and his eyes blinked open and looked up at me.'

She smiled up at him then, her eyes spilling over with tears. 'He was beautiful, Luca, you should have seen him. His skin was almost translucent, and his tiny hand wrapped around my little finger, trying to hold on.'

Her smile faded. 'But he couldn't hold on. Not for long. And all I could do was cuddle our baby while his breathing slowed and slowed until he took one final, brave little breath...'

Oh God, he thought. Their baby had died in her arms after he had been born.

Oh God.

'Who was with you?' he whispered, thinking it should have been him. 'Your father? Lily? A friend?'

She shook her head and whispered, 'No one.'

And through the rising bubble of injustice he felt at the thought that she had been alone, he thought of the man on the farm who had no idea why his daughter had suddenly rushed off to Sydney barely a moment after she'd arrived. 'Your father didn't know?'

'I couldn't bear to tell him. I was so ashamed when I found out I was pregnant. I couldn't bear to admit that I, the product of a one-night stand, had turned around and made the same mistake my parents had. So I went back to university and hid and pretended it wasn't happening. And afterwards...well, afterwards...I couldn't bear to think about it, let alone tell anyone else.' She looked up at him with plaintive eyes. 'Do you understand? Can you try to understand?'

'You should have told me. I should have been there. You should not have been alone.'

She gave a laugh that sounded more like a hiccup. 'Because you would have so welcomed that call, to tell you I was pregnant, that you would have rushed to be by my side.' She shook her head. 'I don't think so.'

And he hated her words but he knew what she said was true.

'No,' she continued, 'I would have told you. Once the baby was born. But my parents married because of me, and look how that turned out, and I didn't want to be forced into something I didn't want, and I didn't want you to think you were being forced into something you didn't want.'

'You said that,' he said, remembering that night in Venice when she had so vehemently stated that a baby was no reason for marriage. 'So you waited.'

She nodded and swallowed, her chin kicking high into the stiff wind. 'Well, maybe…maybe also in part because I was in no hurry to see you again anyway after the way we had parted. But I knew I would have to tell you once he was born.' She stopped and breathed deep as she looked down at the tiny grave framed in iron lace. 'But when he came too early…when Leo died…I thought that would be the end of it. That there was no point…'

She shook her head, the ends of her hair whipped like a halo around her head as she looked across at him, the pain of loss etched deep in her amber eyes. 'But it wasn't. And I'm sorry you had to find out the way you did. I'm so sorry. Everything I've done seems to have turned out badly.'

'No,' he said with a sigh, gazing down at her while another set of waves crashed into the rocks behind, almost drowning his voice in the roar. 'I believe that's my territory.'

She blinked over watery eyes, confusion warring with the pain of loss.

'Come,' he said, tugging her by her hand to her feet. 'Come and walk with me a while. I need to talk to you and I'm not sure Leo would want to hear it.'

With the merest nod of her head, she let him lead her down through the cemetery, to where the cliff walk widened into a viewing platform that clung to the edge of the world and where the teeming surf smashed against the rocks with a booming roar.

She blinked into the wind, half wondering if she was dreaming, if she'd imagined him here with the power of her grief, but no, just a glance sideways confirmed it was no dream. He stood solid alongside her, his face so stern as he gazed over the edge of the continent, it could have been carved out of the stone wall of the cliffs.

It was good to see him again.

It was good he'd come to meet his son.

It hurt that he hadn't said he'd come to see her but it was good he had come. One final chance to clear the air surrounding their baby's brief existence.

Maybe now they could both move on.

Maybe.

They stood together in a silence of their own thoughts all framed by the roar and crash of water while Luca wondered where to begin. There was so much he had to explain, so much to make up for. The spray was refreshing against his skin, salty like his tears, but cleansing too. Strange he should think that, when he couldn't remember the last time he'd cried.

And with a crunching of gears inside his boarded up heart, he did.

When the news had come of his parents' deaths that foggy night when their water taxi had crashed into a craft with a broken light.

So many years ago and yet the pain felt so raw, unleashed by whatever had unlocked his heart.

Whoever had unlocked his heart.

Valentina.

He watched the waves roll in, in endless repetition. Only to be smashed to pieces against a wall of rock so hard the sea seemed to be fighting a losing battle.

Except it wasn't. Here and there boulders had fallen free, or whole sections of cliff had collapsed into the sea, undercut, worn away and otherwise toppled by the relentless force of the water.

Today he felt like that cliff, the seemingly indestructible stone no match for the constant work of time and tide. No match for a greater force.

He turned to that greater force now, a force that had been able to come back from holding her dying child in her arms to confront that child's father and seemingly accede to his demands, all the time working away on him while he crumbled before her.

And suddenly he knew what he had to say. 'Valentina,' he said, taking her hands in his, cold hands he wanted to hold and warm for ever, 'I have wronged you in so many ways.'

She smiled and he, who deserved no smile and certainly none from this woman, thought his newly exposed heart would break. 'I'm glad you came to see Leo.' He noted that she didn't dispute the fact that he'd wronged her. But there was no disputing it. He knew that now.

'I came to see you too,' he said, and her eyes widened in response, 'to see if you might understand just a little of why I acted as I did, even if those actions are unforgivable. I know I could not hope for your forgiveness, but maybe a little understanding?' He shrugged. 'When I was a child,' he started, 'my parents were both killed in a boating accident. You saw their tombs.' She nodded. 'Eduardo and Agnethe took me in, gave me a home. I went to them with nothing. My father had just invested everything he had in a start-up company he would be a key part in. With his death, it folded and all but a pittance was lost.'

'I understand,' she said. 'Lily told me you had lived with Eduardo as a child. You must have felt that when Eduardo married Lily that you lost your inheritance a second time around. No wonder you wanted the palazzo back so desperately.'

He laughed a little at that. 'Is that what you think? I

think I was too young to worry about any lost fortune back when my parents died. But it would have been useful later. I did worry about Eduardo and the palazzo. He was one of Venice's grand old men, but no businessman, living on his family's reputation while his fortune dwindled.

'I knew as I grew older that the palazzo needed major structural work, but there was never the money and when Agnethe died Eduardo missed her dreadfully and I think he forgot to care.

'I promised him then that I would pay him and Agnethe back for taking me in, by fixing the palazzo and restoring it to its former glory. I studied and I worked day and night to make it happen.'

'And then he went and married Lily.'

He smiled thinly at that. 'You could put it that way. She refused to consider my plans to restore the palazzo, she made short work of the limited funds Eduardo had at his disposal.'

Tina nodded, the strands of her hair catching on her lashes in the wind, and he ached to brush them away, but it was too soon, he knew. It was enough that she let him hold her hands. It was enough that she did not protest at the circles his thumbs made on her skin. 'That does sound like Lily.'

'Once the property was in her name, I tried to buy it. She refused again. But she came to me when she needed more money. It seemed the only way to get her out.'

She took a deep breath. 'I can see it would have been hard to shift her otherwise. Thank you for telling me this, Luca. It does help me understand a little better.'

'It is no excuse for the way I treated you.'

'I guess you were still mad at me for slapping you and walking out.'

'A little,' he admitted, until he saw her face and he

smiled ruefully. 'Maybe more than a little. But I have a confession to make about that time.' His hands squeezed hers, his fingers interlocking with hers. 'You bothered me that night, Valentina. You got under my skin. You were too perfect and you shouldn't have been—you were Lily's daughter after all and I didn't want to like you. I wanted somebody I could walk away from and I knew I couldn't stay away from you, unless you hated me.'

She shook her head, a frown tugging her fair brows together. 'And yet you did hold it against me.' But he took heart that her words weren't angry. Instead they searched for understanding amidst the tangle of revelations, as if she was searching for the one thread that would pull the knots free. He took heart that she was still listening and tried to find her the key.

'Because it suited me to. Don't you see? By blowing it out of proportion, by making it your fault, it gave me an excuse to get you to Venice, and to legitimise it by calling it vengeance. And it was easy to be angry, because I was mad at Lily for letting the house fall into such disrepair, and I hadn't forgotten you, and that made me even madder.

'I am sorry I said what I did. It was designed to drive you away. It was hurtful, just as the words I said before you left Venice were designed to hurt. And why? Because I needed to believe the worst of you, that you had destroyed our child.' He felt her flinch, as if reliving the pain of his accusations but he just squeezed her hands and pressed on. 'I'm so sorry. Because just as it worked that night we spent together, my ugly words worked only too well, and this time drove you from Venice.' He shrugged and looked up the hill towards the grave. 'I guess it is only just that I should be the one who paid some of the cost too, by never knowing of my son's existence until now.'

A wave crashed on the rocks below, sending spray high,

droplets that sparkled like diamonds in the thin sun before spinning into nothingness.

'I can never make up to you all the wrongs I have committed,' he said. 'I'm so sorry.'

For a few moments she said nothing, and he imagined that any time now she would pull her hands from his, thank him for his explanation and justifiably remove herself from his life once again. This time for good.

But her hands somehow remained in his. And then came her tentative question. 'Why did you need to drive me away so very badly?'

He looked into her eyes, those amber pools that he had come to love, along with their owner. 'Because otherwise I would have had to admit the truth. That I love you, Valentina. And I know you will not want to hear this from me—not after all that has happened—all that I have subjected you to. But I had to come and see you. I had to ask if there was any way you could ever forgive me.'

She looked up at him incredulously. 'You love me?'

He wasn't surprised she didn't believe him. It was a miracle she hadn't slapped him again for saying it. 'I do. I'm an idiot and a fool and every type of bastard for the things I've said to you and done to you, but I love you, Valentina, and I cannot bear the thought of you not being part of my life. When you left Venice, you took my heart with you. But I know I am clutching at straws. That you are too good for someone like me. That you deserve better. Much better.'

'You might be right,' she said, fresh tears springing from her eyes, and his freshly opened heart fell to his feet. 'Maybe I do deserve better. But damn you, Luca Barbarigo, it's you who I love. It's you I want to be with.'

Could a man die of happiness? he wondered as he cradled her face in his hands, letting her words seep through his consciousness, all the way through the layers of doubts and impossibilities, all the way through to his heart. 'Valentina,' he whispered, because there was nothing better he could think of to say, not when her lips were calling.

He loved her.

Tina could see it in his eyes, could feel it in his gentle touch. Could feel it in the shimmer of sea salt air between them and in the connection of his heart to hers.

Their lips meshed, the salt of their tears blending with the salt of the sea, and she tasted their shared loss and the heated promise of life and love.

'I love you,' he said. 'Oh God, it's taken too long to realise it, but I love you, Valentina. I know I don't deserve to ask this, but will you do me the honour of becoming my wife?'

His words, his rich voice, vibrated through her senses and her bones and found a joyful answer in her heart, her tears a rapturous celebration. 'Oh, Luca, yes! Yes, I will be your wife.'

He gathered her up and held her tight, so tight as he spun her around in the boom and spray from another crashing wave, that she felt part of him. She was part of him.

And when he put her down on her feet again, it was to look seriously into her eyes. 'Perhaps, after we are married, if you like, then maybe we could try again. For another child. A brother or sister for Leo.'

She shuddered in his arms. 'But what if…' He looked down at her with such an air of hope that it magnified her fear tenfold. 'I'm afraid, Luca,' she said, looking up the hill towards the plot where their one child already lay. 'Nobody knows why it happened and I don't think I could bear it if it happened again. I don't think I could come back from that.'

'No.' He rocked her then, wanting to soothe away her fears. 'No. It won't happen again.'

'How do you know that?'

'I don't. I wish to God I could promise you that it won't happen again, but I can't. But what I can promise you is this, that if it did happen again, if life chose to be so cruel again, that this time you would not be alone, that I will be there alongside you, holding your hand. And this time your loss would be my loss. Your tears would be my tears. I will never let you go through something like that alone again.'

The sheer power of his words gave her the confidence to believe him. The emotion behind his words gave her the courage to want to try.

'Perhaps,' she said plaintively, lifting her face to his, 'when we are married...'

And he growled at the courage of this woman and he pulled her close and kissed her again and held her tight, against the wind tugging at their clothing and the spray from the crashing waves—against the worst that life could throw at them.

And knew that whatever came their way, their love would endure for ever.

EPILOGUE

THEY were married in Venice, the wedding gondola decked out in black and crimson with highlights of gold. The cushions were made of silk and satin, the upholstery plush velvet. And while the gondolier himself looked resplendent in crisp attire, propelling the vessel with an effortless looking rhythm, it was to the bride sitting beaming alongside her proud father that every eye was drawn.

It was the bride from whom Luca couldn't tear his eyes.

His bride.

Valentina.

She stepped from the vessel in a gown befitting the goddess that she was, honey gold in colour, a timeless one-shouldered design, skimming her breasts before draping softly to the ground, both classic and feminine, the necklace of amber beads Luca had given her at her throat.

They married in the Scuola Grande di San Giovanni Evangelista, the opera house where they had seen *La Traviata*, the night Tina had felt the ground move beneath her feet and realised she had fallen in love with Luca. Her father gave her away, passing her hand to Luca's with a grudging smile, before taking his place in the front and curling his fingers possessively around those of his guest, none other than Deidre Turner. Tina smiled, happy for her father, happier for herself when the service began, the ceremony that would make her Luca's bride.

And if the wedding was magnificent, the reception was a celebration, held in the refurbished palazzo where Luca had grown up. Now restored to its former glory, its piers strengthened and renewed, its façade was as richly decorated as it once had been, befitting one of the oldest families in Venice.

'It's such a beautiful wedding,' said Lily to her daughter with a wistful sigh as the pair touched up their lipstick in the powder room together. 'But then you look beautiful, Valentina. I don't think I've ever seen such a radiant bride.'

Tina hadn't been able to stop smiling all day, but now her smile widened as she turned towards her mother. 'I love him, Lily. And I'm so very happy.'

Her mother took her daughter's hands in hers. 'It shows. I'm so proud of you, Valentina. You've grown into a wonderful woman, and I'm just sorry for all the grief I've caused you along the way. But I promise I will be a better mother to you—I am the same person, but I am trying to change, I am trying to be better.'

'Oh, Lily.' Tears sprang to her eyes and she blinked them away as Lily swung into action and passed her tissues before she tested the limits of her waterproof mascara.

'And now I've made you cry! *Sacre bleu!* That will not do. So let me tell you something instead to make you smile—Antonio was so moved, he proposed to me right after the ceremony.'

Tina gasped, her tears staunched by the surprise announcement. 'And?'

'I said yes, of course! I can't hope to change everything about me at once.' And then they were both reaching for the tissues, they were laughing so hard.

'Lily's agreed to marry Antonio,' she told Luca, as he

spun her around the ballroom's centuries-old terrazzo floor.

Luca smiled down at her. 'Do you think Mitch will agree to give her away too?'

'I don't know,' she reflected, as she watched her father spin past them with Deidre, their gazes well and truly locked. 'There's a good chance he might be otherwise *engaged*.'

Luca laughed, and hugged her closer. 'You don't mind then, that you might lose your father to another woman?'

'Not a chance. I'm happy for him. Besides—' she turned her face up to his '—look at all I've won. I must be the luckiest woman in the whole world.'

'I love you,' he said, whirling her around. 'I will always love you.'

His bride beamed up at him, felt her amber eyes misting. 'I love you too,' she pledged, 'with all my heart.'

His eyes darkened, his mouth drew closer, but she stilled him with a fingertip to his lips. 'But wait! That's not all I have to tell you. There's more.'

She leaned up closer to his ear and whispered the secret she'd been longing to share ever since she'd found out, and Luca responded the way she'd hoped, by whooping with joy as he spun her around the floor in his arms until she was drunk with giddiness. And then he stopped spinning and kissed her until she was giddy all over again, but this time on the love fizzing through her veins.

And both of them knew the day could not have been more perfect, and yet still it was nothing compared to what happened seven months later.

Mitchell Eduardo Barbarigo came into the world bang on time and boasting a healthy set of lungs. True to his word, Luca was by Tina's side, clutching her hand, sponging her brow or rubbing her back or just being there, the whole time. True to his word, she was not alone.

And just as true to his word, her tears were his tears, except this time they were tears of joy. Tears of elation.

Tears of love for this brand new family.

* * * * *

INNOCENT OF HIS CLAIM

JANETTE KENNY

For as long as **Janette Kenny** can remember, plots and characters have taken up residence in her head. Her parents, both voracious readers, read her the classics when she was a child. That gave birth to a deep love of literature, and allowed her to travel to exotic locales—those found between the covers of books. Janette's artist mother encouraged her yen to write. As an adolescent she began creating cartoons featuring her dad as the hero, with plots that focused on the misadventures on their family farm, and she stuffed them in the nightly newspaper for him to find. To her frustration, her sketches paled in comparison with her captions.

Though she dabbled with articles, she didn't fully embrace her dream to write novels until years later, when she was a busy cosmetologist making a name for herself in her own salon. That was when she decided to write the type of stories she'd been reading—romances.

Once the writing bug bit, an incurable passion consumed her to create stories and people them. Still, it was seven more years and that many novels before she saw her first historical romance published. Now that she's also writing contemporary romances for Mills & Boon she finally knows that a full-time career in writing is closer to reality.

Janette shares her home and free time with a chow-shepherd mix pup she rescued from the pound, who aspires to be a lap dog. She invites you to visit her website at www.jankenny.com and she loves to hear from readers—e-mail her at janette@jankenny.com

CHAPTER ONE

"IT's done." Henry returned the telephone to its austere black cradle with a decisive click, his face as stoic as the marble busts in David Tate's executive office in central London. "The takeover of Tate Unlimited is complete."

Delanie sat perfectly still and stared across the desk at her father's massive, empty chair. Most women thrust into her situation would be a puddle of tears. Fretful. Scared. But she felt curiously numb. Detached, as if she was watching someone else go through the death of a parent, the subsequent ordeal of a swift hostile takeover of his corporation and now a very uncertain future.

Though she'd been unable to display grief at his funeral, she had at least shown respect. Considering her relationship with her father, even that was a lot.

"My bid to exclude the house and my family's personal assets?" she asked, holding onto the hope that she had salvaged something from her father's empire.

Henry, who'd been her father's attorney for as long as she could remember and who she'd affectionately called Uncle Henry all of her life, shook his head, his papery lips pulled into a thin line that sent her hopes plummeting. "All gone. However the new owner has trumped your bid to buy Elite Affair with a counter offer."

"What does he want?" she asked.

Not that it mattered. Her only means to negotiate a deal in

the first place hinged on selling the vintage cars. But those were gone, leaving her with nothing tangible to trade or sell.

"His solicitor wouldn't say, stating the owner will inform us of the details upon his arrival," Henry said.

Of course, more waiting. More drama added to this corporate piracy.

She huffed out a weary breath and pushed to her feet, smoothing her dress over her hips. Fittingly, she was garbed in a somber black Dolce and Gabbana sheath, although it made her pale complexion seem waxy and lifeless. Right now she felt bloodless but was too angry to surrender.

The fall of her father's company had been inevitable, yet she'd hoped that the corporate dragon breathing fire down on them for the past two weeks would have the decency to show respect. That he would at least listen to her request. That the unknown entity hiding behind the group called Varsi Dynamics was, in fact, human and not a machine or monster.

Now she wasn't sure. She wasn't sure of anything.

It would be so easy to toss in the proverbial towel. Certainly people would understand that losing both parents and every worldly thing she possessed in such a short span of time was simply too much for her to bear. But her pride wouldn't let her give in to pity and pride was all she had left.

Narrow shoulders squared, she strode to the draped window and gathered her courage around her for this meeting with the tycoon who had gobbled up everything her father had owned. Everything she owned and valued as well, damn him!

She flung back the drapes and stared at the cold rain streaking down the mullioned windows. Steel-gray clouds barred the sun from making an appearance.

The gloomy weather was appropriate to laying her father and his wretched empire to rest once and for all. If she could just get back what was hers....

"Do we at least now know who's behind Varsi Dynamics?" she asked as she faced her father's loyal attorney.

"No." Henry consulted his Baume & Mercier watch, a gift for service long ago. The brown leather band now seemed too bulky and masculine for his bony wrist that was only slightly bigger than her own. "But we shall soon find out. He's scheduled to arrive at quarter past two."

Any time then, she thought. "Good. I want to get this over with and go home."

Only she didn't have a home anymore. She had nothing. So where would she go? Impose on friends? Pound the streets looking for a job?

Delanie tried to tuck an errant strand of hair behind her ear but the tremor that continued to rock through her undermined the effort. She gave it up with a heavy sigh and let the pale gold strand fall as it had repeatedly done at the cemetery.

If she were prone to outbursts then this would be the ideal time to have one. What kind of man would demand that this meeting be held in the closed offices of Tate Unlimited on the heels of her father's burial?

Perhaps a visceral man with horns and a tail. Clearly he was a man without principles.

The man behind Varsi Dynamics had launched his takeover on Tate Unlimited in her father's last hours. Before her father was interred at the Tate family plot at Sumpton Park, the corporate shark had gained control of her father's assets, right down to the furniture in the mansion and the fleet of Rolls Royces in the garages.

"I imagine the new owner will take great delight in personally firing everyone on staff," she groused as she stopped behind the burgundy leather chair her father had ruled from.

Henry fidgeted with his crimson-and-gold striped tie, the first sign that he wasn't quite as calm as he let on. "Actually, his solicitor assured me that all Tate employees would remain on staff through a six-month vetting period."

She blinked, that news the one ray of sun on this gloomy day. "That's a surprise."

"Indeed," Henry said, consulting his watch again. "Time to go below stairs to meet and show him up. Wouldn't want the gent wandering around the building and getting lost. Will you be all right alone?"

His concern brought a bittersweet smile to her face. "Yes, I'll be fine."

Henry gave a crisp nod and left, his gait swift and sure for a man his age.

Silence thrummed in the room that held only bitter memories. No, she wouldn't miss Tate Unlimited. But Elite Affair, the company her father had swindled out of her, meant everything to her. It was her dream. Her means to support herself. Her freedom from a man's control.

She was anything but fine, she thought as her palms pressed into the sumptuous leather back of the executive chair.

The scent of spice wafted in the air. Her father's aftershave. Faint, as if he'd just stepped out of the office.

The old urge to run pinged through her like a cold pounding rain and she shivered. To her father, a woman's main purpose was to marry well and produce an heir. A male heir, according to the verbal barbs he'd flung at her mother for failing to uphold her duty.

In his eyes, Delanie was no better. Her fingers dug into the leather as his biting diatribes played over and over in her mind. A failure. A liability. No better than her mother.

If he hadn't blackmailed her to stay on this past year she would have left. In hindsight she should have done that, for she'd ended up with nothing anyway—unless by some miracle she could meet the new owner's counteroffer.

The *ding* of the elevator echoed dully down the corridor. Masculine footsteps pounded the marble floor like an advancing army. Her pulse rose with each step.

The waiting was over.

He was here.

Chills skipped up her spine, but she forced herself to stand straight and greet this next hurdle straight on. Deep breath in, slow exhalation. But even that failed to calm her racing heart or lessen the knocking of her knees.

As for offering a serene smile, she wasn't about to attempt one. Only a fool would smile at the shark swimming toward them.

Henry's voice drifted to her, so clear she knew he was standing in the corridor outside the waiting-room door. "Miss Tate is in her father's office. If you'll come this way, sir."

"That will be all," replied a deep masculine voice that ground Delanie's thoughts to a screeching, nerve-grating halt.

No! Her mind must be playing cruel tricks on her.

But there was no mistaking that husk of an Italian accent that she hadn't heard in ten long years except in her dreams. That she'd wished never to hear again.

"Sir," Henry sputtered. "I insist I be on hand..."

"Leave us!" The clipped order blew open the lid on painful memories she'd tucked away long ago.

The man from her past was here. But why? Was he the corporate raider, the one with the wherewithal and ruthless bent to strip everything from her?

Her gaze swept the room to find a way out; her pulse raced so fast she was light-headed. Were the walls closing in on her?

No, just her past.

The waiting-room door slammed shut, likely in Henry's face. She jumped in heels that suddenly pinched, her skin pebbling and her heart thundering with each determined step that brought Marco closer.

Footsteps stopped outside the office door. She swallowed hard. Had Marco paused to straighten his tie—a quirk he'd done often because he detested wearing one? Or, on a wilder thought that mirrored her rising hysteria, was he sharpening his teeth for the proverbial kill?

Her heart thundered, her body swayed as the dizzying rush of memories swirled around her like a choking fog. Each second nipped along her skin, chipping away at the confidence she tried desperately to shore up.

The man she'd thought never to see again stepped into the office and shut the door behind him with a deafening click. Her traitorous eyes drank him in: tall and commanding, broad shoulders racked tight. Breathtakingly handsome.

Piercing dark eyes set in a classic face drilled into her, impaling her to the spot. "*Ciao,* Delanie."

Her fingernails dug into her father's chair, likely scoring the leather. But it remained her only shield against the enemy.

Enemy... In her wildest imaginings, she had never guessed that the mystery owner of Varsi Dynamic was Marco Vincienta, her ex-fiancé. The man who'd held her heart in his powerful hands and crushed it without remorse.

There could only be one reason for him to take over Tate Unlimited and demand that she meet him here a scant hour after her father's funeral. Revenge.

She swallowed, her throat parched, the spacious room shrinking as the powerful throb of his aura reached out to encircle her. Trap her.

"Marco," she said, her voice catching over his name that she'd once said lovingly, the emotionally wounded man that she'd foolishly thought she could heal with her love.

He looked larger, stronger, colder. His lean torso was in top physical form, more so than memory served. His wealth of dark hair that she'd loved running her fingers through was clipped short in a fashionable style, yet an errant curl strayed onto his broad tanned forehead to hint at his rebel soul.

He was far more handsome and intense than she remembered. Far more dangerous-looking. Hungry. Like a caged wolf she'd seen at the zoo, its cool gaze scanning the crowd, searching for easy prey.

Only Marco stared straight at her. The look of a predator who'd tracked down his quarry. Who had it cornered and was moments away from pouncing.

Perspiration beaded her forehead and dampened the deep V between her breasts. It took supreme effort to stand straight and keep her head high, refusing to show fear or any weakness.

"So you are the man behind Varsi Dynamics," she said.

A rapacious smile curved his chiseled lips that had once played so tenderly over her eager flesh, awakening sensations she'd never felt before or since he'd exited her life. Sensations that maddeningly still caused heat to curl in her belly.

She hated that odd loss of self-control, that awareness of him on that level. Hated him as much as she'd once loved him. Perhaps more now that she knew he'd been the one to put her through such hell the past few weeks.

"It is one of my lesser acquisitions."

"Lesser?" She couldn't hide her surprise.

The wolf's smile widened. "Hard to believe that the young bastard you and your father stole a company from amassed a fortune and the power to take down a titan."

"I had nothing to do with what my father did," she said, earning a snort from him. "Everything I felt for you was real."

"Yes, just like your tearful confession of family abuse, revealed after I confronted you and your father with the truth, after I said I was done with you." His dark eyes were void of emotion. "It was too little too late. Perhaps if you'd told me your story before you betrayed me…"

"I never betrayed you," she spat. "Why are you so blind to the truth? Why must you think the worst…"

He sliced the air between them with a hand and she stammered to a halt. "History. What happened then has nothing to do with why I'm here now."

She forced her chin up and met his cold gaze head-on. "That's rather difficult to believe after you've systematically stripped me of everything."

The tailored sleeves of his jacket pulled into perfect pleats as he crossed his arms over his chest, his face an impassive mask. He was a stranger, worlds away from the young Italian she'd lost her heart to. An older, harder version of the dynamic lover who'd broken her heart.

"I'm in need of your services," he said sharply.

She blinked, stunned speechless. As a wedding planner? Lover? Did it matter when either was cruel to ask of her?

"Is this a joke?"

"Not at all," he said. "I want you to come to Italy with me today."

For a moment she couldn't think, couldn't get past those same words he'd spoken long ago. Come to Italy with me... Leave the hell of her life. Leave her mother at her father's mercy...

She couldn't do it then. She wouldn't now.

"No way," she said. "The only reason I honored your order to be here today was to hear your counteroffer to my bid for Elite Affair."

One dark brow winged up. "This is my counteroffer. Come to Italy and plan a wedding. If you please the bride and me then Elite Affair will be yours."

Could it be that simple? No, there would be nothing simple about being around Marco, seeing him fawn over his bride.

It would be emotional hell for her. Torture. But, she thought, her mind catching on the carrot he dangled before her, in the end she would gain Elite Affair—if she could trust him to uphold his end of the bargain.

Her eyes met his intense ones and her foolish heart fluttered. It was a dangerous game. But right now she had absolutely nothing to lose and everything to gain.

"All right. But I can plan your wedding from London and send one of my consultants to ensure the events go off perfectly."

He shook his head. "No. You will be there from start to finish or the deal is off."

She shoved her father's massive chair aside and rounded

the desk, facing him. "Why? What does it matter as long as your bride is happy?"

He drove his fingers through his hair, then pinned her with a look so intense she had to lean against the desk to keep from swaying. "Because the bride insists that you be there to oversee every detail."

"And you would do anything for your bride," she said.

"*Si.* I want her day to be perfect."

Exactly what every groom should want, except this man had once asked her to marry him. The man who had vowed to stand by her. Believe her. Protect her.

Marco had failed miserably at all three. What was to stop him from stringing her along to get his way?

"Not good enough," she said. "I demand a guarantee in writing that I'll get my company back when the work is done."

"No. You get the company if your work is satisfactory to the bride."

"And if she nitpicks?"

"You have a reputation for pleasing the most finicky client."

"Within reason," she clarified.

He almost smiled. "You'll be amply compensated for your time."

And make a fool of herself over him again? She shook her head, having been down that rocky road before, having trusted him before. Never again.

"Forget it. I'll never agree to that."

"Don't make vows you can't keep," he said.

"Trust me, I can keep this one!"

He glared at her, a stone pillar of a man who had once been turgid hot flesh and blazing passion in her arms. Ancient history.

They had been a bright nova. They'd come together in a cataclysmic crash of passion only to fade into cold darkness when it ended. He'd hurt her more than she'd thought possible. Was still hurting her, she thought sourly.

"I never knew you, Marco, but then that's how you wanted it," she said, letting him see the pain and anguish that must be evident in her eyes. "You put up walls and shared very little about your past or your fears, and the dreams you wove for our future were hazy."

"Yet you were willing to marry me."

She bit her lip, wanting to deny it. But she couldn't. "I was young. Naive. I trusted you." Loved him.

Marco's brow snapped into a V as he jerked his gaze from her and mouthed a curse. Then he presented a broad rigid back to her, fists clenched at his sides.

She hadn't expected a like confession from him. That wouldn't be Marco. So why were tears stinging her eyes?

Dammit, she'd held her poise and dignity throughout the funeral. She certainly wouldn't give Marco the satisfaction of knowing how much he'd crushed her again. How close she was to crumbling into a heap.

Head high, she marched toward the door. There was no reason to stay, no use to try and negotiate with him. That would be up to Henry now.

No home. No job. Nothing but her pride.

"I am not finished with you," he said.

"Tough," she said, relieved her voice didn't betray her heartache, that her knees didn't buckle. "I'm finished with you."

A few more feet and she was closing the door behind her with that same resounding click she'd heard as he'd entered. A sob caught in her throat but she managed to choke it back as she ran across the waiting room toward an uncertain future.

CHAPTER TWO

MARCO wrenched the door open with nearly enough force to pull the heavy oak panel off the bronze hinges. Amazing that just a few minutes in Delanie Tate's infuriating company could fling him right back into that chaotic mix of emotions he'd tried to run from all his life.

His disposition was soured by the fact his body stirred at being near her again. That his heart thundered despite the anger cracking like sheet lightning along his nerves.

No woman but Delanie had ever brought those explosive emotions out in him, but with that intense desire came fear. A cold choking fear that he'd never understood until he'd returned to Italy ten years ago and yanked the dark shroud off his past.

He should let Delanie go. Cut his losses now and go home. But as his eyes locked on her trim backside running across the waiting room, he knew he couldn't let her go. Not now. Not when he'd promised his sister that he would return to Italy with Delanie Tate.

He wouldn't gain her compliance by crossing swords with her. But he damned sure wasn't going to beg for her help either.

A smile flicked over his lips. He held what she wanted most. She would be the one begging.

"How much does Elite Affair mean to you?" he asked, just as she was a step away from sailing out the door.

She stopped, one hand pressed to the open doorjamb while the toe of one impossibly high black heel remained poised to push her out the door. Even in unrelieved black mourning, she was sexy as hell. And those damned shoes…

The strong, perfectly curved length of her leg and dainty foot in those take-me-now shoes brought back memories of her wearing similar footwear and nothing else. His body stirred, his blood heating to a most uncomfortable level. If not for the steely snap to her slender shoulders and the cool, almost hostile gaze she flung at him just then he would think the pose was staged to entice him.

"Well?" he prodded when she simply glared at him.

"You're enjoying your victory at my expense."

"Don't flatter yourself," he said. "My goal was to take down your father's empire."

"Which you did. Don't expect me to congratulate you."

He crossed his arms over his chest and leaned against the doorjamb, enjoying this side of her. When he'd met her she'd been a combination of playful and meek, leaning more to meek in her father's shadow.

But in the ensuing years Delanie had acquired bite and verve. The way she held herself and her ability to closet her emotions intrigued him. Not that he wanted to be intrigued again by this woman.

She'd tricked him once. He would never be so foolish as to totally trust her again.

Remembering that betrayal zinged an old burning sensation across his heart. "Are you going to answer my question?"

"Elite Affair means a great deal to me and you know it," she said, slender shoulders straight and back painfully stiff.

"Then use your head. If you walk out that door now you will toss away any chance of regaining total control of the business you built."

She went pale, or perhaps it was a trick of the light. "After what you've done, how can you expect me to trust you?"

"I don't," he said. "This is strictly business. I've taken the initiative to draft a mutually beneficial contract. Are you willing to listen to terms or do I fire your employees and liquidate Elite Affair?"

"You'd do that to a profitable business?"

"In a heartbeat."

Her small hands bunched at her sides and the mouth he'd dreamed of kissing into submission in the dead of night drew into a tight unyielding knot that slammed straight into his gut.

Dammit, he'd expected a tearful confession that she *had* worked with her father against him, followed by his magnanimous offer to hire her for his sister's wedding, with Delanie's reward being a fat check plus title to her company. But she was resisting him at every turn. Showing spunk and a stubborn bent that challenged him—aroused him.

Not that he would back off no matter what she said or did. He'd come this far and there was no retreat. No concession.

His gaze locked with hers and he caught that flicker of doubt. It was a battle of wills and in that he had the upper hand because he held what she wanted most. Elite Affair.

"Fine. We talk," she snapped, not sparing him a glance.

She had conceded as he'd expected her to do. So why didn't he feel victorious?

Delanie slammed the door she'd been about to escape through and strode back into her father's oppressive office, passing him with a swish of her long hair. Ever the reigning princess.

He loosed a smile, enjoying the sight of her full bottom beneath her unbecoming black dress. His gaze remained on those long dainty legs that were deceptively strong, that had once clung tightly to his hips in the throes of passion.

Certainly if he put his mind to it he could have her back in his arms, back in his bed. And that was a complication he had no intention of taking on. Too much was at stake to risk satisfying his libido no matter how tempting. And she damned sure was tempting!

Ironic that the only passion between them now was anger and that shimmered off her in sizzling waves. Even that set his pulse racing, he admitted, sobering instantly.

If only he could cease wanting her more than he'd ever wanted a woman. If only he could purge her from his system once and for all.

He gave his French cuffs a tug and followed her into the room, shutting the door and his emotions firmly behind him. She visibly jumped and he swore.

"Relax," he said. "I don't intend to pounce on you."

"Excuse me for not trusting you," she said, still presenting her painfully straight back to him.

He fisted his hands, resisting the urge to cross to her and force her to face him. Touching her would be a major mistake.

"That goes both ways, Delanie."

She whirled to face him, features pinched tight. "If you distrust me so, then why do you want to negotiate with me?"

"I don't," he said frankly. "As I told you before, you are the bride's choice."

"And you'd do anything to please her."

"Yes," he bit out, "but—"

"Including corporate rape," she interjected, chin thrust out and accusing eyes fixed on him.

He stiffened, the explanation poised on his tongue forgotten. "My takeover of Tate Unlimited was aboveboard."

"Perhaps," she said, chin up. "But your motive was revenge, proving you're no better than my father."

His fingers wadded into fists. "Never compare me to him."

The warning was given in the strong, flat monotone that always convinced his opponents to switch topics. Color instantly bloomed on her too-pale cheeks, like vibrant English roses blooming amid snow, but her chin remained up and her gaze glittered defiance.

"Are you denying you acted out of vengeance?" she asked.

"No. But if I was in the same league as your father I would overextend Tate Unlimited until it was destroyed, as he did to my vineyard."

Lines creased her delicate brow. "What?"

He drove his fingers through his hair and swallowed a curse. "Do not pretend you weren't aware of its downfall."

"I had no idea." She shook her head, voice soft, big blue eyes wide. "Please tell me the truth."

The look, the plea… That's all it took to shift his plans off kilter. To get him thinking about her. In his arms. In his bed.

Her innocent act was worthy of an award, he thought grimly.

"You were vice-president of Tate Unlimited. How could you not know when you had access to all corporate records?" he asked.

Color flooded her face and she looked away. "It was a token position. I served as his hostess at business functions and, as he termed it, a charming diversion to his potential clients during intense initial meetings."

He wouldn't allow himself to believe her, no matter how much he might want to. "Fine. Play innocent. It doesn't matter."

Her fists landed on the plush back of the chair. "I am not *playing* innocent. I am ignorant of what my father did to your family's company once he gained control, or why he would destroy something he obviously wanted so badly."

Her wide eyes pleaded with his, open, unguarded. He huffed out a breath. Swore.

"Sagrantino grapes are prized throughout Italy and the world and my family's winery grew the best. It was our legacy but few had heard of us outside of Italy because we couldn't produce enough to satisfy world demand." A muscle pulsed along his lean jaw. "That's why I sought your father out. I needed financial backing as well as a noted exporter who could place our wine worldwide. Once he had wrested control of my family's company, he destroyed it with gross mismanagement."

"I'm so sorry he did that to you."

"As am I, because his impatience and ignorance destroyed the vineyard."

It was time to let the past drop into the black hole of his memories and hammer the lid back on it. He was in control of all that David Tate had owned. That evened the score as far as he was concerned.

As for Delanie, she was back in his life only because of his vow to please his sister. Once she finished planning the wedding, it would be better for both of them if they never saw each other again.

"Your small company has achieved a degree of favorable notoriety," he said.

She gave him a long appraising look. "I'm surprised you noticed."

"It was brought to my attention."

His gaze drilled into hers as she stood behind her father's chair. "I'm giving you the chance to gain sole ownership of Elite Affair, debt-free, by successfully planning a lavish carte blanche wedding that will be photographed and reported worldwide."

She went absolutely still, eyes widening like saucers. "Why are you willing to hire me with our history between us?"

It was a sound question, especially considering what he'd done—storming the citadel and winning. "You are my sister's choice because of your company's promise to work with the bride to make her wedding special. Every plan you do is unique."

She crossed her arms beneath her bosom and gave the most unladylike snort, as if his compliment meant nothing to her and that almost made him smile. "Does your bride know that you are entrusting arrangements for her wedding to your former lover?"

He shook his head and let a rusty chuckle escape. This bolder side of Delanie was a welcome switch from the demure girl he'd known.

"I am not that trusting," he admitted. "The bride is my sister, Bella, and she wants someone who will understand her needs and abide by her wishes. She needs your special touch, Delanie."

Her eyes widened again and the faintest flush stole over her cheekbones. "I wasn't aware you had a sister."

"I didn't know myself until eight years ago." His hand cut the air, dismissing the topic from further inquiry. "It is complicated."

"I've discovered that many families are 'complicated' in ways that have some impact on an upcoming wedding," she said. "That's one reason we are selective in our clientele."

"Is that the only reason why you turned Bella down when she attempted to hire you two weeks ago?" he asked.

Her too-pale lips parted. "You can't be thinking that I knew she was your sister, because I swear that isn't the case. And even if I had known, my assistant handles all the initial calls. The moment he discovered the wedding was to take place in Italy, he would have politely declined and wished her well."

Which, according to Bella, is exactly what had happened. "So what will it be? Your agreement to plan Bella's wedding for title to your company or do we part company now?"

She bit her lip and frowned, then huffed out a breath and nodded as if coming to grips with her decision. "I'll do it. I'll have Henry send a contract to your solicitor by the weekend and we can go from there."

"That's too late. The wedding is two weeks from now."

"That's not nearly enough time," she sputtered. "Two months is not sufficient to orchestrate such a lavish affair."

"If we wait two months it will be clear why the bride is marrying so quickly. Understand?"

Her cheeks flushed a charming pink but she gave a jerky nod. "Yes. Well. That doesn't leave us much time."

"No," he said. "I had my attorney draft a contract for your review. Once you sign we can be off."

She stiffened up again. "We?"

"I'm in a time crunch and must return to Italy tonight. You'll come with me and oversee the details there."

"I can't," she said in a strained voice he'd never heard before, that touched something kindred in him. "My business and assistants are here."

"There is nothing that can't be done via the internet or phone," he said. "You'll have the best of both at your disposal."

She cupped her palms to her face, her slender shoulders trembling once. Twice.

That tremor had him fisting his hands to keep from reaching out to her, enfolding her slender form against his length. And that would be a mistake for then she would know how much she'd affected him.

Dammit, he wasn't going to let her get to him.

"Your answer, Delanie," he said. "Do you come with me? Or is the deal off?"

She pressed her lips together, throat working. "After all that has happened between us, do you honestly expect me to trust you and drop everything?"

"Yes, because I am entrusting you to organize the most important day in my sister's life."

She looked away, stilled, then she bobbed her head and he hoped to hell that meant she understood, that she would cease fighting him.

"I prefer my own contract," she said.

"As do I."

Her chin came up again and her gaze clashed with his. Only the tremor in her lower lip belied her total control.

"My contract is designed for my purposes but you are entitled to make minor changes to it if you like," she said.

He most certainly would do that. Ever since the disaster of dealing with David Tate, Marco had learned to manage his own affairs to the letter.

But this concession was doable. Perhaps even wise, for he would know what she expected and would be able to mount a countermove if necessary.

This time he held control and he would have Delanie close at hand again. And why the hell was he entertaining any thought of being close to her again?

His gaze raked over her, his brow furrowing. The black dress she wore encased the petite figure he remembered with aching clarity. She appeared gaunt and fragile. A deception, he was certain.

Marco paced to the heavily draped window and swore, painfully aware of what was at the heart of it. She'd intrigued him from the start. She still did.

But that didn't matter now. It was all in the past, and it would stay there. He had control over that part of him now.

Having her in Italy would prove that. By the time his sister was a happily married woman, Marco would have no doubt in his mind that walking away from Delanie had been the right choice ten years ago. He could finally purge her from his system.

"Fine. Give me your contract and I'll read it on the plane," he said, the decision easy as it suited both their purposes. "Now let's leave."

Delanie bit her lower lip again. No was the easy answer.

But he was holding out her dream on a silver salver. He also held her employees', really her only friends, future in his hands. She couldn't refuse.

And if she was honest with herself, a part of her didn't want to walk away. She could easily blame that lonely part of her heart that still held Marco Vincienta close, the part of her that wondered why he'd found her so lacking. That deep-in-the-night dream that his desertion had all been a horrid mistake and that they truly were meant for each other.

She was a fool for entertaining such fanciful thoughts, even for a moment, but she'd always been a fool for love where Marco was concerned. At least by taking this job she would be opening doors for herself in the future. That was her dream. That was what she would focus on instead of the tall handsome Italian whose touch made her bones melt.

"Okay," she said. "It won't take me more than an hour to pack."

He broke eye contact the moment her agreement was out, snapping a strong wrist up to consult a watch that looked masculine and expensive. "We leave now. I will buy you whatever you need once we get to Italy."

And that was the end of that argument, concluded before she could get her anger up. She made a quick stop at her minuscule office to collect the passport she'd needed for her dealings with Henry, her laptop, a contract and the jeans, jersey and comfortable sandals she'd left at work in case she decided to begin cleaning out her father's office today.

With the lot of it crammed into a small carryall along with the few toiletries she kept on hand there, she let Marco escort her from the building, barely having the time to thank Henry before she was ushered into a gleaming black sedan.

She pressed a hand to her stomach, the drive through London a blur while Marco sprawled beside her and talked on his mobile, speaking a language she barely recognized as Italian. Not that it would have mattered if she spoke it fluently. Each time the car zoomed around a corner, the steely length of his leg brushed hers and her mind simply shut off as another emotion exploded in her, one that had lain dormant for ten years.

But even if they hadn't touched, his presence simply commanded every inch of space. Commanded every second of her attention, leaving her all too aware of him as a powerful man.

Ruthless. Driven. She could see the end effect of what she'd glimpsed in him years ago.

Knowing she was powerless in his company played along her nerves until a discordant hum vibrated through her to leave her stomach knotted. Even shallow breaths pulled his essence deep into her lungs, bringing a flood of memories that made her throat clog with emotion best left untouched. In these close confines she was doubly aware of his control, his power, his sensuality.

Shifting away from him the best she could only brought his intense brown eyes slewing back to her. Her cheeks instantly turned red—she knew they must be because she felt the fire burning her skin.

"Is something wrong?" he asked when she had inched as far from him as possible.

Wrong? He had the gall to ask that when his large muscled form dominated the interior of the auto? When he'd taken everything from her?

She lifted her chin, aware diplomacy was necessary to avoid further conflict. "I was just giving you space."

His gaze narrowed, his lips pulling into an uncompromising line. "Are you? Because to me it looks as if you're avoiding my touch, even if that touch was no more than my arm or leg brushing against you. Accidentally brushed you, I would add."

What could she say to that and maintain this fragile peace? The truth. They'd had a wretched history of avoiding the truth when honesty mattered most. But then when she had been honest with him, he had still walked away from her. He had been the one to turn his back on her.

"Use your head. Less than an hour ago you stormed into my life and took everything from me in the wake of my father's burial," she said with a telling quaver in her voice that had her clenching her fingers in frustration, a habit she'd developed as a child when her father was venting his anger on her mother.

She'd been so good at hiding her emotions from her volatile father. But she'd failed miserably at that with Marco.

He knew when she was angry, hurt, cautious. But he never could guess the reason for her trouble and she'd been too ashamed to tell him everything.

Her cheeks burned at the old memory. In that regard he'd been right to accuse her of lying to him. To be angry. If only he had believed her when she finally revealed her shame...

"I'm physically and emotionally spent, Marco. You've won. I've agreed to come to Italy and plan your sister's wedding. But that's all you'll get from me," she added. "Is that clear?"

"Extremely! I want nothing more from you than what was agreed upon," he said, shoulders snapped into a rigid line.

"Good. I don't want any misconceptions," she said.

"There was never a doubt of your role or of mine," he said as the sedan thankfully came to a stop at the airport, ending the torture of him jostling against her time and again. "Ten years ago you were looking for a rich man with status, a man who would measure up to your and your father's precise standards. I was not that man then nor am I now."

She gaped, flabbergasted. "You can't believe that!"

"It is the truth."

He couldn't be more wrong, but to admit that would prompt questions she wasn't about to address. Her trust had been broken not once but twice by this man. She wasn't about to put it out there again.

Not that it mattered. He'd already slammed out of the car, leaving her alone and trembling. She pressed a hand to her middle and slumped against the seat.

A private jet—she'd never been able to tell one from the other—sat on the tarmac to her left, its stairs lowered to admit passengers. It didn't dawn on her that this was Marco's plane until she saw a crewman carrying her small duffel onto it.

Her door was wrenched opened a heartbeat later and cool brown eyes flecked with gold stared down at her. "Let's go."

She gave a nod and tried to extract herself from the car without his help. He mouthed a curse and assisted her to her feet, his large hand enveloping hers before she could protest, his skin warm against hers, his touch gentle and strong. Heat sped up her arm yet she shivered, liking his touch far too much and hating herself because of it.

The moment she gained her footing he dropped his hand from her and motioned her toward the plane. The message was clear: he didn't wish to touch her any more than she wished to be touched.

A lie, if her libido had a say, which it most certainly did not. She crossed the tarmac quickly and hoped once inside she could find a seat far removed from him.

Not a problem, she realized as she mounted the stairs and stepped into the private lair of an Italian wine baron. The interior was dressed in a classic, yet understated, design resplendent in rich browns, ivory and gold.

The flight attendant motioned Delanie to take a seat. She bit her lower lip—so many to choose from. Twin flight chairs. A large curved sofa that was far too intimate. Farther back more chairs and a table, likely utilized for meetings. Beyond that an open door that showed a glimpse of a bed.

Wishing to stay as far away from a bedroom as possible, she claimed one of the deep gold chairs up front with a smile to the attendant and a quick glance at her traveling companion. He passed her without sparing her a glance, the thick carpet muffling his steps yet cluing her in that he preferred the rear of the plane.

Fine by her, she thought irritably as the strategically positioned cushions conformed to her tired back and tense shoulders. He could shut himself up in his bedroom for all she cared. The lack of his presence after such a trying hour would be a welcome pleasure.

"We'll take off immediately so please fasten your seatbelt," the attendant told her before disappearing into a cabin up front.

Delanie obeyed without complaint and tried to relax, not an easy feat as she'd never been a seasoned traveler. In the Tate household, the only member who took holidays was her father.

Perhaps this wouldn't be so bad. The interior was quiet and comfortable and the chair was an absolute dream. If she managed to control her stress levels as the plane reached cruising altitude and leveled off then maybe she could nod off en route.

God knew she was tired enough to fall asleep standing up. The past week of dealing with doctors and attorneys and worried shareholders had drained her of her last reserves.

But total rest was still denied her.

Perhaps she could have dozed off if Marco's voice hadn't drifted to her. If her body hadn't come awake at the deep timbre that left her shaking.

He spoke in clipped Italian delivered so fast and fluently that with her meager knowledge she couldn't begin to translate. Was he really so much like her father, always engaged in some deal? Or was he delivering the news to Italy that he'd succeeded, that he'd brought Tate Unlimited to its knees?

That he had the millionaire's heiress in tow with the contract that she'd agreed to do his bidding safely in hand?

All of the above, she thought as a small degree of hysteria rippled through her. Could she have dreamt up a more intense working relationship? No!

Marco was the billionaire who had trumped her tyrannical father's millionaire status. He was the antithesis of power. He was her boss for the next two weeks.

He was the only man she'd fallen in love with. The only man she had ever loved physically and emotionally.

A hysterical laugh stuck in her throat as the plane sped through the clouds, carrying her into the unknown with a man who was more stranger to her than ever before. A man she'd hoped to cling to in the dead of night, who would be there for her until the day she drew her last breath. The man she'd spun dreams on.

Her only lover. Her hero.

Unwanted tears stung her eyes and she blinked them back. How very wrong she'd been.

Hopefully, once they arrived in Italy he would take himself off so she could breathe again. So she could think. So she could do her job and then escape back to London with sole ownership of her business in hand.

Only then could she focus on her career. On her future. On living in peace. That's all she wanted.

All she had to do to have that was endure two weeks in the company of the man who still left her weak-kneed. Who tormented her dreams in the dead of night.

She could do it. She had to. Failure wasn't an option.

CHAPTER THREE

Two hours into the flight, Marco ended the conference call and rubbed his gritty eyes. Sleep had been sporadic all week, a fact that could be blamed on the alluring beauty seated primly in the front of his plane.

His gaze zeroed in on her with unerring accuracy. She hadn't moved much since boarding the plane. Had she dozed off? Was she simply enjoying the flight, content knowing that she would get exactly what she'd wanted all along?

He shifted and damned his restlessness. It shouldn't matter to him if Delanie Tate was pleased or not. He'd never set out to spite her and he damned sure hadn't attempted to placate her.

In fact, before his sister's interference, he'd hoped to avoid her entirely during this shift in power. Delanie was a page from his past and he intended to keep her there.

Page? A wry smile tugged at his lips. No, she was a chapter at least. Perhaps even a book of pure trouble.

Still he hadn't wished to reread that episode anytime soon. But Bella's stubborn insistence on having Delanie as her wedding planner forced him to chose between pleasing himself or his sister.

He snorted. That had been no contest.

His sister's happiness came first.

That had put Delanie right back into his life.

While he'd been prepared to deal with her on a business level, he hadn't anticipated he would still find her unbelievably attractive. He'd never anticipated his body would react so at her nearness.

It was frustrating. Annoying. Unacceptable.

Dammit, he was a man in charge of his emotions. In control of his sex drive.

So why the hell was he shifting restlessly on the leather chair?

He swiped a hand down his face. This unwanted reaction to her was unacceptable on far too many levels.

If he had taken Delanie at her word, which he did not, he would have ordered the plane back to London and have her escorted off. He would have gladly let her plan his sister's wedding from there, thus freeing himself of her alluring company.

But he couldn't trust her. She'd betrayed him before when she'd sworn she loved him. There was nothing between them now but animosity on her part, and wariness on his own.

Since Elite Affair had turned down his sister once and then him a second time when he had upped the offer of money, he was left with one choice—force Delanie's hand. His takedown of Tate Unlimited was the perfect opportunity.

There was no other recourse, he reasoned, refusing to take pleasure from watching the dim light play over her hair. She worked for him now. More so than other contractors he was in league with, she needed to be watched and made accountable.

The only way he could achieve that was by maintaining total control of the situation. That was best done by having her under his thumb.

Easy enough to accomplish. Or it should have been.

Being physically close to Delanie was a totally different matter that he still didn't feel comfortable dealing with. But he would.

She aroused him on a deeper level than he liked and no amount of avoidance would change that. Even distancing himself from her on the plane hadn't worked because she'd been on his mind the entire time.

He swore and scanned the contract she'd pressed on him earlier. Since it was straightforward and clear, he signed it without ceremony and left his chair.

"Your contract is precise yet fair," he said, breaking the silence as he came to a stop behind her.

She started in her chair and looked back at him. The dark of her eyes nearly swallowed the clear blue.

"Thank you," she said. "I see no reason to make a straightforward business arrangement complex."

Her voice held that breathy quality that lapped around his control like warm waves, threatening to erode his defenses. It was so tempting to relax and be taken out to that sea of passion they'd frolicked in long ago. Too tempting.

"I'm of a like mind," he said, planting his feet firmly in the here and now as he dropped onto the seat across from her.

The most charming flush stole across her cheekbones and he paused. Except for the unnatural stiffness in her narrow shoulders and the tilt of her head, she looked very much as she had when they'd met.

The years should have hardened her. Should have shown on her face. But all he saw was a reluctant surrender and a proud bearing that he admired.

"Tell me about her," Delanie said, her gaze fixed on his again.

He looked away so she wouldn't see he was softening to her again, that his control over remaining impassive was slipping through his fingers like warm grains of sand.

"My sister?" he asked, then smiled when she nodded. "Bella is beautiful and willful and far too seductive for her own good."

"Yet you love her."

He sobered at that assessment. Love. He had loved his grandparents. Had loved his mother and tried to love his cold father—a wasted effort. He'd been consumed with Delanie but had he loved her?

No, it couldn't have been love. Infatuation. Lust. When the truth came out he'd had no difficulty walking away from her.

So why did she cross his mind in the dead of night? Why did he catch himself comparing every woman he met with her?

His chest heaved as the answer skirted his mind—an answer that he always ignored, just as he always ignored that old gnawing sense of emptiness when it threatened to yawn away in his soul. Or the skitter that streaked up his spine.

Like now.

"Bella is my responsibility," he said. "I care for her."

"That's cold."

"That's reality. Bella resents me."

She blinked, her clear eyes fixed on his as if she could read his soul. "Why?"

He shifted on the seat, uncomfortable delving into this. Yet what was the use in holding his silence? She would find out soon enough from someone in the village or at the villa. He might as well be the first to break the news.

"Bella thought she was Antonio Cabriotini's only bastard," he said simply.

"Antonio Cabriotini?" she parroted.

"Our biological father," he said, glancing her way to gauge her reaction.

She shook her head and frowned. "I thought your parents were married."

Such naiveté. "The man who raised me, who gave me his name, was married to my mother but I wasn't his son. When he found out, he withdrew the closeness I'd always had with him."

For a moment Delanie couldn't breathe. Couldn't wrap her brain around what he was telling her. And then finally she got it with a breathless wham to her midsection.

She finally understood the reason behind those broad tense shoulders attempting a careless shrug, the motion as abrupt as a salute. His illegitimacy was the reason for the pain she caught lurking behind those dark fathomless eyes, pain at having the father he'd loved ripped from him. That was the change in him she couldn't quite put her finger on.

"How long have you known this?" she asked.

"Eight years."

The words were shot out without feeling, his gaze boring into hers now. Hard. Cold. Defiant.

But she heard the underlying pain in his voice as well. Caught the tiny tick of hurt that snapped like a sail along his taut bronzed cheek.

Her heart gave an odd thud and her hand shifted, a blink away from reaching out to him. She caught herself with a trembling clasp of her own hands.

How wrongly would he take it if she offered compassion? Considering their past, she doubted he would take it well. Yet hadn't they moved beyond the past pain? Weren't they old enough and wise enough to understand nothing untoward was meant by it? Now wasn't the time to dissect it to find out.

"I see," she said, nerves stretched so tight they hummed.

"Do you?" he asked. "Because I don't understand how my mama who claimed to have loved my papa could be unfaithful to him. I do not understand why nobody saw fit to tell me the truth until after my parents' deaths."

Hearing the anger in his voice, that telling drawl when he told her this, made her insides cramp in an oh-too-familiar pang of understanding. No wonder he had no faith in love. He would never open himself to an emotion he believed caused only pain. And wasn't she just as guilty of holding back from him? He was right. That was in the past. There was nothing she could say when Marco had never believed her anyway.

"You would likely be surprised by how many families hold dark secrets," she said, cheeks burning and stomach knotting at the troubled memories of her own childhood.

He snorted. "Nothing surprises me anymore."

How sad that he had become more jaded. But then, so

had she. Wasn't she afraid to trust? To surrender her heart and soul?

She shifted on the chair while her mind shoved away from that train of thought. "I gather your sister knew of her paternity before you did."

"By a month or so." He drove his fingers through his hair, sending the thick waves in disarray.

She caught a breath as an old memory ribboned through her of doing the same to his wealth of dark hair. Of holding him close to her on a sun-kissed beach, laughing with him, kissing him in a slow, deep burn until the world blurred to only them.

Ten years ago she'd been a hopeless dreamer, desperately wanting a hero. Her innocence had convinced her that when she looked deeply into his warm brown eyes she believed her world was complete with him in it.

She shook off those idyllic yesterdays like a cool rain on chilled skin and chanced a glance at him, hoping he wasn't looking at her in some sort of horror. But he stared off, brow furrowed, clearly troubled by something else.

"Did you know her?" she asked, grasping the thread of their conversation by its tail.

"No. We were strangers coming from vastly different backgrounds which complicated matters more. Since the start Bella has resented that I was named her guardian until she reached twenty-five," he said, clearly not of the same mind.

Delanie felt a commiserating pang with his sister, knowing how badly she'd ached to break free of her domineering father, hating that she'd waited and waited for her own dawn of independence. "How old is she now?"

"Twenty," he said, sliding her a knowing look.

The same age she had been when she'd met Marco. Willful. Emotional. And tangled in a wretched triangle with her parents, dreaming of freedom yet unwilling to put her frail mother at risk to grab what she wanted.

"Tell me more about Bella," she blurted out.

He shrugged, this time the movement less tense. "As I said she's young. Spoilt. Resentful."

"Of you?" Delanie guessed.

He laughed, but she caught the pained treble, the hint of worry that had her wanting to leave her seat and go to him. Hug him, comfort him. Sanity prevailed and she didn't, but it wasn't easy knowing his elite world wasn't perfect. And hadn't she hoped that would be the case? She was suddenly glad for the subdued light on board that hid the heat scorching her cheeks.

"Bella resents me, resents the world," he said, dark eyes on her again. "She needs a strong hand."

Of course he would think that! But hearing him admit he was controlling his sister proved her fears long ago were right. Or did they? Was she still using that as an excuse to hold back from giving her all again? From trusting?

She stared at the floor, admitting she'd lost herself in his arms that first time. Basking in the afterglow of love was new. Terrifying.

Still she'd loved Marco. She'd hoped that she was simply mistaken. But the second time they made love was more consuming, more earthshattering to her heart. Her soul.

My dear, I love your father, and he loves me in his own way, her mother had told her as she recuperated from a volatile night spent suffering her father's anger.

Delanie never forgot that night. Never forgot that love could hurt. That love could strip a woman of her independence. Perhaps even her sanity.

No love was worth that, Delanie had decided.

That realization had kept her from committing fully to Marco again. And wasn't she right in thinking that in time he would have slipped further into the role of dominator, perhaps even going to the depths her father had sunk to? That she would relive the hell her mother had had throughout their marriage?

Single was safer. Single was being free. So why was her body craving his possession again? Why was she so weak around Marco Vincienta?

"I seriously doubt your sister needs a man dominating her," she said and was instantly pinned in place with his fierce scowl.

Her heart raced but she hiked her chin up, determined not to tremble over the past that still bound her, refusing to cringe at Marco's command as she'd seen her mother do with her father countless times. Or worse, whimper when he physically abused her.

"You are an expert on these matters because?"

Delanie didn't understand why on earth she had thought that the intervening years might have finally made him believe her. Still, he'd asked so she would answer.

"My father was quick to rule with an iron hand or fist depending on his whim." He'd used it liberally on her mother to gain Delanie's compliance.

A ripe curse exploded from him. "I told you never to compare me to David Tate!"

"Then stop acting like him."

He frowned, brows drawn in a deep forbidding V over the classic slope of his nose. Time hung suspended between them, her heart supplying each tick of the seconds that raced past.

His fingers bunched into fists at his sides and her stomach flipped over. Ease up a bit. Marco won't hurt you. At least not that way. She knew it in her heart, her soul.

"Are you saying Tate hit you?" he asked, his dark gaze probing hers.

For an instant she almost thought he cared that she might have suffered physical abuse, though for her the emotional barbs scared her just as much. But she'd heard her father apologize for his deplorable behavior for too many years, and watched him break his promises.

"No, he never hit me," she said. "As I already told you, Father reserved his punishment for my mother."

"A lot can change in ten years."

That was an understatement considering she'd found herself trapped in an untenable situation. Since he hadn't believed her then, why show concern now?

She huffed out a breath, his curiosity annoying. Insulting even. It no longer mattered to her what he thought. She certainly didn't owe him an explanation.

His gaze narrowed, hardened. "Answer me."

Again with the demands. But avoiding the issue was more troubling that it was worth. Nothing could be gained by ignoring him.

"A lot can remain exactly the same as well," she said. "But to satisfy your curiosity, I stayed to ensure that my mother wasn't abused. It was the only promise that my father never broke to me."

Marco clenched his teeth against her bare-faced lie. He knew she was lying. Had known ten years ago. But if she was so insistent on pursuing her lies, then he would see how far she would go with them.

"What kept you there after her death?"

"You still don't get it, do you? My father did to me what he did to you. He gained control of my business and the only way I could get it back was to abide by his agreement. I was two months away from getting my company back from him when you launched your takeover."

She glared at the rich, powerful man who held all the cards and tried to forget there had been a time when she'd loved him with each breath she took. When she'd wanted to believe his every word. Wanted to trust him fully. A time when she wrestled between fear and desire.

"Now I'm doing your bidding to gain title to what is mine," she said.

His gaze remained remote. "You'll be amply compensated."

"I'll hold you to the letter of the contract," she said.

He smiled, the gesture brief and calculating. "As will I, Miss Tate. Which is why we will stop at the villa first so you can meet Bella and complete your survey."

Without another word he rose and walked to the rear of the plan, the soft snick of a door the only indication this inquisition was over. That he'd finally left her alone.

She crumbled in the chair and rubbed her forehead, emotionally spent. Despite his resentment of her, or perhaps because of it, he'd given her a golden opportunity to reclaim Elite Affair.

He was following her contract so far, so she couldn't very well complain on that quarter either. Still she wasn't about to let down her guard around him.

This was business. Nothing more. For that reason alone she had to keep her guard up. Had to see this event through to the end. Had to watch that he didn't double-cross her—that once the job was completed, Elite Affair reverted solely to her one hundred percent.

Only then would she be able to start over. To make a life for herself. To be independent for once in her life.

All she had to do was get through the next two weeks.

Moments after the plane smoothly landed at the San Francesco d'Assisi airport on the less hilly outskirts of Perugia, Marco escorted Delanie to a waiting sedan and they were off. He rarely used a driver unless he was entertaining a fellow businessman, preferring to handle the wheel himself down the *autostrada* as well as on the roads that bypassed walled towns and sliced through the patchwork of medieval fields of produce.

But the combination of too little sleep and the emotional upheaval of being near Delanie again curtailed that urge. He tapped a fist on his thigh, still vexed by the latter.

He should not find her attractive. He sure as hell shouldn't begin to believe her lies about her troubled childhood, not when he'd learned the truth. If David Tate had been the beast Delanie swore him to be, her mother would have broken free when she'd had the chance.

He needed his thoughts on the present. His relationship with Delanie was just business, pure and simple. That fact alone called for space between them. Though once they were in the backseat of the car she took that to the extreme and scrunched against the door as if waiting for the chance to jump free.

"I repeat, I am not going to pounce on you," he said.

Her gaze swung to him, a bit wild and overly wide. "I know it's just... You're so intense. So angry still."

He scowled, disliking that he was letting his emotions reign. She was so nervous he literally felt every quick breath she sucked in until his own equilibrium was spinning.

"My apologies then," he said. "It has been a very long day without sleep."

"For both of us." She heaved a sigh and directed her attention beyond the auto again. "It's beautiful here."

"*Il cuore verde d'Italia.* The green heart of Italy." He loved it. Respected it. Nurtured the land to the best of his ability and it rewarded him with kingly yields.

"You've always lived here?"

"For some time now," he said, not inclined to share more of the details of his life with her.

There was no point in it.

She faced him, her perfectly shaped head lifted, pale brows pulled over the proud tilt of her nose. "Your vineyards. Are they near here?"

"The vineyards I inherited or the land your father destroyed?" he asked when he knew damned good and well that the latter was what she meant.

Two swaths of red streaked across her cheekbones. "It always comes back to that, doesn't it?"

"It is not something one forgets."

"Or forgives," she said, frowning. "I'm so sorry Father did that—"

"Save it," he snapped. "I'm in no mood to hear your apology or excuses."

She shut her mouth, hurt he had jumped to conclusions when what she'd been about to say was "to us." Yes, it was horrific that her father had spitefully ruined the business that had been in Marco's family for generations. That he'd added another emotional scar to the ones Marco already suffered.

But the greatest tragedy of all was that Marco saw her as the enemy too, that he had refused to believe her then, that he couldn't find it in him to trust her now.

You don't trust him anymore either.

How funny he'd accused her of lying, of betraying him, when he too had broken his promise. He'd shattered her trust in him.

She heaved a sigh, sick at heart that nothing had changed. They were still two wounded souls, hurting each other because that was easier.

"I'm curious about the vineyard my father destroyed," she said, making herself clear.

He stared straight ahead, annoyed she was continuing her questions, vexed that the ripple of pain reflected in her clear blue eyes got to him, made him believe her innocence if only for a moment.

All an act. It had to be. And if he was wrong? If she was truly ignorant of her father's schemes? If she'd been blackmailed to comply with Tate's dictates?

What did it matter now? Too much had happened between them. He was more jaded than ever before and she was as well or she wouldn't be this cautious, this remote.

"Fine," she huffed out, crossing her arms and staring militantly out the window. "Forget I asked."

He caught himself smiling at her show of temper, admiring

that steel that ran down her spine. A gentleman would comply with her request. But he was no gentleman.

"It is roughly twenty kilometers south of the villa. Half an hour by car." He stared at her profile, willing her to face him. "Less if I'm driving."

She continued her vigil out the window but he thought some of the tension eased from her narrow shoulders, that the slightest hint of a smile teased her soft lips. "How long before we reach the villa?"

"It should not take more than twenty minutes," he said, answering as calmly as she'd asked, keeping his tone low, intimate, as she'd done.

It didn't require a response and she didn't offer one. That was for the best. More than ever he needed to get back to the reason she was here.

Theirs was simply a working relationship. Anything beyond that was too great a risk.

Yet instead of relaxing, his heart accelerated even more during the drive to the Cabriotini villa. The easy explanation was his own unease at returning here, far easier than admitting his thoughts were on Delanie.

The simple truth was this mansion wasn't home to him and never would be. The moment he was away from it, he put the man who'd lived and wasted his life and fortune here completely out of his thoughts.

If he could just do the same regarding the enticing woman beside him. She'd plagued his sleep too often over the years. He'd convinced himself he'd hated her.

A damned lie.

He distrusted her but he didn't hate her. He wanted her with the same fire that had burned in him ten years ago.

The conundrum for him was how to put that fire out?

His gaze flicked to hers and his body stirred more than it had in ages. What the hell was it about this woman? Dare he hope he could get her out of his system? That he could move on?

Overindulgence. Too much of a good thing could sour a man. Perhaps that was what was needed now.

CHAPTER FOUR

DELANIE had caught glimpses of elegant mansions nestled among the hills throughout the drive and had expected Cabriotini Villa to be along the same order. But the moment the auto pulled into an iron-gated drive that swung open automatically, she knew this estate was far grander than any she'd seen so far. Perhaps more so than any she'd visited in England.

For one thing, the villa claimed a commanding view of the valley, perched on a knoll overlooking perfectly aligned fields of grapevines laden with plump purple and blush fruits. On the surrounding fields, groves of olives lined up in precise rows, their leaves shimmering silver in the sun, their black and deep green fruit glistening like jewels.

"Welcome to Cabriotini," Marco said as the driver sped up a long drive flanked by poplars standing like sentinels.

The sun popping through their dense tops created a dappled effect, as if they were waving Marco home. Only instead of a smile he wore a pensive expression as if he dreaded coming here.

"You don't care for your ancestral home, do you?" she asked at last.

"I am only here temporarily—this isn't my home. It's the estate bequeathed to me and Bella by the man who sired us, and it's where we've lived since discovering our paternity."

She blinked, stunned by his vehement tone. "That's a rather impersonal way to refer to your father and your sister."

He cut her a look that made her shiver. "Antonio Cabriotini wasn't my father. His seed gave me life. I never spoke with the man. Never met him though I saw him once from a distance long before I was told I had any connection to him."

An uneasy silence rippled between then. "He must have known who you were."

He shrugged. "I doubt it. Cabriotini didn't attempt to look for his bastards until he was dying. That's when he decided to find an heir."

She offered a thin smile. "He wanted you then."

Marco laughed, the bitter sound mirroring his dislike of his paternity. "Don't paint this into something homey. He detested the thought of leaving his wealth to a distant cousin in Majorca. So he hired investigators to discover if he'd sired any bastards in Italy." He gave a gruff snort. "Cabriotini's attorney hit the jackpot, finding my young sister and then me some months after the investigation was launched."

She winced, her burning cheeks surely as pink as the roses clustered against an ivory wall. "He must have been a very miserable man."

"Cabriotini lived hard and played hard and enjoyed a procession of mistresses. According to them, he made it clear to every women he bedded that he would deny any 'mistakes' that might evolve from a liaison." His mouth pulled into that pained smile again and she shifted away from the car door without realizing she'd done so.

Not that Marco noticed. His gaze was riveted out the window again, his broad shoulders so stiff she imagined them lashed to a steel girder.

She worried her lower lip, wanting to avoid a scene. God knew she'd endured enough of them in her life.

"You haven't been a family for very long then," she ventured, thinking by diverting the conversation to his sister again it could qualify a bit as her doing her job.

"We've never been a family," he said flatly.

"When did you become so cold, so unfeeling?"

"Ten years ago," he said, not even deigning to look at her.

She bit her lower lip and stared at her clasped hands, surprised they were trembling. Of course he would blame everything on that awful night when he'd cornered her and her father in the posh Zwuavé Gardens in Mayfair, accusing David Tate of stealing his family business, accusing Delanie of betraying him.

She'd never been able to forget that ugly scene. Each second of that confrontation was embedded in her memory, each hurtful word tattooed on her heart.

"How could you believe I betrayed you?" she asked as the car cruised down the poplar-lined driveway, taking her deeper into his lair.

Marco snorted, pressing a knuckled fist into the leather seat, accusing gaze drilling into her. "You were the only person I confided in about my grandmother's mental state. You knew I intended to remove her from her role in her own business before she was taken advantage of. You told your father this and he swooped down on her."

As she'd done that night, with her heart threatening to pound out of her chest, she shook her head in denial. "I never told Father anything."

Marco leaned closer and loomed over her. "Then how did he know something that I told only you?"

She shook her head, having no answer. Never in a million years would she have divulged what they'd spoken of in whispers, arms and legs entangled, bare bodies curled perfectly together in a delicious skin-on-skin rub. Their intimacy had been a precious gift to her. She wouldn't have jeopardized that.

But her father would, she admitted, worrying her bottom lip with her teeth, the same question plaguing her mind as well.

She'd been so wrong about this man, certain he loved her, certain he believed her innocence. Certain that he would return for her. But he'd disappeared.

When she'd needed him most, he'd proven to be no better than her father.

That night at the restaurant with Marco and David Tate she'd hardened, realizing with a sinking heart that her father had used her to get to Marco and he'd succeeded. He'd used the one good thing in her life against her—used his daughter.

"What did you do, Father?" she had demanded, ice crystallizing in her veins as she'd confronted her father, his light eyes devoid of any emotion.

"What did I do?" he parroted then laughed, a nasty cackle that taunted—haunted her still. "You know exactly what I did. As you well know, one learns so much through pillow talk."

The insinuation she'd intentionally betrayed the man she loved had her face flaming—not with shame but with anger. She'd known her father was the ultimate manipulator, but she'd never dreamed he would go to such lengths to best Marco.

A huge error on her part. Any man who beat his wife wasn't above using his daughter to his benefit.

"I didn't give you any information," she'd hissed, but her father only gave her that smug smile.

She'd only mentioned her worry over Marco's grandmother to one person: her own mother. But her mother wouldn't have divulged something Delanie told her in private. She wouldn't have betrayed her. Would she?

She'd turned to Marco ten years ago, standing at their table tall and proud and so very angry. "He's lying, Marco. I would never hurt you. Never betray you."

He'd stared at her a long time before he stepped closer, dragging one finger down her cheek that was slick with tears she hadn't realized she'd shed, his palm strong yet gentle as he cupped her chin. She leaned into that hand, her gaze on his, begging him to believe her.

"Then how could your father possibly know things that I shared only with you?" he asked, pulling his hand back, denying her his touch, his trust.

She shook her head, having no solid answer. "He spied on us. He must have."

The anger in his beautiful brown eyes cooled to a brittle glaze that chilled her to the bone. And she knew that the torrid love they'd shared was freezing over.

Marco had backed away from the table, the epitome of arrogant pride. And she held her breath, praying for him to see the truth, waiting for him to extend his hand to her.

Instead, he turned and walked away with brisk determined steps, spine straight, broad shoulders girded in an impossibly stiff line.

She'd pressed trembling fingers to her lips, stilling the cry that tried to escape. Rejection bludgeoned her and she shrank in her chair, humiliated. Stunned. Hurt beyond words.

"That was unpleasant," her father said, returning his attention to his beef Wellington and topped-off glass of port, dismissing her heartache as if it were nothing.

Because to her father, she was nothing. It had never been more clear to her than at that moment.

She pushed to her feet on shaky legs, the scrape of chair legs blaring over the din of happy customers.

"I hate you," she hissed, batting tears from her eyes.

Her father had lifted one sardonic brow then laughed, a dark sound edged with sarcasm. "Of course you do. Perhaps you should hurry after Mr. Vincienta. Beg him to take you back," he said. "I don't need you and neither does your mother."

But her mother did need her.

Delanie could see the retribution gathering in his light eyes and her stomach twisted into a tighter knot. She knew his pattern. He would need to release his tension over being confronted publicly by Marco and now her.

Her mother would pay the ultimate price. Again.

Even so she wove through the restaurant on shaky legs, mumbling excuses as she went, heart thundering in her chest. She had to speak with Marco one more time. She had to make him believe she'd had no part in her father's latest scheme. That she was as much a victim as anyone else.

"Marco!" she cried out as she pushed past the doorman and stumbled onto the sidewalk, her teary gaze frantically searching for him.

He stopped in the arc of light but didn't face her.

Heart in her throat, she gulped a sob and raced to him. Her trembling fingers banded his arm and he stiffened even more.

"I don't know how he found out about your grandmother but I was ignorant of his plan. I played no part in his corporate schemes," she said. "You have to believe me."

He looked at her then with an expression so cold she shivered. "No, I do not have to believe you."

She batted at a tear that leaked from her gritty eyes only to do the same with another. And another. She gave up the effort to stay them and looked at him through a veil of tears.

"I've never told a soul since primary school, but you have to know the truth. Father is abusive," she said.

His brows snapped together. "To you?"

She shook her head and gulped in great drafts of air. "To Mother. He's always abused her, though he was careful her bruises didn't show." Until that last time...

Her fingers inched up his rigid forearm. "I can't leave her. He'll—" She shook her head again, fingers digging into his muscled arm. "I don't know what depths he will sink to this time if I defy him again."

"You're telling the truth?" he asked, his frown fierce.

"Yes," she whispered past dry lips.

"You need to escape his grasp. Come with me to Italy."

When he'd asked her before, in the heat of passion, she'd refused because, while he'd told her he wanted her, he'd never professed his love. He always held back something she couldn't define, she'd just sensed the wall going up. That kept her from totally trusting him as she longed to do.

But now he was giving her a real chance to escape her

hellish life. To be with the man she loved, the man with the wounded heart that she still believed her love could heal. She wanted to go but wouldn't unless specific conditions were met.

"Yes, I'll go with you but not without my mother. I can't leave her to suffer." The guilt of doing so once still plagued her. "Please. I love you, Marco. I need your help. I need you."

Marco jerked his head aside, his rigid posture concealing anything he was feeling. And she'd prayed he believed her. Prayed that he would help her and her mother.

"Go back to your father but say nothing about telling me this," he said. "I'll go to your house now and speak with your mother. Trust me to arrange everything. It will be all right."

She'd swallowed hard. Trust was asking so much, especially with so much at stake. Especially when she was leery of putting her heart and soul into his hands. But she loved him. She wanted to believe he would never hurt her but she needed time—time she simply didn't have.

"Okay," she said. "When will I see you?"

"Soon."

He stood there a moment longer, staring into her eyes before his gaze fixed on her mouth. *Kiss me,* she thought. *Hold me. Convince me everything will be fine. Perfect. Make the fear go away.*

But he did none of that.

In a blink he disappeared into the darkness, leaving her with the unpleasant task of trudging back into the restaurant and facing her father.

"Did you change your mind about leaving with the Italian or did he reject you?" her father asked the moment she eased onto the chair across from him.

She damned the heat flooding her cheeks and averted her eyes so he wouldn't read the truth in them. "He was already gone by the time I got outside."

"Hmm," her father said, cradling his port in one pale hand,

the long slender fingers looking too effeminate to be capable
of inflicting pain.

But she knew differently.

As Marco had asked of her, she suffered the evening in
her father's company. Her nerves jumped like live wires by
the time they returned home but she held onto the belief he
would make everything right. That she and her mother would
soon be free.

She hurried to her mother's room, hoping Marco had talked
over a plan with her. That they would be leaving here soon.
That they would finally be free of David Tate's control.

"Well? What did Marco say? When do we leave?" Delanie
asked in hushed tones.

Small furrows raced across her mother's pale forehead, the
skin so thin and white it was nearly translucent. "I've no idea
what you're talking about."

And so Delanie explained it in a rush, her fragile faith in
Marco withering when her mother gave her a pitying smile.
"He never came, dear. He never called."

"But he said—"

"Men are the kings of false promises," her mother interrupted, her fragile blue-veined hand patting Delanie's in a
conciliatory gesture that failed to comfort. "You should know
that by now."

Yes, she should know it. Did know it. But she'd begun to
trust Marco.

"Mother, did you ever mention what I told you about
Marco's grandmother?" she asked.

"No, not a word," her mother said, but looked everywhere
but at her. "Why do you ask?"

Delanie waved a dismissive hand. "Just curious. It's just
that I told nobody but you and yet Father has learned of it."

Her mother had smiled. "You should know by now that the
walls here have ears."

Yes, of course. A maid must have overheard and told

someone. That's how the information had trickled back to her father.

Delanie had gone to her room that night, refusing to sob. Tears solved nothing. She'd crawled into bed and curled into a ball, vowing never to fall victim to love and a man's control again.

Yet, ten years later, here she was as the car stopped under the portico of the palatial villa, blinking eyes that burned with unshed tears. Heart aching in an all too familiar pain that she thought she had buried long ago.

A glance at the tall Italian who'd just pushed out of the auto gave her the answer.

Years ago Marco had simply stormed out of her life, turning her tenuous trust in him to dust as he walked over the shards of her broken heart. Now he was back, causing her to doubt her mother's loyalty. Making her want to lean on him all over again. The odd pang in her chest confirmed the one thing she'd feared most. She was still vulnerable to Marco's magnetic charm. Still not over him.

This time she would guard her heart.

Marco stood a moment stretching his long legs. His gaze climbed the gray walls of Cabriotini's Italianate villa, the red tile roof gleaming in the late-afternoon sun and the well-tended lawn with artistically designed flower beds overflowing with bright yellow and orange blossoms.

His time living here was about over. Two weeks and he would move to his home. In two weeks he wouldn't be haunted by the stigma of this villa. Or by Delanie Tate?

The hint of a smile tugged at his lips as he rounded the hood. He opened her door and extended a hand, challenging her to accept his manners or publicly snub him.

There was a long pause as she sat huddled on the plush seat, sunlight dancing down the length of her lovely legs encased in the sheerest hose, the skin pale. Were they still as smooth?

Sexy legs. That was the first thing he'd noticed about her before discovering how luscious the whole package was—full breasts, lush, inviting lips, soft, yielding body begging for sex.

"We manage a sparse staff," he said, dragging his gaze back to hers. "But they'll see that your reasonable needs are met."

"I don't need or wish to be waited on," she said, slipping her small hand in his and exiting with the grace befitting quality.

"It's breathtaking," Delanie said, her silken wrap slipping down her arms as she extracted her hand from his.

He just caught himself from grabbing the shawl. From easing it around her narrow shoulders and stealing a caress.

"Yes, breathtaking," he said, his gaze on her.

Her face was uplifted to the sun, one hand shielding her eyes, her golden hair fluttering in the warm breeze scented with ripe fruit. Both were slightly sweet. Intoxicating.

His stomach tightened another notch, but fighting it was as useless as trying to ignore it.

Delanie Tate was still the most beautiful woman he'd ever met. Still stirred something in him that he hadn't truly understood himself. That he couldn't control.

Oh, there was attraction. Lust even. But the odd feelings churning deep inside him went beyond that.

She took him to a level he didn't understand. Didn't trust.

Hell, he couldn't trust her to abide by her word. Which is why he had to keep her close. Had to make sure she planned his sister's wedding right down to the last canapé and curled bit of ribbon, that she saw it through to the end.

She looked at him then, cheeks pink from the sun, lush lips holding a tentative smile.

He sucked in a breath, ignoring the urge to drag her into his arms. Hold her. Kiss her.

"You won't miss living here, will you?" she asked.

"Not one bit. I look forward to moving into my home." He motioned to the door. "After you."

She studied him a moment longer before striding toward the door. He took a breath and followed, keeping his gaze trained on her glorious hair instead of her inviting backside.

"Will you continue to keep in close contact with your sister or are you ready to push her out of your life as well?" she asked.

"Why the concern?" he shot back.

She stopped at the door and faced him. "You've made it clear you have never been a family man and yet you've lived in a place you dislike for years. Now you've gone to the trouble to force me here to plan your sister's wedding." Her gaze locked with his. "Why do all that? And don't spout duty!"

He rubbed the bridge of his nose and heaved a sigh. She couldn't know how much he wanted to rid himself of this place or why. How reluctant he was to open his heart to Bella—the sister who was a stranger in so many ways.

All his life he'd tried to be a good grandson. A good son. A good man to one good woman—Delanie.

But in the end he hadn't been good enough for any of them. His aged grandmother had trusted a stranger over him. His mother had let him live a lie and his biological father had shunned him.

And Delanie...

Delanie had betrayed his trust. His love. And yet she still plagued his thoughts over the years.

The one who got away, he thought with a mocking smile. Only that wasn't the truth.

Sobering, looking at her now standing before him so proud and vexed, he could only admit the truth. She was the one he'd pushed away. Ruthlessly. Furiously.

Wisest thing he'd ever done or biggest mistake of his life? That question nagged at him at the oddest times, but he'd never been more determined to discern the truth until now.

To do that he needed to spend time alone with Delanie.

"It's not Bella I wish to distance myself from," he said at

last, his eyes never leaving hers. "It's this place. It symbolizes a pattern of life that I fell into naturally, just like the man who sired me."

She stared at him through narrowed eyes, mouth drawn in a tight bow. "You were following in your father's footsteps?"

He gave a curt nod, the admission coming hard. "I was certainly headed that direction after the collapse of my business. Cabriotini's death changed that pattern of life. Changed me."

"For the better?"

"That depends on who you ask," he said. "Come. I'm sure you would like to find your room and rest."

"Actually I'd like to meet your sister first. The sooner I can get started formulating plans for her wedding the better."

Not what he expected to hear but he had no objections. Bella could be another matter.

"Of course."

He asked the housekeeper to summon his sister then led Delanie into the salon awash with sunlight thanks to a bank of tall windows. The French doors had been thrown open to the patio, admitting a warm welcoming breeze sweetened with the spice of ripe grapes.

Yet the only scent teasing his senses to distraction was the floral one wafting around Delanie. She was still in his blood, but where he really wanted her was in his bed, willing and hot for him.

Soon, he thought as he crossed to the liquor cabinet. "Would you care for a drink?"

Definitely, but dulling her senses around Marco could be a huge error on her part. More than ever she needed to keep her wits sharp. If she ignored the sudden sexual overtones radiating from him then just maybe she could muddle through being close to him.

Still, she heard herself ask, "Is it one of your labels?"

"Our premiere sagrantino," he said, handing her a glass of glistening torrid red wine. "Eight years old and entering its prime. Or would you prefer something less robust? A merlot perhaps?"

"No, the sagrantino will be fine."

She took the glass from him, careful not to touch his fingers, careful not to find too much significance in that remark. It was no surprise that he remembered her favorite wine. It stood to reason that her adversary would use something she liked to lull her.

Adversary... Her eyes flicked to Marco's dark enigmatic ones and she suddenly couldn't breathe, couldn't do anything but clutch the fine stem of the glass between her fingers.

She ran her tongue over her lips as the intensity in his eyes burned her from the inside out, the heat so strong she feared he would devour her.

This awareness between them had always been there. Always had been strong. But even knowing that hadn't prepared her for the onslaught of emotions. She'd been so sure anger at him would kill her desire. But it hadn't.

"To Bella's wedding," he said, raising his glass.

A trickle of awareness skipped up her arms and legs and she shifted, edgy, needy, instantly aware of the change in him. Was this how a hare felt being stalked?

She stiffened but lifted her glass to his, the melodic ting of crystal resonating in the air while a different awareness played over her nerves, leaving them humming.

"Yes, to your sister's wedding," she said, well aware he was the master of manipulation when it came to her.

He drank, the bronzed column of his throat working, the seductive bow of his lips stained by the dark wine. She stared, unable to move, to do anything but remember a time when they'd found a secluded glen and come together, drinking red wine from cheap glasses and each other.

Her skin tightened at the memory of him laving it off her body with his tongue. How his eyes had locked with hers, blazing with heat and lust and what she'd thought was love. He'd thrust into her deeply that day, making them one, making her feel whole and cherished and loved for the first time in her life.

"Are you sure you wouldn't prefer a different wine?" he asked, breaking the spell that held her as tightly as chains.

She flicked him a smile, hands thankfully steady on the wineglass. "No, I was just tangled in thoughts."

"About?"

About what could have been if they hadn't splintered apart.

Wasted energy. Nothing could come of them together again, but that didn't calm the deep hum that vibrated through her, hot and thrumming with a pulse that was so needy. Even knowing he'd never loved her, she had never been able to forget him. Never had been able to think of letting another man touch her.

She would surely never trust so easily again.

"I was thinking about all I need to do." She swirled the dark wine before taking a sip.

Her senses exploded to life while the alcohol went straight to her head. Just like the man staring at her giving her that bubbly, fuzzy feeling that coursed through her veins.

"Lovely," she got out a bit breathlessly.

"I am glad you like it." He moved closer, almost prying her glass from her stiff fingers then backing her up against the sun-warmed expanse of wall oh so easily. "The fruity taste lingers on the tongue while the tart acidity awakens the palate, don't you think?"

He was going to kiss her. She read it in the dark smoky glint of his eyes. Sensed it in his obviously aroused body pressing close to hers. And, God help her, she wanted that kiss. Wanted his mouth on hers, his hands stroking her body.

Her heart raced like the wind and her mind spun in a bizarre panic. She couldn't let it happen and yet that's exactly what she wanted him to do. Kiss her. Mold her to his length.

"Our relationship is strictly business," she said, clapping a palm against the steely wall of his chest, desperate to stop this, to avoid a repeat of history that would fling her right back into the hot swirling depths of consuming passion.

"It can be whatever we wish," he said, stepping so close her scent swirled about him like silken scarves.

"No. You're wrong."

She held her ground, looking up at him with eyes that had known pain, known heartache. One night long ago he'd glimpsed the beginnings of that grief and believed it, got lost in her need and his own. He wasn't gullible now.

Yet instinct told him that what he read in her eyes was real. This was a reflection of pain learned one way—by experience.

"Why so wary?" he asked. "I've abided by all you asked."

"I've had little cause to trust anyone."

Hadn't they both? "A lesson learned from your father?"

Her chin came up, her gaze frosting. "And from you."

He flinched as the salvo struck his heart. "How can I possibly be blamed for your distrust?"

Dammit, were those tears in her eyes? No matter. He wouldn't let them influence him again.

Ten years ago he'd fallen for her sob story until the truth had won out. It was a painful reminder of how devious a woman could be, a lesson learned from his mother's infidelity.

Nothing learned in his recent investigation of Delanie swayed him to believe her now. She'd tricked him, betrayed him...

"You said you would come for me," she said. "You promised to help me and my mother. But you lied."

His fingers tightened on the glass until they numbed. That was the last thing he expected her to bring up.

"No, that most certainly wasn't a lie," he said.

"Then why didn't you come for me? Why didn't you call?"

Because he'd found her out to be the liar. The one using him in a new way. Yet now he had trouble dredging up that same level of distrust. He found himself questioning what had once seemed so clear.

He drove his fingers through his hair, hating this sense of uncertainty. Is this a hell similar to that his own father had lived with? That had left Marco feeling isolated as a teen? Abandoned? Unloved?

"Papa, why do you ignore me? Why do you and Mama argue all the time?" he'd asked soon after they'd moved to Umbria.

"Ignore you? I'm a busy man," his father had said. "Ask your mother why we are like this," his father would say.

And when Marco had, his mother would burst into tears.

Just as Delanie had when confronted with her betrayal.

Yes, revenge had sounded sweeter than the succulent sagrantino grapes ripening in his vineyard to Marco. He'd lived for this moment. Planned it well. But the reality of forcing Delanie to do his bidding tasted as bitter as fruit harvested far too soon.

The impulse to touch her was too strong. Too overwhelming to ignore. He brushed back errant strands of hair that looked and felt like silk, careful not to touch her skin. Careful not to spook her.

"I did come, Delanie," he said. "I made arrangements to spirit you both away and met with your mother as I'd promised. But when I offered her sanctuary she refused."

"No. Mum wouldn't have done that."

He ground his teeth. If this were a man continually calling him a liar... But it wasn't. It was Delanie, the sweetly feminine thorn in his side.

"Believe what you will," he said, well aware she would anyway.

She set her glass down and pressed both palms to her temples. "This makes no sense. Father abused her. Why would she refuse the chance to escape that life?"

"Your mother denied everything you told me," he said, his eyes boring into her suddenly startled ones.

"No!"

He shrugged. "It's the truth."

And Delanie looked into his eyes and knew it was so. He'd come for her and her mother. But her mum had sworn to her that Marco had never come. Never called.

The last bastion of her childhood crumbled before her eyes into dust, clinging, choking, leaving a remnant of deceit that couldn't be easily wiped away.

That night she'd believed her mother, her confidant. While her heart had been breaking, it had never crossed her mind once that her mother would do anything to harm her. Deceive her.

Delanie pressed trembling fingers to her temples where a headache threatened to pound to life, sickened by the truth that loomed before her. Had the mother she'd sacrificed her own freedom for betrayed her confidence? Used her?

The walls have ears, her mother had told her whenever she would question how her father knew of her plans. And she'd believed her mother, she admitted, hands falling to her sides.

Poor naive fool, she chided herself.

My God, her mother had been the one who'd alerted David Tate to Marco's ailing grandmother. *She'd* told him about Delanie's plans and concerns for her own company, setting the stage to halt her independence. Her mother had stolen her chance of happiness with Marco, all because she would not leave the abusive husband she loved and whose horrific temper she constantly made excuses for.

"I don't know who or what to believe anymore," she said, turning to the window, more confused and hurt and angry than she'd ever been in her life.

"It's difficult when lies are buried among the truths."

So true. It was glaringly clear that both her parents had manipulated and lied to her all her life. Her trust in her mother had made it so easy to play into her father's hands. To give him control over her future while destroying Marco's legacy.

This truth cut deep and bled.

She cast him a quick look then glanced away, unable to meet his steady gaze for long, afraid she would see pity in his eyes. "I don't have the heart even to try anymore."

"It's not like you to give up."

Strong hands cupped her shoulders. His offer of support?

God knew she desperately needed a strong shoulder to lean on now. But Marco? He'd betrayed her as well. He could be using her now.

She shrugged him off and scooted aside, heart thundering and skin tingling. "Don't touch me. Please."

"*Cara*—"

"Am I interrupting a private moment?" a woman asked, her tone holding a hint of amusement.

Delanie stared at the women. She was young and pretty, though the petulant bow to her mouth and the annoying snap of masticating chewing gum kept her from being a raving beauty or an ingénue.

"My sister, Bella," he introduced.

"Delanie Tate," she said.

The younger woman flashed a wide smile. "Good. You're finally here. I'm about to go out of my mind dealing with these old traditionalists."

Delanie flicked a look at Marco but he merely shrugged. It was the first time she'd seen him look uncertain.

She faced the bride. "I gather you would prefer a modern wedding."

Bella bobbed her head. "Heavens, yes. It's a joke for me to wear virginal white."

Heat burned Delanie's cheeks, but she continued smiling and jumped at the chance to get through this crucial meeting with Bella now. Once she knew the young woman's wants she could get to work on a proposal. Far away from Marco Vincienta.

"Please, let's sit and talk," Delanie said, motioning to the seating area where a sumptuous cream sofa was flanked by overstuffed chairs. "What are your preferences as to color?"

Bella slumped onto a stripped chair, pulling her bare feet beneath her. "Pale blue." She frowned. "Or green."

"Both are lovely choices," Delanie said as she took her electronic notebook from her purse and eased onto the sofa close to Bella, ready to fill the blanks in on her unique form. "With your dark coloring, you would look stunning in either though the green would truly bring out the gold flecks in your dark eyes."

Eyes that were strikingly similar to Marco's. They must have their father's eyes, she surmised, though she refrained from saying that aloud.

"I would love that," Bella gushed.

A glance at Marco found him watching his sister, dark brows drawn over his classic nose and muscular arms locked over his broad chest. Delanie had expected impatience but he seemed as interested in what his sister said as Delanie.

She shook off the distraction that was solely Marco with a discreet cough, vowing to ignore him. "I gather you'd like nontraditional flowers as well?"

Bella nodded. "Anything but roses or calla lilies or anything else that someone has declared as symbolizing everlasting love."

Ah, that was a telling remark if she ever heard one. But she didn't press the point now with Marco watching them like a hawk.

She was here to please his sister. Not him. He'd already told her money was no object.

Delanie made a few notes, already having an idea of an avenue to pursue. "Where will the ceremony be held?"

"The cathedral in the village," Marco said.

"No! I will marry in St. Antonio de Montiforte or not at all," Bella said.

An uneasy tension pulsed between the siblings. Delanie

cleared her throat, having dealt with similar matters in the past.

She faced Marco. "You hired me to plan a wedding that would please your sister, to do as she wishes. That means that she decides where to exchange her vows. Correct?"

Marco mumbled something, likely a curse. "Fine. Have the wedding in Montiforte. Force your guests to drive an hour to your wedding and back here for the reception. Unless you have changed your mind about that as well!"

"We want to hold the reception in Castello di Montiforte," Bella said.

Marco scrubbed a hand over his mouth and shifted, and for a moment Delanie almost felt sorry for him having two women tear down his plans. But his refusal to believe her still rose like a wall between them, bolstering her determination to keep her distance from him.

He heaved a sigh. "Perhaps since the gardens are less than perfect it is best to hold the reception there."

"I knew you would understand," Bella said, then smiled such a serene smile that Delanie nearly laughed.

Marco snorted but kept his thoughts to himself.

In short order, Delanie went over a few more points to ensure she had no doubts as to the bride's preferences.

"That should do it," Delanie said. "I'll contact you if I have any questions. And please, if you want anything changed, no matter how insignificant it seems, let me know right away."

"I will." Bella clapped her hands together and rose. "Thank you for agreeing to plan my wedding after all."

"Thank your brother," Delanie said. "He convinced me to travel here."

Bella squealed and ran to her brother, throwing her arms around him with a hug that looked comfortable. "Marco, *grazie!* It will be perfect now. Oh! I must tell my fiancé. You will take care of Miss Tate?"

"Very good care." He gaze flicked to Delanie, his smile going from brotherly to something knowing and hot.

A zillion butterflies took flight in her stomach and she pressed a hand to her middle before taking a breath. She couldn't stay here at the villa while she was planning a wedding that was taking place an hour away. She couldn't stay anywhere near Marco without having to battle her desire every moment.

"I have a tremendous amount to do in short order," she said as she stuffed her electronic notebook back in her purse. "Which is why I must relocate to Montiforte. "

"You're serious?"

"Very." She rose and faced him, and damned her suddenly weak knees. It simply wasn't fair that he had this effect on her. "I would appreciate it if your driver would take me there now so I can get settled in. I want to start early in the morning with the arrangements."

He crossed his arms over his chest and lifted one mocking brow. "Why do I have the feeling you are anxious to get away from me?"

"I'm sure I wouldn't know. The driver?"

"I sent him home for the night."

"Then I'll ring for a cab."

"That isn't necessary."

She slapped her hands on her hips and fumed. "I suppose you have a better idea?"

His widening smile was a sensual promise that every nerve in her body recognized and responded to with a quickening sizzle through her blood. "Of course, *cara.* I'll take you to Montiforte and personally see you settled in."

CHAPTER FIVE

EMOTIONS whirled like a vortex within Delanie, leaving her shaking. Being in Marco's company for another hour was the last thing she wanted. But suffering the sexual allure of his body again was preferable to staying in this villa with him in residence, knowing he was just down the hall.

If only she could fully trust that she would walk away from this in total control of her business. But she couldn't.

Her father had used her. If Marco had told the truth, then her mother had lied. Even then, there was the fact that Marco refused to believe her.

She bit her lower lip, trying to get entranced by the ribbons of sun streaming over the undulating hills. If only she could find more appeal in this sunset instead of the man beside her.

Impossible to do with him behind the wheel of the powerful red sports car. Ferrari? Bugatti? She hadn't a clue.

No matter how hard she tried, her gaze kept flicking back to his hands on the leather-wrapped wheel. Hands that she remembered all too well coaxing oh-too-ready responses from her body with equal ease.

"You will have absolute privacy here," he said.

Twilight bathed the hills in shades of amber and crimson by the time they reached the walled hamlet of Montiforte. An ancient castle dominated one end of town and an equally aged church filled the other.

In between rose a collection of oddly shaped buildings, some standing nearly atop the other. All faced a small square piazza where a lichen-covered god stood on an equally aged stepped pedestal next to an old well.

"I didn't expect Montiforte to be so small and medieval," she said.

"It is one of the oldest settlements in Umbria. Come, the village market is still open. You will need supplies at the villa."

She climbed out before he could assist her this time and walked with him to the lone shop. The sweet fragrance of ripe grapes hung in the air, but Marco's spicy scent dominated. Just like the man.

The shopkeeper greeted him by name, but the rest was lost to her as they lapsed into a rapid flow of Italian. She took the time while they visited to wander around the small shop.

The savory smells were feasts in themselves. Balls, ropes and small wheels of cheese hung amid an array of sausages.

Canted tables held an assortment of fresh fruits and vegetables. She leaned over a baker's case filled with baguettes, fat rounds of breads and a selection of rolls. One round loaf caught her eye.

"The *torta di testo* is delicious toasted and drizzled with olive oil," Marco said, standing beside her holding two cheeses and a string of sausage. "It is good for sandwiches as well."

The shopkeeper nodded and brought out a basket filled with the round flat bread. His smile encouraged her to choose.

"Thank you," she said, selecting several and trying not to recall a similar day outside London when she and Marco had stopped in a shop for a takeaway lunch, deciding spontaneously to turn it into a picnic instead.

And they'd feasted the better part of the day on sweets and savories and hot kisses, getting more intoxicated on each other than on the wine. One look at him now was proof he could do so again.

A hot swirl of heat curled low in her belly and she frowned, annoyed her thoughts always splintered off into something torrid with him. It would be so easy to fall into his arms, his bed.

But with pleasure came heartache. She'd learned that lesson well. Even the unspoken promise of pleasure she glimpsed in his eyes could turn on her like a viper.

"This is really more than enough," she said.

"Who knows? You may have company."

Like him? Her throat went dry at the thought of entertaining Marco in a villa, just the two of them. There had been a time when she would have done anything to get him alone.

"I'm sure I'll be far too busy working to receive guests," she said, pulling out her wallet to pay for her purchases.

"Meals are included in your contract," he said, giving the shopkeeper a look that had the man turning from her.

There wasn't a thing in the contract regarding meals and they both knew it, but again arguing would only raise another passion. Best to let that issue rest.

She was already tired from the journey and stressed to the max by being with Marco again. "Thank you then."

Outside her gaze drifted over the stone buildings and narrow streets and walkways rising like steps up the hillside. There was just enough sun to give the village a Monet aura with bluing shadows creeping over stucco washed a mellow gold by the setting sun.

"There is a bistro near the castle that serves amazing food," he said as he joined her, his shadow swallowing her whole much as she knew his passion would do if she surrendered to it. "I suggest we eat before you retire to your residence."

And wouldn't that be cozy? Her sharing an intimate meal with the man she still found far too desirable.

She diverted her eyes from the magnetic draw of his. "I'm far too weary from the journey to enjoy it. Besides I have ample food to sustain me should I get hungry."

Over the thud of her own heart she heard the melodic strains of a mandolin, the music floating on a cooling breeze.

But she felt no chill, not with Marco standing so close, not when his nearness warmed her from the inside out.

"Very well then," he said. "Another time."

Not if she could avoid it.

He pressed a hand to her back and she swallowed a gasp as heat flooded her, spiraling out from his splayed fingers to flow through her in sultry waves. No, she had to keep her distance from this man who was already taking far too many liberties.

She hurried to the car and climbed in, not waiting for him to assist her. He hissed a curse and closed the door after her, and she took a breath then another as he walked around the front of the car, one strong, well-boned hand riding the sleek hood.

In moments he threw himself behind the wheel and they were off, the car winding up the hills lined with poplar and flanked by fields of grapes, their leaves a burnished gold hiding grapes that looked black this time of day.

Marco handled the powerful car with ease, seeming so arrogantly sure of himself that her nerves tightened another notch. She was no match for him. Never had been.

How funny that he accused her of betraying him, using him, when she'd been the vulnerable one, caught up in the magnetic pull of the dashing Italian. In the span of several weeks, he'd romanced her and proposed marriage.

While she desperately waited for him to come for her, he'd deserted her without explanation. Left her to believe her family's lies.

She'd lost her heart and her will to trust in love again. Lost control of her company and her life. Regaining it had became her goal. Her only vow was to avoid Marco should their paths ever cross again.

Yet here she was with him again, trying valiantly to subdue the stirrings of need inside her. She searched for gaping holes in everything he told her yet found nothing more than shadowed valleys.

She wanted to hate him, but her heart wouldn't let her. So

she hated herself for her inability to get over him, for not purging him from her system long ago.

"We're here." He stopped the car in front of a villa bathed in a burnished gold swath of sunset.

Her stomach tightened. "Is this a bed and breakfast?"

"No." His shirt glowed white with the sleeves rolled up and his tanned muscular forearms bared. "It is a private villa above Montiforte."

"A rental then?" she asked, thinking the fee must be exorbitant and glad she didn't have to pay the cost.

"It is yours for your stay here."

He extracted himself from behind the wheel with predatory grace and she stole a deep breath to steady her nerves, her entire body surrendering to a tremble as she blew it out. The trunk opened and closed, jarring her to move. But her door opened just as her hand was reaching for it.

She stared up into his eyes that were darker than sin and for the life of her she couldn't speak, couldn't move.

His hand reached for her and she froze, forgetting to breathe. "I won't bite."

Ah, but he had. Delicious nibbles along her limbs that she remembered with sensual clarity.

For the second time she placed her hand in his and left the car. Thankfully he let go of her first, reaching for the bag of groceries she clutched in one hand.

"I've got it," she said, stepping back.

He stared at her another moment before he motioned to the villa, his teeth wickedly white in the fading light. "Let's get you settled. A housekeeper comes twice a week. She'll be in tomorrow morning."

"Thanks for the warning."

Her skin tingled, nerves pinging wildly as she marched up the winding walk to the arched door. What was the matter with her that she couldn't squash thoughts of them entangled?

It was over. Done. She was here to do a job. Nothing more.

Her fingers closed around the antique brass knob but the door was locked. He reached around her to work a key into the lock, his spicy scent enveloping her and sending her senses on another spiraling jolt.

She turned, thinking to scoot away and give him room to open the door. Instead he caged her in with an arm to the door at her back and his hard unyielding length at her front.

His warm breath fanned her cheek and she bit back a moan. "Back off."

"No way."

His teeth flashed in a wolf's smile a heartbeat before he claimed her mouth with a possessive hunger that sparked a firestorm in her blood, that flung her right back to when Marco had first swept into her life like a hot tropical storm and spun her static existence on its head.

Distantly she heard a muffled thump. Her bag? She didn't know. Didn't care.

His arms banded around her, hauling her close, molding her to his length. His gaze burned into hers, melting her resolve. Every nerve in her body came awake, snapping and sizzling.

She wanted his kiss even though she knew it was wrong of her, even though she knew it could throw open the door to old pain. Her palms pressed against the unforgiving wall of his chest, but instead of shoving him away, they relearned the impressive contours of toned muscles.

His kiss commanded. Consumed. Her rigid admonition to keep him at arm's length caught fire and burned to ash as her fingers splayed, exploring the breadth of the man who haunted her dreams.

He was broader, more muscled, more dominant than before. More arrogantly male than any man she'd ever met, but she couldn't find the strength or reason to resist him, couldn't do anything but press against him and return his kisses with a matching heat, like a flower unfurling its petals to the glory of the sun.

One hand held her head just so, fingers threaded through her hair while the other stroked down her side, grazing the side of her breast, the dip of her waist and flare of her hip, setting off sensations she'd hadn't felt in too long.

She stirred, restless for him to do more than tease. To slip a hand between her thighs and ease the ache building inside her to the point she feared she would explode.

But he did nothing more than hold her tight and plumb the cay of her mouth. The spicy taste of him on her tongue was a delicious bubble that fizzed through her blood like champagne.

And popped as he pulled away, his smile smug. Victorious.

Why shouldn't he be since he'd beaten down her defenses with little effort?

Her face burned but her body chilled. She pushed away from him and stormed inside, whirling to face him, fingers taking a punishing grip on the open door.

"Leave me be, Marco. Get it through your head that I want nothing to do with you."

Near-black eyes drilled into her, his desire evident. "Then why did you kiss me?"

"Consider it a weak moment that won't happen again," she said. It could lead nowhere but to more hurt for her because she wasn't one who could have an affair without emotions. "I'm here to do a job. Not to delve into casual sex with a former lover."

He smirked. "You could have fooled me."

She hiked her chin up and shoved the door shut, refusing to dignify that remark. All she wanted now was privacy so she could sort through the tangle of emotions tugging at her.

He caught the heavy panel before it arced halfway and pushed it wide. "We aren't done yet."

"I disagree. Now please leave so I can focus on your sister's wedding, or have you forgotten that's why you forced me to come here?" She swept up her bag of groceries and stormed into the salon, hoping the kitchen lay through the wide arched opening ahead.

Her instincts were right, amazing considering the steady thud of his steps on the terra-cotta tiles that should have sent her running. Despite the dark open-beamed ceilings, the villa was surprisingly light, the kitchen especially so thanks to arched double doors that opened onto the terrace to let the last rays of the setting sun arrow through their multi-paned glass panels.

"I have not forgotten," he said, his voice so close that she knew he was right on her heels.

She placed her bag from the market on the large brick bar topped with the same warm terra-cotta tiles and whirled to face him. "Then please, leave me in peace."

His lips pulled into a thin line, but it was the windows slamming down on his desire at the same time as rigidity stole over his features that fascinated her. He looked every inch the unforgiving ruthless businessman.

To think she'd been so close to letting him command her body again. Far too close to risk being in his company much longer.

"How long do you really think you can go on denying what we both want?" he asked.

"Forever," she shot back.

He straightened and crossed his arms over his chest. "You will change your mind."

Damn his arrogance! Damn it that he was right! If she spent much time with him she would crumble into his arms, into his bed. That kiss had proved just how weak she was around him.

That admission shamed her. Hadn't the pain of having her father and then Marco betray her been enough?

And if he was telling the truth? If Mother did lie to him that night, sending him away with the belief that Delanie had been in league with her father?

She shook her head. What did it matter? True love wouldn't dissolve at the first sign of trouble.

Marco should have believed her. He should have returned to her, confronting her with what her mother had said, because if he had...

She would have left with Marco that night. She wouldn't have wasted the last ten years of her life.

If she could believe Marco...

"I won't change my mind," she said, painfully aware she couldn't turn back the hands of time, that she couldn't regain what had been lost.

He deposited her overnight bag on the terra-cotta floor, his gaze riveted on her. A few feet separated them but the magnetic pull between them was just as strong as ever.

"We'll see," he said, the firm lips that had ravished hers curving in a knowing smile.

That's all it took to set off a deep quiver that arced between her hipbones and mocked her ability to refuse him for long. They both knew her mind could say no but her body was a traitor, wanting him still.

She grabbed her overnight case and stormed toward the back of the house, hoping she would find a bedroom with a solid door. "Thank you for arranging for me to stay here. You know the way out."

That was met with silence which didn't surprise her. She just prayed he would leave, that he wouldn't remain here to tear down the already shaky wall surrounding her defenses.

Escape through the first door to the right seemed most prudent. She closed it behind her and ran home the old-fashioned bolt to keep Marco out.

And then, finally, she took a deep quivery breath and sagged against the door. The bag slipped from her hands and dropped. She closed her eyes and listened.

A lifetime seemed to pass before she heard the purr of a powerful engine. It had to be Marco leaving as she'd asked, though the only way to know would be to return to the dining area.

She grabbed her bag and pushed away from the door, then simply stared at the huge bed that dominated the room. A bit much for a rental and far larger than what she needed, but she wasn't about to complain.

Once she'd put her change of clothes in a dresser drawer, she ventured back into the dining area. The house was quiet with one lamp on in the salon. Nobody was here but her and her lingering memories.

Still, she opened the front door and stepped out onto the terrace, scanning the area shrouded in shadows. Lights winked at her from the village below, but there was no sign of Marco's flashy red car.

He'd left.

She trudged inside and secured the locks on the door, then moved to the ones off the dining area and did the same. A yawn slipped from her followed by another.

When had she eaten last? She couldn't remember. Her stomach had been in too tight a coil on the flight to risk food. Now she was simply too tired.

She needed sleep, but first needed to deal with the food she'd bought. Or Marco had bought. Did it matter at this stage?

It took a moment to put the fresh vegetables and fruit on a plate. Another to slip the cheese and sausage into the refrigerator.

That already had food in it? She blinked. Straightened.

Was this an added service like posh hotels? You pay for what you use? Or forgotten items from the last renter?

She shook her head and let loose another yawn. It was a matter she could deal with tomorrow.

Moments later she secluded herself in the big bed, on the verge of exhaustion. A muffled sound threatened to snap her out of it, but the sleep pulling at her was too great for her to stay alert.

Quiet. All was quiet. The doors were locked. Marco was gone from the house. She hoped he would be absent from her dreams as well this night.

The decisive closing of a door brought Delanie wide awake. She sat up in the sumptuous bed and blinked, stunned that the sun was already up.

The echo of footsteps on the tiles drifted to her. She tensed. Alert. Someone else was in the villa.

It took a moment for her mind to clear. It must be the housekeeper Marco had mentioned.

She let out the breath she'd sucked in and headed for the en suite facilities. A quick shower would wash away the last dregs of sleep, a necessity since she did need to get started planning Bella's wedding today.

With luck her path would rarely cross a certain arousing Italian's for the next two weeks. Now if she could just keep him from intruding on her thoughts.

After giving her hair a quick towel-drying, she dressed in black jeans, a turquoise jersey and sandals.

By the time she had her morning tea and fruit, her fine hair would be dry and she could set off to the center of Montiforte. With luck she could hitch a ride with the housekeeper.

An afternoon spent in the village would be the ideal time for her to combine personal shopping with a brief investigation of what was readily available there. When she was exhausted, she could either rent an auto or hire a cab to drive her back to the villa.

The second she stepped into the kitchen, awash in sunlight, she saw the housekeeper busy dusting in the salon. A plate of flaky pastries were set out on the kitchen bar with a jar of some dark berry jam beside them.

Her mouth watered and the hollow pang in her stomach confirmed she'd gone far too long without food. But then, she'd been too upset on the flight even to think about eating.

"Good morning," she greeted as she stepped into the kitchen to make a pot of tea.

The housekeeper stopped dusting and humming and looked up with a smile. "*Buongiorno, signorina!* Please, enjoy the *cornetto* with jam," she said, motioning to the counter.

"Thank you, I will."

She sat at the bar and ate a pastry topped with a sweet berry jam accompanied by an invigorating cup of morning tea sweetened with honey. This was the type of casual breakfast that she'd never been allowed to enjoy in the manor she'd grown up in.

Eating with the help was unheard of by both her parents. Forbidden, a lesson she learned late.

The few times she'd been caught in the kitchen chatting with the help, they had both been punished. She shifted, frowning as she tried to remember faces of servants that suddenly no longer worked for them. And then there were the more painful remembrances of workers who ceased treating her with familiarity.

Sitting here now while a housekeeper she didn't even know hummed and worked and chatted with her was a refreshing change. It was like living in a real home.

"These are delicious. Where did you buy them?"

The older woman laughed. "I make. It was my nonna's recipe, handed down from her mother." The woman waved a hand as if it progressed even further back.

"How lucky," Delanie said and meant it, earning her another smile.

She had absolutely no talents handed down from generation to generation. Or at least none that she would carry on.

"Have you lived in Montiforte long?" she asked the housekeeper.

"All my life," the woman said, returning to her work as if it were perfectly natural to do so among tenants. "My family has worked in the Toligara vineyards for generations." She frowned. "Signore Vincienta's grandfather was a good man who died too young. If he had been alive, the Toligara lands would never have been stolen. It was a bad three years in the valley working for the Englishman."

Delanie's face burned, not needing to know the man's name. She knew. Just like she knew how badly things had been under her father's care.

"It must have been a dreadful time," she said.

The housekeeper bobbed her head. "All is good again now that Signore Vincienta is managing Toligara."

Marco, of course. Interesting that such a stern man was so well loved by the people. That the business didn't bear his own arrogant name. But perhaps he was a better steward of the land and his employees than lover?

She pushed that arousing thought from her mind, but not before a giddy tightening streaked inside her. "Does your husband work in the Toligara vineyards?"

"No, the olive groves," she said. "I clean signore's house once a week."

"Really?"

Delanie strolled to the double doors and looked over the inviting terrace to the rolling hills beyond. Why would a billionaire only keep a weekly housekeeper when he could certainly afford fulltime staff? But then she recalled he maintained a minimal staff at Cabriotini Villa as well. Penury? Or was there another reason he shunned being waited on?

She shook her head, annoyed her thoughts were continually turned to Marco. But then it was clear he had a fan in his housekeeper, Delanie thought sourly.

"Is there a taxi service in Montiforte?" she asked.

The housekeeper laughed. "Montiforte isn't large enough for that."

"I had hoped to hire one to take me to the village."

"Why?" the housekeeper asked. "It is a short walk down the hill before you are on the upper alleyway of Montiforte."

"Oh. I hadn't realized it was that close," she said. The drive up had certainly seemed endless. But then time seemed to crawl when she was alone with Marco.

"I will clean your bedroom and en suite now, okay?" the housekeeper said.

"Yes, of course." She waved the woman on. "Do you have another house to clean today?"

"Oh, no. Signore pays me enough that I can work here one day a week."

The housekeeper disappeared into the bedroom, humming the same lilting tune she had earlier.

Delanie took three steps after the woman then stopped dead. No, she had to have misunderstood the housekeeper. This couldn't be Marco's house.

But as she turned in a slow circle, taking in the details she'd overlooked last night, it was clear this wasn't a rental. This was a home, with a few framed photos on the fireplace mantel and other personal touches strewn around.

But a billionaire's home?

No, it couldn't be. This quaint farmhouse nestled in the hills couldn't be where Marco lived.

Still, to be sure, she marched into the front bedroom and flung open the closet door. His spicy scent enveloped her as a dizzying surge of awareness spiraled up her limbs.

As if that weren't proof enough, suits, trousers, shirts hung in precise order. All were clearly high-end garments. All were his size.

She spun around, face flaming as her gaze flicked over the huge bed freshly made. The dresser with a minimum of clutter atop it. The jacket he'd worn yesterday was tossed haphazardly on a chair.

Her fingers tightened on the doorknob. Her blood cooled, glazed over with ice.

Damn him! He'd brought her to his home and had had the audacity to spend the night in the room next to her.

Fine! One night spent in his company didn't qualify. But she certainly wouldn't spend another with him in the next room, not when he'd made it clear that he desired her. Not when her body was at odds with her convictions, readily melting at his slightest provocation.

"Do you know where I might find a bed and breakfast or inn close by?" Delanie asked, standing in the bedroom she'd used last night and realizing the paintings on the wall were authentic.

Wealth. It had been all around her yet she'd failed to recognize it.

"You are leaving?" the housekeeper asked.

Delanie smiled. "It would be more practical if I stay right in town."

The housekeeper shook her head and returned to dusting. "There are two in the village but you won't find a room. The wine festival begins in a few days."

Montiforte would certainly be teeming with people and would have the best of the region on display. That could make planning the wedding far easier.

But to stay in the villa with Marco? To be secluded here?

An ache streaked across her midsection again and tightened. Desire. It had been so long since she'd felt it this keenly. Ten years to be exact.

No, she couldn't do this. Couldn't be close to him again.

"How far away is the nearest village?" she asked the housekeeper as she burst into the sunbathed kitchen.

Silence answered her. The room was empty.

A quick check of the salon confirmed she was the only one here. Her shoulders slumped. The housekeeper had left.

The housekeeper who came weekly to Marco's house.

She jabbed her fists at her sides. How could she have been so blind? How had she not known he was sleeping in the room next to hers?

CHAPTER SIX

DELANIE grabbed her bag which held all she would need for planning and breezed out onto the terrace.

Walking was invigorating. Walking just might clear her head of those unbidden, unwanted thoughts that kept intruding about Marco.

And even if it didn't, she needed to go to Montiforte and make sure there wasn't a room to be had.

The heels on her sandals clicked on the terra-cotta tiles that spanned the terrace. She frowned, wishing she had a more substantial shoe for the walk but the only other footwear she had with her were black pumps.

So personal shopping was high on her agenda as well.

As she reached the edge of the patio, the grandeur of the area literally took her breath away and pushed all other worries to the back of her mind. This was heady stuff for a girl raised in the city.

She shielded her eyes and stood as close to the edge as she dared. For as far as she could see, the beauty never ended.

Autumn painted the undulating countryside in a patchwork blanket of varying greens and golds. Interspersed among the hills were villages, clusters of buildings stacked into the hillsides.

In the distance she glimpsed a river winding through the valley, its details muted by distance into a wash of greens and blues, like a Monet painting come to life. On the rolling hills stretched neat rows upon rows of vines, all laden with plump grapes so dark a blue they gleamed nearly black in the sunlight.

She breathed in the fresh air as she stood where the hill dropped off into a gentle slope, the trail leading downward to nothing more than a graveled meandering path wide enough for two. The day was beautiful and calming, the sun warm on her face and arms with the breeze just cool enough to make the exertion of a walk pleasurable.

In moments she slipped under the charming Roman arch crusted with lichen and onto a narrow path that wound down the hill. Gray stone crunched underfoot and the trill of song-birds sang to her from high in the trees. The tiered gardens built into the hillside still overflowed with small orange and yellow blossoms, their color emphasized by gold and rust leaves.

But despite the allure on the terraced hillside and the spine of mountains looming in the distance, Marco remained in her thoughts. He had always been a fever in her blood and now was no different. In fact, now might be worse.

One touch, one taste only left her wanting more. Even though she knew it was folly, knew she would be the one hurt in the end, she couldn't banish the dreams of lying in his arms just once more.

Clearly she was mad. What else could explain why she was attracted to the man who'd hurt her?

She shook her head and moved on, focusing on the curved stone archway of a building that protruded from the hillside, its side covered in vines. A truck was parked nearby, its bed heaped with harvested grapes.

Her gaze fixed on the man striding toward her, broad shoulders squared and face drawn in a scowl that was darker than midnight. Marco, she realized, even before she got a clear look at his face.

He wore jeans so faded they were nearly white and a black

sweater that molded to his muscular chest and hugged his lean hips. His attire was so casual and so worn he could have passed for the lorry driver.

Her skin pebbled as fluttery ribbons of awareness wrapped around her, holding her tight to the spot. With effort she squared her shoulders and lifted her chin, determined to meet him head-on. To be practical and all business.

His hot gaze paused for a moment on the flimsy sandals dangling from one hand to her very bare feet. One brow lifted.

Her toes curled as did something low in her belly.

"Beautiful but impractical," he said.

She wasn't sure if he meant her in general or the straps of leather that she slipped on her tired feet. "I didn't have anything else but heels which would have been dangerous. If you would have just let me return home to pack—"

"Why are you here?"

Well, what did she expect? Pleasantries? A warm greeting?

"I am on my way to Montiforte," she said and managed a polite smile. "Why didn't you tell me the villa was yours?"

"There was no reason to." He glanced at his watch with a scowl. "I'll drive you to Montiforte."

"That's not necessary. Your housekeeper told me it was an easy walk," she said, the breathy catch in her voice mocking her stamina.

The last thing she wanted to do was be alone with him. If he hadn't kissed her, if her body hadn't so readily responded, she might be able to suffer through his company. But after having his hands on her, his lips devouring her own and setting her blood on fire, she couldn't risk it. He was simply too dangerously appealing and those memories she'd never been able to purge from her thoughts were rushing forward, tempting her with wild ideas of how good it could be with him.

"I insist. Come. Let me show you the winery and then we will have lunch," he said.

"Marco, I must get to town." Must get away from him while she could, while she still had the will to resist him.

"You can spare a half hour," he said. "There is a bistro in Montiforte that serves excellent fare. I insist you join me."

Of course he would. The cosmic force that was solely Marco engulfed her, threatened to wash her out into an uncharted sea that terrified her and enticed her.

"I appreciate the offer but I have a lot to do." Like visit the shops without Marco's company, without sharing lunch with him which sounded far too much like a date. "Time is short to get everything in order."

He waved her worry away. "As it is for me, overseeing the harvest as well as finalizing preparations for the festival. But we both must eat. As for wine, it goes without saying that we will serve our label at the wedding, but you should sample it so you are aware what foods would best be served."

What to say? She had every reason to trust in their contract that precisely detailed her duties and her reward for complying, but the fact that he'd lied about owning the villa kept her suspicions alive.

Her father had excelled at rescinding offers and finding loopholes in contracts. She had no idea if Marco had become just as ruthless.

"Point taken," she said. "The housekeeper mentioned the festival, but I hadn't realized it coincided with harvest and the wedding."

He threaded fingers through his thick hair. "Yes, too much happening at once. And not just here but throughout Umbria. It's maddening."

"And now a wedding," she said, and wished that his smile hadn't warmed her so. But it had and there was no denying her attraction to him.

"*Si*. This way." He laid a hand at the small of her back and urged her forward.

Her skin burned beneath his palm, the heat seeping into her

bones and leaving her weak-kneed. But she forced her legs to move, taking each step with care and hoping he didn't notice how much his touch affected her.

The interior of the winery was a welcome distraction, a beautifully vaulted space with warm terra-cotta floors and ancient-looking frescoed walls that simply took her breath away. "This is absolutely gorgeous."

"My great-great-grandfather built the winery and a local painter did the walls. Generations have added on to the structure but none have touched the fresco."

"Nor should they ever."

"Precisely. I made necessary repairs once I'd reclaimed it, but for the most part this building is as it had been four generations ago. Come, let me show you the rest." He slipped his arm around her shoulders and escorted her through the room, accompanied by the gawks of onlookers, as if it were the most natural thing to do, as if they hadn't been separated for ten years.

An electric shiver eddied through her, bringing every sensation awake. Her blood hummed from the contact, from the promise in his touch and from the memory of pleasure untold.

She hated that he still had this effect on her even though she savored this connection. The contradiction in her baffled her and she hated that as well. Hated that he could control the situation and her, hated that a part of her would always want this closeness.

He stepped from her and she just caught herself from grabbing him and holding on to this fragile contact. Her face burned at the admission. Thankfully he was busy moving something out of the walkway so he didn't notice her flush.

She tore her gaze from the man who commanded too much of her thoughts and gave her chilled arms a brisk rubbing. The room was stacked to the arched ceiling with oak barrels, and a pungent aroma hung in the air.

"You are cold." He grabbed a man's jacket off a peg and

swept it around her shoulders before she could protest wearing a communal garment.

His scent drifted off the fabric and she stilled, knowing this was his. Another puzzlement that was solely Marco.

She had never thought a man in his position would hang his coat among the workers' rough jackets. Yet common sense told her that he would need this if he spent any amount of time here and she knew he must. Knew that Marco wasn't just a man to spout orders or supervise—that he was one who would lend his back to a task as well.

And that only served to remind her that she really had never known Marco Vincienta at all.

"Thank you," she managed, clutching the jacket close and welcoming the warmth. "I didn't realize the winery was so large."

"It is deceiving from the outside. This is actually a natural cave that has been used by the Toligara family for centuries." He motioned above them to the network of round pipes. "I've made substantial changes to modernize the winery. These pipes carry the new wine to the casks."

"Why so many?"

"Each is a different type of wine, and they must not be mixed."

"Wow," she said, lowering her gaze to find him watching her with eyes that held an intimacy she didn't wish to explore here with her defenses already in tatters. "How badly did my father damage it?"

"The winery and olive groves suffered minimal damage. But the vineyards…" He paused and a shadow crossed his eyes. "There were few vines left alive and those needed much nurturing. Each day that I struggled to rebuild I hated your father more, not for his stealth in acquiring my family's business but for maliciously destroying it."

"You hated me just as much or more," she said.

He moved toward her with predatory grace, eyes locked

with hers. She tried to make her shaky legs move but they got the message late, managing to do no more than shuffle back a fraction, his advancing steps besting her retreating ones.

"I tried to but I could not," he said, the scratch in his usually controlled voice catching her by surprise. "What about you, *cara?* Do you hate me still?"

Her back slammed against the wall, the stones cool and hard against her spine, his gaze hot and probing hers. That familiar tingling danced over her heart, her belly, before settling low between her legs. She clenched her muscles, willing the needy sensations away, but that only made the ache more intense, more demanding.

The woodsy scent that was uniquely his enveloped her. He was far too close. Far too powerful. Far too tantalizing.

"I have no feelings toward you at all."

"Not even desire?" he asked.

"No, none," she said with surprising nonchalance.

His gaze drilled into her and she squirmed, her insides twisting and her heart hammered against her ribs. "You're lying, *cara.* The rapid pulse in your throat tells me your heart is racing. Your eyes are dilated with your need and your nipples are peaking through your shirt. If I put my hand between your legs would you be wet for me too?"

Damn him! Was she that transparent? "I'm here to do a job, Marco. Get that through your head. Nothing more."

He smiled but that left her more uneasy. "You do realize you cannot escape the inevitable," he said, a note of amusement ringing in his voice that echoed in the cavernous keeping room.

She was realizing far too much being alone with him. Feeling far too natural with him. It was bad enough her body betrayed her, weeping for his touch, throbbing for the press of his steely length against her.

But to think the past could have easily gone a different route terrified her.

"I don't know what you're talking about."

"Yes, you do," he said. "Us."

"There is no us," she said, her upthrust palms warning him to back off.

Marco filled her vision, filled her world. His gaze probed so deeply she shivered as his intimate touch whispered over her heart, her soul.

He planted both palms on the wall behind her, forcing her to draw her hands in to her breasts to keep from touching his oh-so-admirable chest. How easily he caged her in, towering over her, standing so close she could see the tiny flecks of gold light his dark eyes with a sensuous glow that made her body cry for him.

Marco was everything she had always wanted and everything she should avoid in a man.

That was never more evident than now. So why did her body refuse to listen?

"Yes, there is an us," he said, stroking his thumb along her jaw and smiling when she surrendered to a shiver. "There will always be us."

She shook her head and crushed her fists against her traitorous heart. Pride kept her from admitting he was right, and right now pride was all she had to cling to.

He pushed away and extended his hand to her, his gaze challenging. "Come. Our table is waiting."

"I've lost my appetite." Delanie smoothly ducked beneath his arm and strode toward the door, determined to walk the distance. To run if she must.

Marco allowed a small smile and enjoyed the enticing sway of her hips. "Where are you going?"

"To Montiforte."

"I'll drive you," he said, catching up with her easily before she'd made it halfway across the entryway.

"Thanks, but your housekeeper assured me it wasn't a long walk."

"I will take you."

That stopped her, as if his order had strings to pull her up short. She glanced back at him, body stiffened, not fully turning. But it gave him a clear view of the ripe fullness of her breasts pushing against her top.

A rosy flush kissed her neck and cheeks—from desire? Anger? Perhaps a bit of both over the way he bested her every attempt to avoid him.

The harder he pushed the more she pulled away, like magnets fighting an invisible force. But he wasn't about to back off.

He wanted her in his arms, in his bed where she belonged. At least for as long as she was here. Maybe this time when they parted he would be able to pluck her from his memory.

"Don't you have work to do?" Delanie asked.

"Nothing that can't wait," he said, exchanging a nod with his astute PA standing in the shadows who instantly disappeared to rearrange his schedule.

Her eyes, a clear blue that rivaled a Tuscan summer sky, met his and he found it difficult to draw a decent breath. The indecision reflected in her gaze clutched at his gut.

"Well, I do have things to do, mainly getting a wedding planned in short order," she said.

"You can begin after lunch," he said.

Her mouth thinned and for a moment he feared she would refuse. "Fine. We will eat and then I will get to work."

She resumed her rapid walk toward the door. He tarried a moment, enjoying the view of her firm bottom cupped in tight black denim.

Marco suffered the heaviness in his groin and strode after her. Outside he pressed his palm to the luscious small of her back and escorted her to his red Bugatti.

In moments he guided the sleek sports car down the hill toward Montiforte. "You won't find a room in the village."

"That's what your housekeeper told me."

"You don't believe her."

A beat of silence pinged between them. He could be a gentleman and remove himself from his house, giving her the privacy she sought—the distancing from him.

But he wanted her. Wanted? No he *had* to have her again. And he would have her, he vowed, allowing a smile.

Delanie looked through the window at the workers in the fields and heaved a sigh, her insides a jumble. "I know your housekeeper is probably right about the accommodations in Montiforte but I need to check."

"Then do, but know that even if you find a flat, you're better off staying at my villa."

"Better for whom?" she asked, shooting his arresting profile a glare. Why did he have to be so damned sexy?

His lips quirked in a half smile. "As I said earlier you are only prolonging the inevitable."

There it was again, that assurance that she would fall into his bed. Her faced heated, her breath quickening, her body so tightly wound with need she could scream. She couldn't ignore the pulse of need between her thighs any more than she could deny the emptiness in her arms. The longing for his lips on hers.

This was hell, and heaven would be found in his arms. But a romance with him would lead nowhere.

It couldn't, because she would not let herself slip under a man's control again. And yet she still wanted that carnal connection. Craved it. She still yearned for the crush of his powerful body on hers and the pinnacle of pleasure when he thrust into her, when passion took them to the beyond.

Sex. That was all Marco wanted from her. And—if anything—that was all she would allow herself with him, she swore on a shiver, knowing it would be glorious, fabulous sex.

"Your arrogance knows no bounds." She looked down at the hem of her top and cringed to find she'd wadded it in her fists. "Love was never part of the equation for you, was it?"

He snorted, his fingers tightening on the wheel, the muscle in his cheek ticking frantically. "Love. Woman do their damnedest to get men to give their hearts to them and men know that the fastest way to get a woman into bed is professing such devotion. I was not one of them. Ever."

"No. That was never a promise made and broken by you."

He sliced her a look so intense she felt her skin grow moist. "Are we back to doubting the other's word?"

"When did we ever fully trust the other?" she said.

His silence was answer enough.

He was her weakness. Her addiction. Her damnation? Time would tell on that one.

She had craved his love, wanted him, but had been too young at the time to realize that he wouldn't change. That love was an emotion he wouldn't or couldn't feel.

And still knowing all that she couldn't banish him from her thoughts. Couldn't stop comparing every man she met to Marco Vincienta and finding them all lacking.

She'd memorized every moment she'd been with Marco—the salty tang of his skin, the husk in his laugh, the electric golden gleam in his dark eyes when they were one, a heartbeat away from reaching nirvana.

Ten years was an awfully long drought to endure, even for a woman who'd only known one man. Too long.

"You're too quiet," he said. "Angry?"

She shook her head. "No. I'm resigned to the fact that you're a vital man and are used to getting what you want."

"Not always."

His right hand rested easy on the steering wheel, his control unmistakable, yet his big body was relaxed, almost as if he were one with the car, a powerful, pulsating thrust of energy that caught her up in his midst.

"That's hard to believe," she said.

"I didn't get you, *cara,*" he said bluntly, and her thoughts ground to a jarring halt again.

"We were lovers."

He shrugged. "Briefly. I wanted more." He slid her a knowing look. "We were good together."

She'd thought so too. She'd spent endless nights dreaming of a future around this man.

"What we had is over," she said, needing to make that clear.

"Not necessarily."

He offered a cold proposition yet it stirred something hot inside her. Emotion and need shifted like tectonic plates in an angry sea, stirring up a tempest of sensual awareness that she hadn't felt in years.

This was what she'd blocked from her thoughts, tossed away like something to fear. This aching, gnawing sensation in the pit of her stomach told her something exciting was about to happen. That was the cause of the flush of heat and tingle of skin that swept over a woman when she was attracted to a man and was ready to act on that desire.

And she was attracted to Marco.

She would be lying if she said otherwise. The first instant she'd laid eyes on him she'd been lost, swept away to distant shores and silken sheets with just a caress, just a look. One kiss and she'd been lost.

He was her Prince Charming, her critical judge and the lover she carried in her heart. Now she had the chance to relive that glorious time with him one more time.

Dare she?

"It's over," she said, and hoped that it was so. "We're not the same people we were then."

"Perhaps that is for the best."

She chewed her lower lip, wishing she could be sure. There

was simply no way to know the type of man Marco had become in so short a time.

And where did that leave her?

The lush, hilly scenery passed by in a blur, the patchwork of olive groves and vineyards lost in a dark haze much like the picture she saw of her future. It had been so long since she'd allowed herself to dream big, to think in terms of just herself.

To be selfish.

Acting on her deepest desires now would be selfish. Dare she take what she wanted, even though she would likely leave Italy and him with a broken heart?

Too soon Marco zipped through an arched gatehouse flanked by a lane of rugged brick buildings. Green-, red- and maize-painted shutters hung at the tall windows, most open in midafternoon.

Clusters of potted plants sat by doorways and on crowded iron fire escapes that clung to the old buildings, their flowers sparse now. The brick-lined street narrowed and rose, slanting up against the buildings to the next level dominated by a piazza and fountain positioned right in the middle.

A moment later he wheeled the sports car under an arched portico covered with golden vines decorated with crimson leaves. He climbed out with fluid grace and opened her door, his hand firm and possessive as he helped her extract herself from the low-slung car.

Large white umbrellas shaded the street-side tables covered with white linens, the entire perimeter ringed with massive pots holding bushes, trees and a few flowers too stubborn to take their annual rest. "This doesn't look like a bistro to me."

"They have expanded the past year," he said, his hand at her back guiding her inside where a smiling maître d' greeted them.

"I have your table ready, Signore Vincienta," the man said. "Follow me."

She managed a glimpse of exquisite murals hanging on

exposed brick walls as they were led up a narrow flight of stairs to a private room. A cozy table for two sat before the tall windows, its linen cloth fluttering in the warm breeze.

Her stomach was doing much the same, thanks to Marco's hand still pressed to the small of her back. Their table was off in a nook, quite private. A perfect table for lovers, she thought as they took their seats.

He snapped his linen napkin open and flung it on his lap as the waiter appeared at his elbow. "Orvieto to start with antipasto," he told the waiter, but his gaze flicked to hers as he added, "It's a semisweet white, renowned in Umbria."

"That would be lovely," she said, fussing with her open napkin.

"*Tagliolini al tartufo bianco* for two," he told the waiter, his gaze still on hers.

She nodded her agreement for she really didn't care. It would be pure luck if she could manage a meal with her insides in such a twist.

He frowned, studying her closely. Her narrow shoulders were set in a tense line. Her smile looked strained. But she wasn't running, wasn't rebelling. *Patience,* he told himself.

"Relax," he said after he waved the maître d' on with a wine order.

If only she could…

She cleared her throat and took in the breathtaking vista of rolling hills beyond the aged walled village, but the thought that had taken root in her mind left her too giddy with nerves to appreciate its raw beauty. "I've given much thought about— us," she settled on, still hesitant to put a cold label on his proposition.

"Have you?" he asked, leaning back in his chair so he could admire her. "What have you decided?"

She met his gaze with the practised smile she'd used countless times in the course of entertaining her father's potential clients and affected her most cosmopolitan tone, hoping it would mask the riot of emotions running rampant inside her. "We're adults now. If we have an affair it must be discreet and brief, lasting no longer than my stay in Italy. It also must be safe for both of us."

The bold proposition had no sooner left her mouth than the waiter strode in and went straight to Marco, decanting a bottle of wine and pouring a suitable splash in his glass. His gaze narrowed on her for a taut moment but that was the only sign her words had had any effect on him and not necessarily a good one.

As was expected, he tasted the wine with a precision that had not been so defined years ago. A nod gave the waiter permission to pour and leave.

Marco leaned back in his chair, his wineglass cradled in one hand, his eyes locked on hers. Perspiration beaded her brow and dotted her bare shoulders.

"I agree. No strings. No surprises," he said at last, raising his glass. "A toast."

Face heated and body trembling with uncertainty, she dug deep for control and slipped her fingers around the heavy stem of her wineglass. She raised it and forced a calm smile that she certainly didn't feel.

"To?" she dared to ask, heart pounding and mouth desert dry.

He rocked forward, the movement as fluidly predatory as a jungle cat's. "To our affair."

With the clink of crystal and dueling of intense dark eyes with her own wide ones, her fate for a few weeks was sealed.

Marco drank, the bronzed column of his throat working, his gaze hot and fixed on hers. A flush stole over her skin, as intimate as a caress.

It was done. They would be lovers, and knowing Marco it would be soon. Perhaps even tonight.

She brought the glass to her lips with a hand that trembled, and took a drink, swallowing more than the ladylike sip she'd intended. A surge of heat swept over her as much from the alcohol as from the man and the need he stirred in her.

Already his essence was threading through her. And they had done no more than kiss once. She didn't want to guess how deeply embedded it would be after they made love.

"You still don't trust me," he said, and that brought her gaze snapping up to his again.

She didn't deny it. "That goes both ways."

He swirled his wine and smiled, a relaxed gesture that belied his power. "*Cara,* must I remind you that I have trusted you to arrange my sister's wedding?"

Good grief, but he was serious. "Yes, you trust me so much so you are living in the house with me, watching my every step."

His smile widened as he leaned forward, a glint in his eyes that stirred memories of them together, entwined. "I am living in the same house with you because I want you in my bed every night. Every free chance we have. There is no other reason."

The waiter bustled in with plates of food, his flurry of movement a welcome distraction for her to gain some semblance of calm. Not that she could with Marco staring at her with such intensity. Not that she could have formed a coherent sentence at that point.

Her body shook from the promise in his words, the hungry look in his eyes. It had come down to this, or maybe this had been his plan all along.

Force her here. Seduce her. Then walk out of her life again, this time forever.

She set her glass down and stared at her plate, knowing her nervous stomach wouldn't tolerate food. Still she sampled it, more to keep her hands busy and her gaze off Marco.

It was her choice. She could continue to fight her magnetic attraction to him and suffer a stressful, miserable stay in Italy or surrender to this raging desire and spend the next two weeks in his arms.

Either way her heart would break when they said their final good-byes and she returned to London, but by becoming his lover again there would be no regret. She would have had one last sizzling fling with Marco.

Besides this wasn't some stranger who failed to stir her interest or desire. This was Marco, the man she knew intimately. The man she loved.

Love. It had no place here, not in an affair. She could expect nothing from this but pleasure. The final closing of this chapter in her life when his sister's wedding was over and she returned to London alone.

"You are eating less than a bird," he said, having consumed a good portion of his meal.

"Sorry. I'm not hungry for food."

There was only one thing that would ease the tight coil pulsing in her belly. Sex.

She took a sip of wine and ran her tongue over her lips, all the while holding his gaze with hers, hoping he wouldn't laugh at her attempt at seduction.

The potent promise swirling in his eyes was more intoxicating than the wine, both leaving her head spinning, both sending heat coursing through her. But only he had the power to turn her into this soft wanton, breasts heavy and nipples tightening into hard buds.

Only Marco could make her hunger for sex. That's how she had to look at it. Anything else would simply crush her.

Marco took a drink of the rich wine, letting time drag out, watching as a bead of sweat dared to trickle down her slender neck. Nerves. She was a jumble of them. An act? Another contradiction that was solely Delanie?

"That is an innuendo that begs careful consideration," he said.

"If you feel that is necessary," she said, making some flippant wave of her hand.

"You don't?"

"Why wait when our time together is brief?"

Her voice had gone soft with a husk that left his blood pulsating with raw need. Years before they'd come together in a cataclysmic explosion of desire, wanted only the moment, wanted only what pleased them at the time.

Now they were adults, capable of setting barriers as well as tearing them down. That's just what she'd done, torn down the last fence separating them.

Sex between them wouldn't be new. They knew what to expect going into it, knew it wouldn't last. Knew that despite good intentions, somebody could walk away from it hurt.

"Let's get out of here," he said.

She nodded, her gaze lowered, her fingers fidgeting as she dropped her linen napkin on the table. "Yes, please."

For the second time, he noted that quiet reserve which was at odds with her agreement that they embark on an affair. But he wasn't going to dwell on that or on her sudden jitters. Or on the fact he was approaching sex with her as he would a mistress.

She deserved better than that. *They* deserved more as individuals and as a couple.

And he would see that she was treated like a queen—in his arms and out of them for the duration of her stay.

He rose silently and helped her to her feet, absorbing the tremor that shot through her when he grasped her elbow. That first teetering step she took, nearly wrenching free from him, demanded he tighten his hold on her.

"Sorry," she said, swaying slightly before gaining her balance on the same low sandals she'd worn walking down the hillside to the winery. "I'm okay now."

He wasn't convinced. "How much wine did you drink?"

She sent him a helpless look that caught him by surprise,

like a punch to the gut driving the air from his lungs. As though she trusted him.

"I'm not sure," she said, delicate brow puckered. "Every time I looked my glass was full."

His lips thinned, more annoyed at himself for not paying attention to the overzealous waiter. If he had, he certainly would have cautioned her for imbibing a bit more than necessary.

He slipped her hand through the crook in his arm, holding it there a moment when she jolted.

"Thank you," she said, relaxing but refusing to meet his gaze.

"My pleasure."

And it was, he admitted.

He heaved a sigh and got them out of the restaurant without much notice other than from the curious onlookers who recognized that Montiforte's most eligible bachelor was with a beautiful woman. Once in the car, he whipped through the streets toward the highway that would take them into the foothills.

"How do you feel?" he asked, flicking her a quick glance to find her curled a bit on her seat, head nestled against the leather back and dreamy eyes fixed on his.

She smiled, and a jolt of heat shot to his groin. "Very relaxed now. And you?"

"Fine," he gruffed out, shifting slightly to ease his growing torment.

But she wasn't looking at him. She was looking at the shadows creeping down the mountains into the valley.

"We will be there soon." Closer now that he was on the winding road that wound up from town.

"That's good."

He reached over and grasped her hand in his, something he'd done years ago with her. Something he'd only done with this woman. Her fingers twined with his, small and silken and lost in his big grip.

"I've missed this," she said, voice drowsy, fingers tightening on his.

He gave her hand a squeeze and something—emotion?—did the same to his heart. "So have I."

The evening was turning out to be warm, with a balmy breeze. The woman beside him was hot, willing. Relaxed.

He maneuvered the wheel with one-handed precision, his blood running as hotly as the high-powered engine slicing through the night.

Five more minutes and then he zipped down the poplar-lined drive to his villa.

"We're here," he said, killing the engine.

The silence was deafening, but the brilliant smile from a full moon shone down on them, showing Delanie with eyes closed, fast asleep.

He pressed back in his seat, his annoyance vanishing as he drank in her beauty. A smile tugged at his mouth. It was all he could do to contain his laughter at the irony of her capitulation and overindulgence.

Tonight would not be the night. But soon, he thought as he slipped from the car. As he gathered her in his arms and strode into the house, making straightway for the master bedroom.

Soon.

CHAPTER SEVEN

DELANIE stirred, opening her eyes a mere slit and saw nothing familiar. Sunlight flooded the room and she winced, snapping her eyes shut and pulling the bedsheet over her head with a groan.

Snippets of last night pinged through her memory. Too much fine wine. Too bold a decision. A long, seductive drive to the villa with Marco controlling the moment and her.

Another groan whispered from her as she pressed her face into the soft down pillow, forcing herself to relax, to let the tension seep from her. But that was denied her as a spicy scent filled her senses. Familiar. Seductive. Masculine.

Marco, of course.

She levered up on her elbows, staring at the place beside her, knowing his scent wouldn't be that strong unless he'd spent substantial time in this bed, holding her in his arms. The slightest indent visible in the pillow proved he'd been here.

That spicy scent that was uniquely his, that she'd never been able to forget, was all around her. On her bare skin.

Her breath came fast as she scrambled for the sheet, her gaze flitting around the large bedroom. Marco's, she recognized now.

Sunlight flooded through the windows to stream across the polished wood floor and wash over the clean modern lines of the furnishings. Her jeans and jersey were draped over a chair back. Her sandals lay willy-nilly on the floor.

She swallowed hard and slowly stretched, her skin chilling as she did a quick mental inspection of herself. He'd stripped her to her skin, not the first time but the first time she had no memory of it.

But they hadn't been intimate. She was sure of it.

If they had, her body would be replete with pleasure instead of humming with the same tension. She wouldn't be this tight physically or emotionally.

"Buongiorno," he said, striding into the room bearing a tray, his muscular body as bare and bronzed as his feet.

She damned the telling shiver that rippled through her in one long delicious wave, knowing full well they'd slept in each other's arms, skin against skin. "Good morning."

He set the tray down on the bed with a wink and climbed in beside her as if it were the most natural thing in the world. And at one time it had been.

But that thought came and went like lightning as she tried not to look at the naked man beside her. The strong, lean body she'd admired ten years ago had developed into sculpted slabs of muscle befitting a Roman God. Bronzed. Beautiful.

"I have fruit, brie and croissants." He popped a grape in his mouth and held another out to her. "It isn't much."

"It's fine. Lovely, actually," she said, taking a deep blue grape from his outstretched palm, rattled by his buff body and good mood in the face of her humiliating performance last night. "I'm sorry about drinking so much."

He shrugged one well-hewn shoulder and chewed, the frown pulling at his brow there and gone. "These things happen. You were tired and the waiter was being generous. We have tonight to look forward to."

She swallowed, shifting and nearly groaning at the throb between her legs that begged for release, a need that had erupted the second he'd walked into the bedroom and stretched out beside her.

"Yes, of course. I expected you would want to get reacquainted this morning," she said, damning the heat that burned her neck and cheeks, a red flag of embarrassment that warred with the carnal flush burning her pale skin.

He leaned so close she could see her obvious lust reflected in his eyes. Her cheeks burned even more, and the need inside her was so unbearable she thrashed her legs, hoping he would notice, praying he would touch her there and relieve the ache.

"As much as I would enjoy making love with you long into the morning, now is not the time," he said, trailing a finger down her neck, the upper curve of her breast and circling a nipple that grew hard and aching at his touch, that had her leaning into him. "I want to savor every second adoring you and I refuse to be rushed."

In the quiet wake of her bold capitulation and her ensuing inelegant behavior at the restaurant, the last thing she wished to do was show how malleable she was in his hands. Yet here she was, breath hitching, her breasts full and her very core crying with need for him.

"I want that too," she said, digging deep to find the strength to tear herself away from him, to sweep her shredded dignity around her like a sturdy wrap.

But she couldn't pull her gaze from his, couldn't scramble away when he leaned in, his big hands gliding up her bare arms, dredging a shiver from her that had nothing to do with the chill air and everything to do with the hot hard man.

His warm inviting breath on her face had her lifting her face to his in greedy invitation. She'd waited for this for so long. So long…

Her lips parted, heart hammering beneath her breasts. His mouth met hers with a groan, a soft brush of lips that fizzed in her blood like the finest champagne, sweet and intoxicating and going straight to her head.

"Marco," she breathed against his lips, her fingers splayed over his bare chest, the muscles hard, the skin hot and smooth, the sprinkling of dark hair crisp and slightly damp beneath her palm as she slid a finger down the chiseled contours of his body to his length thrusting hard against her thigh.

He sucked in a breath, pressing himself against her palm. The same insistent pulse she felt in him thrummed between her legs and deeper into her core where she ached for him to be. In her, part of her.

"Tonight," he said, grasping her hand and pulling it away.

His breath sawed hot against her neck, sending delicious chills rippling over her skin. It had been too long since she'd felt this wicked, this easy with a man.

He dropped one last lingering kiss on her too-sensitive skin, then sauntered away, his bare buttocks tight, his legs long and muscled. She clutched the sheet in both hands, the soft fabric abrasive to her sensitized nipples, trying to focus, trying to shake off the sensual haze swirling around her like early-morning fog.

She clenched her thighs together and stifled a groan, wanting him so badly she physically ached. Don't gawk at him. But she couldn't tear her eyes away from such masculine beauty. Couldn't forget how that strong body had felt on her, in her.

Modesty would goad most people to dress in private but Marco clearly didn't possess such inhibitions. He unabashedly stood in the opening of the dressing room and thrust long legs into navy trousers before shrugging into a pale blue shirt.

And she sat on the bed transfixed, drinking in every second. Branding it all on her memory.

His mobile trilled no more than twice before he answered and moved into the shadows. He was too far from her and his voice was pitched too low to understand a word, but the sudden tensing of his broad shoulders alerted her that the news wasn't good.

"I should return before dark," he told her, striding from the dressing room without glancing her way.

And just like that the playboy she'd dined with last night and had a teasing respite with this morning was gone, hidden behind a custom-made suit that was undoubtedly Italian and clearly tailored to fit his admirable physique.

"I have a lot to do as well," she said—starting with a trip to a women's clothing shop.

"*Si,* the wedding," he said, pausing at the door. "A selection of clothes and shoes will be delivered for you today."

Just what a rich man would do for his mistress. That tainted what they'd agreed on. Brought it down to a level that made her skin crawl. Yet wasn't that what she had agreed to? A brief affair? To be his mistress for two weeks?

She seized a quick breath, chin held high, as the bubble of euphoria inside popped to rain ice on her blood. "Thanks, but I prefer choosing my own clothes."

"I prefer buying these gifts for you," he drawled. "But if you wish, consider them as compensation for dragging you from London with the clothes on your back."

"Fine. Thanks." She would purchase her own clothes and when she left she'd take them and leave his behind.

His brow furrowed as he executed a perfect knot in an indigo silk tie and snugged it to his throat with a quick twist of his wrist. "Just so you know, I have never brought a woman here before."

What was she supposed to say to that? *You're kidding... Thank you...*

In the end she said nothing because her libido was shorting out her brain cells with the way his gaze was fixed on her, peeling away the sheet she clutched to her bosom, kissing skin that was moist and flushed with desire.

How could he make her nearly come with a look?

The control she'd had the past ten years was nonexistent now in the face of his potent sensuality. Which made this entire job all the more challenging to endure.

But she would get through. She wanted to get through it!

She had to do a stellar job, had to garner the top publicity this wedding would offer her. Had to have this last fling with Marco because…

Because she wanted him.

She'd willingly added an affair to her list of things to accomplish here because of that burning desire. Selfish and carnal and so unlike her, but that was the truth.

Her only saving grace was the ability to hide the emotions rioting in her, a knack perfected as she'd suffered the company of businessmen eager to align with Tate Unlimited. Men who'd thought the fast track to getting to the top of Tate Unlimited was to woo her. But she'd kept them all at arm's length, earning the reputation of being an ice princess. All but Marco.

"Give me a ring if you need me," he said.

"I shall," she said, managing a smile.

He stared at her a long assessing moment before striding from the house. But she didn't draw a decent breath until she heard the powerful roar of the Bugatti racing away.

Dusk cast a surreal glow over the vineyards stretching to the foothills and had turned the tiled roofs of Montiforte a fiery red by the time Marco returned from Rome. It had been a stressful day and he was eager to conclude it and return to Delanie.

But that would have to wait, thanks to a problem at the Toligara press. The man who always oversaw issues like this was off to Arezzo for the night with his wife of thirty-five years, celebrating their anniversary.

Though Marco hated postponing his evening with Delanie, he wasn't about to ruin a trusted employee's happy occasion. Besides, his time with Delanie should be savored like fine wine, savored to its fullest.

In bed and out of it.

He tugged his phone from his pocket and punched in her number, one that he'd put in over a month ago but had never called. "Are you through for the day?" he asked when Delanie answered with a hesitant greeting.

"Almost. I am finalizing the date for a fitting and should be back to the house in thirty minutes or so," she said. "Are you there?"

Was that a note of dread in her voice?

"No, I have just reached Montiforte," he said. "There was a problem at the oil press that needs my attention. I've no idea when I'll return home."

"Oh, I'm sorry to hear that."

"That is good to know," he said, smiling. "How did your day go?"

"Productive. I've arranged for Bella's first fitting with the dressmaker tomorrow and should have sample arrangements of flowers ready for her approval by then as well. Tomorrow I'll see that all is in readiness for the church, then I'll tour the castle where she wishes to hold the reception."

As her contract dictated, she told him about the businesses she'd contacted, her preferences for each and why she'd chosen to work with locals.

"I was amazed at what was available here and their willingness to adapt. It's a good start," she said.

He smiled, hearing the enthusiasm in her voice. "It seems you have everything in line."

"There is still much to do," she said. "Bella expressly stated she did not want the men in tuxedos so I spoke with the tailor. But she's also decided she wants a blend of traditional and modern so I'll arrange a very relaxed Mediterranean theme."

"I doubt the groom will complain about the lack of formality," he said, and neither would he.

"Just what I thought as well," she said. "There are two photographers of note in Montiforte and both of their works are good. But I'd prefer gathering samples to show Bella since each one has a far different style."

"My sister is quick to speak her opinion," he said.

She laughed. "That is obviously a family trait."

He laughed, enjoying this banter. Enjoying her.

"True. I want you, *cara*. How is that for expressing my opinion?"

He heard her breathing, quick and hurried. "To the point. Honest, and I appreciate honesty."

"As do I," he said, serious again.

"Good, because I want this as well," she said in a whisper that hummed through his blood.

A new tension surged between them in waves. Hot and intense. A tension that had nothing to do with his sister's wedding and everything to do with their affair.

"I regret this postponement," he said.

"There is always tomorrow."

Every nerve in his body screamed for release tonight. Now. His biological father would have let the workers deal with the mess at the mill and gone off to meet the lady.

Which is exactly what he would not do, he vowed as he neared the olive press. This was his company. His problem to solve.

Ah, but if he just had a few more minutes to at least talk with Delanie…

"Have a good evening, *cara*," he said as he killed the engine.

"Yes, you as well."

"Delanie," he said, rolling her name over his tongue, savoring it as he had hoped to do to her tonight.

"Yes."

"Tomorrow will be our time," he said. "We'll start with dinner."

And end up in bed.

She didn't reply, but then no words were necessary. Tomorrow he would have her in his arms where she belonged.

* * *

As busy as she'd been all day, she should have fallen into an exhausted sleep. But here it was near two in the morning and she was still wide awake.

Delanie hugged her arms to her bosom and strolled back to the glass doors that opened onto the terrace. A bloated moon bathed the hills in a wash of silver, the effect almost magical.

It was a vista one wouldn't easily tire of, she thought.

The hum of an engine broke the stillness a heartbeat before headlamps cut through the night. Marco's Bugatti, winding back up the hill. She recognized the deep purr of the powerful engine.

Even if she hadn't, some sense told her that Marco was returning home. The velvety hush of the night drifted around her, as darkly sensual as the man behind the wheel.

She chafed her bare arms, trembling like a leaf caught in the wind, burning inside with an emotion she hadn't felt in years. An emotion she never wished to feel again for Marco Vincienta.

Yet it was there. Intense. Demanding.

A true mistress would greet him at the door with open arms. She would be wearing one of the sexy outfits he'd had delivered today, clothes she had no intention of wearing.

His mistress would lead him to the bedroom and satisfy the ache throbbing between them. But that wasn't her.

The car rounded the curve, the headlights sweeping across the front of the villa. She bit her lip and stepped back into the shadows, shaking, knowing she couldn't do it.

It took but a moment to return to her room. Another to close the door silently as the metallic click of his car door echoed in the night.

She crawled into bed and lay stiff as a board, waiting. Trying to listen to his footsteps over the pounding of her heart.

Come to me, she silently willed him.

The front door opened and closed. Steady steps made their

way across the living room. Another door opened and closed. Close, but not hers.

She bit her lip again, restless. It wasn't too late. She could go to him still.

Who was she kidding?

He'd rebuffed her the first time she'd flirted with him ten years ago, choosing his own moment to catch her alone with her defenses down. He'd rejected her the night he'd left her and England.

No, she simply couldn't make the first move again. Not tonight. Maybe never.

Marco stepped onto the terrace the following morning, muscles snapping taut as he watched Delanie stroll along the perimeter of an olive grove, her mobile pressed to her ear. A light breeze sent her long hair rippling down her back in a golden waterfall of silk. The full sun kissed her bare arms and legs with a honey-gold light.

Tonight she would be his. Tonight he would know if that curtain of hair felt as silken draping his arms, his chest, his groin. He would know if her smooth skin tasted as sweet as pomegranates on his tongue.

Dammit, he'd spent a miserable night staring at the ceiling, fighting the urge to go to her. As badly as he wanted her, he knew a coupling then would be less than satisfying.

His fingers tightened around the cup of coffee he held, his chest pillowing out as he inhaled heavily. Nothing had changed. She was the only woman he had ever burned this intensely for, still ached to kiss, hold, drive into her with all the passion simmering in his soul.

She was the one he'd come to care about. The one who'd roused a fury in him he hadn't known he possessed.

His gut pinched. A jolt scraped over his nerves and lifted the hair at his nape.

The anger resulting from Delanie's lies was a fool's emotion yet he couldn't deny its existence any more than he could deny his desire for her. The fact it plagued him now confirmed he'd yet to trust her fully.

Trust. Such a simple word. Such a difficult thing to achieve with another person. Impossible with Delanie.

He sipped his coffee. Huffed another terse sigh and welcomed the flood of sanity that washed to sea those darker, selfish thoughts.

Delanie Tate was here on business. And he had every right to stand here and watch her, to drink in her beauty and poise until he was sated.

And so he did.

Her stride was sure yet unhurried. But there was something about her posture that screamed tension. The slight bowing of her shoulders. The lowered head. The free hand that splayed and fisted before the call obviously ended and she just stood there, staring at her mobile.

His brow furrowed. Something was wrong. Personally? The wedding?

It was the last that prompted him to make a quick call to his PA to clear his schedule for the day and night. He had no idea of her plans, but whatever they were he had no intention of letting Delanie do it alone.

If there was a problem brewing he would do all he could to help her. He would go with her as silent support. To smooth the way for stubborn merchants. To be with her, watching her at work in her world.

When her day was finished, they would celebrate with a bit of *vino* and a lot of *amore.*

He smiled. That couldn't come soon enough.

This driving desire would ease the more they were together. When she left him this time, he would be ready to see her go.

And if he was wrong...

He set his empty cup down and stormed down the steps,

refusing to consider that this plan could backfire on him, that he could end up burned again by the same woman.

She stopped on the edge of the flagstones, her gaze widening on his across the expanse, looking a bit windblown and sexy as hell. Looking flustered as well.

A silky blue blouse draped over full breasts and peaked over nipples that he longed to caress, kiss, draw deeply into his mouth. Her simple tan skirt hugged her hips to a point just above her knees, exposing a good length of strong creamy legs.

New clothes. Items he wouldn't have chosen, yet on her they were alluring.

"At work already?" he asked.

"Yes, your sister rang moments after I stepped out here," she said, a telling frown marring her smooth brow. "Bella refuses to consider either local photographer, insisting I hire someone who can capture what she feels."

He swore, certain his sister was being temperamental just for the pleasure of it. Just because she could.

"She is being unreasonably difficult," he said. "She is beautiful. In love. With child. That won't change no matter who takes the pictures."

"No, it does matter. If she's uncomfortable it will show in her pictures," she said. "She wants me to visit a photographer in Florence. A childhood friend that she's hesitant to contact herself."

"Why?"

"I gathered their last parting was painful and not mutual and she fears he will refuse her," she said. "But Bella wants him to take the shots for her wedding, reception and some honeymoon pictures."

"What was he to her?"

"I don't know." She sighed. "I thought I could find that out when I phoned him, but he demands to talk face to face with the bride and groom or the wedding planner before accepting the job. Bella wants me to appeal to him, so I need to travel there today. Depending on how well things go I may not return until quite late tonight or early tomorrow."

He scrubbed a hand over his mouth, believing her. This is what she was reputed to do best—ensure that the bride was pleased. But to let her visit this photographer alone? Spend a night in Florence? Unacceptable!

"Fine. We leave whenever you are ready."

Her lips parted and the pulse point in her throat thrummed wildly. "We?"

His smile widened, tempted to lave and kiss that warbling pulse until she moaned. "I assure you I won't be in your way."

Her gaze narrowed and he braced himself, expecting her to argue. But it would do her no good. He wasn't about to let her out of his sight for long.

As if reading his mind, she squared her slumping shoulders. "I am equally sure you will be, but given the circumstances I have little choice. Give me a moment to gather my things."

He smiled, ready to give her all the time she needed.

Delanie hurried into her room and hoped her haste gave the impression of diligence instead of escape. Mercy, how would she get through a day and possibly a night in sunny, sensual Florence with Marco at her elbow?

Her senses were too raw around him, her desire for him growing stronger by the day. Why had she agreed to be his mistress for the duration? Where was her backbone?

She pinched her eyes shut, hating the hollow ache in her heart that confirmed she was vulnerable to him. A future with Marco was out of the question.

Though he refused to acknowledge any similarity to her father, she saw the parallels. Marco dominated everything in his life, his world. Those tendencies could take an ugly turn and she could end up tied to a man like her father.

She wouldn't repeat her mother's mistakes and suffer in silence, chained by love.

Now more than ever she needed to prove to herself they were only good together for the short term, that she hadn't made a horrid mistake ten years ago. That she wasn't making one now.

When she left him and Italy, it would be with the assurance that she'd been right. They made great lovers. That was all.

She would return to England and tuck her memories of Marco into a secret place in her heart. Move on with her life.

Closure, at last, would be hers.

And if she was wrong?

An hour later she was in Florence, having worked on last-minute plans on her electronic notepad while Marco drove and spoke with his PA via his mobile. But it was still a struggle for her to keep her mind on her work with him sitting beside her, effortlessly commanding the Bugatti as they whizzed up the winding *autostrada* with the Apennines rising to her right while lush vineyards and olive groves and a meandering river stretched as far as the eye could see.

The fertile landscape and fresh air were a feast. The man beside her remained the decadent dessert she hungered to savor.

When she'd first met him so long ago, she'd fallen as much in lust with him as love. Perhaps more so.

Now she was seeing the man he'd become. Powerful. Ruthless. More fascinating than any man she'd ever met.

She still desired him, not with that wild hungry craving of youth. But with a woman's appreciation of his strong, honed body and keen mind.

It would be so easy to fall back into an intimate relationship with him. So tempting to lose herself just once more in his arms. So easy to convince herself that an affair could develop into something lasting.

It was an illusion she must definitely guard against.

He already held her business in his grip. She dared not let him claim her heart again as well.

But how could she stop the inevitable?

She cast his beautifully sculpted profile a surreptitious look. Desire ribboned around her but it was the warmth stealing around her heart that confirmed she was already doomed.

"You've been terribly quiet," Marco said, feeling her gaze stroking over him yet again.

His blood raced, sending a surge of heat to his already uncomfortable groin. This woman was torturing him just by being near. And he had the entire day to spend with her in Florence!

"The photographer has samples on his website and I took the opportunity to study them and make a few notes," she said, slipping her slim notepad back into her oversize bag.

"I trust you're impressed with his work."

"He's very talented."

What she hadn't said raised his curiosity. "He is someone you would hire then."

Her brow creased, fueling his misgivings. "I'll know more once I've met with him."

"If you feel he's not right, we can turn around now."

"And disappoint Bella? No way." She inhaled sharply, her chin coming up in that bulldog determined way of hers that he admired and disliked in equal measure. "I intend to make this appointment and judge his talents for myself."

He smiled, his fingers stroking the steering wheel as he crossed the River Arno, the deep blue water reminding him of Delanie's eyes when she climaxed. And wasn't that a hell of a thing to remember when he was already tight with lust for her?

"We should arrive at the photographer's studio shortly," he said, trying to think of anything but the woman beside him.

She stiffened, the sudden chill in the car making his skin bead. "I don't want you interfering in my business."

He held a palm toward her. "I am there as nothing more than your assistant."

"Are you crazy?" she asked. "Everyone in Italy must know who you are from the press."

He scowled, his teasing mood and desire freezing over instantly. "I have avoided the press since my rise and I intend it to stay that way. Trust me when I say I won't be telling a photographer who I am."

CHAPTER EIGHT

MARCO'S promise needled Delanie as he traversed the congested narrow streets of Florence with the skill of a Formula 1 driver. The gray stone mass of the ancient city with the occasional building painted yellow or green failed to draw her interest away from the colorful man behind the wheel.

It seemed inconceivable that someone who'd risen to such power and who'd inherited a millionaire's business could escape notoriety. But he'd done that, choosing to hide his identity behind a ghost corporation.

She could understand the need for anonymity in his business dealings. But why did he feel the same need to stand in the shadows in sunny Italy?

Moments later, he smoothly parked near the Signoria Square with its impressive Neptune's fountain that she'd read about in school. Though fabulous to see, the statue's generous physique paled beside Marco's.

She surrendered to a delicious shiver as the object of her delight and turmoil escorted her up a narrow passageway on rugged stone stairs that had climbed the sides of gray stone buildings for centuries. Though serviceable, they hadn't been made for dainty heels that seemed to find every little glitch and imperfection in the stone.

She stepped wrongly a heartbeat later and swayed, but Marco caught her up with a strong arm around her waist.

Her breath caught and every nerve in her body zinged as if shocked.

"These steps are wicked," she said, trying to extract herself from his steely hold.

"Perhaps I should carry you the rest of the way," he said, his breath warm and welcome on her face.

Too welcome.

She got her balance and eased from him. "Perhaps I should take off my shoes."

His lips pulled into a smile that sent her insides tumbling. "Isn't that how we met?"

"I—I don't remember." She slipped off her slings and hurried up the steps, leaving him and that memory behind her.

But not for long.

Marco was beside her an instant later and so was the sweet erotic memory of the first time they'd met. Holland Park, on what must have been the hottest day London had seen in decades.

That's where Marco found her. He'd followed her from her father's office and found her barefoot at the edge of the water that moved calmly around her ankles.

"I'm fairly certain going into the water is forbidden by the park officials," he'd drawled, his Italian accent lending his voice a very seductive tone that whispered over her bare arms and legs and left her tingling.

She'd whirled to confront him and was temporary struck dumb as she realized her intruder wasn't a park attendant or a constable but a very handsome, very virile stranger. "Most likely you're right."

"Want to talk about it?"

Nobody had ever asked her if she needed a shoulder to lean on or cry on. Her father issued orders. Her mother begged her for support.

But nobody ever asked Delanie Tate if she wanted to talk about what bothered her.

It was so unheard of, such a phenomenal event that she left the water's edge and crossed to the handsome stranger with a breathy, "Yes."

That day she'd fallen into Marco Vincienta's arms and his bed—another first for her. She shirked off her fears of trusting a man, turning to putty in Marco's capable hands as he whisked her away into passion she'd not known existed.

In less than a week she'd lost her heart to him. And she was terrified because she was swiftly becoming emotionally dependent on a man, just like her mother. Marco had been so dominating, so aloof, yet so passionate with her.

That fear that she would repeat her mother's hell had been the one thing that kept her on edge, that stopped her from fully trusting him, even though her body loved his touch, his kiss.

And that wounded look in his eyes had melted something in her. Left her wanting to hold him. Heal his hurts.

Now she saw how wrong she'd been. How she'd let fear cloud her vision. Marco was ruthless, able to mete out vengeance to those who deserved it. But he wasn't mean. Wasn't abusive. Wasn't vindictive.

Marco Vincienta was the direct opposite of her father. And she loved him still, maybe more than ever before.

Now he pressed his hand to the small of her back, hot and possessive. She gasped and whirled around, skin on fire.

Big mistake, she realized a heartbeat later. The cold rough stone wall was at her back, a massive pillar to her right, and filling the narrow void was Marco.

"You're lying, *cara mia*," he said, hands bracketing her shoulders to hem her in, head bent close so only she heard him. "You remember those first days together when we gave and took equally, just like I remember them."

Her heart raced, her mind spun those memories of when she'd fallen in love with Marco to life. When their passion had terrified her. When she'd thought she could hold back from surrendering all to him and still hold on to the man.

She'd convinced herself Marco could do business with her father and keep their relationship separate. That beside him, she could continue to protect her mother. How very wrong she'd been.

Yes, she remembered the joy, the passion. A tingle raced up her spine as she focused on the beautifully masculine sculpt of his mouth. How she'd struggled the first time to hold a part of her from him. How she'd failed then.

Now she was stronger. Resisting him should be easy. But her knees quaked and her blood hummed the longer she stared into his eyes, reading the passion, the promise, the purpose. Was he going to kiss her? Out here on the street? Was she going to let him?

No, she couldn't let herself go again. She slammed both palms against his chest and shivered at the power and heat radiating from him into her. Moisture gathered under her breasts and between her thighs.

"What difference does it make if I do remember?" she asked at last. "Nothing has changed."

"Hasn't it?"

How could he ask such a thing? "Not the things that mattered. You are still holding back, as I must."

She ducked under his arm and ran up the steps on legs that shook, every nerve in her body humming with the awareness that he was right behind her. That he could, if he wanted to, catch her again. That she was right there on the verge of surrendering to passion. All over again.

This time she wasn't sure if she had the strength to stop herself from getting lost in his passion again. From losing her independence. Her sense of self-worth.

Dammit, she wouldn't be an emotional puppet like her mother, letting a man rule every aspect of her life. This was why she feared she would never be able to have that type of relationship again.

The photographer's gallery was the fourth level up and

she pushed inside without waiting for Marco. But she knew the instant he entered the shop behind her because her skin tingled, craving his touch again.

She shook off thoughts of him and took in the cramped gallery. Ivory plastered walls were covered with a multitude of framed photos ranging from breathtaking landscapes to the most realistic portraits she'd ever seen.

None were staged. In fact, the majority were candid shots. The range of emotion captured on the people's faces spoke to the feelings trapped inside her. Longing. Fear. Love.

"Look. That's Bella." Marco pointed to a framed photo set apart from the others as if it held a place of honor.

The young girl in the portrait stared down at them with guarded eyes. Eyes that looked far too old for her age.

Delanie pressed a hand to her heart, mouth dropping open. Marco had told her Bella had come from poverty but she'd never truly considered what that meant. She hadn't realized Bella had had to work as a child.

The picture showed stained clothes that hung on her small frame, her thin arms holding a large tray of fish draped with linen, the burden seeming too great for one so young and frail.

Heat swept up Delanie's cheeks, a burning wash of shame such as she'd never felt before. She hadn't had the ideal childhood, but she had been given every material convenience available. She hadn't had to work. Hadn't wanted for anything but frivolities.

"I just want to cry when I stare into her eyes," she said.

His palm rested on her lower back, softly, but this time she didn't jolt. Didn't pull away. This time she wanted this connection to him, wanted to share the agony and anger that coursed through him.

"Bella was twelve when Cabriotini's lawyer found her living with the fishmonger." His fingers splayed on her back and she couldn't help but lean into him. "Her mother had died three years before and he was her stepfather, the closest thing she had to family. He'd remarried but kept Bella, allowing her room and board in exchange for helping him in his shop."

She faced him, and her heart ached at the bleakness etched on his handsome face. He cared more than she'd thought possible. And if he was capable of caring that much for his sister…

As quickly as the thought popped into her head she pushed it away. She didn't dare let herself hope for more with him no matter how much compassion he showed his sister.

"At least they found her and got her out of that life," she said, her palm stroking the line of his clenched jaw, content for now to share this special moment with him. "What you've done for her, though, is wonderful. You gave her a home and family."

He snorted, relaxing marginally. "I did what Cabriotini should have done years before. He knew Bella was his daughter yet he did nothing to help her."

"Why?"

"Because she was female and a young unschooled one at that," he said.

Exactly what her own father would have done. Delanie had spent her whole life feeling second-rate because of her sex. Because her father had believed only a man could run his corporation.

But not Marco. He'd set his sister up as co-owner of Cabriotini Vineyard. He gave her the mansion, preferring his villa nestled in the hills.

And another misconception about Marco fell away, revealing a man with a big heart. With compassion. A man she could trust?

"May I help you?" a young man asked.

"I have an appointment with Carlo Domanti," she said.

The young man speared Marco an assessing look before turning back to her. "Delanie Tate, I presume?"

"Yes," she said, suddenly beset with nerves by the way this man boldly scrutinized her.

Marco thrust his hand out and introduced himself, offering no more than his name. If it rang a bell with Carlo, he didn't let on.

"That picture," Marco said, pointing to his sister. "I want it."

Carlo locked his arms over his chest. "It's not for sale."

"Everything has a price," Marco said.

She winced, all too aware that he'd found her price and used it to gain her compliance—in and out of bed.

The photographer's gaze narrowed on Marco. "Why do you want it?"

"That girl is my sister."

Carlo flung a hand in the air and spat out a stream of curses. "That is a lie! She does not have a brother."

"Bella didn't know about me then." Marco got right in the photographer's face. "I was unaware of her as well until several years after that picture was taken."

Carlo studied him, brow furrowed, arms locked over his chest. Finally he gave a nod, and Delanie blew out the breath she'd been holding.

"I will consider your offer," Carlo allowed, but it was obvious by his scowl that he wasn't convinced.

Marco's mouth hinted at a smile. "I assure you it will be a profitable deal for you."

If the photographer was tempted by money, he certainly hid it well. But at least the throbbing tension had eased enough for her to finalize this business.

"Mr. Domanti, I take it you know Bella?" Delanie asked.

The photographer bobbed his head. "We were born in the same village in the same questionable circumstances."

Bella's insistence that Delanie find this particular photographer made sense now. "Then you're long-time friends."

"I remember when she was born. As she was the only girl, I made it my duty to watch her the best I could. But she was rebellious. Stubborn. Proud. The last time I saw her, spoke to her, was when I took that photo." His gaze narrowed on Marco again. "I left her as she wished but I never forgot her. Where is she? Is she all right?"

"She is well and about to become a married woman," Marco said.

"That's why we're here. Bella wants you to photograph her wedding," Delanie said.

The photographer threaded long lean fingers through his mop of curly hair. "You work for Bella?"

"I do," Delanie said. "Now if we could sit down and negotiate the terms, number of photos…"

Carlo slashed the air with a hand, a gesture so reminiscent of Marco in a mood that she nearly laughed. It must be a universal language for Italian men.

"I would do it for free for Bella," Carlo said.

"Bella wouldn't want that," Delanie said before Marco could interject anything.

Without further delay she quoted a figure well above the normal rate, all the while removing the contract from her portfolio. "If you would just read and sign this, we're all set to go."

Carlo didn't hesitate, giving her very straightforward contract a quick read. He signed it with an artistic flourish.

Moments later Marco was ushering her out the door, but not before he offered the photographer a staggering sum of money that was reluctantly accepted. All for that one poignant picture of Bella.

"It's touching that you want that portrait so badly," she said as they started down the stone stairs.

"There is nothing endearing about it. I don't ever want to forget the wrong done to us both," he said. "And I sure as hell don't want to risk it falling into the wrong hands either."

"Paparazzi?"

He gave a crisp nod. "In her condition, she doesn't need bad press and neither does her fiancé."

"I can't argue with that logic."

He stopped, forcing her to do the same. His mouth quirked in an utterly charming grin that sent her senses somersaulting.

"What? We are in agreement?"

She couldn't stop her smile, couldn't find a reason to pull away from him. "Surely it's a quirk of fate."

He laughed, a deep rich sound that coaxed her to do the same, to let loose with him. There had been few times when they'd laughed together, when they'd been this free and light of heart.

But as much as she reveled in his smile, his touch, as much as she yearned for his kiss, she knew she was treading on dangerous ground with him. She wasn't a starry-eyed young girl any longer.

She knew heartache followed sweet bliss, that as much as they meshed in bed, out of it they clashed. Now that she'd glimpsed another side of Marco, she was even more vulnerable to him.

"I'm anxious to tell Bella the news," she said, hoping he readily took her hint to leave Florence.

His smile was wide and totally unexpected. "You are making her dreams come true effortlessly. Bravo."

"Thank you."

They fell into step on the street, making their way through the growing crowd toward the Bugatti. Delanie smiled to herself. For a man who wanted to blend in, he certainly missed the boat by driving such a flashy car.

"What amuses you so?" he asked as he assisted her into the low passenger seat.

She spread her arms. "This. It's the red flag you wave in defiance of your attempt to remain the anonymous billionaire. Deep down you want to be noticed."

His smile fled, his body going painfully stiff in a blink. "You're wrong. Italian men adore performance cars. I own it because I can."

He shut the door soundly on the car and his emotions as well. Shutting her out.

She wet her dry lips, hesitant to follow him into his dark place. That had been their pattern but she was tired of it.

"You dreamed of owning a car like this when you were a boy working in the fields," she said after he slid behind the wheel and sent the Bugatti whizzing down a warren of narrow streets.

He cut her a look that was so boyish and charming she smiled. "It is true. The precise make and model don't matter but the flashy cars were always red. Always fast and always driven by the man who was in charge of his world."

"Then you have achieved your goals," she said.

He shrugged. "Not all."

What else could he want? A wife? Children? Love?

She refrained from probing. She didn't want to know how he intended to live his life after she returned to England. Didn't want to think about him losing his heart to another woman.

With effort, she focused on the reason she had come to Italy. Bella and her wedding. He would move mountains to please his sister and it was her job to make sure all went smoothly.

"Traditionally the father of the bride gives his daughter a special token on her wedding day," she said, sliding him a look to gauge his reaction. "It would be nice if you stepped into that role for her."

"I am giving her a vineyard and a villa," he said, jaw set.

She flexed her fingers when she longed to curl them into fists and pound the dashboard. "I was thinking of something more personal."

"It is that important?"

"Marco! Of course it is. This is your sister and she will hope to have a personal token from you to remember this special day."

"Ah, a memento." He frowned, nodded. "Very well. What should this gift be?"

She just caught herself from reaching out to him, from laying a commiserating hand on his arm. "A piece of jewelry would be lovely. Something for her to treasure."

"Good idea. We will visit Ponte Vecchio," he said.

Moments later he whipped the car down a narrow cobbled street and parked. But he didn't budge, save for the tightening of his fingers on the steering wheel as he stared at the gray buildings stacked neatly on top of each other. She wondered if he even noticed the people traversing the street, or if he was lost in some memory again.

What bothered him about this place? she wondered, seeing nothing remarkable or disturbing about Florence. It was a fairly large city but not nearly as hectic as London or Paris.

"Change your mind?" she asked.

"No, just thinking. Come."

He helped her leave the car and escorted her down the walkway toward the bridge. The closer they got to it, the more people they encountered. Yet his tension seemed to ease.

"What is this place?" she asked at last.

"This is the home of the most renowned goldsmiths in all of Italy. You will help me choose a gift," he said, smiling.

"I would be happy to."

The shops on the bridge were stuck together as if glued. It seemed as if no attempt had been made to make the buildings uniform in size, and several protruded over the deep blue river as if hanging on for dear life.

Delanie knew the feeling as she clung to Marco's hand, aware he was a powerful yet very tentative lifeline. As they strolled along the walkway with the stone wall to her right and shops clustering the Ponte Vecchio ahead, he told her the fascinating history of the goldsmiths of Florence extending back four hundred years.

She smiled, the sun warm on her face while a cool breeze

from the river whispered around her shoulders. Coupled with the enthusiastic man beside her it was a perfect moment, one she'd never thought she would share with him.

"I feel as if I'm in the company of a tour guide," she said, half teasing, but it coaxed another smile from him.

Her heart skipped a beat and warmed. Ah, such a very sexy, very handsome tour guide.

"How is it that you know so much about Florence?"

He shrugged, not that tense lifting of broad shoulders that he'd affected the past week, that she hated. No, this was the boyish hike that she found endearing and that hint of old pain she saw in his eyes showed a glimpse of the man she'd fallen so desperately in love with years ago.

And heaven help her but she was doing it again. She was utterly helpless to stop her heart from melting.

"My grandfather Vincienta owned a decanting shop on the edge of Florence. It was beyond the new bridge to the left." He pulled her to the wall and pointed downriver, but to her the land blended, all looking the same. Besides, she was more fascinated watching the emotions flickering like a movie on Marco's face, a face that was for once open and relaxed.

"Nonno wasn't a savvy businessmen. If a friend or a kind face wanted *vino* or *olio* and promised to pay later, he would give it to them on good faith. The debts mounted, so much so that my papa couldn't hold on to the shop after his father's death."

Marco gave a deprecating laugh, but it was the hand tightening on hers that made her flinch, not from pain but from the frustration that coursed from him into her. She sensed whatever change had happened then hadn't been a good one.

"Mama's father, Nonno Toligara, offered Papa a job in his small *olio* press and vineyard, but Papa got a better offer from Antonio Cabriotini. My mother begged Papa to refuse the offer but he took it anyway because he never wished to work for family again, especially not my grandfather who had not wanted him for a son-in-law in the first place."

"Was your father aware that you... I mean that you weren't his child?" she settled for, her voice hushed as they started across the bridge.

"According to my nonna, it was a year or more after he went to work for Cabriotini when Father discovered the truth, though my family still kept it from me. I did not understand why life at home changed. Why my parents fought more. Why my papa purposely spent less and less time in my company."

"How could he ostracize the child he'd raised since birth?" she asked, her other hand coming up to his arm, the muscle so tense she felt as if she were grasping a stone pillar.

He stopped in the lee of the arch leading onto the bridge, his gaze so bleak and pained she wanted to cry. "Papa held to old-world beliefs and I was a bastard in his eyes. A constant reminder of his wife's betrayal. Though they argued fiercely and he ignored me as much as possible, he never physically mistreated me. In fact, he did me a favor."

"How can you say that?"

"Papa discouraged me from working with him at Cabriotini's vineyard or for my Nonno Toligara. He insisted I get an education. That I learn business so I wouldn't repeat the mistakes of my ancestors," he said. "I balked at first, thinking if I worked with my father it would strengthen our relationship, that we would become close again. A few months after I began secondary school, my parents died in an auto accident and I was sent to Montiforte to live with my Nonni Toligara."

"That's so tragic," she said, a fist pressed to her heart.

One shoulder lifted. "Yes, but a blessing as well. They saw that I got an education, both at the winery and press and later at the university." His fingers tangled with hers. "Come."

What could she say to that? That they would be proud he'd done so well? That he'd done the impossible insofar as he'd regained the family business and made it far better?

It seemed wiser to keep those thoughts to herself as he led her onto the bridge, his hand tightly clasping hers. Ponte Vecchio teemed with people, from single shoppers to mothers with children to couples strolling hand-in-hand.

It was unlike any place she'd seen before. The vibrant colors of the awnings over some shops and the array of finery glistening in the line of windows left her as excited as a child at Christmas.

When they walked past the breaks between buildings, she caught a breathtaking view of the river winding though vineyards and olive groves painted in muted golds and bronze with the shadow of mountains in the distance. It was a vista painters coveted, yet her gaze was drawn time and again to Marco.

He stopped before a shop framed in wood, stained a rich patina by much polishing. A bank of bay windows overflowed with a stunning array of gold jewelry, its glow blinding in the late-day sun.

"This is the place," he said and dragged her inside.

Delanie craned her neck as she passed a glass case with the most dazzling array of gold bracelets, the size and intricate designs begging a second look. But the next showcase was just as stunning, just as breathtaking as the other.

Everywhere she looked, her gaze fell on the warm liquid sensuality of ultra-fine gold. Or on one arrogantly gorgeous Italian who had yet to release her hand.

"Is it really all eighteen-carat?" she asked Marco as he caught a clerk's eye.

"Yes, all the goldsmiths here pride themselves on selling the highest grade gold." He bent over a case. "Which one do you think Bella would like?"

She pointed to a display of pendants suspended on fine twisted gold chains. "Any of these freeform designs should appeal to her."

"I like the middle one," he said.

She smiled in agreement. "I think that will be perfect for your sister."

Marco nodded to the patient clerk and the older man hurried to comply. Delanie grasped the opportunity to put distance between her and Marco, to focus on the array of jewelry instead of on the doubts that were hammering away at her, an insistent ache that left her shaken inside, left her questioning everything to do with him.

How different her life would be if the lies hadn't gotten between them. If she had walked away from her business and her family. If she were his wife instead of his lover....

"You like?" Marco asked, appearing at her elbow with that same maddening stealth that had stolen her heart so long ago.

With effort she tore her gaze from the dark liquid languor glowing in his eyes to the warmth of the gold pendant suspended from an equally exquisite chain. "It's fabulous. I've never seen anything quite like the chain or the pendant."

"They are unique blends of modern design and fabled Florentine craftsmanship," he said, smiling, relaxed, his command of his world so appealing. "In many ways, the Etruscan influence still runs deeply here."

In the craftsmanship and the people? She'd read about the indigenous people while in school but had trouble dredging up any specifics. Not so for Marco.

But then he'd been born here. He'd been surrounded by this curious mix of old world and new most of his life. The rich cultural wealth that flowed alongside the Apennines coursed in his blood as well.

That only proved again how little she'd known about him ten years ago. How little she'd attempted to learn about his life.

Her cheeks heated as she admitted to herself that she'd been too selfish to think beyond her own world.

She bit her lower lip, the gold before her blurring into a liquid burnished sea. The life she'd wanted was close enough to taste, to embrace. So why did her heart ache at the thought of leaving here? Leaving Marco?

"Which piece would the lady like to see?" the clerk asked, appearing on the other side of the case as if by magic. As if expecting Marco to buy more of the lavishly expensive jewelry.

For her? Not on her life! She would make love with him but she would not take a token of gold back to London.

Her fingertips grazed the polished edge of the case, blinking frantically to disperse her sudden tears. "Nothing, thank you. I'm just window-shopping."

Marco edged closer, his arm touching hers lightly, yet sending her insides into a tumble all the same. "Come on. You must like one piece more than the other."

With Marco so close and behaving so charmingly again she was having trouble thinking straight. If she didn't know better, she would swear he was flirting with her. But that was preposterous. Wasn't it?

She rubbed her left temple, frustrated she couldn't concentrate on anything but Marco standing so close. His unique scent drifted in a silken glide over her skin, leaving her trembling.

Marco in his most arrogant persona she could deal with. But when he was like this, sweet, sexy, attentive, she couldn't think of anything but falling into his arms, holding him, kissing him, loving him. Dangerous thoughts to have for a man she intended to walk away from—for good this time.

"Can't decide?" he prodded.

With effort, she shook off the drugging effect that was totally him and pointed toward the pendant she'd been admiring earlier. Only as her vision cleared, she realized that the necklaces were no longer there.

She scanned the case, a frown pulling at her brow. When had the clerk exchanged the tray of pendants for rings?

The little man was quick to hold up a stunning ring for her inspection, carefully setting it on the velvet pillow. Her

breath caught and her pulse raced. She'd never seen such delicate gold filigree or such an amazing rainbow of fire reflect-
ing off one diamond.

"It's exquisite," she said.

The clerk made an appreciative sound. "Would the lady
like to try it on?"

"No!" She pushed back from the case, glancing at Marco,
then the door. "I'll wait outside for you."

With that she fled the shop and the sweet lure of the man
she feared she would never forget.

CHAPTER NINE

MARCO credited a good deal of his swift success to the fact that he relied on his gut instincts. So far they hadn't let him down. He saw no reason to defer from that course now when the object of his desire was in sight.

Or more specifically, his desire was sitting beside him as he raced back to his villa. His suddenly silent, suddenly edgy object of desire.

There had been a major quake between them as they'd walked onto Ponte Vecchio. For some reason he had yet to understand, it had erupted in the jeweler's shop when the clerk assumed that Delanie was his fiancée and had trotted forth the tray of rings.

Delanie had been mellowing toward him all day, even giving him that look that was a green light aimed directly at him. Then, the second the clerk pulled up the engagement ring Delanie had been admiring, she had pulled away. She had actually run from the shop.

What madness had come over him to stand by and watch? Why hadn't he been the one to immediately pull her out of the shop when the engagement rings were trotted out, ending any speculation of what she meant to him?

Those questions nagged at him as he followed her out, finding her standing in the arched opening of the bridge, wind threading through her hair.

"What is wrong?" he'd asked, pulling her behind a pilla
where they had a modicum of privacy.

"It was so hot in there," she said, her gaze turned to the
river. "Didn't you notice?"

Then before he could reply, she'd slipped from him agai
and walked back to the stone railing. By the time he'd joined
her, she was smiling, though he saw a note of strain around he
expressive eyes and the lovely mouth that he longed to kiss.

"I love this view," she said.

"So do I." But he wasn't looking at the fertile hills or the
haze of the Apennines in the distance.

He was staring at Delanie, his gaze worshiping her, de
vouring her. A sudden swift stab of longing twisted in his
gut as he stared at her.

In less than a week now, Bella would be married and Delanie
would expect him to make good on his deal with her. She would
return to London with the success of a much-publicized wed
ding in her portfolio, in full control of her business.

Both of them would go on with their lives. Except he wasn'
ready to see her go.

Though they shared a refreshing lunch later, all spontane
ity was gone the moment they got in his Bugatti for the drive
home. The closer they'd gotten to his villa the more remote
she had become.

He flexed his fingers on the steering wheel, annoyed and
frustrated. As they neared Montiforte, he sensed Delanie slip
ping away from him.

If he didn't do something to stop this soon, she would lock
herself into some secret place that he couldn't reach. He would
lose her again before he truly had her.

But what if she stayed? What role would she play in the life
of a man who had sworn never to marry? Mistress?

No, she wouldn't do that. She wouldn't stay. So he had to
make the most of this opportunity.

"Do you need anything from the village?" he asked.

"Everything is done and progressing on schedule," she said. "It's just a matter of checking in with the vendors and the bride daily until the wedding day."

Minutes later they were at his house nestled in the hills. Before they got out of his car, he knew exactly what he was going to do. There would be no altering it this time.

"Thank you for the lovely day," Delanie said as she stepped into the sunbathed patio.

"It was my pleasure."

He stopped in the doorway, shoulder braced on the jamb, gaze savoring the enticing view of her very firm, very sexy backside. His pulse kicked up, his groin tightening.

"You have done a remarkable job," he said.

"Thanks," she said, not slowing. Fleeing, nearly.

He flexed his fingers, aware there would be no going back, jaw firming with his decision. "We will celebrate your success tonight."

She came to a stiff halt by the chaise, hand gripping the plump backrest. "That isn't necessary."

"I disagree."

He pushed away from the door, crossing to her in three strides. His palms grazed her shoulders and he damned the silk that kept him from feeling the velvet of her bare skin.

"We need this celebration, Delanie. Just us," he said.

He heard her swallow and was startled to find his own throat felt just as tight, that his nerves were not as unruffled as usual. She did this to him, kept him off balance just that fraction, rocking the stable foundation he'd carved out.

No other woman had ever left him so on edge. Just Delanie. She'd done it from the first moment they'd met, when she'd given all to him that first time before letting fear choke her. He'd had no idea how to deal with it then.

He wasn't entirely sure now, but he knew passion churned deeply in her, passion that she felt for him. His fingertips tingled with the need to touch her, hold her, release that need in her that coursed through him as well. A whirlpool of unrest swirled in his gut, a gnawing hunger that only she could sate.

She faced him then, eyes wide and cheeks kissed with a rosy flush. "You want sex," she said frankly.

"I wanted you the moment I stepped onto Ponte Vecchio with you," he said, hand cupping her head, canting her face gently up to his. "Perhaps even sooner."

And then his lips were on hers, hot, ravenous. Flames exploded in his blood, a firestorm of desire that licked through his veins.

He slipped an arm around her narrow waist and pulled her flush against him, the sizzle in his blood popping like a champagne cork in his head.

His skin was on fire, the hot tips of her breasts branding his chest. Her scent was on him, in him, blotting out the world, blotting out everything but her. This moment. Them.

This is how it had been between them before. It was how it was meant to be: a fire of consuming need and blazing heat that they danced in when they were wrapped in each other's arms.

She was his. He knew it in his gut, his soul.

He only had to convince her of that. Coax her to soften, to surrender. To realize that this was where she was supposed to be.

With him. By his side. In his bed.

His lips traced the curve of her jaw, her slender neck, her delicate stubborn chin before settling over her sweet mouth in a kiss that sang through his veins. The rightness stealing over him dashed any doubts.

This was right. This was what should be. Surely she knew that. Felt the depth of emotions rejoicing within him.

She moaned, bowing into him as if to remind him how well their bodies fitted together. Not that he needed a reminder. He recalled every delicious moment he'd spent with her; the memories tormented his sleep.

Yet another sign she was the only woman for him. Yes, he'd had other lovers in the ensuing years. Lovely women he'd romanced. Women he'd treated well but who weren't around for long. Women who failed to compare to Delanie Tate.

Weeks after being with them, he had trouble remembering their faces. But not Delanie's.

He remembered everything. How her pupils darkened when they came together. Her breathy pants. Her touch, her scent, the beat of her heart against his.

He pulled back, breath sawing heavily, blood raging like a swollen river. "I want you, *cara mia.*"

"I want you as well," she said, the husk in her now-breathy voice the most erotic thing he'd ever heard.

He leaned back further, just enough to stare into the dreamy depths of her eyes, her pupils dilated, her lips plump and wet from his kisses.

He cupped her hips and yanked her against him, rocking his engorged shaft against her softness. "I want to make love with you until we are too weak to move, until we have freely spent our passion. And then, after we have rested, we will do it again. And again."

"Yes," she said, her voice a sexy huskiness that played over his senses in sweet abandon. "Let's make love all night long."

She flung her head back with a gasp and threaded her fingers through his hair, her nails scraping his scalp, the match to flint that sent a firestorm raging through his blood. Heat flared, roared through him with every erotic grind of her hips against his hard length.

Still she held part of herself back, denying him his conquest. And so he cast off his own reservations and kissed her with all the passion trapped inside him.

A moment passed, then another. Finally her very proper veneer went up in ash, revealing the earthy soul of a woman lost to abandon. Lost to him.

He gritted his teeth, sweat beading his brow as pressure

pounded through his veins so fiercely he feared he would ex
plode. Feared the fire raging in him would burn him to a crisp.

Structured thoughts scattered under the blaze of desire
sweeping over him. He could barely draw a decent breath,
but he dug deep to clutch the cold steel in his spine to temper
his lust. To hold on to a modicum of control.

His body ached for a quick tumble to ease the mountain
of tension stacked inside him like the village houses against
the hills. One fracture was all it would take to break free the
desire he'd dammed up for too long.

Once would never be enough with her. A taste would only
leave him hungering for more. And he would have it, a long
sensual feast of the senses to last the night and beyond, to fog
the issues he avoided with her, that he refused even to con
sider with another woman.

Her kisses turned wild, the rake of her fingernails stoking
the fire in him. If he didn't know better, he would swear she
was more ravenous for this than he was. Would think it had
been far too long since she'd reveled in this sweet pleasure
with a man. But that couldn't be.

Even if it were true he refused to dwell on it now. Thoughts
of her with anyone but him were poison in his soul, danger
ous and undermining.

She was in his arms now. Soon she would be in his bed
where he intended to keep her until this driving need left him.
A night, a day. Maybe two and this urgency would be gone.

For now he would enjoy her. For now she was his. For now
they were together.

His fingers bit into the inviting curve of her hips covered in
the slim tight skirt. "I will explode if I don't have you soon."

"It's okay," she said, nipping his chin while drilling the
hard points of her nipples into his chest. "I can't wait much
longer either."

He stripped off her blouse and skirt with hands that trem
bled, then helped her rip his shirt off his heated body, unable

to bear her tender attempts. Though cool air whispered over his flesh he still burned deep for her.

When was the last time he'd been this desperate to possess a woman? Ten years ago, he thought without hesitation. Ten long years ago with the same enchanting woman.

The air crackled with electricity, making each touch a sensual jolt that left him trembling inside. He was burning up with unquenchable need, and the beautiful blush kissing her cheeks, neck and the full breasts that heaved in tempo with his ragged breaths told him that she wanted this just as much. Wanted him.

Yet he dragged out this long-awaited foreplay a bit longer by simply caressing her with his gaze. Knowing it would be sweeter in the end. Going as far as he dared, then pushing the boundary a bit more but finally taking her into his arms and kissing her, stroking his hands up and down her bare back.

Her hands were just as busy, sliding down his sides, her fingertips skipping over the firm globes of his bottom. An avalanche of sensations zipped over his heated skin and he faltered, tossing his head back to gasp for air.

"You are magnificent," she said, clutching his length with small knowing hands that threatened to bring him to his knees.

"Cara," he said on a hiss, afraid to breathe, to move for fear she would stop. "You are killing me."

"Softly comes this death," she said, kneeling before him, fingers still worshipping his sex.

Then her mouth touched him there, the shock so electric he jolted. Perhaps cursed. Perhaps said a prayer as her lips trailed up and down his length until he wanted to howl with the pleasure thundering through him.

He treaded his fingers through her silken hair, holding her close, straining for control that was fast spiraling away from him.

This was sweet erotic torture, and it was something he never allowed for it put the woman in control. It stole the power from him. Stole rational thought and replaced it with earthy need.

But he'd taught her this soon after they met, encouraged her to explore him because he'd thought it would loosen her inhibitions. It had to a degree, but she'd relished the control, her ability to give him pleasure while holding back giving her all to him in turn.

That had begun the pattern of their intimacy that had kept them apart, that would throw up a wall between them now unless she totally surrendered herself to him.

So he held back now, tense muscles jerking with the hunger for pleasure. His skin burned, too hot, too tight, certain to break if he didn't find release soon.

It would not be this way.

That was the lone thought on his mind as he dug deep and found the strength to stop this sweet torture.

"Not now." He jerked her to her feet and dragged her flush against him.

"But…"

He silenced her protest with a kiss that conquered. Demanded.

She hesitated. Stiff, caught off guard. Then a sound bubbled from the back of her throat and she met his kiss with equal fervor.

He slid his palms over her sexy bottom and trailed his fingers down her thighs. The cool silk of her tender skin sent a shiver rocketing through him.

His blood hammered so loudly he felt rather than heard her needy moan. But he gave her no rest, stroking the delicious curve of her hips, the lush fullness of her bottom, the slick seductive folds between her trembling legs.

"Oh, God," she said, clutching his shoulders, back bowing to push her bosom and sex closer to him.

"Yes," he said thickly, coaxing her on with deeper strokes

of his fingers and trying like hell to hold his own desire in check.

It was hell and heaven, extracting more stamina from him than he thought was possible. His limbs ached, his muscles knotted. Sweat poured off his brow and down his back. His sex throbbed, ready to burst.

"Marco!"

"Let go, Delanie. Let go like you did the first time."

"I can't," she said, voice cracking.

"You can. Do it. You won't regret it, *cara.*"

He held her as passion warred with her fear, as her fingers dug into his shoulders, her gaze locked with his. Triumph surged through him as desire finally glazed her eyes, as her lovely body rippled in erotic surrender and his patience paid off tenfold.

It had been too long since he'd enjoyed watching a woman reach her passion. Too long since he'd felt this sense of awe. Too long since he'd been gifted with Delanie's full passion.

Her fingernails dug into his flesh so hard she likely drew blood but he didn't care. His lips curled in male satisfaction, chest puffing with the assurance that he'd been the one to give her such pleasure. That he'd gained the same just watching desire sweep her up in its honeyed maelstrom.

The strength of her climax left her in sated bliss and he caught her, cradled her close. But what caught him by surprise was the swelling of his heart, the warmth that stole over him as he looked down at her, a rightness that was unlike anything he'd felt before, even with her.

A thread of fear pulled through him and tightened his gut. He didn't want to feel emotion this deeply. Didn't want those tender emotions clawing at him, trying to burrow in.

What he'd had with Delanie was history. This was their time to part amiably. To be adults and admit there never would be any future for them together. To savor each other and this moment.

He blocked everything from his mind but the fact he was overly aroused and had a very naked, very willing woman in his arms. This was sex and he would make sure it was the best sex either of them had ever had.

They would part without regret before the wedding. The past would be just a fond memory.

"I can't wait," he said, setting her on the counter, the bedroom simply too great a distance in his condition.

Her legs parted in invitation and her fingers dug into his shoulders. "Neither can I."

He pulled her forward and thrust into her, and a deep satisfied growl rumbled from him. Being in her wasn't enough. He had to kiss her. Had to parallel the sensual assault with his mouth. Had to hold her and stroke her soft flesh.

But he sensed no complaint. Nothing but sweet surrender.

The last was something he never allowed in a lover. But this was Delanie. This was something that was reserved only for her. That he'd waited to experience for far too long.

They were both lost in desire, their bodies moving in rhythm, knowing where to stroke, to touch, to bring the most pleasure.

It vaguely occurred to him that they were equally dominant now. That they were in perfect sensual sync. He took, she gave, and vice versa.

They were matched. Perfect together?

That was the last thought on his mind as she climaxed and he gave over as well. The lone thought that locked his knees and kept him standing as wave after wave of pleasure coursed through him.

She clung to him, limp, sated. He laid his face aside hers, his breath tortured as he fought to regain sanity after the little death.

And he *had* lost his sanity, he realized, as he slowly eased from her. When had he been this irresponsibly horny?

"Dammit," he hissed, muscles taut with anger.

"What's wrong?" she asked, her voice having a drowsy, sexy edge that was making him hard again.

"We—" He pursed his lips and made a slicing motion with his hand. "I didn't think to use protection."

Which brought a whole host of what-ifs into play, foremost being what if he got her pregnant? The answer was obvious. He would not sire a bastard. No way. They would have to marry and pronto.

Her hands slid around his hot, tense nape. "It's all right. I'm on the pill and I assure you I'm clean."

His breath left him in a whoosh, taking the tight coil of tension with it. She was protected. Not trying to trap him into marriage.

"That," he said, kissing her forehead, her nose, "is very good to know."

"I thought you would approve," she whispered against his neck. "That was bloody awesome. In case you're wondering, once won't be enough."

He tipped his head back and laughed, something else that he never did with a woman after sex. Delanie joined him, free, relaxed.

No strings. No commitments. Just pleasure. That was all this was. So why did he feel a moment's annoyance? Why was he a bit disappointed to hear she'd had the foresight to protect herself against pregnancy?

He shrugged off the damned doubts that had no place in this moment. "This time, we will make good use of the bed."

This time, on legs that thankfully didn't shake, he carried her into the bedroom and proceeded to show her how much he enjoyed every delicious inch of her.

Delanie stirred, stretching like a lazy kitten. A twinge of discomfort streaked across her hipbones and she winced, stilling until the moment passed.

It had been this way every morning for the past three days,

each day and night spent in sensual wonder, each new day better than the one before.

Last night had certainly been no exception. She pinched her eyes shut, face heating to an uncomfortable warmth as each delicious minute flashed before her eyes.

They had made love well into the wee hours of the morning, not pounding urgent coupling but a slow, deep coming together that touched something in her she wasn't even aware of. Sometime in the early hours of the morning they'd finally fallen into an exhausted sleep.

She'd never felt closer to him. Never been so close to giving up anything and everything for him.

Yet Marco had left their bed before dawn. Perhaps he was on the terrace drinking coffee.

Or, she thought as she slipped from the bed, he was in his office working.

She would have enjoyed indulging in a hot bath but she needed to find Marco first. Talk to him. Gauge his mood.

In moments she was dressed in jeans and a lightweight sweater, attire perfect for a day spent here at the house. She padded to the door, wincing again at the tenderness between her legs and the abrasive rub of her lace bra against her nipples.

Her nerves tautened as she stepped into the kitchen, where the doors were thrown open to let in a gentle breeze. Her gaze took in the open area and the salon beyond. No sign of him.

Then, distantly, she heard the low rumble of Marco's voice drifting to her on the breeze. He was outside, speaking to someone in Italian.

She strode to the door and paused, catching sight of him pacing the length of the terrace, his mobile phone pressed to his ear. Words flew from him like bullets. Though Delanie couldn't keep up with the conversation, she sensed by his clipped tone that he was upset.

"Okay," Marco said, free hand fisted at his side. "Tell her I will be there in a few minutes."

Her stomach knotted as much from the tension in his voice as the fact he would leave the villa soon. So much for expecting an intimate morning together.

But then the timing of such things was rarely left to the mistress, she supposed. He would come in. Tell her about his change of plans and she would see him when it was convenient for him. Not her.

She crossed to the kitchen and splashed coffee in a cup, needing the caffeine jolt to her system. Though she'd intended to adopt a cosmopolitan demeanor regarding their affair, she simply couldn't do it.

It wasn't even a hard admission to make. She'd known from the start that she couldn't regard sex with Marco as a casual thing, especially if she stopped holding part of herself back. But there was no graceful way out now.

Her shoulders bowed as she walked toward the door, a smile trembling on her lips as she stepped out onto the terrace. A very empty terrace. Empty garden. Empty pool area.

She frowned. He hadn't come back into the house. Had he zipped off in his red sports car without a goodbye? Without a word to her?

That was simply unacceptable behavior! She set her cup of coffee down beside his half-drunk one and rounded the house, thinking she just might catch a glimpse of him peeling down the winding drive in his sleek red auto toward the "she" who needed him so much. But the Bugatti was right where Marco had parked it last night.

Baffled, she retraced her steps to the terrace. Just as she was ready to turn toward the door, she caught a blinding flash of white moving in the hills above the house.

She shielded her eyes and focused on the figure.

Marco? Yes, the more she watched the more sure she was of it. He was taking the trail upward and would soon be out of sight. Who was he going to see? Whose call had the power to send him out like this on foot?

A female neighbor in need perhaps? A convenient lover?

Delanie fisted her hands, welcoming the swift jab of anger that finally prodded her feet to move. She was well onto the track winding into the hills before it struck her that the wisest course was to fob this off and leave him to whatever lady had snared his fancy.

But curiosity was a cruel companion to jealousy and both were playing hell with her emotions right now. So she struck out after him, determined to find out where he'd gone in such a rush that he couldn't even leave her a note.

Staying on the well-maintained trail took her to a lovely clearing a good two kilometers above Marco's house. The stands of cypress and perfect lines of lofty poplars kept this little area well secluded, the perfect place to secrete away a mistress.

Her gaze took in the small farmstead. Instead of livestock, which she hadn't expected to find anyway, her gaze lit on several dozen medium-sized lanky dogs lazing in a fenced enclosure.

A woman with a dog kennel was the last thing she'd expected to find. How odd she'd never heard more than a few barks in all the time she'd been here.

She looked toward the barn, which she guessed was the heart of the operation, and just caught sight of Marco going inside. Without thinking that she was now trespassing or at the least spying on her lover, she struck out toward the barn as well.

Her heart was racing like the wind long before she stepped inside a small room furnished with a half dozen utility chairs and a counter that looked suspiciously like a reception area of sorts. She followed Marco's voice into the adjacent room where he knelt beside a tan dog. A woman of modest years with a stern countenance stood behind him with a perplexed look on her face.

"How long has she been like this?" Marco asked, brow furrowed as he ran a gentle hand over the dog's sleek coat.

"I found her this way this morning," the woman said. "The knee is completely displaced. Surgery might give her full range of movement again but at her age…"

Marco flung the woman a glacial look that made Delanie shiver. "Then operate. I have made it clear that Rifugio del Cuccia was built for the animals and that means prolonging their quality of life as long as it is humanly possible."

"Very well," the woman said. "I will operate on her this afternoon."

The woman walked off but Marco remained crouched by the animal. He stroked the dog gently and crooned so softly Delanie had to strain to hear the soothing melody, so rich and warm she pressed a hand to her mouth to stifle a sigh.

But the old greyhound responded, giving a weary wag of her tail. The dog lifted her head once to look at him before moaning and lying back down with a contented sigh.

Delanie's throat tightened and her eyes misted. And her heart… Oh, God, her heart flooded with warmth.

The animal loved him and he was clearly protective of the dog. Yet she never recalled him talking of animals the entire time she had known him. Just another slice of Marco Vincienta that he kept hidden from the world. A very compassionate side that she'd never seen to this degree.

She eased back toward the door, feeling very shallow for the earlier negative thoughts that had consumed her, compelling her to follow him. Feeling far too weak-kneed as well.

What she wouldn't give if he would show that much love to her!

But he couldn't. Or wouldn't.

She'd known from the start that leaving him would hurt. That she still loved him.

But she hadn't realized until this moment that walking away from this wonderful man would surely kill her.

CHAPTER TEN

"You don't have to leave," Marco said, still not looking up. "I'm not going to bite your head off for following me."

She grimaced. Another second and she would have been gone. Instead she scrambled for composure and a steady tone.

"No, you'll just sic the dogs on me," she said, aiming for a tease.

To her relief he smiled, a boyish grin that made her heart thump harder. "There's not a vicious one in the kennel, *cara*."

Again, she saw a different side of Marco as she crouched on the floor in a kennel making light conversation. The tension that had bonded to her suddenly came unglued. She shivered at the naked freedom of losing the encumbrance, of allowing herself to simply relax around him again.

An odd thing to admit after the intimacies they'd shared last night. She chafed her upper arms and glanced at her surroundings.

Kennels side by side down the perimeter, separated from each other by solid walls, had pet doors that opened into the fenced yard. A few dogs dozed in their cages but none as listlessly as the greyhound sprawled at Marco's feet.

"I didn't mean to intrude on a private moment," she said.

"You're not. I should have invited you to come with me," he said. "At the least, I should have told you why I had to rush off."

But he hadn't. His thoughts had been on the dog he obviously cared for instead of the woman he'd romanced all night.

Yet she couldn't fault him.

"It's all right. I take it this place is yours," she said.

He gave a crisp nod. "I bought this old farm several years ago and refurbished it into the dog kennel you see it today." His hand stilled on the listless greyhound, his smile tender. "Zena was one of our first guests."

"She's special to you then."

"Yes, but not like you think." He continued to pet the dog, seeming in no hurry to move or avoid her questions. "She was a champion, setting records with the amount of races she won in four years and deserves a luxurious retirement."

She shifted, her smile fading. "I wasn't aware you were involved in dog-racing."

Dark, narrowed eyes drilled into her and a muscle jerked along his jaw. "I never have been, at least not as a proponent of the sport. Their less-than-humane practices to the animals sickens me. The dogs earn billions for their owners yet are treated abominably. That is part of the reason I built this rescue shelter."

Zena moaned and lifted her head and Marco instantly focused his attention on the animal. The dog responded by stilling with a weary exhalation.

His broad shoulders relaxed, his hard features softened. It was all she could do to keep from going to him, rubbing the taut muscles, soothing him as he was comforting the dog.

"I just assumed…" She rubbed the chill from her arms again. "My apologies."

That earned her a negligent shrug. "It's ok. You made the same assumption most make considering my biological father had a penchant for gambling."

Delanie bit her lip, debating whether to let the subject drop or pursue it. There was certainly more to it. More that bothered him or else he wouldn't have gone to all this expense.

Wouldn't have been so emotionally invested in building a shelter just moments from his home.

"Do you mind if I join you?" she asked.

"Please, sit," he said, and the dog did no more than cast big brown eyes her way. Eyes that had clearly seen too much hurt and very little of the affection she was reaping now.

She bit her lip as she eased down on the other side of Zena. "I've never been around dogs."

He looked up. "You never had a pet?"

An image of chasing a dog flickered in her memory. "Mother was given a puppy once. He looked like a puff of fur and was so soft and so full of life." Too full of life for her household.

"What happened to him?"

She frowned at her clasped hands. "Father told us he had to find a new home for the dog because his allergies prevented close contact with animals of any kind."

He snorted. "Did you believe him?"

"Back then I did," she said. "But now? No."

Her gaze lifted from the dog to the man and her breath caught as her gaze locked with his dark somber eyes. The last thing she needed now was his compassion.

"What about you?" she asked. "Did you grow up around animals?"

"We had a dog when I was a boy. A mongrel, really."

He cracked a smile and her heart ached as she imagined him playing in the streets of Florence with his pet. Ached because she envied him that memory when her own was so fleeting.

"Tell me about your dog," she said. "What was his name?

"Sebastian," he said. "He followed me home from school one day, so scrawny he was little more than matted fur over bones."

"So you took him in," she said.

"Yes. Mama gave him scraps and he made himself at home on our back stoop."

His features softened, his eyes glowed, as he launched into a slice of life about a poor Italian boy on the winding cobbled streets in Florence, running with a mutt of a dog. Laughing. Free. Enjoying his childhood with parents who were passionately close at that time.

A gnawing pain that was simply jealousy for what he'd had and she hadn't popped up in her, as ugly as a sudden pimple on a cheek or chin. A mark to ignore or treat, and she struggled to do either.

At one time she'd pitied him for the dire straits he'd come from. But in truth it was she who'd lived in emotional poverty in the mansion in Mayfair. No matter how hard she tried she couldn't remember her mother and father laughing, together or apart. Couldn't remember the wealthy Tate family doing anything for the sheer enjoyment of it.

The only time she'd truly lived was when she'd met Marco. He'd pulled her out of her staid life and showed her a world bright with promise. He'd been exciting and loving and powerful.

When he'd left her, she'd retreated to what she'd known— protecting her mother as best as she could. Enduring.

Her budding career as a wedding planner became her only outlet. Through it she lived vicariously, enjoying others' happiness without risking her own heart again.

Sitting with Marco on the floor of a fabulous dog shelter terrified her more than she wished to admit. Her heart beat too fast, her thoughts whirled like a tempest, all centered around the man who had stormed back into her life and forced her really to look at her existence.

Gaining her independence had been all she'd wanted for so long. It still was her goal.

Entertaining thoughts of Marco remaining in her life was moot. Nothing had changed between them.

She deserved more than a one-sided affair of the heart. He couldn't open his heart to love. Or was there hope that would change?

That thought remained front and center in her mind as she reached out to stroke the dog. The stiff coat was surprisingly soft, much like Marco: He projected a hard exterior but clearly had a much softer spot in his heart for animals.

The dog was a breathing, needy connection between them because it was safer to touch the dog than each other. Safer than opening herself up to those feelings that were already battering down the door she'd locked them behind.

"I'm jealous of your memories of a happy home and family," she said.

He shrugged, and she coveted even that careless surety he affected without effort. "I have good ones and not so good ones. There are more chapters of the latter than the former."

"Mine range from bad to indifferent," she said, though she suspected her bad memories outweighed his. "But you had more than just parents at odds. My maternal grandparents died long before I was born. My father was estranged from his family."

He frowned. "So you were cut off from kin?"

She nodded. "Henry sent word to a younger sibling of Father's upon his death, but they didn't respond."

"That's wrong."

"Perhaps, but it was proof that Father reaped what he'd sown with family and business associates," she said.

She was spared saying more as the veterinarian strode into the room, her dark blue surgical scrubs a sign she was ready to operate. The woman didn't spare Delanie a glance.

"Marco, we are ready for Zena," the veterinarian said.

He shifted to a squat, his gaze on the dog as Delanie rose to her feet. "Should I carry her for you?"

"Grazie." The veterinarian held the door open. "Bring her in here, please."

He gently lifted the dog in his strong arms and disappeared through the door with the veterinarian trailing him. The metal panel closed with a clang.

Delanie paced the room and rubbed her bare arms again, debating whether to stay or to go back to the villa. She had no desire to witness a surgery though she suspected Marco would remain here until Zena was on the road to recovery.

She slipped out the door and headed to the path that wound back to Marco's house. Yes, she was running away, even though she couldn't run far from her troubles.

Once Marco had time for her, he would seek her out. Wine her. Dine her. Seduce her until she begged him to make love to her—to ease the torment of desire.

And when they'd rested, she would welcome his passion all over again.

Stolen days of bliss, that's all she had with him.

Halfway down the hill she paused at the breathtaking vista of Montiforte far below. She drank in the beauty like one famished, convinced she would never tire of letting her gaze wander the hills and quaint villages where hustle and bustle were foreign concepts.

How odd that she, the girl who had craved the excitement of London, would come to appreciate the quiet beauty of this landlocked part of Italy. Not once had she pined for her typical breakneck routine that was mired in the city. She had rarely thought of her friends.

An anomaly.

She'd been busy planning the wedding, getting to know the village and the people who were always quick to help. Then she'd gotten caught up in Marco's charisma, lost in his arms, addicted to his passion.

Too soon it would all end and she would return to her world. She would have the company she'd sacrificed years of her life to regain. She would lose Marco all over again.

Her shoulders slumped, her stomach knotting. Why

couldn't her heart race with excitement over finally gaining what she wanted? Why was the world she'd known less appealing than this laid-back lifestyle?

"It's a beautiful sight, no?" Marco said.

She let out a yelp, startled he'd sneaked up on her. "I thought you would stay with Zena."

He shook his head. "She is in good hands." His gaze roamed her length, as intimate as a caress. "What are your plans for today?"

"I have none," she said.

He slipped an arm around her, pulled her into the heat and hardness of his body and she melted against him effortlessly. Her heart leapt to life, thudding hard in her chest. Her breasts grew heavy, the nipples peaking to aching awareness.

"Then let's return to the house and enjoy the time left us. Okay?" he asked.

Asked!

She smiled and hoped he couldn't tell it was pained.

He offered the one thing he could give her without reservations. With total honesty. Passion.

Denying herself the pleasure wouldn't make leaving him any easier. A heart couldn't break any more than it had, could it?

"How can I say no?" she said.

Something had changed between him and Delanie in the shelter and damned if he could put his finger on it. But he didn't like it.

Her smile was just as warm as the sun. Her fingers still clung to his with the same urgency. Her eyes still burned with passion.

Yet he felt the distancing between them as if she were leaving him now instead of in a few days. That would come soon enough. For now, while he had her here they would make the most of their time together.

He would know for sure before she left him again if his pride had cost him the most important thing in his life.

"That sweet spicy smell. Is it coming from that flower over there?" she asked, pointing to a light purple bloom that had newly unfurled its petals.

"Yes, the much-prized *zafferano*," he said, and at her pulled brow added, "Saffron. It grows wild here and has been a major export for centuries."

"It's so delicate."

Much like Delanie, he thought, smiling. "Ah, but she is stingy with her treasure. *Zafferano* is the world's most expensive herb."

"Our chef made saffron rice," she said.

He snorted. "As does the world. But a saffron risotto with cinnamon pork—" He kissed his thumb and forefinger. *"Delizioso."*

Her kissable mouth pulled into a playful smile but it was the fingers tightening on his that sent a surge of heat blazing through him. "Okay, where do I sample this delicacy?"

One jerk brought her slamming against him, full lush breasts to hard heaving chest. He kissed her mouth quickly, then swooped back for another one, longer this time, lingering over her as one would a scrumptious dish.

"At my house, of course," he said, his voice thickened with his growing need to have her. Not any woman. Her. "With a stop in the village for ingredients."

"Who is going to cook this delicacy?" she asked as he inched toward the crocus and plucked off the three reddish stigmas.

He held such a treasure, yet it paled in comparison to the woman. She was the rare treasure.

"Me, of course," he said as he picked his way back to the trail, careful not to tread on new tender shoots. "I am not just a pretty face!"

She laughed, a rich playful sound that lifted the weight of

worry from him. They had this. The spontaneity of lovers that had not faded with time. But was it enough?

It had to be.

Delanie Tate wanted love. Wanted hearts and flowers. Wanted a man who would let her spread her wings and fly independently of him.

Marco simply couldn't do that. He couldn't allay his doubts that she would return to her lies. That in the end, she would find a man more dashing, more amiable than he and would betray him.

No, all he had with her was her time in Italy planning Bella's wedding. He intended to make the most of it.

He pressed a fortune's worth of fresh herb into her hands. "I will have you know that one of my early apprenticeships was cooking, and I was damned good at it."

"You're good at everything," she said with a smile.

If only he could be…. But nothing had changed.

"I am just a simple Italian," he said, and she laughed harder.

"There is nothing simple about you," she said, her teasing smile a balm to his doubts.

Hand in hand, they wound their way to the house, stopping for the occasional kiss. Each one lasted longer, firing his blood and numbing his mind well before they left the trail.

A drive to the village netted a selection of vegetables, a loaf of crusty bread and cuts of prime pork.

"You're serious about cooking for us," she said.

"Very. I will make a risotto that will melt in your mouth," he promised on the short drive back to the house.

"I'm embarrassed to admit I'm horribly inadequate in the culinary arts," she said, helping him carry their fare into the house. "Did your mother teach you?"

He smiled at that thought and poured two glasses of rich sagrantino. "My nonna taught me. She was an amazing cook. An amazing woman with only one fault—she was too trusting."

Her eyes swam with intense hurt, but it was the touch of

her fingers urgently gripping his hand that made his heart lurch. "I'm so sorry my father maliciously destroyed your family's business."

He shrugged, the fury that usually swept over him thankfully absent, leaving only the slow burn of deceit on his tongue. "I am too. But it's over. He is dead. The winery and olive press are mine again. And you are here with me."

She bit her lower lip and he caught the barest tremor shaking her before she managed a smile. "I'm glad we had this time together. That we've cleared the air of misconceptions."

His hand closed over hers, his pulse gaining speed as he stepped closer and cupped her cheek with his other palm. Her gaze lifted to his—open, questioning. Hesitant?

"Our affair doesn't have to be temporary."

She wet her lips, the pulse in her throat fluttering as wildly as his own. "Yes, it must end. Unless your feelings toward me have changed."

He couldn't breathe, couldn't think beyond the fact she'd called his hand, that she expected a declaration of his feelings before she would consider staying here.

It's what he'd known she would do all along. So why had he brought it up when he knew the answer would push them further apart?

"Nothing has changed," he said honestly, dropping a kiss on her nose, her chin, her mouth. "Especially not my hunger for you."

She held herself stiffly for a moment, then lifted her face to his. Was that a flicker of pain in her eyes?

He couldn't tell, and she drove the question from his mind by threading her fingers at his nape, bowing her body into his length. She kissed his chin, then nipped the flesh, sending a flash fire of desire racing through his blood.

"Then I suggest we enjoy good food and each other," she said, definitely taking the lead this time.

He ran a hand down her back, damning the soft barrier of clothes that kept him from caressing her silken skin, dragging her body flush against his with an urgency that totally lacked finesse. His mouth settled on hers, as hot and hungry as he'd been for her years ago. Maybe more so because having her again was better than a memory, richer, hotter.

She was a fire in his blood, making him burn from the inside out. His shirt clung to his slick back and chest. His jeans were a nagging constraint to his sex.

"We have on far too many clothes," he said, tearing his shirt off and flinging it aside.

"Way too many," she said, her voice a breathy huskiness that fired his libido another notch.

She raked her nails down his chest to his waistband, the white-lacquered tips he liked to see against his darker skin slipping beneath to graze the tip of his erection. He hissed in a breath and went still, praying for control.

"I am too full with want for you," he said.

"It's okay," she said, dragging his jeans down and kneeling before him. "I feel the same."

"Maledetto!" he hissed as her lips skimmed his hot hard length, her small fingers urgent on his skin.

He locked his knees and tipped his head back, giving her free rein, knowing by the blood roaring in his ears and pounding through his veins that it would be brief. The first part of his release jolted through him, his fingers threading through her hair as a shout exploded from him.

Somehow he remained standing until the last tremor rocked through him. He pulled her up into his arms, crushing her against his chest.

"You are a vixen."

"And you are a sorcerer, catching me up in your spell."

If only I could, he thought.

If he had that power, this would be the beginning instead of an interlude. She would be his forever.

He pushed the nagging thought from his mind. A flick of his fingers released the snap of jeans that hugged her rounded bottom as he'd longed to do on the long walk back to the house. But they were too snug to drop on their own. Like skin. Hot. More arousing than any model he'd seen, than any woman he'd ever crossed paths with.

He should forbid Delanie to ever wear them in public, he thought as he hooked his thumbs over the band and peeled them down, his skin riding her hipbones, catching the tiny band of her thong as well.

Sweat beaded his forehead, his chest warming quickly as well. Had sex ever been this erotic before? This much sensual torture?

He didn't know. Couldn't remember. But his sex jolted again, aching with the need to be in her.

"I love this," she said.

His ego swelled, his thoughts blurring in a haze of lust. He hoisted her onto the counter and spread her long sexy legs by riding his palms up her thighs, nostrils flaring as he caught her scent, insides tightening as she opened to him like a rose kissed by the morning sun.

"That is because this is heaven," he said, whisking her top and bra off and filling his palms with the creamy swells of her breasts, convinced this was as close to paradise as he would ever get.

His first flick of his tongue over a hardened peach nipple had her surging forward, wrapping her legs around his hips. The jolt of her moist sex against his belly shocked his system while pumping moisture to his engorged tip.

Yes, foreplay was over.

He cupped her lush bottom and slid her close, mouth bonding with hers in an explosion of raw lust. White lights exploded from their touch, blazing red as his sex found her wet, hot core and thrust in hard.

The world stopped for an instant, electricity streaking up and down his length, holding him in that erotic chasm for an instant. Heaven and hell.

No woman had ever brought him to such heights, made him feel so intently. He hated it as much as he craved it, ached for it.

She climaxed first, screaming his name. His hoarse shout, a benediction, a curse, he didn't know, burst from him a heartbeat later.

All thought left him then, replaced by a torrent of sensations that roared through him with cataclysmic force.

"Marco," she whispered against his shoulder, her hands clutching him tightly as if she feared she would tumble off the earth if she didn't hold on.

"I have you," he managed to get out, dredging deep to find the stamina he needed to carry the most precious thing he'd ever held in his hands.

Delanie. To his bedroom.

Each step was agony, taking a lifetime. But he got there and collapsed with her on the bed.

"You are amazing," she said and planted a kiss on his temple, lips sliding down his cheek even while her small hand sought and found his sex. "Amazing."

She made him believe that perhaps he was when blood rushed again to that part of him. The lethargy that had bound him was cut free, replaced by the beginning surge of desire.

He smoothed hands that shook just a fraction down her back, savoring the curve of her hip, the firm globes that filled out her jeans so very well. "I intend to spend every day I have with you right here."

"Good plan," she said, kissing her way past his belly, sliding lower to find his length that pulsed with need.

All rational thought fled him then, replaced by a nirvana he had known too seldom. But it felt right.

Everything felt right with Delanie.

No matter what, he damned sure wasn't letting Delanie go this time.

A week had never passed so pleasurably or quickly. They ate, they drank, they made love.

On the morning of the wedding, Delanie couldn't believe it was over. Didn't want to face the fact that their idyll was history.

Her contract would soon be satisfied and her affair with Marco would end. And then the heartache would truly set in.

She pressed a hand to the gnawing ache in her stomach. The only way she would be able to get through this day was to stay busy and stay away from Marco. So far so good.

But then, she thought as she stepped from the guest shower, he'd yet to rouse from their bed.

She dressed quickly in a beige shirtdress that was comfortable yet stylish enough to get her through the morning. Winding her still-damp hair in a French twist sufficed, and a bit of mascara helped divert attention away from the red streaks in her eyes. A bit of blush gave her unusually pale cheeks much-needed color.

So did the red patent belt she cinched around her waist. Stepping into matching red patent pumps and adding a strand of red beads with matching earrings completed her business attire.

"You are up at an ungodly early hour," Marco said.

She gasped, shaken to see him lounging against the door-jamb, his dark eyes unreadable, his jaw rigid. How long had he been watching?

"Today is the wedding so it is a workday for me."

He snorted. "Your bag looks packed."

"For the most part," she said. "I wanted as much done now as I could since I'll be busy all day."

There was nothing welcoming about the muscular arms crossed tightly over his bare chest either. Strong arms that had held her close to his heart last night, that were now hard with tension.

Her gaze followed the dark hair that arrowed over his washboard abs, disappearing under faded jeans that rode indecently low on his lean hips. How could he look angry and sexy at the same time?

"Why are you doing this, *cara?*"

"Because my job will be completed and there is no reason to remain in Italy any longer."

He muttered something in Italian that she couldn't guess. Just as well, for it was likely a curse.

"There most certainly is a reason." He waved a hand between them. "This thing between us is not over."

So close to the words she'd longed to hear. But she didn't want *close* anymore. She wanted the words, wanted to hear passion and his heart behind them.

All or nothing.

"This thing?" she repeated, and he jerked his hand back and stared at some point beyond her. "Can't you call it what it is? A love affair? Or is using the world *love* as much a problem for you as professing what's in your heart?"

His impossibly broad shoulders stiffened with military precision. His eyes burned with something she'd never seen before—an emotion that left her shaking inside.

"Love is nothing more than a word to me," he said. "A word without substance. A word that deceives."

She lifted a hand, right on the verge of reaching for him. Of cupping the jaw set like stone. Rubbing a thumb over lips that were pulled into a thin disagreeable line.

But she reined that impulse in and reached for her bag of

toiletries instead. She tossed them in her case with hands that shook, and she blinked her suddenly stinging eyes, desperate to stay the tears that threatened.

Crying would solve nothing. She'd learned that long ago.

"You're wrong, Marco," she said. "But until you stop fearing the emotion that can free you, you'll never believe in its power. There will always be something missing from your life, something you can't buy or take over."

He snorted. "If you say so."

She shook her head. Sighed.

At least Marco was being honest. He wasn't promising her something he couldn't give her.

For that reason alone she respected him. Loved him even more, which made the pain of leaving him all the more intense.

But one-sided love was worse than an arranged marriage. She'd seen it in her parents but she hadn't understood how a woman could accept such a situation until she'd experienced it firsthand with Marco.

But, unlike her mother, she wouldn't settle for less than all his heart.

Her time with Marco was over. Now she would begin the process of filing those special memories of them away so she could pull them out and cherish them when her thoughts were clearer, when her heart wasn't aching so much.

"I trust you'll have my paperwork ready for me today." She walked to the doorway he filled so completely, expecting him to at least be a gentleman and move.

He didn't budge, but the muscle along his jawline quivered. She had her choice of trying to push past him or stop. She stopped.

"If that is your wish," he said, his upper lip curling with obvious distaste.

Her wish would be for this to be a bad dream. When she awoke it would be to Marco vowing to love her forever. But that wasn't going to happen.

She tried for a professional smile. "It is."

Because she simply couldn't spend another night in his arms. Already her stomach cramped and her nerves felt raw and frayed at the thought of leaving him. At least if she was busy all day, she could rush to the airport tonight and be gone before her heartache truly set in. Before she surrendered to the flood of tears that were sure to come.

"Anything else?" he asked, voice flat. Emotionless. Sounding as empty as she felt inside.

"I need transportation to the villa to ensure all is well with Bella's wardrobe, then back here so I can oversee that events will run smoothly at the church and the castle."

"Fine," he said, pushing away from the doorway and storming back toward his bedroom. "I'll drive you."

She opened her mouth to argue and then promptly snapped it shut. Avoiding him was going to be impossible so why try?

CHAPTER ELEVEN

MARCO remained silent and brooding as he drove her to St. Antonio de Montiforte Cathedral. She half expected him to abandon her while she double-checked the wedding preparations, but he waited for her, likely impatiently.

The tense silence continued to pulse like a frantic heart beating as he ushered her into his flashy sports car and sped down the highway toward Cabriotini villa. It promised to be the longest hour trapped in an auto that she'd ever endured.

Delanie managed the first ten minutes or so by staring out the window, admiring the scenery. After that she was torn between remaining quiet or making an attempt to talk to him. Neither felt right to her, not when they were at such odds after being so close.

Not when the silence screamed inside her head.

One glance at his set jaw and wounded eyes tore at her heart. She swallowed hard and wadded her fingers together to keep from reaching out to him.

A clean break was needed here. That meant no touching. No softening. Yet she couldn't be that cold, that unfeeling. Not when she felt his pain as deeply as her own.

"I never intended to hurt you or be hurt," she said. "Please believe that."

He didn't answer for the longest time, then finally heaved a sigh and then another. "I know," he said, his voice hushed yet catching. "We seem to excel at inflicting pain on each other."

"Yes," she said, her voice cracking, her chest so tight she could barely draw a breath.

He fell silent again, but then there was nothing left to say. Nothing left to do but get through this day without shedding any more emotional blood.

Once at the villa, Delanie was relieved to find Bella a serene, glowing bride-to-be. Her gown fitted perfectly as did those of her attendants. They were a charming gaggle of young women, some seeming thrilled to be part of such grandeur.

There was simply nothing more for her to do here but ensure that the bridal party would arrive on time. Marco was in charge of that, and she sought him out. No surprise, he was outside standing beside his car.

"I trust you'll be on hand to see that the bride and her attendants arrive at the church on time," she said.

"Her chauffeur will deliver her and her friends in a white limousine, and the housekeeper will see that all leave the villa on time." He nodded to his Bugatti. "If you're ready to return to Montiforte, let's go."

Delanie took a fortifying breath and complied. As on the drive up, silence reigned and tension rose like an ice mountain between them as they sped back to Montiforte.

Marco wheeled under the portico at Castello di Montiforte, and a valet rushed to open her door. She managed a smile as she faced Marco. "Thank you for escorting me about today."

"My pleasure," he said. "The day isn't over. I'll wait for you."

A fact she was all too aware of. "Don't bother. I'm sure you have things to do and I look forward to the walk back."

His eyes narrowed, but their intensity burned stronger. Hotter. "As you wish."

She managed a smile and quickly exited his car, but her legs shook so badly she feared they would give out as she hurried inside the castle. Once there she was able to take a breath, to steer her thoughts on what she must do. That pulled her out of her emotional tumble and allowed her to focus on her job, on doing what she did best.

All the preparations were going well or were finished. All her plans had fallen neatly in order. Her only task was to oversee that nothing unforeseen cropped up to cause a problem.

She refused to think of one sexy Italian as a problem now. Her personal life and her profession could not collide and crash now, not when so much was at stake.

Delanie bit her lip and discreetly checked her watch. In a little over an hour the wedding would commence, followed by the reception. Her hours left in Italy were few. This time tomorrow she'd be back in London.

Her company and her life would be hers to command again. She'd be free of a man's control. Independence would finally be hers.

It was what she'd always wanted, yet there was no excitement in her victory. No reason to gloat.

Not that she could with her heart in tatters.

Love. If she were a cynic like Marco she would swear off ever allowing that emotion into her scope again. But she'd tried to do that with him. And she'd failed.

She downed her head and started up the trail toward the villa. But no matter how many times she mentally went over her checklist, Marco remained the last person commanding her thoughts.

Every second she'd spent with him tormented her. Dammit, she shouldn't be plagued with indecisions now.

They'd struck a bargain. Stuck to it. If she was the weak link and let her heart get involved, that was her problem.

She was making the right choice in leaving. So why did it feel so wrong?

By the time Delanie reached the villa she trembled with nerves scraped raw. Her gaze lit on the Bugatti.

Her body quivered with need and worry, but she tempered

her fears and faced her demons full-on. She stepped into the villa, her gaze searching for him.

Marco stood in the salon, wearing a pale gray suit specially tailored for those broad shoulders that she'd caressed and clung to, the trousers conforming to lean hips that had moved so sensuously with hers. His shirt was black, the bride's choice and befitting the rebel in him.

And she adored the look. Her foolish heart rejoiced at the sight of him. A lonely ache wrapped ghostly arms around her, their touch imagined but not felt.

She shivered, feeling nothing. Knowing that her memories of him were tucked away. If one moment of fabulous sex was enough then she would be blissfully happy. But it wasn't.

It never had been. It never would be, which was why she had to put distance between them now.

"A moment, please," he said as she started to walk past him.

It was a demand, not a question. But then that shouldn't surprise her.

She pushed out a tight breath and stopped, knees locked and toes curling in her sensible flats. "Is something wrong?"

"No."

He crossed to the window, presenting a stiff back to her as he stared through it. She worried her hands together, dreading to know what he wanted to tell her less than an hour before they were to leave for the wedding.

"Is Bella all right?" she asked, worrying that something was wrong, that she might have failed.

He flipped a hand, the motion abrupt. "Bella just called me en route to the church. She is stressed and nervous but otherwise fine."

"Good," she said, hand to her heart. "I was afraid you had bad news."

He faced her then. Grim-faced, solemn and giving her no reason to think that still wasn't the case. Her nerves twitched as he pulled an envelope from his breast pocket and held it out to her.

"You've done everything you said you would do to ensure Bella had the wedding she wanted." His gaze stroked her length once, twice, so personal, so intimate she shivered as if his fingers and hands and tongue had stroked over her willing flesh. "More, actually. There is no reason for me to forestall honoring my promise to you."

By sheer determination, she willed her hand not to tremble as she took the envelope from him, careful not to touch the long blunt fingers that had played over her skin. She slid a nail under the seal and pulled out the papers.

Her mind went numb as she stared at the check and the obscene number of zeros. He'd promised a fat check for professional services.

But this— This was a fortune, far more than she would ever charge a client. Far more than her struggling company was worth.

It was an insult. Wasn't it? A payoff?

Then her gaze landed on the very legal contract. She skimmed it once, heart racing as its significance sunk in.

Elite Affair was hers. All shares reverted to her name only. Her baby. All hers again.

"Why did you do this?" she asked, waving the check, certain the combined value of it and the whole of the company trumped any amount he would give a mistress he'd just dismissed. "What's the catch?"

"There is none."

She sucked in a breath, then another, her mind spinning. "That's hard to believe. Father taught me nothing was free. Nothing good came without a price."

"And I told you to never compare me or the way I work to your father."

"Trust," she said. "We never had that."

"The best lesson my father taught me was never to trust a woman," he said.

"Experience taught me never to trust a man you loved, whether he was a relative or a lover."

His mouth pulled into a flat line and his eyes narrowed to slits, yet enough anger shot from them to make her take a cautious step back. "Point taken. Again. But this is given freely because you deserve a bonus."

"Oh? Then I overreacted," she said and meant it, knowing she'd crossed the line, that she'd insulted him without cause. "I'm just—" How to say it? "Flabbergasted you would do this."

He gave a quick hike of one broad shoulder. "It was wrong of me to hold this over you when it is clear to me now that you were ignorant of your father's plan to destroy me."

She stared at the papers and shivered, far colder inside than she'd been at her father's funeral. But then, this parting was a far different type of grief.

Her father's death had brought relief. Closure.

This parting brought sorrow. No matter how good they'd been at one time, no matter how much better they were in bed, it wasn't enough to make him tear down the walls around his heart. And if he couldn't do that, their passion wasn't enough to make her take him as he was.

She deserved more. They both did, but she was the only one who recognized it.

"That isn't our greatest obstacle, is it?"

He shook his head. "No. We want—expect—different things in a relationship."

He couldn't even bring himself to say *marriage*. It wasn't in his immediate future, and love— Well, love was never part of their equation, at least not mutually.

She wanted his heart. He wanted her body.

On the heels of their brief affair, his largesse came off as a perk for services rendered for work above and beyond the contract. All she'd ever expected was her due, but to argue the point now, before the wedding, just wasn't done.

With strength that was fast slipping, she reminded herself she was the professional here. Making a scene would ruin everything and voicing her opinion would cause a scene.

"Yes, you're right," she said, and managed a smile.

He scowled, his nod coming in an abrupt jerk, his steps toward the door stiff. "I must go to the church now. I'll arrange for a driver to be at your disposal for the rest of your stay."

"Thank you," she managed, waiting for a surge of relief to flow over her.

He stopped on the threshold, fingers splayed on the door frame. "It is I who should thank you." He cut her a look then was gone.

She clutched her hands together, feeling empty. Deserted.

The thud of his footsteps across the terrace was a dirge in her head, signaling the end of their time together. Her shoulders bowed. The raw pain lancing across her heart was simply too much to take after days of so much laughter and passion.

She stared down at the papers that would change her life forever, that gave her the chance to do exactly what she had always wanted. Why wasn't she dancing with joy? Why was she so damned miserable?

The powerful engine on the Bugatti broke the silence, its purr cracking the ice that had held her immobile. She blinked, but her eyes still filled with blinding silent tears.

Somehow she stumbled to the chair by the window, her composure deserting her the second she dropped onto the cushion. Scalding tears poured from her eyes and she let them fall.

If he had insulted her she could have clung to her pride and annoyance and gotten through this. But how could she cope with his polite indifference?

She couldn't and she wasn't about to keep trying.

For the first time in years, she let herself cry over the fact that she and Marco simply couldn't make it work. That they were dynamite in bed. That he could give her anything in this world except the one thing she desperately wanted—his love.

So she cried it all out now, well aware her day wasn't over with him. That she still had hours to get through.

When the emotional storm ended, she hurried to her room and changed clothes, slipping into a simple blue sheath a shade darker than a spring sky.

It fitted her well but was modest. Businesslike. The type of thing she always wore while working. So unlike the lovely dresses and gowns crowding the closet, clothes that Marco had ordered. Clothes she'd refused to try on, let alone wear.

She slipped her feet into taupe pumps and gave herself one last critical look in the mirror. A pale woman with sorrowful eyes stared back at her.

Not the look she wanted to present at the wedding, but how could one erase those lines of heartache? And even if she could, who would really care?

Still, a repair of her makeup, including eye drops, hid the redness in her eyes and minimized the puffiness. A dash of peach blush restored color to her too-pale cheeks.

It was good enough. For the most part, she would be dealing with the workers, not the guests. Surely not Marco. She would do all she could to avoid him, and if their paths crossed and she didn't look her best, so be it.

Their business was concluded. Her wisest course was to do her job and get out of Italy as she'd planned.

Without hesitating, she placed the call to the airline securing a one-way ticket to Heathrow tonight. Then she left her room and focused her thoughts on one thing—ensuring that this wedding went off as perfectly as she'd planned it.

"Marco, why do you look so sad on the happiest day of my life?" Bella asked.

Delanie was the easy answer, and the one that would only prompt a multitude of questions.

"Sorry, my mind was on business," he said, forcing a smile which came easier as his gaze lit on his sister. He wasn't in a mood to answer questions, not on the day that he'd just received word from his CEO at Tate Unlimited who'd found David Tate's hidden personal documents from ten years ago.

The news chilled him. Sickened him. To think he'd believed Tate's lies instead of Delanie. Ass. He'd been a total ass for far too long. *No more!*

Bella looked like a princess in her ivory silk gown that shimmered with threads of ice-green and gold. With a hint of makeup and her hair caught up in some sophisticated style, she was absolutely breathtaking.

"Business," she scoffed, and added an indignant lift of her chin.

He could not help but chuckle. "Tending to business is what has given you a livelihood as well as a dream wedding befitting such a beauty."

She beamed. "I *am* beautiful, yes?"

For a girl born in poverty, she'd learned quickly the nuances of perfecting a haughty demeanor. Of being rich.

"Yes," he said. "You will stop hearts."

Bella clapped both hands together. "There is only one heart I wish to stop and then make race. Giamo's."

The groom, the man she'd fallen in love with and into bed with, was a vineyard worker she'd met right after she'd turned twenty.

Marco had moved out of the estate and into his own home in Montiforte, believing his sister was capable of living by herself. An error on his part, perhaps. But Giamo was a good hardworking man and one Marco believed would one day run the family winery.

Now Bella laughed and twirled before him like a child, looking carefree and far from the expectant mother or bride. Her young-heiress persona was belied on the fact that she still giggled, still could be found in the gardener's shed playing with kittens, still looked too damned young to be a wife or a mother.

"Delanie is wonderful," Bella said, clasping her hands to her bosom, totally unaware how mention of Delanie made his own heart stop and stutter. "You paid her well?"

"A fortune." Which wasn't a lie. He owed her that and more and not just for her work in planning this wedding.

Bella planted her hands at her waist, her expression suddenly fierce. "Don't let her go, Marco. She is perfect for you. She would make you a wonderful—"

"Don't say it," he warned, cutting her words off.

"But—"

He slashed the air with a hand, hushing her, the playful mood shuttered. "There is no *but*. Miss Tate has done a fabulous job planning your wedding just as you requested. Now she wants to return to her job and her life in England."

His sister scowled. "You're making a horrible mistake letting her go."

"No, I'm giving her what she always dreamed of having," he said and believed it. He'd hurt her enough.

Bella tossed both hands in the air, sending her veil fluttering around her bare shoulders, before fixing him with a pitying look. "You should give *yourself* what you've dreamed of having, Marco. Then you and Delanie would both be happy."

Bella flounced out the door without waiting for his reply, not that he had one acceptable to voice. In fact, his little sister had rendered him speechless with that observation. How could one so young be so wise?

He pressed the heels of his hands against his burning eyes and muttered an oath, sick inside over his lack of emotion.

There had been a time when he had believed money could buy anything. Had believed that once he was rich, he could make Delanie happy. And then, of late, had believed that he would only find peace solo.

Now he knew that was a lie.

Delanie didn't want his wealth. She wanted his love and that was the one thing he didn't know if he could give her.

He'd shut off that emotion years ago, swearing he would never suffer a marriage such as his parents had had, that emotional hell that bound them together and made them—and him—miserable.

"Never be so foolish as to love a woman," his father had told Marco after a particularly violent fight between his parents. "Find a woman who satisfies you in bed, for that is all that a man can expect to have from a woman or a wife. *Amore* poisons. It slowly kills."

That same night, his father had stormed out of the house to find his wife. Only, neither of them had come back.

He shook his head, the pain of that memory faded, replaced by the impending loss of Delanie again. She'd been on his mind since he'd left her this morning.

At the church, his gaze honed in on her the moment she arrived, dressed in an elegant dress befitting a CEO. His chest tightened, his pulse raced, his blood running thick and hot.

He wanted her. Would always want her. But would he cross to her? No!

One of the ushers motioned to him. "It's time."

Marco nodded and followed the man to Bella, who stubbornly refused to look at him.

"I would make her life miserable," he whispered to Bella.

She looked at him with eyes that were suddenly sad. "Oh, Marco. What will it take to make you see that she loves you and that you love her?"

The first strains of "The Wedding March" prevented him from answering that question. He presented his arm to his sister.

"Smile, Bella," he said. "This is your moment."

She held his gaze for a moment then smiled. But the full

force of her beauty didn't shine until they started down the aisle and Giamo turned to face them.

He felt the tremble go through Bella and saw the adoration shining in her eyes and in the groom's. It was a look much like the one Delanie had given him not so very long ago. A look he'd dismissed because the power of it terrified him.

Now the thought of losing that forever scared him more. While everyone's attention was on the bride, his searched out and found Delanie.

Dammit, he wanted her as he'd wanted no other woman. She was his equal in bed and out of it.

But love?

He wished he knew what that emotion was. What it felt like to be caught in its grip. Wanted to know if he was even capable of such feeling.

No great change coursed through him. No miraculous sense that love had suddenly bloomed in the desert that was his heart. No epiphany revealed itself to soothe his soul.

He tore his gaze from hers. For the first time in years, Marco Vincienta felt like a failure.

The sun had set hours ago yet the massive chandeliers hanging from the beamed ceiling cast a mellow glow over tables draped in white linen. Celebrants ate and drank and laughed freely while the wedding singer warbled love songs.

Delanie hovered on the fringe of the massive ballroom, pleased that it had been a perfectly beautiful wedding for Bella and Giamo. The reception at the castle was lovely, with the paparazzi kept outside while Carlo Domanti moved through the crowd, capturing this special day for the happy couple.

A select number of pictures would find their way into the media. Delanie had been promised that a few others would be available to her for advertising purposes.

Everything she'd wanted, needed, to relaunch her business

with flare was now hers. Like the bride, she should be celebrating today as the happiest day of her life.

She *should* have been.

It was sheer torture to know she was excluded from Marco's
life now. Her choice. Her hell.

Would it always be this way? Would she always be the fool
around this arousing Italian?

If only her gaze didn't constantly swing to him. If only
her heart didn't seize and her breath catch at the sight of him
laughing and mingling with the guests.

Though for the last hour, he'd been absent. She worried
her hands and scanned the crowd. How long did it take for a
broken heart to mend?

"This could last all night," came a deep rich voice just behind her.

"Marco," she said, whirling, hand over her thundering
heart.

She stared at him, suddenly tongue-tied. Unbelievably at
a loss for words.

With effort, she rallied her wits and managed a smile, hoping only she knew that her lips trembled. "You startled me."

"My apologies." He cradled a wineglass in each hand and
handed her one.

She took the glass, her fingers barely brushing his. A jolt
shot into her veins to set her blood on fire.

He raised his glass to her and smiled and her heart did a
tumble again. *"Brava!"*

"To the happy couple." She tore her gaze from his intense
scrutiny and focused on the wine, on taking a cordial sip
without choking up.

A sudden quietness wrapped around her like a ribbon and
had her taking a step closer to Marco before she realized it.
His gaze darkened, his lips curving just a smidgeon.

"Cara," he breathed, head bending toward hers.

"Evviva gli sposi!" a guest shouted.

Delanie jumped back from Marco as others joined in with applause and shouts. She raised her glass in the traditional toast, but her heart was still thundering.

If the guest hadn't chosen that moment to salute the bride and groom, Marco's lips would have captured hers. Despite her intentions she would have let them. Welcomed them.

She would have melted in his arms.

The music started up with people hurrying onto the dance floor to form a huge circle.

"Marco, please join us," Bella shouted.

He waved to his sister and extended a hand to Delanie. "You will come too."

Delanie shook her head and retreated another step. "No! I have two left feet and would truly prefer watching. Please, go and enjoy this with your family."

For a moment she was certain he would protest. That he would insist on her participation. But she watched thankfully as he shrugged and strode toward his sister, walking away from her as he must.

Delanie sucked in a breath, painfully aware the time had come for her to leave. That the longer she stayed, the more she risked being seduced by Marco again.

Her job here was over.

Nobody would notice if she left. Nobody would miss her.

CHAPTER TWELVE

AFTER the Tarantella, which seemed endless no matter how enjoyable, had ended, Marco went in search of Delanie. He wasted fifteen minutes before he realized she'd left the castle soon after the dancing began.

No doubt she was exhausted after a day spent overseeing a wedding and reception. The tension he'd added fuel to was a burden she hadn't needed either.

But then that type of behavior should be expected from an ass, and he'd done all in his power the last two days presenting that very image to her. No longer.

He wasn't done with her by a long shot and this time she would hear him out.

The second he fulfilled his duty and saw his sister and brother-in-law off in the wee hours of the morning, Marco sped back to his villa. A gentleman would have waited until morning to confront her, but Marco had proven time and again he was not fully of that league.

Without hesitating, he went straight to Delanie's room. He gave one sharp knock on the door then pushed inside, too impatient to wait for her to rouse from sleep and welcome him in.

Or tell him to go to hell, which was what he deserved!

The dim light from the hall stretched into the room and across the bed—the neatly made bed.

"Delanie," he called out, flicking on the light.

A quick scan of the bedroom confirmed what he already knew in his heart. Delanie was gone.

The only trace of the woman who had occupied his thoughts was the new clothes he'd bought for her, still hanging in the closet untouched.

He stood in the middle of the room, fists bunched at his sides, chest heaving. She'd been so anxious to leave Italy and him that she'd done so tonight.

Not that he blamed her for running off. He was the one responsible for that. He'd driven her away.

He sucked in air, hands fisted, chest heaving as he fought the demon inside him. Letting her go was easy. It was what he'd always done.

Going after her took something he didn't know whether he possessed, something that terrified him. But to lose her forever…

In moments he was behind the wheel again, speeding toward the *autostrada*. He wanted her back, but convincing her that she belonged with him wouldn't be easy. Impossible perhaps.

Giving up wasn't an option. Not now. It was all or nothing.

He had to succeed. Had to make her believe him. The fear that had held his emotions prisoner was nothing compared to the fear of losing her forever.

Delanie paced the waiting area, wondering how much longer it would take for the airline to ready the plane for boarding. Flight times here at night were obviously an estimate and a rough one at that, but there was no other recourse available.

So she paced and she fretted and she tried to think of anything but the tall Italian who'd broken her heart again. It would take time to get over the hurt. Forever to forget him.

"*Attenzione*. Boarding will commence in ten minutes," the clerk said in Italian, and then in English.

Finally, she thought, reaching for the bag at her feet.

"Delanie!" rasped that deep Italian voice that sent chills up her spine. That awakened every nerve in her body to the powerful throb of his presence.

She whirled around and stared at Marco bearing down on her, his hair tousled and face ravaged. His stark white shirt was open at the neck, the bow tie long gone. And then she saw the worry in his eyes and her blood ran cold.

"What are you doing here?" she asked. "Has something gone wrong?"

Not the greeting he'd hoped for. "No. But we need to talk."

"About what?" she asked again.

"Us."

She stiffened, her eyes narrowing. "I can't imagine why."

He dashed fingers through his hair. "You need to know this. My CEO at Tate Unlimited found a hidden stash of your father's papers. In it were documents about your mother's peculiar accidents and Tate's dictate to ensure they stayed hidden. The mark of an abuser, as you'd said. As your mother denied."

She flinched and stiffened. "Fine. You now have proof of what I told you long ago."

"Part of me always believed it," he admitted. "But there's more. There was a written note from your mother to your father dated mere days before he acquired my grandparents' vineyard. She told him about my nonna's failing health. Of my concern. Your mother was the one to betray your trust."

"I'd already come to that chilling conclusion, but I'm glad you know that as well, not that it makes any difference. Now if you'll excuse me—" She turned to leave.

He muttered a curse. So much for thinking the truth would free them of their pasts. That she would greet him with open arms. That she would be as glad to see him as he was to be near her again.

His old fears rushed forward with the warning he'd heeded

all of his adult life. Fool! Trust a woman with your heart and you will end up hurt.

But he already was hurting, his heart aching, his blood pounding so hard his head spun. All his life he'd believed his father's words had kept him from making a mistake with countless women. Then he'd blamed Delanie's betrayal—or what he'd believed was her betrayal—when that wasn't the case at all.

What kept him from committing to any woman was his lack of feeling for those women whose names were long forgotten. All but Delanie. She broke through his defenses. Touched him, even though he'd denied it years ago.

Up until an hour ago he'd still denied it.

Never again. He no longer doubted her word. No longer doubted the feelings surging through his blood. No longer could stand to be apart from her.

Now he knew what was in his heart. He only had to convince her that he was telling the truth.

He stepped in front of her, blocking her way. "If you have nothing to say to me, then you will at least grant me the courtesy of listening while I talk."

Why was he doing this, ripping her heart apart more just by being here? "Sorry, I have a plane to catch."

She grabbed her bag and darted around him, starting toward the shrinking boarding line. He let her take all of two steps before he grabbed her arm and turned her around.

"The damned plane can wait."

Her jaw dropped open, then snapped shut. "It won't wait, even for your arrogance. I'm not about to miss this flight and have to wait another two hours."

The anger he'd wielded like a shield cracked, falling away. His frown deepened as he read the tiredness in her eyes.

"You can't go, Delanie. You can't leave me."

Her shoulders slumped, her fingers clutching her bag when what she really wanted to cling to was him. Stupid, but true.

That's how badly she had it for him still. That's why she couldn't miss this plane.

"I won't stay," she said, staring into his eyes that seemed darker. More intense. More pained. "I won't be your lover."

His big hands cupped her upper arms and did that slow glide down and back up, setting her skin on fire and threatening to melt her fast-fading resistance. "But that is just what you are, *cara mia.*"

She shook her head and found the strength to push him away. "Past tense. What we had is over. I can't go through that again. Goodbye."

She whirled and ran to the check-in, fumbling to pull her boarding pass from her bag. Just a few more seconds and she would board the plane. A few more would carry her away from Marco before her composure deserted her.

"I love you, Delanie Tate," he shouted.

An arctic blast couldn't have froze her in place any quicker. All thoughts of continuing out the door onto the tarmac and the waiting plane were over.

"What?" she asked, turning to face him.

"I love you, *cara.*"

She swallowed, pulse trembling wildly. "You can't be serious."

"Oh, but I am." He nudged her chin up and dropped a kiss on her lips, fleetingly, yet she burned for more. "I loved you ten years ago but was too damned afraid of becoming the same obsessed man as my father. I clung to that belief the past two weeks when all I could think of doing was spending every day and night with you for as long as I lived."

Her gaze probed his and he let her in, let her see the naked soul before her. The barest smile trembled on her lips.

"You aren't just saying the words. You really do love me as I love you," she said, wonder in her eyes, in her smile.

"With all my heart and soul," he said, his lips finding hers again for a long lingering kiss that chased away her doubts, that freed the man she'd fallen in love with years ago.

"Marry me," he said when they finally came up for air. "Stay in Italy with me and run your company. Be my wife. Mother to my children. Balm to my soul."

Her lips trembled and tears sprang to her eyes. This was no joke. No ploy.

This was the declaration she'd waited a lifetime to hear.

She dropped her bag and threw her arms around his neck. "Yes. God, yes!"

His arms banded around her, molding her to his length, oblivious of the stragglers watching. He had Delanie in his arms, in his heart, right where she belonged.

He kissed her forehead, her nose, her inviting lips. "I will make you happy, *cara mia*. I'll make your dreams come true."

She smiled and cupped his face, tears of joy swimming in her eyes. "You already have, Marco. You already have."

* * * * *

'The perfect Christmas read!' - Julia Williams

Jewellery designer Skylar loves living London, but when a surprise proposal goes wrong, she finds herself fleeing home to remote Puffin Island.

Burned by a terrible divorce, TV historian Alec is dazzled by Sky's beauty and so cynical that he assumes that's a bad thing! Luckily she's on the verge of getting engaged to someone else, so she won't be a constant source of temptation... but this Christmas, can Alec and Sky realise that they are what each other was looking for all along?

Order yours today at
www.millsandboon.co.uk